BARBARA DELINSKY

was born and raised in suburban Boston. She worked as a researcher, photographer and reporter before turning to writing full-time in 1980. With more than fifty novels to her credit, she is truly one of the shining stars of contemporary romance fiction. This talented writer has received numerous awards and honors, and her involving stories have made her a *New York Times* bestselling author. There are over 12 million copies of her books in print worldwide—a testament to Barbara's universal appeal.

STEPHANIE BOND

was seven years deep into a systems engineering career and pursuing an MBA at night when an instructor remarked that she had a flair for writing and suggested that she submit to academic journals. But Stephanie, a voracious reader, was only interested in writing fiction—more specifically, romance fiction. Upon completing her master's degree and with no formal training in writing (her undergraduate degree is in computer programming), she started writing a romance novel in her spare time. Two years later, in 1995, she sold her first book, a romantic comedy, to Harlequin Books. In 1997, with ten sales under her belt to two publishers, Stephanie left her corporate job to write women's romantic fiction full-time. She now writes contemporary romantic comedies. Stephanie and her husband live in Atlanta, Georgia.

BARBARA DELINSKY

STEPHANIE BOND

IN TOO DEEP

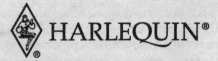
HARLEQUIN®

TORONTO • NEW YORK • LONDON
AMSTERDAM • PARIS • SYDNEY • HAMBURG
STOCKHOLM • ATHENS • TOKYO • MILAN • MADRID
PRAGUE • WARSAW • BUDAPEST • AUCKLAND

ISBN 0-373-83544-2

IN TOO DEEP

Copyright © 2003 by Harlequin Books S.A.

The publisher acknowledges the copyright holders of the individual works as follows:

HAVING FAITH
Copyright © 1990 by Barbara Delinsky

IT TAKES A REBEL
Copyright © 2000 by Stephanie Bond Hauck

CONTENTS

HAVING FAITH   9
Barbara Delinsky

IT TAKES A REBEL   221
Stephanie Bond

HAVING FAITH

Barbara Delinsky

1

"JUST WAIT." Laura Leindecker's voice was soft and riddled with pain. "You'll see. He comes across as being honest and charming, and that's what people think he is. That's what I thought he was. For twenty-four years, that's what I thought." She swallowed hard in a bid for strength. "But I know better now. He's not what he seems. He cheats and he lies."

Ignoring the headache that was part and parcel of late afternoon on a hell of a day, Faith Barry came forward, bracing her elbows on her desk. "Did he come right out and confess to having an affair?"

Laura swallowed again. "He had no choice. I found the note. It was right there in the pocket of his trenchcoat. I'm sure he meant for me to find it. He was the one who asked me to take the coat to the dry cleaner, and he knew I'd check the pockets."

"How did he know that?"

"Because I always do it. Bruce is a tight-wad, still he leaves money in his pockets." She frowned. "I think he does it to test me. He's always telling me that I don't really work. But what does he expect," she asked, growing beseechful, "when he has me doing this, that and the other for him all day long? It takes time to see to his custodial needs. But that's my job. So I check his pockets." She paused. "Only there wasn't any money this time." Her voice shook. "Just the note."

Faith nodded, which, aside from injecting an occasional question, was pretty much what she'd been doing for the past fifteen minutes. Laura Leindecker's story wasn't a new one. Faith heard similar ones often, and though the details might differ, the anger, the hurt, the sense of betrayal were the same.

Faith hurt for her. She knew that her questioning didn't help. Still, it was a necessary means to an end. "Can you tell me what the note said?" she asked gently.

Laura looked at the carpeted floor while she gathered her wits. Keeping her lids lowered against humiliation, she said, "'Better than ever. Next week, same time, same place.'" Her eyes rose, filled with hurt. "It was written on notepaper from the Four Seasons. That's our favorite hotel. We've eaten at the restaurant there a dozen times in as many months, and I'm not exaggerating. And he had the gall to take her there."

"To the restaurant?" Faith asked. "Do you think he'd risk that kind of exposure?" She knew of Bruce Leindecker. Most Bostonians did. He'd made his name in real estate, and while he was far from a mega-mogul, his face was well-known.

"I wouldn't put *anything* past him," Laura cried in a moment's lapse of composure. "No decent human being would risk that kind of exposure, but then no decent human being would cheat on a woman who's been faithful and loving and giving and patient and understanding and solicitous for twenty-four years!"

Faith had to marvel at Laura if, indeed, she'd been all those things for so long. Faith had been married for eight years, and in that time she'd only managed to stay faithful. Somehow, all the rest had gone down the tubes—but mutually so. The divorce had been amicable.

"Do you have children?" she asked. She thought she remembered reading about some, but she wasn't sure.

"Two," Laura told her and let out a defeated breath. "They trusted him, too, though it's a miracle. I can't begin to count the number of times over the years when he was to be at a football game or a dance recital and then didn't arrive until the janitors were closing up." She paled when a new thought hit. "I wonder how many of those times he was with a paramour. There were so many opportunities. So many late nights. So many business trips."

"Did you ever suspect anything?"

"No. I told you. I trusted him. I was a fool." She pressed a finger over her lip. When that was ineffective in stanching her tears, she took a handkerchief from her purse, pressed it to her nose, then dabbed at the corners of her eyes.

Faith remembered the first time she'd had a client break down in her office. She'd wanted to put her arms around the woman and tell her everything was going to be all right, except it wasn't true. That particular woman was on welfare, had two preschoolers and chronic asthma, and didn't know how to balance a checkbook, let alone fill out a job application.

Laura Leindecker's situation was different. She was older, for one thing, early fifties, perhaps, and the children were probably grown. She was also more formal, very pretty, elegant in an understated way. She seemed in good health, but Faith knew looks could be deceiving. One thing was sure, though. She wasn't on welfare.

Still, she was in pain. Rich or poor, it didn't matter. Infidelity hurt. Betrayal hurt. The pending dissolution of something that had stood for nearly a quarter century hurt.

Faith waited until Laura was in control again. Quietly she said, "I know that this is all very difficult for you, Mrs. Leindecker, but if I'm to represent you, I'll have to know more. When you confronted your husband with the note, when he admitted to having the affair, how did he react?"

Laura brooded on that for a minute. "He was charming."

"Charming...how?"

"He acted totally humbled. He apologized. He said he'd made a mistake. He almost cried." She shot a teary glance skyward. "Bruce has never cried in his life. Calm, even-tempered, in control—that's Bruce."

"Perhaps if he nearly cried, it's a sign he was truly sorry."

"No. It was an act."

"Maybe he's only now realizing the ramifications of what he's done."

"No doubt," Laura agreed a bit facetiously. "He's wondering where he's going to sleep tonight. I told him I'd call the police if he tried coming home."

Faith was uneasy with threats, particularly ones that would be impossible to enforce. Unless Laura could show that her husband posed a physical danger to her, the police wouldn't do a thing—except report the call in the local newspaper the next week. Once a domestic quarrel went public like that, things were harder to resolve.

"Where were you when you told him this?"

"In his office. When I found that note, I dropped everything and raced right in there. I've never been so angry in my entire life."

Faith could believe that, since Laura struck her as being a relatively sedate soul. But humiliation and hurt often found an outlet in anger.

"He kept telling me to quiet down," Laura went on. "He didn't want anyone in the office to think something was wrong." Her gentle voice went higher. "This is a man who has a weekly tryst with a woman who isn't his wife at a hotel where any number of people can recognize him, and he's worried about being embarrassed at work?" And higher. "Well, what about me? Do you think I'll be able to show my face ever again in that hotel and not be mortified?"

"You will," Faith assured her in a calming tone. "Given who and what your husband is, he was probably discreet."

"At the Four Seasons?"

"There are ways. A room can be taken by the woman. The man arrives after her. No one has to know what floor he goes to or what business he's on. It's simple."

"It's disgusting."

"Yes, but it's done all the time, and with no one the wiser save a wife who finds a note in her husband's coat. Do you have any idea who the woman is?"

"He refused to tell me."

"Do you know how long it's been going on?"

"He wouldn't tell me that, either. He's protecting her. He's afraid I'll go after her in a divorce suit."

"You don't need to go after anyone. Not in this state. The fight won't be about the divorce, just the settlement."

"And I want a big one," Laura said in a show of bravado. "I sacrificed the best years of my life for that man. He was a nobody when I met him. I stood by him through the early years. I was patient. I gave him support. I saw that his needs were filled—" She stopped, looking stricken. Then she grew defensive. "Yes, I *did* fill his needs. It's not my fault that he had to further prove his virility. He should have known better. This is going to cost him."

"It's going to cost you, too, Mrs. Leindecker," Faith felt compelled to point out, albeit gently, "and I'm not only talking about my fee. I'm talking about the emotional pain involved in divorce. You may feel that nothing can be worse than finding a note in your husband's coat pocket, but that's not so. If you decide to file for divorce, things could be harder than you imagine. You'll be alone for the first time in twenty-four years. Have you thought about that? Is it what you want?" She let the question sink in for a minute. "And beyond the emotional, there's the physical settlement. If your husband agrees to your demands, that's fine. If he doesn't, the trouble's just begun."

Laura eyed her warily. "You're trying to talk me out of this. Why?"

"Because that's my job."

"I thought your job was to represent me. You have the reputation of being a tough lawyer who fights hard for her clients. I'm willing to pay you to fight hard for me. Why won't you?"

"I will, if that's what you truly want. But as a lawyer, I have a moral obligation to try to salvage the marriage before we end it." She couldn't stress the point enough. "As an officer of the court in this state, I have an *ethical* obligation to do that. No-fault divorce doesn't mean that the marital gates should swing open and shut with the flick of a finger." She paused. "Some people come to me after years of marital counseling and months of discussing divorce. You and your husband haven't done either of those things—at least, not to my knowledge. Have you ever had marital counseling?"

"No."

"Have you ever considered divorce before?"

"No. I told you. I trusted him. I was completely taken in."

Faith looked down at her hands, laced and unlaced them, then sat back in her seat. "You had a shock this morning when you found that note. Sometimes a shock like that starts certain wheels moving. They pick up speed and propel you towards something that, if you were to stop and really think about it, you might not want."

Laura clutched the lip of her purse. "I want a divorce."

"You haven't even slept on the thought."

"I want a divorce."

"Are you sure that there isn't the slightest chance of a reconciliation?"

"Yes, I'm sure. I can't trust Bruce anymore. I want a divorce. Will you represent me?"

Faith recognized stubbornness when she saw it, but she had a stubborn streak of her own. "I'll represent you, but only if you go home and think really hard about what you want to do. Today's Friday. If by next Tuesday you still feel that there's no hope for the marriage, I'll help you get your divorce." When she saw Laura pull a checkbook from her purse, she held up a hand. "Wait until Tuesday. If the divorce is what you want, I'll take a retainer then."

"I thought you'd want the money now," Laura said in surprise. "Aren't you afraid that after taking up your time today, I may turn around and go to another lawyer?"

Faith smiled. It was a tired smile, subdued by her headache, not in the least bit smug. But it held pride. "You may, and that's your choice. I think, though, that I offer something unique. I'm a woman and I'm tough. I also happen to get along with most every judge I've faced, and that's what's different here. I'm not strident, like some of my colleagues. I'm not militant. I'm a professional, and a professional gets results. So if results are what you want, you'll be back."

LAURA LEINDECKER LEFT shortly after that, which was none too soon for Faith who immediately went off in search of a painkiller. Her secretary didn't have any, but she'd half expected that, since Loni was as close to a flower child as a 1990's woman could be. She was sweet and extremely capable, and Faith found a nostalgic charm in her dedication to all things natural and pure, but she had no painkillers.

Nor did Monica, the colleague with whom Faith shared the suite of offices and Loni.

So Faith returned to her desk, determined to beat the headache with sheer willpower, and set about answering the phone calls she'd deliberately left for the end of the day. Several of them were difficult and required adjunctive calls, such as the one to the client suing for custody of her eleven-year-old son, whom she'd just learned was picked up for shoplifting in the local five-and-dime, or the one to the client who had shown up in a hospital the night before with injuries from a beating given her by the husband who, by order of the court, had been forbidden to approach her.

Sheer willpower didn't have much of a chance against emotional situations like those, and by the time Faith hung up the phone, her headache was no better. So she closed her eyes, put her head in her hands and concentrated on relaxing. But it had been a hard week, and her tension reflected that. She was grateful it was Friday.

Though she had plenty of work to do over the weekend, the pace of weekend work was different.

Buoyed by that thought, she reached for a small recorder to dictate several letters. Loni had left for the day, which was fine for the letters since they didn't have to be typed until Monday. It wasn't so fine for the phone. Before Faith had a chance to turn the line over to the answering service, she received back-to-back calls that were both tedious and time-consuming. By the time she finally hung up the phone, she'd just about had it.

That was when the buzzer rang in the outer office. Someone was at the front door of the suite, locked now that Loni was gone. For a minute, Faith considered ignoring it. She considered curling up in a ball in the corner of the sofa, burying her aching head under her arms and shirking every legal responsibility she had. Last time the buzzer had rung after hours, though, it had been a seventeen-year-old girl who had seen Faith on television and wanted help in stopping her parents from making her abort the baby she carried.

Rubbing her temple, Faith left her office. She was barely into the reception area when she felt a wave of warmth. The face beyond the glass door was a familiar one, not a client, but a friend.

She opened the door and smiled up at the tall, dark-haired man who stood there. "Sawyer," she said, almost in a sigh. She slipped her arms around his waist and gave him a hug. "How are you?"

"Better now, sexy lady," he drawled, squeezing her tightly. Then he held her back. "Am I interrupting anything?"

"Work. Always work."

"You work too hard."

"Look who's talking," she scolded, but she was delighted he was there. Taking his hand, she drew him into the office. "I haven't seen you in months. How can that be, Sawyer? We work in the same profession. We work in the same specialty. We even work in the same building. Why don't we ever bump into each other?"

"Good question," he decided. "I think you're avoiding me."

"Me? But you're my best friend!" When he arched a brow, she amended that to, "My best boy friend." When his mouth quirked, she said, "Male friend. My best male friend. I wouldn't have made it through law school without you. Or made it through those early days at Matsker and Lynn. Or had the courage to leave there and go out on my own."

"The feeling's mutual, Faith. You know that." He gave her a quick once-over in appreciation of the fact that she looked professional but individual. Both qualities applied to her practice as well. "I'm proud of you," he said with a grin. "I'm really proud of you. You've done well for yourself."

As she held his gaze, her own grew melancholy. "I suppose."

"What do you mean, you suppose? Look at your practice."

"That's what I've been doing. All week long."

"And you have a headache," he said, suddenly seeing it in her eyes as he'd done countless other times when she'd been under strain. "And," he went on, "you don't have anything to take for it. Why don't you ever buy aspirin?"

"I do. It's at home."

"But you don't need it there. You need it here." Taking her shoulder, he ushered her to the sofa and pushed her down. "Stay put. I'll be right back." Before she could protest, he was out the door and jogging down the hall to the stairs.

She had to smile. Sawyer wasn't an elevator person any more than she was, which was, in fact, how they had originally met. Uptight but eager first-year students, they had literally bumped into each in a stairwell at the law library. Once they'd picked up the scattered books, papers and themselves, they'd started to talk. Though Faith had been black-and-blue for a week from the encounter, the friend she'd found in Sawyer had been worth the discoloration.

She took elevators more now, particularly after hours or when she faced a climb of four or more flights in high heels. Sawyer's office was six floors up. But he was a man, a tall, broad-shouldered man who wasn't worried about rape. Nor was he wearing high heels.

Chuckling at that thought, she put her head back, closed her eyes and sat quietly. In a matter of minutes, Sawyer was back with the pills in his hand. He took a cup of water from the bubbler and waited while she swallowed the aspirin. Then he leaned against Loni's desk with his long legs crossed at the ankles.

"It really *is* pretty amazing," he remarked.

"What is?"

"That we don't run into each other more. I miss seeing you. How've you been?"

She nodded and smiled. "Not bad. Busy. That's good, I guess."

"It is good. How are things at home?"

"Quiet," she said in a voice that was just that. "Lonely sometimes, but it's better this way. More honest. Jack and I went in different directions. For too long we pretended something was left, but it wasn't." She rested her head against the sofa back, but her eyes were fixed intently on Sawyer. "You know what I mean, don't you."

Sawyer knew. And he knew Faith knew he knew, because she'd known his wife. Joanna had needed something else, too. They were married soon after he returned from Vietnam, and for two years she nursed him back to health physically and emotionally. She was good at her job. He had recovered, gone through law school and entered a profession in which he thrived. Joanna hadn't known what to do with the strong and independent man he became. In the end, she found someone who needed her more.

"She married him," he told Faith.

"The fellow with MS?"

He nodded. "She'll devote her life to him. I admire her for that."

"Do you talk with her often?"

"Nah. She's busy. I'm busy. She knows she can come to me if she ever runs into trouble. I owe her a lot. I think I'll always feel that way. But we weren't very good at being husband and wife, and after a while, the constant trying was a strain."

Faith thought about the irony of two divorce lawyers being divorced. "Makes you wonder, doesn't it? Did we go into this field because we knew firsthand the pitfalls of marriage? Or did we see the pitfalls of marriage *because* we went into this field?"

"Had to be the first," Sawyer decided without pause. "We were both having doubts about our marriages even back when we were in law school."

"Not really doubts. Frustrations, and they weren't all that bad. It's just that we talked about them, you and I. Some people don't. Some people suffer year after year in silence. Just this afternoon I met with a woman who wants to end a twenty-four-year marriage. She was telling me that—"

He held up a hand. "Shhh. Don't say it."

"There's not much to say, just that she never thought to—"

"Careful, Faith. That woman is one of the reasons I'm here."

Faith frowned. "Laura Leindecker?"

"Bruce Leindecker. I'm representing him in the divorce."

"You're representing Bruce Leindecker?" Faith repeated. Slowly she sat up. As understanding dawned, she broke into a cautious smile. "You and I—" her finger went back and forth "—are going to be working together?"

"Yup."

She dropped her hand to her lap, and her smile widened. "After all this time. I don't believe it." In the next instant, the smile vanished. "Can we do it? Don't we know each other too well?" But she answered herself in the next breath. "No. There are no grounds for conflict of interest as long as neither of us compromises his client by saying too much. Right?"

"Right," Sawyer said. He folded his arms across his chest.

"Good thing you stopped me a minute ago."

"Uh-huh."

But she was confused. "Who told you I was defending Mrs. Leindecker?"

"Mr. Leindecker."

"How did he know? It's been barely two hours since the woman walked out of here, and we don't even have a formal agreement."

"She seems to think you do. The minute she left you, she called her husband to gloat."

Faith squirmed a little inside. "Gloat—was that his term or yours?"

"Does it matter?"

"Yes. Because it's wrong. Laura Leindecker was angry and hurt. Even if she was the type—which I don't think she is—I doubt she was up for gloating."

"You underestimate the woman," Sawyer said like a man.

"Have you ever met her?"

"No, but her husband knows her well. It sounds like gloating is among the mildest of her faults."

"Sawyer, that man cheated on her," Faith argued, immediately taking the side of her client, which was the rule of thumb in discussions between lawyers. "She's been a loyal wife for twenty-four years and—"

"She has a martyr complex. She's prim and proper and not very flexible when it comes to her husband's business demands. Don't let her con you into believing that she's an angel, Faith. No man turns his back on an angel."

Faith's jaw dropped. "I don't believe this. Are you saying that he was *justified* in philandering?"

"No. All I'm saying is that there are two sides to every story."

"Precisely. That's why we'll take this case before a judge and, if need be, a jury."

"Or settle out of court."

"Or not handle it at all." Her voice mellowed. "Look what just happened. We have to be careful, Sawyer. When we're together we talk. It would be all too easy to discuss things we shouldn't." She chewed on her cheek for a minute, then rose from the sofa and walked to the far side of the room. "This isn't the way I imagined it. I always wanted to work on the *same* side as you. I thought maybe we'd represent codefendants in some kind of civil suit." Turning, she started back toward him. "I don't want to fight you."

He arched a brow. "You can always tell Mrs. Leindecker that you won't represent her."

"But she has a right to representation."

"Let someone else do it."

She stopped talking. "You'd like that, wouldn't you? And your client would like it. He's scared. That was why he called you so quickly. He's scared, because he knows I fight hard." She rather liked that thought. She didn't like the next, though. "Is that why you stopped in here, Sawyer? Did you come to try to talk me off this case?"

"Absolutely not," Sawyer said, coming to his feet. "I want to work with you, even if we are on opposite sides of the case. I've heard you're good. I want to see how good. But if working against me will inhibit you—"

"Why should it?"

"Because we're friends."

"Will our friendship inhibit *you*?"

"Of course not," he said crossly. "A client is a client. Every one deserves the best I can give."

"Should I be different? More partial? More emotional? Should I be making any less of a commitment to my clients than you make to yours?"

"Take it easy, Faith. You're making something out of nothing."

"No," she said, but more thoughtfully. "I know you, Sawyer. Remember the hours we used to spend talking? Remember the times we discussed sexual stereotypes? Remember the times you confessed that you believed women were too emotional for certain types of jobs?"

"I was talking about the presidency of the country, and I still feel that way."

"And I still think you're wrong."

"Fine. Good. I respect that."

She came closer. "I also think your opinions go beyond the presidency. You think women are too emotional, period."

"Not true. Just too emotional for certain jobs."

"Like the presidency."

"I've already said that."

"Or Chairman of the Board of General Motors?"

"What woman is interested in cars? Chairman of the Board of General Foods, now there's a possibility...."

"Sawyer, that's awful!" she cried. She was standing directly before him, hands on hips, chin set. "Talk about stereotypes. You don't have to be interested in cars to be involved with General Motors. You have to be interested in big business and in profits, and if you try to tell me that women aren't economically savvy, I'll scream."

He did his best not to grin. "Calm down, Faith. You're getting too emotional."

"Too emotional?" she echoed, but she saw the humor of the situation. And she couldn't be angry at Sawyer. He was too nice a guy. "Why is it that when a man raises his voice he's being emphatic, but when a woman does it she's being emotional? Answer me that, Sawyer Bell."

"It's all in the voice. A man's voice—raised—is forceful. A woman's is shrill."

"Is that how you see it in the courtroom?"

"Sometimes."

"And it turns off the judge?"

"Or the jury, or both."

"But we lady lawyers are winning cases. How do you explain that?"

His eyes twinkled. "You lady lawyers who are winning cases have learned to be less emotional and more emphatic."

"That's a compliment, I take it?"

"Definitely."

"Do you see those few female execs of Fortune 500 companies as being more emphatic and less emotional?"

"No doubt."

"But they couldn't be President of the U.S. of A."

"Not yet. They may have come a long way, but they still have a long way to go."

"And women like Margaret Thatcher, Indira Gandhi and Golda Meir?"

He grinned. "They weren't trying to rule countries dominated by male chauvinist pigs."

Faith laughed. She'd forgotten how much fun talking with Sawyer was. As parochial as his views of women were, he knew it, even ridiculed it. In that sense he was probably one of the most liberal men she'd ever met.

Slipping an arm around her shoulder, he drew her to his side. "You laugh, Faith. I like that."

"How can I help it? You're irresistible!"

"So are you." His grin gave way to a look of open-eyed hope. "Come with me tonight. There's a tribute for Dewey O'Day at Parker's. It's going to be boring as hell, but I knew the guy. He gave me good coverage when he was with the *Herald*, so I really have to go. Come with me."

She made a face. "Boring as hell, huh? That's not a great selling point."

"Me. You'll be with me. You'll be helping me survive."

"Sawyer, I hate those things."

"So do I, but I have to go." He cupped her shoulders.

"If you go too, we'll have fun. It won't last more than an hour or two."

"Or three. I know these things. They drag on forever."

"We'll sneak out before the speeches begin. In the meantime, there'll be food and booze."

"I don't drink."

"Neither do I, so we'll each have one and we won't be bored at all."

"That sounds totally irresponsible."

"So?"

"What about the case?"

"What case?"

"The Leindecker case. Maybe we shouldn't be seen together."

"That's crazy. We're friends. And colleagues. There's no reason why we can't spend time together. We won't be discussing clients, will we?"

"No."

"So? What do you say?"

"Oh, Sawyer." She let out a breath. "I have so much work to do."

"On Friday night?"

"Yes, on Friday night."

"Do it tomorrow."

"I have other stuff to do tomorrow."

"So you'll have a little more. Come on, Faith. Live a little."

She looked dubious. "At a tribute to Dewey O'Day?"

"With *me*. We'll have a good time. I promise."

Faith tried to think back to the last time she'd had a good time. It seemed ages ago. "You promise?"

"I promise."

2

THE ROOM WAS PACKED. Everyone who was anyone in Boston political circles was there, as well as members of the business and professional communities who had at one point been touched by Dewey O'Day. That was no small number; the man had been the nose of the *Herald* for forty years. Faith suspected as many people were there to butter up his successor as to pay tribute to Dewey himself. Sawyer confirmed it in a low drawl as they meandered through the crowd.

His whisper swelled to a full voice when he extended a hand to an older man who smiled as they approached. "Senator Cooperthorne. How have you been?"

"Fine, Sawyer."

"Do you know Faith Barry? Faith, this is Peter Cooperthorne, State Senator from Winthrop."

Faith offered her hand and a cordial smile. "It's a pleasure, Senator."

"The pleasure is mine. Good taste, Sawyer. She's a fine-looking woman. Is she yours?"

Sawyer shot Faith an amused glance. "Uh, no. She's a friend. Actually, a lawyer. Actually, a very skilled lawyer. I'm surprised you haven't heard of her. She's something of an authority on family law."

But family law wasn't Peter Cooperthorne's thing, as Faith discovered when he quickly launched into a discussion of the city's latest union dispute. Actually it wasn't so much a discussion as a monologue, and a rambling one at that. Sawyer, who did occasionally dabble in labor law, took the first opportunity to excuse himself and guide Faith away.

"Hot air," he side-mouthed to her. "The man doesn't know diddly about labor psychology, but he has an endless supply of hot air."

"He is the consummate politician," she side-mouthed back, then smiled at a familiar face. "Hi, Tommy. How goes it?"

"Great. But I haven't seen you in a while. You don't come visiting anymore."

Faith sent him a dry look, then made the introductions. "Tommy Lonigan, Sawyer Bell. Tommy is with the Probation Department," she explained to Sawyer. "We've had, uh, mutual clients."

Tommy wasn't leaving it at that. "Faith is the best thing to show her face in the Somerville Court House in years."

"I can believe that," Sawyer said. "Nice meeting you." With a light hand at Faith's back, he started her moving again. "Don't know how he'd know about years," he said under his breath. "He looks like he's fresh out of high school."

"UMass. And he's been out for three years." She nodded at another familiar face, but didn't stop. When Sawyer swept two glasses of wine from a passing tray and handed her one, she took it. They walked on.

"Sawyer!" A dapper-looking man stopped them. Sawyer introduced him as a former client; Faith recognized him as one of the city's major philanthropists. "So you're paying tribute to old Dewey, too?"

"Sure," Sawyer said. "He's been fair to me."

The man leaned closer and lowered his voice. "Wish I

could say the same, but he has a chip on his shoulder when it comes to money. He knocks me in his column every chance he gets, and if it isn't me, it's my car or my house or my art collection. As far as I'm concerned, he should have retired twenty years ago."

"If you feel that way," Faith couldn't help but ask, "why are you here?"

"Because I'm a good sport. And because the governor's showing up later and *he* likes old Dewey." He winked at her, clapped Sawyer on the shoulder and moved on.

Faith looked at Sawyer. "At least he was honest. What do you think he wants from the governor?"

"Probably a job for his new son-in-law. From what I hear, the kid's a real dud." He chinked his wineglass to hers. "Cheers."

"Cheers." She took a swallow and let Sawyer guide her on.

They stopped to greet a mutual acquaintance, a TV reporter who covered the State House and who, when he was off duty, covered himself to the exclusion of most other topics of conversation. Faith thought him a self-centered bore, which she promptly told Sawyer when they finally escaped.

"Not only that," Sawyer announced, "but he sleeps with a teddy bear." He took another swallow of wine.

Faith nearly choked on hers. Laughing, she looked up at him. "A teddy bear? How do you know that?"

"He had an affair with one of the lawyers in our office. She saw the bear."

"Now that's interesting," Faith decided. "Not boring at all." But it was the exception to the rule. For another hour, they wound their way through the crowd, and though they were often stopped by fellow lawyers and other acquaintances, they were never tempted to linger in any one circle for long.

Then the speeches began. "Let's leave," Faith whispered. She and Sawyer were at the back of the room, shoulder to shoulder against the wall. They'd had two glasses of wine apiece, and while they weren't quite tipsy, they weren't quite not. "I'm hungry."

"How can you be hungry?" he whispered back. "You ate a full plate of hors d'oeuvres."

"They were puny and, besides, you ate half of them."

"I did?"

"You did. What would you say to some Peking ravioli and a little Kung Pao shrimp?"

"I'd say, 'Ah so.'"

Faith snickered.

He leaned closer. "Shhh. You'll disturb the MC."

"The MC," she whispered back, "is a lousy speaker. His voice doesn't carry. I can't hear a word he's saying. Who told him to be MC anyway?"

"He's the Speaker of the House. He can do what he wants."

"Except speak."

Sawyer snickered.

"Shhh. You'll disturb the MC."

"You want to listen? I thought you wanted to leave."

"Can we?" she asked, eyes lighting up.

"Not yet. I want to hear Dewey."

"But he'll be last. I know how these things work. A million of his cronies will stand up—"

"Not a million. Maybe a dozen."

"At least a dozen, and they'll tell all kinds of lies—"

"Not lies. They'll talk about his good points and joke about his bad points." He paused. "Yeah, they'll lie." He paused again. "Want to go?"

She grinned. "I thought you'd never ask."

Without another word, they worked their way to the door, crossed through the lobby and went out into the night. A cold blast of air might have cleared their heads some, but the weather was mild, as New England autumns could unexpectedly be. So, light-headed and light-hearted they headed down School Street.

"Not Chinese," Sawyer said, as though he'd been debating the merits of Kung Pao shrimp ever since Faith had mentioned it. "Want to go to Houlihan's?"

"On a Friday night? We'd never get in."

"Sure we would. All it takes is a ten slipped into the right hand."

But Faith didn't want to go to Houlihan's. "I've been there for lunch three times in the last two weeks. How about Seaside?"

"Talk about lines getting in."

"Talk about slipping a ten—won't it work there?"

But Sawyer didn't want to go to Seaside. "I represented the wife of the owner in a scruffy divorce. Her husband's a bastard. On principle I avoid the place."

Faith could understand that. "How about Zachary's?"

"Too far away. I want to walk. How about the Ritz?"

She screwed up her nose. "Too stuffy."

"And Zachary's isn't?"

"How about the Daily Catch? I want to go to the North End. I feel like squid." She caught his eye. "Do you like squid?"

"I have been known," he said, "to be so mesmerized by the taste of the body of the thing that I forget and leave the tentacles dangling down my chin."

Faith sputtered into a laugh. She looped her arm through his. "You're fun to be with. Jack would never say anything like that. He'd never *do* anything like that."

"So why did you marry him instead of me?"

"Because I didn't know you when I married Jack. Besides, by the time I met you, you were married to Joanna."

Sawyer grunted. "She never laughed. She smiled sometimes, but she never laughed. She wasn't the type." They turned onto Washington Street and he declared, "Squid sounds just fine. I'm in the mood for the North End. Think there's a festival going on?"

"If there is, we may not get into the Daily Catch."

"We'll get in."

"You're slipping tens again?"

"Don't have to. I represented the owner when the city was giving him liquor license trouble. We won. He loves me."

Faith tried to decide whether she'd heard about that case, but her mind wasn't as sharp as usual. What she did decide was that it didn't matter whether she'd heard about the case or not. "Why is it you have all these illustrious clients? Mine are nowhere near as exciting."

"So why are you on television all the time?"

"Because I'm attractive, articulate and female." She tugged at his arm and drew him down Water Street. "I want to go home and change first. I'll stick out like a sore thumb walking through the North End in a silk dress and heels, and my feet hurt."

Sawyer was feeling thoroughly agreeable. He had no problem with changing clothes first. And she did have a point. The North End was best enjoyed wearing sneakers. "I'm at Rowes Wharf. You're at Union Wharf. If we stop at my place first, yours is right there on the way to the North End."

So it was decided. They talked as they walked, laughing most of the way once Sawyer got started on jokes. He had a knack for telling a story, could put on an Irish brogue, an Arkansas drawl or a Brooklyn bark with equal skill, and his repertoire was endless. Some of the jokes were funnier than others, some dirtier than others. Faith was muzzy enough to laugh at anything.

By the time they reached his condo, they were feeling quite good, which was why Faith didn't refuse him when he uncorked a chardonnay and poured her a glass.

"I don't drink," she reminded him as she took a sip of the wine. "Mmm. This is nice."

"It should be. It was a gift from a friend's wine cellar on the occasion of my settling a malpractice suit for him." He sampled the wine, then arched an approving brow. "Not bad."

"Not bad at all. Go change. I'm hungry."

Setting his glass on a coffee table, he headed down the hall. "Make yourself comfortable. I'll be right back."

Faith wandered across the living room. The decor registered in the back of her mind as being modern enough, pleasant enough, coordinated enough. The object of her interest, though, was the view from the window. The harbor's darkness was broken by the lights of passing boats, by buildings flanking the water, by the airport. She could see plenty of boats and buildings from her place, but she had nowhere near as good a view of the airport. Sipping her wine, she watched a plane take off, another one land, a second take off, a second one land.

She loved traveling. She'd done some when she'd been growing up, when her father had still been paying the bills and she'd still had the time. After that, she'd slacked off. Traveling with Jack hadn't been much fun. He wanted to see all the places she'd already seen, busy places like London and Paris, where he could plan out a daily program and sightsee from morning to night. She tried to understand that his job wasn't as demanding as hers. He worked in his father's business, and there was nothing particularly riveting about the manufacture of cardboard boxes. Her job, on the other hand, was both busy and challenging. Her idea of paradise was a long stretch of white sandy beach, a frothy fruit punch and a juicy novel.

So, after a while, she hadn't encouraged Jack to make travel arrangements. She'd contented herself with a week each summer in a rented house on Nantucket, plus whatever legal meetings she could spare the time to attend. But she missed the anticipation of going somewhere new, somewhere just to play.

"Like the view?" Sawyer asked, coming up behind her. He'd changed into jeans and a sweatshirt, and was carrying his wine.

"Oh, yeah." She looked him over. "Not bad, Sawyer. You're staying in shape. Still running?"

"Sure am."

"Every morning?"

"Bright and early. Boston's great at six. Just me and the pigeons and the street cleaners and the dozens of yuppies who live around here and think it's cool to run." He chinked his wineglass to hers. "Cheers."

"Cheers," she said and took a drink. "But you're not a yuppie."

He swallowed his wine. "Nope. Know who is, though?"

"Who?"

He grinned smugly. "Wally Ahearn."

Faith couldn't believe that. "Wally Ahearn? No way. Wally Ahearn was so antiestablishment he was nearly outlawed on the law-school campus."

"But he got his degree."

"Yeah, wearing a gauzy something his guru lent him. Wally Ahearn a yuppie? He *runs*?"

Something about the way she said it—and about the image of Wally as they remembered him in the guru's gown—made them both laugh. Sawyer forced himself to sober, but only after he'd taken a healthy drink of wine. "Trust me, Faith," he said in a trustworthy voice. "Wally no longer looks like a walrus."

"Okay, chalk walrus, and if he's a yuppie, he can't look like a hippie, but I can't, I *can't* see him wearing three-piece suits." She frowned. "He's not actually practicing law, is he?"

"Nope."

"I didn't think so. I always imagined he'd go off to the hills and raise honey bees, or something. Somehow a law degree didn't fit him." She raised the glass to her lips.

"He's a proctologist."

Faith's wine went down the wrong way. Putting a hand on her chest, she began to cough. Sawyer slapped her back, stopping only when she'd caught her breath. "Why do you *say* things like that?" she cried.

"Because it's true." When she gave a final cough, he said, "Take a drink. It'll help." She took a drink, then a deep breath, and when she'd finished doing that, he drew her to the sofa. "Sit."

"I can't sit," she said. "I want to go home and change, then get something to eat." But she sat. After a minute, she began to laugh. "A proctologist? That's too much."

Sawyer retrieved the wine bottle from the counter that separated the kitchen from the living room. "Have I ever lied to you?"

"No, Sawyer."

"I'm an honorable man." He refilled her wine glass, refilled his own and sank down into the chair across from her. "The last of the good guys." Leaning forward, he chinked his glass to hers. "Cheers."

"Cheers," she said, and took a drink. As the wine warmed her senses, she thought for a minute. "You and Larry O'Neill. The saviors of our class. Where's Larry now?"

"Springfield, Illinois. He's doing tax work."

"I can believe that. He has a big family to support. How many kids now?"

"Eight."

"No!"

But Sawyer nodded. "So help me, eight kids."

"He had three when we graduated, and that was nine years ago. He's been busy."

Sawyer laughed. "His wife is the busy one. Do you remember her?"

"Charlene? Of course, I remember Charlene. She was always pregnant. Still is, I guess." She raised her glass. "To Charlene."

"To Charlene," Sawyer said and took a drink. "So how about you, Faith? Do you want kids?"

"Sure I do. I want twelve."

"Twelve!"

"Three sets of twins and two sets of triplets."

"I can't picture it."

"Why not?" she asked, sounding hurt. "Doctors can do anything nowadays. I put in my order, they get out their little test tubes and their little petri dishes, I get my kids."

"Ahhh," he said sagely.

"That's right, ahhh. So how about you?"

"Me? No way. I'm not getting pregnant with one, let alone twins and triplets. Don't want to ruin my figure."

She laughed, and a grin remained long after the sound

had died. She sat back in the sofa, feeling more relaxed than she had in months and months. "You're fun, Sawyer. How could I have forgotten that?"

"Out of sight, out of mind."

"But we always had such good times. Remember the lunches we had with Alvin Breen? Or the seminars we went to? Remember the time we served on a panel together in Pittsfield?"

"Do I ever," he said. There was a wry twist to his lips and a playful gleam in his eye. "You were the only woman, and you took advantage of it to the hilt. You wore a bright red dress, bright red shoes, bright red lipstick, bright red nail polish, and you sat there looking like a perfect piece of fluff. Boy, did you fool them. Their mouths dropped open when you began to speak."

Faith sipped her wine, then said with an innocent tip of her head, "It wasn't my fault they thought I was dumb."

"You let them believe it, you shameless hussy."

"They *chose* to believe it. Most men do."

"Doesn't it make you mad?"

"Mad? When I get such satisfaction seeing them with egg on their faces?"

Sawyer threw back his head and laughed. "I love it," he said, then sat forward. "You're remarkable." He chinked his wineglass to hers. "To you."

"To me," she said with a grin and, with a flourish, finished her wine. She was feeling delightfully warm. Any rough edges that were left over from the week had melted away.

Sawyer rose, took the wine glass from her and set it on the table, then grabbed her hand and drew her up. "Let's go. I'm hungry."

"I think I'm a little high."

"Me, too. We need food."

Minutes later, they were heading down Atlantic Avenue in the general direction of Faith's place. "This is fun," he announced. "I haven't done anything spontaneous in a long time."

"Me, neither. My life is predictable. There's work, work and more work."

"Ever get tired of it?"

"Yup. Then the phone rings, I get a new case and I'm revived."

They walked along at a jaunty pace.

"You're not really representing Dorothea Winchell, are you?" Sawyer asked.

"Sure am."

"She's a fraud."

Faith wasn't at all offended. "Uh-uh. She loved the man. She was with him for ten years. Ten years. And in that time, she took a lot of abuse."

"He chose not to leave her anything in his will."

"He had Alzheimer's. Did he choose, or was he unable to choose? Or did his children prevent him from choosing?"

"You'll lose," Sawyer warned, but playfully. That was the kind of mood he was in.

Faith was in a similar mood. "Losing is relative. As his common-law wife, she has a right to a little protection. We won't get all we're asking, but something is better than nothing." She sent a perky look up at him. "And you're a fine one to be talking. You're representing John Donato. Now, if that isn't a lost cause, I don't know what is."

He was undaunted. "It's a *great* cause. Donato puts up a building. Halfway through construction, the city council finds an obscure code that says the building can't be that tall. Donato is expected to lower the building at a million dollar loss. The city owes him."

"From what I hear," Faith drawled, looking off toward the Aquarium, "Donato obtained his original permit in a slightly, uh, unorthodox manner."

"Y'heard that, did ya?"

"Yup."

"Who'd you hear it from?"

"I'm not telling. Is it true?"

"Now, if I told you that, it'd be a violation of lawyer-client privilege."

"I won't tell anyone," she whispered loudly.

In answer, he wrapped an arm around her waist and pulled her close. Their hips bumped. Laughing, they adjusted their gaits to match, and walked on. To the left, the lights of the Marketplace lent a gaiety to the night. To the right, the Harbor was unusually serene. They felt peaceful, happy, totally at ease with the night and each other, and because of that, they talked about things they might not have normally discussed.

Such as the people they'd dated since their respective divorces.

"Brandi Payne? You actually went out with Brandi Payne?" Faith asked in good-humored disbelief as they turned into Union Wharf.

"Sure did."

"I hear she's a bitch."

"You hear right. She gives new meaning to the term swelled-headed. I suppose you have to give her some credit. She came in as the Channel 4 anchor when the station was trailing the other two, and she's brought it to the top. But full of herself? Whew!"

"What possessed you to go out with her?"

"We have a mutual friend. He had a party. We met. I

asked her out. I wanted to see what the private persona was like, and boy, did I ever. We ran into Alec Soames and Susan Siler at the restaurant. They were in town to do a signing at the Ritz, and they happen to be a stunning couple. Brandi didn't like that much. She wants all eyes on her. The comments she made to Alec and Susan about their book were bad enough, but the fuss she made about what table we were going to have and whether the service was good enough and whether the butternut squash soup had too much salt were downright embarrassing."

"Poor Alec and Susan."

"Poor Sawyer."

Faith was grinning as she opened the door to her condo. "What I want to know," she said, punching out the code to turn off the alarm, "is whether you took her to bed." When the alarm didn't stop, she frowned, concentrated, punched out the code a second time.

"That's a very personal question."

"You're a very personal friend. Damn, what's wrong with this?" The alarm was still humming, waiting to be disengaged. Slowly and with deliberation this time, she gave separate emphasis to each digit in the code. Still the alarm resisted. "I don't believe it," she cried.

"Are you hitting the right numbers?"

"I'm hitting 4-3-8-3. That's my phone number." She put two fingers to her forehead and closed her eyes. "Alarm code. 8-2-9-2." She had punched in the first two when noise exploded around them. The noise died just as suddenly when she entered the last 2. She grinned up at Sawyer. "There. All better. But you didn't answer my question. Did you sleep with Brandi Payne?"

"No, I did not."

"Why not? She has a great bod."

"By the time we finished dinner, I was so turned off by

the woman herself that I didn't give a damn about her bod." The phone rang. "Good timing," he said and started toward it. Abruptly he stopped. "Uh, it's yours."

Laughing, Faith turned into the kitchen and answered it. "Yes?" She grew serious. "Emergency 24?" She frowned. "My alarm. Oh, my alarm! I'm so sorry. That was a mistake. I confused my phone number with—no, no, there's no need to call the police. The code? Uh, uh, 3-6-5. Yes. Thank you." She hung up the phone and looked at Sawyer, who was leaning against the door-jamb. "They wanted to make sure I was okay. Wasn't that nice? If I hadn't given them the right code, they'd have called the police. It's a very clever system. As you can see, none of my neighbors have come running to the door to see whether it's me or a burglar in here." She thought for a minute. "Maybe I need a dog. You know, something intimidating. A watchdog."

"But you're afraid of dogs."

"How do you know?"

"I was with you once when you were attacked by a poodle. Don't you remember? It was four or five years ago. We'd just come from lunch at Dini's, and there was this adorable little—"

"Adorable, nothing!" Faith cried, remembering the day. "That dog was vicious! It was coming right at me with its teeth bared."

"You *thought* it was coming right at you, but the fact was that it was headed for a schnauzer behind you. And it didn't have its teeth bared. It was grinning." He chuckled. "Boy, were you scared."

"And you laughed. You laughed at me."

"I couldn't help it. It was funny. You're always so se-rene-looking, even when you're in court, and then this little dog comes along and—"

"I'm going to change," she interrupted. "I'm hungry."

"Good idea. What's this?"

She had taken a bottle from under a cupboard and was putting it in his hands. "Champagne."

"I think I've had enough to drink."

"So have I. But this is special champagne. It was given to me by Dennis and MaryAnn Johnson when we finally found the right baby for them to adopt. The agencies had given them trouble, because Dennis was convicted of marijuana possession eighteen years ago. Not a spot of trouble since, still he has a record. So we went the private route. It took two years, but the baby is perfect." She grinned. "So this is happy champagne. Open it."

Sawyer looked at the bottle. "Happy champagne, huh?" He was certainly happy. "Why not. You go change, while I open it. I'm feeling underdressed."

Faith leaned close, stretched up to his ear and whispered, "Better underdressed than undressed." She came back down, eyeing him quizzically. "I've never seen you undressed. Do you know that, Sawyer? I've never even seen you without a shirt on. Why didn't we ever go to the beach?"

"We were too busy."

"We went to movies. You and Joanna and Jack and me. Why not to the beach?"

"The beach is for vacations. We never vacationed together."

"Why not? It would have been fun."

"Maybe we didn't trust ourselves. Go change, Faith. I'm hungry."

"Mmm. Me, too," she murmured and went off toward her room.

Sawyer managed to uncork the champagne without too much trouble. He had more trouble finding fluted glasses, then laughed when he realized what he'd gone looking for. Faith wouldn't have fluted glasses any more than he would. A few wine glasses, yes. Wine glasses were good to have on hand in case company popped in with a bottle. Fluted glasses were for more sophisticated drinking, and since Jack hadn't imbibed any more than Joanna, there were no fluted glasses here.

So he took two wine glasses, filled them with champagne and ambled into the living room. It was small and didn't have much furniture, but what it did have was in good taste. Faith had that. Joanna didn't, which wasn't to say that he hadn't liked the house they'd shared. It had been an old thing on the outskirts of Cambridge. They'd bought it soon after they married, thinking that renovating it would be good therapy for Sawyer, and it had been that. He'd taken pride in stripping and staining the woodwork, putting in a new floor, updating the kitchen. It had given him a sense of accomplishment. Joanna's satisfaction came through his—and through filling the place with homespun things. Nothing matched. She had no eye for style or design. She created a cozy clutter that, unfortunately, began to grate on Sawyer when he grew to want breathing space.

Faith's place, small though it was, had breathing space. He was amazed that he thought so, since he'd had enough wine to create the illusion of closeness and warmth, but he felt perfectly comfortable here.

He walked around the sofa and perched against its back, which ran parallel to the glass sliders that looked out on the harbor. Actually, he mused, the view was sideways. It took in as much of the city as the harbor. As for details, he couldn't see many. The glass was reflecting the room behind him more strongly than anything else.

"Cheers," he said, and held one of the wine glasses out

toward his reflection in the glass. He was about to take a sip when his reflection was joined by Faith's. She was wearing jeans and a sweatshirt, and without her heels, seemed suddenly more petite. "Come," he told her reflection. "I want to make a toast."

"Another toast," she breathed. Rounding the sofa, she came to his side and took one of the glasses. "Cheers," she said.

"*I* want to make the toast."

She stopped the glass an inch before her mouth. "Okay. You make the toast."

"Cheers," he said and took a drink.

She laughed, declared his toast, "Profound," and sipped the champagne. "Ah," she said when the last of the bubbles had slipped down her throat. "Nice. Did you miss me?"

"Sure did. I was trying to look out your window, but I couldn't."

"Wait," she said. Holding her glass to the side, she went back through the room and turned off the light. "There." She returned to the nook he'd found behind the sofa. "Like it?"

He stood and moved close to the glass. "Oh, yeah. It's different from mine. You can see the city. And the boats in their slips. You even have a patio."

"You have a balcony."

"This is different. Must be the trees. How did you manage to get trees in here?"

"Sanguinetti Landscaping. They specialize in potted things. Nice flowers and shrubs and plants and stuff. I wanted green."

He turned to look at her. She was faintly lit by the reflection of the city lights, and seemed almost ephemeral.

"You're a very wise girl. I don't understand why some man hasn't snapped you up yet."

"I've only been divorced for a year."

"But you're a catch." He returned to the sofa and sat close by her side. "Didn't someone tell me you dated Paul Agnes for a while?"

"Twice. We went out twice."

"Didn't like him?"

She sipped her champagne. "Not enough."

"To go to bed with him?"

"Right. That was pretty much all he wanted. Why was that, Sawyer? Why *is* that? I thought times had changed. I thought AIDS had put the fear of God into singles. But sex has been the one thing that's first and foremost on the minds of the men I've seen since the divorce. Not that I've seen that many. I'm not in a rush to get involved with anyone. I'm busy with work. I rather like being able to come and go as I please. And I'm not lonely, except sometimes a guy will ask me out for dinner or to a show and it sounds like fun. So I go. And it is fun, until we get back here and he wants to come in. If I say no, he's angry. If I say yes, he's into touchy and feely before you can blink an eye, and when I say no to that, he's doubly angry. So I'm damned both ways. It shouldn't have to be like that."

Sawyer, who'd been sampling his champagne, set the stem of the glass on his knee. "Know what your problem is?"

"No, what? Tell me. I want to know."

"You're too pretty."

"There's no such thing."

"There is, and you are. You're a striking woman. It may be the way you dress. Or the way you carry your-self. Or your confidence. You're feminine without trying to be. It's hard for a man to look at you and not think of sex."

"You don't."

He took a larger swallow from his glass. "That's 'cause you're Jack's girl. You've always been off-limits to me, so I look at you other ways. I know how intelligent and creative and honest and fun you are to be with."

She sent him a glowing smile. "You are my favorite man." She slipped an arm around his waist and raised the other, glass in hand. "To you," she declared.

"To me," he echoed.

They both drank deeply of the champagne. Sawyer slipped from her side. "Hold still. Don't move." He half-walked, half-ran back to the kitchen, scooped up the champagne bottle and was back.

"Maybe we shouldn't," Faith whispered as she watched him refill their glasses. "I'm hungry."

"Me, too, but we haven't finished with the toasts." Setting the bottle on the floor, he sat beside her again and raised his glass. "To Jack and Joanna."

"Why are we toasting them?"

"Because they're not here to toast themselves."

"But why do they have to be toasted?"

"Because they're good sports. They put up with us." He chuckled, then pulled a straight face. "To Jack and Joanna." He chinked his glass to hers.

"To Jack and Joanna," Faith said and took a drink. Since there were two people in the toast—and since Sawyer seemed to be doing it—she took a second drink on the heels of the first. "Sawyer?"

"Umm?"

"Maybe we should fix them up."

"Jack and Joanna? Nah. Wouldn't work. Joanna's too maternal."

"Jack's paternal. It would be great."

"Only if they had a kid, but they'd never make it in the sack."

"That's an awful thing to say, Sawyer!"

He considered that for a minute. "Yes. I'm sorry." He looked at Faith.

She looked at him. "You're not sorry at all."

"No."

They laughed. This time it was Sawyer who slipped an arm around Faith's waist. "I can tell you anything. Do you know how nice that is?" He tugged her close to give her a hug, but somehow they lost hold of their perch on the back of the sofa and half-slid, half-fell to the floor. That made them laugh harder.

"Ahhh," Sawyer groaned through his laughter. "Are you okay, Faith?"

"I'm down, but not out," she declared with mock pomposity. More humbly, she said, "Something spattered on my sweatshirt. Am I bleeding?"

"That was champagne. Com'ere." He helped rearrange her body so they were tucked snugly against the sofa and each other, facing the world beyond the glass sliders. Taking only a minute to replenish their glasses of any champagne they may have lost in the fall, he picked up where he'd left off.

"You're special. I don't know any other woman I can do this with. I really can tell you anything. Anything."

From time to time, one word slurred into the next, but it was subtle, too subtle for Faith, in her own less-than-sober state, to notice. "Tell me something," she said. She tapped his chest with her finger. "Tell me something you wouldn't tell anyone else."

He lowered his voice to a whisper. "Joanna was a lousy kisser."

"A lousy kisser? But she was a nurse. What about all that mouth-to-mouth—"

They burst into hysterics, leaning over one another in laughter. Sawyer was the first to recover. "Honest to God, I don't know how she ever did that. When it came time to kiss, she didn't open her mouth. I couldn't get her to open her mouth."

"And I'm sure you were persuasive."

"I tried. She didn't like the feel of it. So I stopped trying after a while." He looked down at her face in the darkness. "Was Jack persuasive?"

"No. He was punctual."

"Punctual? What's punctual got to do with kissing?"

"Jack was a systematic lover. Certain things were to be done certain ways at certain times, and that was that. Kisses were a meeting of the mouth. They started out as pecks. After seventy-seven seconds of that, they became smooches, and after two minutes and ten seconds of that, they got wet. They stopped completely when he began to pant."

"Sounds like a dog," Sawyer observed, and they broke up again. This time when they sobered, Faith set her wine glass aside. Levering herself up with a hand on his chest, she faced him.

"Show me," she ordered. "Show me how you kissed her."

Something in the back of Sawyer's hazy mind told him that would be wrong. "I can't. I've forgotten."

"Then show me how you kiss, period. I'll bet you're good. I want to know what a good kiss is like."

"So do I."

She cupped his face with her hands. "Kiss me, Sawyer. Show me how you do it. Please?"

Sawyer looked at her upturned face, so dimly lit as

they sat on the floor behind the sofa. He looked out at the city, where thousands and thousands of people were enjoying each other, and he wanted to enjoy himself, too. He *was* enjoying himself.

But he wanted to kiss Faith.

For a long moment he thought, or tried to think of the reasons why he shouldn't. But he was high. He couldn't come up with a single one.

3

"HOW I KISS," he said softly. He raised both hands and slid them into her hair so that he could frame her head and tip it up. "The first touch isn't much more than a token. It's kind of like a hello."

"Is this what you used to do when you walked in from work?"

"No. That wasn't much more than a peck on the cheek, and sometimes it wasn't even that. I thought you wanted to know what a *kiss* kiss was like."

"I do."

"A sex kiss?" he asked, daring it because the wine had loosened his tongue.

"Mmm."

"Okay. First, there's this." He lowered his head, put his lips on hers and moved them just a little before lifting his head again. "It's a way of me finding out if you want to be kissed. Sometimes Joanna didn't. Sometimes she'd turn her head. No way I could miss that message. You, on the other hand—" he gave a skewed grin "—didn't pull away, so I can guess that you want more."

Faith did. "That little thing was just a teaser."

"That's what it was supposed to be. It's supposed to make you want more."

"The first step in persuasion? Okay. So what do you do next?"

"More of the same." Lowering his head again, he did

just that. One light touch after another, each gentle but enchanting, none lasting long enough to provide any deep satisfaction.

Faith liked the way his lips could be firm but still gentle. She liked the warmth of his breath and the faint smell of wine. She liked the feeling of leisure. "Mmm. This is nice. Jack would have already moved on. He had to keep on schedule. But this is nice."

Sawyer agreed. He continued to dole out those fetching kisses, because they were captivating even him. In between, he talked. "Schedules don't work when it comes to sex." He brushed the upper bow of her mouth. "The thing is that sometimes after that first hello you want it hard and fast." He sampled the corner of her mouth. "Other times you want it slow. Sometimes," he said, pausing to kiss her chin, "you want to widen your focus a little. Sometimes a woman's mouth makes you curious about how other parts of her taste." He slid his mouth up to her cheek, then her eye, kissing each lightly. He came down the gentle slope of her nose in an inevitable return to her mouth. "Sometimes," he whispered, "you even want to taste with your tongue." He did that, tracing the curve of her mouth, then sucking in a shallow breath. "Mmm, Faith. You taste very good."

Faith's eyes were closed. She felt as though she were floating, no doubt, she reasoned, on the champagne bubbles that shimmered inside her. "Jack never told me that," she said. Her words were wispy and seemed to overlap. "He never talked when he touched me. He was letting his body do the speaking, only I could never hear the words. Why was that?"

"Maybe because you were concentrating on what was going to happen next. That's what Joanna always did. She didn't want to linger. Move right along, folks. Come on, keep going. She wanted to get on with it and get done as soon as possible. She wanted to get it over with.''

"I didn't want that," Faith protested, then hesitated. "Well, maybe I did. There was nothing inspiring about what was happening. I never enjoyed Jack's kisses. Certainly not the way I'm enjoying yours. Go on, Sawyer. Kiss me more. I liked what you were doing.''

So Sawyer kissed her more, still those same first-stage kisses that he was finding so pleasurable. He knew that the wine had put a glowing sheen on his awareness of the world. He also knew that Faith was a friend, not a sex partner, but that didn't stop him from enjoying the scent of her skin and the dewiness of her mouth. Her lips were soft and pliant, just as a woman's should be. She wasn't reticent, as Joanna had been. Nor was she aggressive, as some other women could be. She let him set the pace, and she responded to it. She seemed very much in tune with him. He liked that.

When he caught a soft sigh slipping from her lips, he opened his mouth to catch it. Her sigh became a gasp, and he quickly pulled back. "You don't like that?"

"I do." She laughed. "I do. It surprised me, that's all. Do it again. I'll be ready this time."

She tried to be, still she wasn't prepared for what happened when Sawyer opened his mouth on hers and gave her the kind of kiss he was primed for. The soft hellos and gently foraging smooches gave way to deeper curiosity. But he didn't have to force her mouth open. It moved with his, reacting to his in all the ways that seemed perfectly natural and utterly right. So he kissed her more deeply, then more deeply again. His tongue found hers, went beyond and around it, swept through the inside of her mouth in a journey that took his breath away.

He gasped for air and tried to steady the fine tremor that shook his arms. "Whew. That's never happened to me before."

"What?" she whispered. She was taking small, short breaths.

"Getting caught up like that."

"You didn't get caught up with Joanna? I always thought men had to get caught up if they were going to be able to complete the sex act."

"Right," he said, "but at different times and levels. Was Jack always ready at the start?"

"Hard, you mean?"

"Hard, I mean."

"Yes. Jack made up his mind that it was time to make love and, bingo, he was hard. I sometimes wondered whether he needed me at all. It could have been anyone under him."

"That's not true. He loved you."

"In his way, but that kind of love had little to do with the sex we had. I'm telling you. It was preprogrammed sex. Nothing like what we're doing now." Her voice dropped to a whisper. "What do we do next?"

Sawyer was still too aware of her taste on his tongue. Taking his hands from her hair, he sat against the sofa back. "Next we take a break."

"Why?"

"Because I need to catch my breath." It was more than that, he knew. It was a tiny voice inside telling him that something was going to get out of hand if he didn't slow down. He was feeling too good. Whether it was the wine or Faith, he didn't know, but his blood was pumping a little too warmly through his veins. And that last, deep, tongue-twisting kiss had done something to his groin.

Things were beginning to feel tight down there. He needed a break.

Reaching for his wine glass, he took a swallow.

Faith was sitting up, eyeing him through the darkness. "You didn't like it," she whispered, and even in spite of the non-sound of her voice, he caught bits of accusation and hurt.

He put a hand to her cheek. "I liked it too well." Slipping his hand down, he caught one of hers and flattened it over his heart. "Feel that? Is that the feel of something I don't like?"

"Could be," she said, pouting. She'd never pouted before in her life. She hated people who pouted and would have hated herself—if she'd known. "People's hearts bang when they're upset or afraid. Could be that you don't want to be doing this, but you feel you have to since I asked. Is that it?"

"No way! If I didn't want to be doing this, I'd get up off the rug and walk away. Do you see me doing that?"

"Maybe you're too tired."

"I'm not too tired."

"Or drunk. Maybe your legs won't work."

He set the wine glass aside. "They work just fine. And I am not drunk," he insisted. He tried to put separate emphasis on each word, but they slurred together. Pulling her across his lap and into his arms, he declared, "I liked what I was doing. I'm going to do it again."

But what he did was different. At least, Faith thought it was. Not that she could remember the fine details of what he'd done before, since the amount of wine she'd drunk robbed her of that clarity, but she remembered the titillation of it. What he did now was even more titillating. It was bolder, more confident, persuasive in ways that had nothing to do with clarity and everything to do with pure sensation. By the time he ended the kiss, she was grasping his sweatshirt for dear life.

"Is *that* how you kissed Joanna?" she whispered between short gasps.

He didn't know. He hadn't been consciously thinking of Joanna. He hadn't been consciously thinking of much but the fire that licked at his nerve ends.

"Maybe we'd better stop," he whispered back. Her head was cradled in his arm. He looked down at her face to find features whose eagerness shone through the dim night light.

"I don't want to stop. I want you to show me more." She bobbed up. With the sudden movement, she swayed. Steadying herself, she sat on her haunches between his legs. "I want to do something."

"What?"

"Touch you. Jack didn't like being touched. He didn't think it was important. He didn't need it to be aroused. But it might have helped me." She averted her eyes in a moment's reconsideration. "Maybe not. Jack had a nice enough build, but there was nothing spectacular about it. Maybe my touching him wouldn't have done a thing for either of us." She looked back up at Sawyer and whispered. "Let me touch you. Just a little." She relaxed her grip on his sweatshirt and flattened her hands on his shoulders. Slowly she drew them toward his neck, back to the top of his arms, almost timidly down over the musculature of his upper chest. And everywhere her hands went, her eyes followed.

She let out a single, clipped sound, halfway between a sigh and a gasp. "Like this," she whispered. "Just like this. So nice."

Sawyer didn't know whether he was more pleased with the look of awe on her face or the feel of her hands on his chest. "Wait." His voice was sounding hoarse. "I'll make it even better." Before either of them could begin to wonder whether they were going too far, he whipped the sweatshirt over his head.

Faith sat back on her heels, looking at what he'd bared. "Sawyer, you're so big!"

"Is that good or bad?"

"Good! Good! I hadn't realized..." Her voice trailed off when she brought her hands up and touched him. His skin was warm, even hot, but she was truly stunned by how much of him there was. She'd known he was well-toned, but she hadn't known he was so broad in the shoulders. Moving in a slow, dreamy way, her hands took forever to cover him. Part of that was because the hair on his chest slowed her down. It created a friction that she found surprisingly exciting. Where the hair thinned and tapered into a narrow line, she purposely kept her hand slow to fully appreciate the firmness of his skin.

Sawyer had never been so erotically charted. He leveled his shoulders, took in a deep gulp of air that expanded his chest even more. With that oxygen feeding his brain, he grabbed Faith under the arms and drew her forward. His mouth met hers in a kiss that, for the first time, held raw hunger.

It should have frightened Faith off, or at least alerted her to the fact of his arousal. But she was too aroused, herself, to think of anything but enjoying more. Wrapping her arms around his neck, she immersed herself in the kiss. Somewhere in its midst, he began to caress her breasts, but that fact was lost amid the overall headiness of what she felt.

"Hold on for a second, babe," he dragged his mouth from hers to whisper. He tried to ease her away but she made a throaty sound of protest and tightened her grip on him. Reaching back for her wrists, he dragged them forward. "Wait. I want to touch you." He held her gaze while he covered her breasts with his hands. After a second he began to knead her flesh. It was the most wonderful thing Faith had felt yet. Her expression told him so.

"Didn't Jack do this to you?"

She nodded. "But it didn't feel like this."

"What does it feel like?"

"Good. I don't know. Really good. Did Joanna like it when you touched her breasts?"

He shook his head. "It embarrassed her. Does it embarrass you?"

Faith swallowed. She was breathing more quickly again, and he wasn't even kissing her anymore. "No. It makes me hot."

"I want to take off your shirt."

"Maybe you shouldn't. Maybe this is enough." But he chose that minute to rub his thumbs over her nipples, which were distinct even through her bra and sweatshirt. "Mmm, do it." She reached for the hem herself, and while she was pulling the sweatshirt over her head, Sawyer unhooked her bra. By the time she lowered her arms, she was naked from the waist up. For a minute, she sat very still looking up at him. Her expression would have been wary if her features were working right, but they didn't seem to be responding efficiently to the commands of her brain. "Is this right, what we're doing?" she managed to ask. She was feeling warm and tingly and more than a little muzzy.

"Oh, yeah," he professed a bit brashly. "We're the best of friends, Faith. Nothing between us is wrong. Here." He held his wine glass to her lips and gave her a drink, then took one himself. Then he set the glass aside and touched her. "You have very beautiful breasts. They stand there, just waiting for me."

"Joanna's didn't stand there?"

"They sagged."

She sputtered out a laugh. "You're awful!"

"I'm serious," he said, but softly. His eyes didn't stray from her breasts, and as he talked, his hand moved lightly, if a bit unsteadily over her flesh. "I didn't really see them much. She kept them well hidden. I think she was ashamed of her body." Raising his eyes to hers, he said, "You're not. I can feel it in you. You're proud to be a woman. That's really refreshing, Faith. Do you know how refreshing it is?"

For a minute, Faith couldn't say a word. He was brushing his fingers over the tips of her breasts. She fancied there was a wire stretching from that point to another point deep inside her. With each brush of his fingers the wire twisted.

"Faith?"

"Mmm?"

"Are you okay?"

"I think so."

"How does that feel?"

"Incredibly—" Her voice caught. She tried again. "Incredibly nice." But just then, the wire snapped. She came forward and up on her knees, looking for his kiss. He gave it to her with just the force she needed, but even before the kiss was over, the hunger had grown. Hugging him tightly, she cried, "Sawyer?" Her mouth was by his ear, her high-pitched cry urgent.

"What is it, sweetheart?"

"Something's hurting. I'm feeling so empty inside that it's hurting. Help me. Please, help me."

Sawyer was feeling the same hurt. It had managed to

surface through the aura of pleasure that was clouding his view of reality. "Shhh, it's okay, sweetheart." He held her tightly for a minute, but the feel of her bare back beneath his arms, not to mention the heaven of her breasts against his chest, drove him on. "Okay," he whispered. He took her mouth in a kiss at the same time that he reached for the snap of her jeans. The zipper was quickly down. She scrambled back to push at the denim and her panties. Together they shimmied both from her legs. Then, while he ran his hands over the parts of her body that were newly uncovered, she hurriedly worked at his jeans.

His zipper was more difficult to lower than hers had been. He was fully aroused, and while that hindered her progress, the discovery excited her beyond belief. No sooner was his fly open when she slipped both hands into his briefs and found the heat waiting there.

"Oh my," she murmured. "Oh my."

"'Oh my' is right," he growled. Tumbling her backward onto the carpet, he quickly shucked his pants. He had to be inside her. There wasn't any doubt in his mind that if he didn't make it fast, he'd die of frustration. Her thighs were open. She rose to meet him when he came between them, and when he entered her, she cried out.

It was the heat. He knew because he felt it himself. It was the heat and the moisture and the wine that made her sheathing so perfect. He tried to savor it, tried to move in and out with the proper understanding of how well she fit him, but he didn't have the patience. He was burning from the inside out, and the only way to fight that was to surge hard and deep toward fulfillment.

Faith was with him all the way. She goaded him on with the movement of her hips, her legs, her restless hands. Their bodies grew damp with sweat, and the sweat mingled. They drove each other ever higher. And when he reached the release he sought, the spasms of his body beat against and between her throbbing.

That should have been the end of it. They should have fallen apart on the floor, done in by drink or exhaustion or sheer bliss. Somehow, it didn't work that way. They did lie there for a minute until they'd caught their breath. But then it was as if they forgot they'd climaxed. Sawyer was still hard inside her, and when he began to move, she gasped in delight.

It took longer this time. Their movements were slower, more drugged, but no less pleasurable. After a time, it was hard to tell where one peak ended and the next began.

FAITH CAME AWAKE very reluctantly the next morning. On the one hand, things were as always. She was in her bed, where she was every morning when the sun rose over the harbor and skipped sideways into her window. On the other hand, things were different.

Her head hurt, for starters. She discovered that when she tried to move it around on the pillow. Her eyes hurt, too. She opened them a slit, immediately realized her mistake and shut them again.

And she was naked. The sheets felt different against bare skin. Moving a hand to her ribs, she confirmed the finding, but that didn't make it any easier to understand. She never slept naked. She was usually too cold for that. Winter or summer, it didn't matter, she always wore something, preferably long-sleeved and ankle length, to bed.

She was warm, though, and for an instant she wondered whether she'd set the electric blanket higher than usual. But she didn't have the electric blanket on. At least she didn't think she did. It was still in storage. And yet she was warm. Gingerly exploring that warmth, she moved her leg. In the process, she discovered two things.

The first was that her muscles hurt. Not just any old muscles, but those in her legs. To be exact, those in her thighs.

The second was that she wasn't alone. Her foot had hit something solid. It was the source of the heat, she knew. She also knew that it had been well over a year since she'd shared a bed with Jack. She hadn't shared a bed with any other person since.

Momentarily ignoring the pounding in her head and the ache around her eyes, she forced herself to look at the side of the double bed that was usually vacant. It wasn't vacant now. A head capped with dark, rumpled hair was in possession of the second pillow. Just below that head was a sinewed neck, below that a pair of broad shoulders, below that a smoothly muscled back that held remnants of a tan.

Unable to take her eyes from that back, Faith took in a quick breath and sat up. She clutched the sheet to her breasts and swallowed once, hard. That was all it took for the events of the night before to slowly begin to filter through the fog that still clouded her brain.

"Sawyer?" she called in a very low, very shaky voice. The second time around, she managed to make it a little louder, but no less shaky. "Sawyer?"

He didn't move. For a split second she wondered whether it wasn't Sawyer after all but a big dummy he'd left as a joke. She'd like that. She'd like the things—pictures, images, flashes of memory—from the night before to have been make-believe.

But no. That was real live flesh, real live Sawyer Bell, real live *naked* Sawyer Bell beside her.

"Sawyer?" she called, this time in a panic. "Sawyer!"

He jerked, then groaned and put a hand on the side of his head.

"Sawyer, get up!" Tugging the top sheet free of the quilt, she scrambled to the side of the bed and wrapped it around her as she stood. When she looked back at Sawyer, he was rolling onto his back. "Get up, Sawyer. Oh please, get up."

He opened his eyes a crack, much as she'd done not so long before. As she'd done, he squeezed them tight again. But Faith wasn't allowing him the leisure she'd had to let memory come calling. "Sawyer." He grunted. "Sawyer!"

He pried his eyes open and focused on her, and for a minute he simply stared, trying without success to make sense out of what he was seeing. Finally he frowned. "Faith?" He knew it had to be her. There wasn't anyone who had quite her face, quite her hair, quite her voice. But he had no idea what she could possibly be doing standing by the side of his bed draped in a sheet.

Then he realized that the setting was wrong. Moving his head by short, pained inches, he saw that he wasn't in his own bedroom at all. His bedroom was done in navies and browns. This one was heavy on whites and hurt his eyes something awful. And the bed was too small. His heel was caught on the bottom edge of the mattress. That never happened with his extra-long king. And he would never, *never* sleep on flowered sheets under a flowered quilt, but unless his eyesight was truly going, that was what he saw above and below his hip. His *naked* hip.

Bolting upright, he winced and caught himself for a minute, then grabbed the quilt from the bed and, though he was plenty warm on his own, wrapped it around him as he hurried to stand on the opposite side of the mattress from Faith. Memory was fast returning, coming in flashes like a strobe tormenting his brain.

"What happened?" he rasped. He hoped she'd tell him that he'd simply had too much to drink, so she'd put him to bed. Somehow, between the look on her face and the images that were flashing in his mind, he doubted that was the case.

"We did it," she whispered in dismay. Then she paused and allowed herself a last-ditch doubt. "Did we?"

Sawyer looked down at the bed. They'd just awoken in it. Clearly they'd spent at least part of the night here. But the pictures flickering into his mind were of someplace darker, like the living room, and someplace harder, like the floor. "Do you see any clothes?" he asked cautiously. He didn't. There was nothing draped over the white wicker chair in the corner, nothing thrown on the white wicker dresser, nothing dropped on the pale green carpet.

"No. I think they may be, uh, in the other room."

Sawyer's headache gave an extra-strong pulse as though in punishment for what the evidence was strongly suggesting. He raked a hand through his hair. "Were we drunk?"

"I don't know. I've never been drunk before. Do you remember much?"

"Bits and pieces."

"Did we...?"

Sawyer tuned into several of those bits and pieces. He remembered talking about Joanna but seeing Faith. He remembered touching her. He remembered that she felt very good to hold. He remembered that she was very tight inside. "I think so."

"Oh Lord." She twisted down onto the bed, putting

her back to him, which gave her a token protection from the embarrassment she felt. She rested her splitting head in her hands. "Oh Lord. I've never, *never* done anything like this. I'm sorry, Sawyer."

"It was my fault as much as yours," he snapped.

She hunched her shoulders. "No need to be snippy about it."

He rubbed a hand over his eyes and was a while in answering. "Sorry."

"Are you always this charming when you wake up?"

"I'm not feeling great. Everything from my neck up is hurting. Even my tongue doesn't feel right."

"Maybe it overexerted itself."

"Look who's being snippy."

For a minute, she sat in quiet dejection. Then she shook her head—which was a mistake. Everything inside seemed to rattle. After another minute's recovery, she said, "I guess I was trying to be cute, only it didn't work." She closed her eyes and whispered, "I don't believe this." Her voice rose. "I don't believe I let all that happen. *Let* it happen. I did it. I goaded you on. I know I did. Why did I do that? I've never been sexually aggressive in my life!"

"You'd had too much to drink. We'd both had too much to drink. Neither of us was thinking clearly."

"But to—make—love." She tripped over the words, as though the sound of them hitting the air made the fact of what they'd done so much more real. "Making love is the most intimate thing two people can do. But we're not lovers, you and me," she cried. "We're friends!"

Sawyer winced. "You don't have to yell."

"We're friends," she repeated, but more softly.

"Some say that friends make the best lovers."

"Or that the best of friendships are ruined when

friends become lovers. I don't want that to happen, Sawyer." She swore softly. "I don't believe this."

"We were tipsy."

"We were awful. Some of the things we said. What we did to Jack and Joanna. That was the *lowest*. Who are we to go on and on about them that way? To talk about the way they made love?" She buried her face in her hands and moaned. "I am so embarrassed."

"We were tipsy."

"They didn't deserve that. Do you think they're off with new lovers, talking about what *we* did in bed? I'd die if I knew Jack was doing that. Some things are sacred." She made a snorting sound. "Boy, we blew sacred, didn't we?"

"The problem is that I know Jack and you know Joanna. We used to go places, the four of us. It's almost natural that we make comparisons."

"It's terrible! How can you condone what we did?"

"I'm not condoning it. But we were tipsy."

"I *know* we were tipsy, still what we did was awful!"

"I know." He held his head. "I take that back. I don't know. Things are coming back to me, and some of them are pretty nice."

Faith whirled on him, but the sudden movement wrenched everything inside her. For a split second she feared she was going to be sick. Mercifully the feeling passed. "I think," she said with her eyes lowered, "that I'd like something for this headache and then a cup or two of very strong coffee."

Both ideas sounded good to Sawyer. He didn't move, though. He didn't want to do anything to anger Faith. She wasn't in the best of moods and neither was he. So he watched her walk from the bedroom with surprising grace, given that she was swathed in a bedsheet. He saw her go into the bathroom and shut the door. It seemed forever that she was in there. He began to wonder whether she was all right, but he didn't move. He simply stood by the side of the bed, holding the flowered quilt wrapped around his lower half.

Finally the door opened and she came out. He guessed she'd thrown water on her face and brushed her hair, because she looked a little more awake. She was also wearing a robe.

"Here," she said quietly. Keeping her eyes low—in deference to her headache rather than deference to him, he was sure—she dropped several tablets into his hand. Then she turned and, walking gingerly, headed for the kitchen.

As soon as she'd disappeared, he took his painstaking turn in the bathroom. When he joined her in the kitchen a short time later, he was wearing the sweatshirt and jeans he'd recovered, with more than a little chagrin, from the living-room floor.

The smell of perking coffee wafted about and would have been welcoming if Faith hadn't been standing so still, facing the counter, keeping her back to him. He slipped onto a bar stool. His legs weren't feeling as steady as usual. The support was welcome.

As he sat there, waiting for the pills to calm the noise in his head and take the raw edge off everything else, he wondered if Faith wanted him to leave. She had every right to be alone if she wanted. It was her house. She wasn't feeling well, and his presence was a reminder why.

But he couldn't leave. The cold water he'd doused his head with in the sink had cleared his mind that much. He and Faith had to talk.

He didn't do a thing, though, until the coffee was done

and she handed him a steaming mug. He'd always thought of life as being more civilized over morning coffee, and Faith's coffee was strong. If it didn't make him more civilized, he didn't know what would. He figured it would also go a long way toward settling his stomach and dulling the ache in his head.

It did both for Faith. After a few minutes, she was able to carry her mug to the counter, take the companion stool to his and face him. "Guess we missed dinner," she said. She was relieved to see that his eyes had the same sickly red look hers did.

"Guess so."

"If we'd had something in our stomachs, the champagne wouldn't have hit so hard."

"Either that, or we'd have been bounced from the restaurant."

She started to smile at that thought, but the movement of her mouth somehow reached her eyes, which still hurt. So she made a quiet sound to acknowledge what he'd said and closed her eyes for a minute. "I feel very foolish," she whispered.

"That's two of us."

"I have never, *never* done anything like this before. I mean, even aside from what we did to Jack and Joanna, the sex was something else." She opened her eyes to his. "I don't sleep around, Sawyer. I never have. There was one guy before I met Jack, and there haven't been any since. Except you."

Sawyer thought about that for a minute. "I'm flattered."

"I didn't mean it as flattery. I meant it to tell you the way I am. I'm not loose. I'm not a frustrated divorcée. I don't go around getting drunk and begging men to make love to me."

"Is that what you thought you did?"

"Yes."

"Well, you didn't. In the first place, you didn't get drunk. If you'd done that, you'd have been incapacitated. You'd probably have passed out. Neither of us was drunk. We were tipsy. That's all."

"Is there really a difference?" she asked.

The faint bitterness in her voice annoyed him. "Yes, there is," he insisted. "There's a big difference. If we'd been drunk we wouldn't have been so lucid."

"Lucid? You think we were lucid?"

"To some extent, yes. The things I said about Joanna were true. I probably shouldn't have said any of them. But they were true. She did a job on me sexually. There were times when I wondered whether I lacked something in that department, since I couldn't make her respond. I never would have planned what happened last night, but once we got going I must have had an inner need to keep going. You were my friend. I'd had just enough to drink. I was loose. I wanted to know if I could turn you on. So maybe I used bad judgment, and I blame that on the drink, but on some level I knew what I was doing." He paused. "My guess is you did, too."

Faith let his words sink in. Much as she tried, she couldn't completely deny them. Quietly she said, "Then we have to accept the responsibility. So that makes it worse."

"Yes and no."

She stared at him. "Explain."

"Yes, we have to accept the responsibility. We're mature adults. We can blame what we did on the wine, but that doesn't excuse it. On the other hand, maybe it wasn't so terrible."

"Are you kidding?" she cried. "Sawyer, we slept together last night! You and me. Best friends. Best buddies. We made love. We went all the way. We scr—"

He cut her off. "Don't say it, Faith. Don't even think it. You're right. We're best friends. Best buddies. We shouldn't have done what we did, but it wasn't some ugly, faceless, nameless thing, and I'm sure as hell not dropping a C-note on your counter and walking out."

Faith flinched. She bowed her head and pressed two fingers to her temple. Feeling quickly contrite, Sawyer gentled his voice. "All I'm saying is that this isn't the end of the world."

"What if I'm pregnant?"

The thought caught him off guard. He swallowed. "Is there a chance of that?"

"Yes. I don't use birth control. I haven't had any need." She grew defensive. "I don't go around doing this kind of thing."

Rattled as he was, her defensiveness hit him the wrong way. "Damn it, I know that, Faith! Will you stop saying it? I *know* you're not loose. I *know* you don't sleep around. I *know* you place value on physical intimacy. We may never have been romantically involved, but I do know you, and better than most, I'd wager."

"You must think I'm awful."

He threw his hands in the air; they came down on his hips. "It takes two to tango, y'know."

"But I kept pushing you on. I kept asking you for more." Her eyes grew moist. "I swear, Sawyer, I've never been like that before."

The tears did it. He'd had no intention of touching her, but when he saw the tears he couldn't sit by and stay physically aloof. Not after what, right or wrong, they'd done. And not when every one of his instincts as a friend and as a man directed him otherwise.

Taking a step to her stool, he wrapped his arms around her. "I want you to listen to me, Faith. You're a bright woman, probably one of the brightest I've ever met. I want you to listen and listen good. Okay?"

She nodded.

He spoke slowly, keeping his voice low and gentle. "I do not think less of you for what we did last night. If anything, the opposite is true. I'm flattered to know that there haven't been any other men but that you let me be the first since the divorce. I'm relieved to know that you're human, that deep down inside you have some of the same needs as me—even if the need is as lousy as criticizing our ex-spouses. I am not disappointed in you. I don't think I could ever be disappointed in you." He paused. "How can I be disappointed when you came so alive in my arms?"

"Sawyer," she moaned.

"Okay. We won't talk about that."

"Don't even *think* about it."

"Fine. What about your being pregnant? When will you know?"

"Two weeks, give or take."

"Then we won't think about that, either, until we know one way or another. There's no point in worrying, and there's no way we can change the chances. If it happened, it's already happened, and if that's the case, we'll sit down together and decide what to do."

Faith couldn't fault his logic. But then, she'd always found Sawyer to be logical. She'd always thought she was, too, which was why she was surprised by her own heightened emotions.

"Sound fair?" he asked, when she remained quiet in his arms.

She nodded. "What do we do in the meantime?"

It was a little while before he answered. He honestly didn't know what to do. "Maybe we ought to go on the way we always have."

"Business as usual?"

"That's right."

"There's only one problem with that. Business as usual means running into each other only by accident. But there's the little matter of the Leindecker divorce."

"The Leindecker divorce."

"Remember? The thing that brought you down to my office in the first place yesterday?"

"I remember." But he hadn't until then, and the recollection gave greater weight to what had happened in the intervening hours. "Oh boy."

Faith knew what he was thinking. "Uh-huh. If we were wondering whether there was a conflict of interest *then*, what's the story *now*?"

Reluctantly Sawyer let his arms fall from around her. He sank back onto his stool. "No different, I guess. We're still okay as long as we watch what we do."

"You can pretend last night didn't happen?"

"No. But I don't know if it'll happen again, and if it doesn't, not much has really changed." He paused. "Has it?"

"I guess not."

"Do you feel that because of last night you'll be less strong an advocate for your client?"

"I don't know. Maybe I won't be as tough a negotiator knowing I'm negotiating with you."

Sawyer narrowed his eyes, which were beginning to feel better. "You'll be tough. Probably more so than usual, if for no other reason than to make the point that you aren't biased by any relationship with me. Of course," he mused, "if you feel uncomfortable about it, you can tell Mrs. Leindecker to get another lawyer."

Faith smirked. "Would that please you?"

"No way. I said I was excited about working with you. I was simply considering your feelings."

"If you're that considerate, you could always withdraw from the case yourself. You could tell Mr. Leindecker to get another lawyer."

"But I want to work with you."

"Against me."

"Against you. It's a challenge, and in that sense both of our clients stand to benefit."

At that moment, Faith wasn't much up for challenges. But in an hour, a day, a week, things would be different. She'd been accepting challenges since she first applied to law school. Fighting prejudice, she'd had to work twice as hard because she was female, but she'd proven herself every bit as good a lawyer as any other she'd run across.

"A woman in Mrs. Leindecker's position deserves the best if she's going to get the respect she's earned," she told him.

"A man in Mr. Leindecker's position *needs* the best if he doesn't want to be taken to the cleaners."

"They were married a long time," she warned. "She's put up with a lot."

"She's *had* a lot. She's lived like a queen."

"Which is how she deserves to be kept. You can't just expect her to go off, get a job and live hand-to-mouth all of a sudden, do you?"

"Come on, Faith. It's not like she's got little kids to take care of—or that she's doddering at the older end of the scale. She's a healthy, middle-aged woman. It wouldn't kill her to work."

"What could she do? She's not trained for anything.

Any job she'd get would pay her a fraction of what your client earns. We're talking the most menial, entry-level position if she had to work. But she shouldn't have to. Not if he led her to believe that she'd always be taken care of. There are things like service and loyalty and unspoken contracts to consider.''

"Tell it to the judge.''

There it was, Faith knew. The gauntlet had been thrown down. And Sawyer Bell was looking at her with a crooked half-grin on his handsome face, waiting, just waiting to see if she had the courage to pick it up.

She wasn't sure whether it was the grin, the handsome face, the need to put last night's folly behind them or the challenge itself that did it. But she rose from the stool, tipped up her chin and informed him in slow, clear words, "I intend to, thank you.''

With that, she reached for the refrigerator door.

4

FAITH MADE a huge breakfast, not so much because Sawyer might be hungry, but because she was. Then, trying to pretend that nothing out of the ordinary had happened between them, she sent him on his way.

Saturdays were work days. On this particular one, she had to go to the grocery for food, the dry cleaner for a drop-off and pickup, the department store for stockings and a refill of mascara. Despite the aspirin, the coffee and the breakfast, she was still feeling a little logy. But she pushed herself. There were things to be done, and if she didn't grab the opportunity, she'd lose it.

She had to smile at that thought; it was the credo by which Jack lived. Over and over he'd said those words during the eight years they'd been married—usually at times when Faith was at her laziest. Since the divorce she'd been more diligent about all those non-law-related things that she would have let ride in the past. Without Jack to keep her on her toes, she had to rely on herself.

So he wasn't all bad, she told herself and knew that it was a way of compensating for how she'd belittled him with Sawyer. In honor of Jack, she even went shopping for a new suit for work, one that was conservative and practical like him, and though she'd probably have picked something more daring on another day, she knew she'd wear it well.

By the time she returned to Union Wharf it was nearly

three in the afternoon. Curled up on the sofa in deliberate defiance of what had happened behind it the night before, she spent several hours making notes on a case that would be coming up for a hearing that week. Then she slipped into a sexy black sheath, made good use of the eye makeup she'd just happened to buy along with the mascara that afternoon, and went to a harvest party at Monica's home in Concord.

The best part, she decided, was the drive to and from Concord. Faith enjoyed driving. She didn't do it often, since she usually walked to and from work, but when she had a case in one of the outlying courthouses, or when she found something to do on a weekend that took her out of the city, she drove with relish. She tuned the radio to her favorite station, the only one in Boston that played country music, and she relaxed. She beat her left foot in time to the music, clapped her hands when a traffic light freed them, hummed along from time to time, even sang aloud when a particular lyric grabbed her.

Monica's party, on the other hand, was a drag. Not that Monica hadn't warned her. Most of the guests were friends of Monica's husband, who was fifteen years older than Monica, who was ten years older than Faith. If those guests had been lawyers, Faith might have had a chance, but the men were in business, and their wives were professional wives. Faith couldn't identify with them at all.

Oh, she managed. She was adept at small talk. Sipping her customary Perrier and lime, she did her share of chatting about the weather, the turn of the leaves, the new musical that had opened at the Shubert, a recently published novel that had the city talking. She listened in on business discussions, knowing that the small bits of information she picked up would come in handy at one point or another in her life. But the talk didn't excite her.

There was nothing lively about the gathering. None of the people made her laugh in delight, and if a party wasn't for laughing in delight, Faith didn't know what it *was* for. For Monica's sake, though, she stuck it out.

She liked Monica. She also respected her. Monica had started out being like the other women at the party, but it hadn't taken her long to realize that if her marriage was to have any chance of survival, she needed something constructive to do. Fortunately her husband understood. He put her through law school and indulged her through ten years of work as a public defender. That was what she was doing when Faith met her. When Faith had decided to leave the law firm she was associated with and go out on her own, Monica was ready for a move.

For five years, they had been splitting the rent on their suite of offices and sharing Loni's salary and skills. Though they often discussed legal issues with each other, their practices were entirely independent. Outside the office, they were friends.

So when, as a friend, Monica had pleaded with Faith to come liven up her husband's party, Faith had agreed. Unfortunately the party needed a kind of livening that Faith, despite her intelligence and quick wit, couldn't begin to accomplish. Still, Faith wasn't sorry she went. The party wasn't a waste. It took up four hours. By the time she drove back into the city, parked her car and safely locked herself into her condo, she was exhausted enough to go straight to sleep.

Unfortunately she'd made a large tactical error. In keeping with the schedule she stuck to in her post-Jack life, she had done no more than make her bed that morning. Sundays were for changing the sheets.

This week, she should have changed them on Saturday. Though she'd aired the bed as always, neatly made it and fluffed the pillows, and though she was tired enough to fall asleep soon after she crawled in, she awoke at four in the morning thinking Sawyer was beside her. And no wonder. The scent of him clung to her sheets. It was so subtle that she wondered at first whether she was imagining it, but the warmth of her body had brought it to life, and she wasn't able to ignore it.

She tried. She tried doing what she'd done all of Saturday, keeping her mind busy enough so that there wasn't room for a wayward thought. But at four in the morning, she couldn't manufacture distractions. There were just the lingering lights of the harbor, the sleeping city, the night and Sawyer.

For the first time, perhaps the very first time since she'd known the man, she allowed herself to take a long, objective look at him physically. It wasn't hard. She might not have thought to heed the details before, still they'd registered. Her mind's eye held an exquisitely detailed picture of him.

He was tall, she guessed six-four or six-five. He'd played basketball in college, she knew because he'd mentioned it once, and though the injuries he sustained in Vietnam had dashed any hopes of a professional career, he still had the body of an athlete. He *was* an athlete. A runner. He'd pushed himself and pushed himself, well beyond the point his doctors had ever thought he'd be able to go, which was a testimony to his will...and to Joanna's, Faith freely admitted. Despite the scars that he'd always carry, he had full command of his body to do with as he pleased.

He was broad-shouldered and narrow-hipped, both of which she'd known forever, neither of which she'd appreciated quite as fully as she had the night before. Though she only remembered seeing his upper body naked, she remembered measuring those parts of him below the waist with her hands. Narrow-hipped, he was, indeed, with legs that could wind forever in and round her own.

Taking in a sharp breath, she put a hand to her chest to calm the wild beat of her heart. But the warmth of her palm served only to remind her of the warmth of Sawyer's hands on her skin. Oh, yes, his hands were warm. They were large and well formed, both strong and gentle.

That was pretty much the way she saw his face, too. Strong but gentle, dark but giving, sober but capable of a buoyant smile. His hair was dark brown and stylishly worn, tumbling over his brow with the least encouragement, and his skin never quite looked as pale as the rest of the world's. There was a ruddiness to it. Like a child, his color heightened with exertion or excitement—or passion, she thought, though she had no way of knowing for sure. It had been too dark in their nook behind the sofa last night to see that.

What she had seen, or felt, was the prickle of his beard. That, too, gave his face a darker, more rugged look, and though she'd never seen him with enough stubble to be called grubby, many times she'd seen a distinct five o'clock shadow. She hadn't thought twice about it before. Now she did, and she decided that it added to the aura of masculinity that surrounded him.

Which was a whole new thought, in itself. Aura of masculinity? He did have that, and he had it in abundance. But she'd never noticed it before, and she couldn't understand why. Surely something that hit her so strongly now had to have hit her on some level before. Maybe, she mused, she'd repressed it. That was an interesting thought.

As she wrestled with it, she could almost see Sawyer

standing back, finding a wry humor in her predicament. She could see his brown eyes twinkling, could see his firm mouth twitching at the corners, could even see one dark eyebrow edging upward into an arch. She tried to be annoyed with him, as he stood there in her mind, but she couldn't. He was a good man. And he was gorgeous.

Uh-huh. Gorgeous. He was. But that didn't change the fact that they were best of friends, had no intention of being involved with each other as lovers, had no *business* being intimately involved if they intended to represent the Leindeckers. And yes, if Laura Leindecker decided to go ahead with the divorce, Faith was in it on her side. In spite of what had happened the night before, she couldn't turn down the golden opportunity of seeing how Sawyer Bell worked.

FAITH STARTED SUNDAY by listing the things she wanted to do. She made it halfway down the list—changing the sheets, doing the laundry, poring through the Sunday *Globe* right down to the crossword puzzle at the back of the magazine section—before Sawyer called.

She recognized his voice at once. It might have been the deep timbre, she mused, or the faint hesitance, or she had to admit that, as much as she busied her mind, Sawyer was still a presence in it. She wasn't sure whether to be pleased he'd called or not, and for that reason she attributed the pickup of her pulse to uncertainty.

"I just wanted to make sure you were okay," he explained in a still-hesitant but gentle and sincere tone. "Somehow it didn't seem right to leave yesterday and not be in touch for days."

She agreed with him and was touched, though not entirely surprised. Sawyer was a considerate man. "Thank you. I'm doing fine." She laughed softly. "I feel a lot better today then I did yesterday. I can move my eyes."

"Mmm. Me, too. After I left you, I came home and slept. Slept on and off for the rest of the day. I've never been hit quite like that."

"You must have been tired anyway."

"Maybe. Still, I don't think I'm ever having another drink."

"Uh-huh," she said, not believing it for a minute.

"I'm serious."

"I'm sure you are. But the holiday season is coming. There are lots of dinners and parties. One drink won't kill you."

"The second or third might."

"Mmm." She thought back to Dewey O'Day's affair. "Why did we do that, Sawyer? Why did we keep taking wine from the tray?"

"We were bored. We didn't want to be there."

"We were laughing a lot. We weren't keeping count of what we had to drink."

"We were giving each other courage. Boy, were we dumb."

"You can say that again."

"Once is enough, thanks. I usually try to be more responsible than we were that night." He paused. "At least we didn't make fools of ourselves at the party."

"The party wasn't the problem. It was all we had to drink after that."

"But if we hadn't drunk what we did at the party, we'd have been more clearheaded afterward. I'd have known not to open that bottle of wine at my place, and you'd have saved the Johnsons' champagne for a better occasion. Now it's gone."

"No loss. Besides, I wasn't about to drink that cham-

pagne all alone, and if I was going to share it with someone, who better than you? You're a friend."

"Am I still?" he asked. The hesitancy she'd heard earlier, gone for a while, was back.

"Of course, you are."

"Even though I took advantage of you?"

Faith sighed indulgently. "Sawyer, you didn't take advantage of me. I asked for everything I got. And no one
forced me to take out that champagne."

"But I'm bigger than you."

She didn't see the connection. He hadn't used physical
force. She doubted he was capable of it where a woman
was concerned. "So?"

"So I should have been able to hold my liquor better. I
should have been that much more sober than you every
step of the way."

"You're wallowing in guilt. Oh boy, are you wallowing."

"Damn right, I am."

"Well, don't. Because if you do, I'll have to. You say
you should have been stronger physically, I say I should
have been stronger mentally."

"Mentally?"

"I should have said no. Traditionally the woman is the
one who has a saner head on her shoulders. I should
have refused another drink the minute I knew I wasn't in
total control."

"But you weren't in total control, which is why you did
what you did."

"Even in *partial* control, I should have known better."
She stopped for a minute to think about what they were
saying. "This goes round and round, doesn't it?"

"Yeah. I thought we'd agreed—" there was a break in

the transmission of his voice "—the blame—hell, my time's up. I don't have any more change."

"Change?" Apparently, he was calling from a pay phone. "Where are you?"

"The Cape. I bought a dilapidated—" there was another break "—summer—I'm fixing it up. Gotta run, Faith. Are you sure you're okay?"

"I'm fine."

"Talk with you soon, then. Bye."

He broke the connection before she could say another word. She pictured him dashing out of the phone booth before the operator could ring to tell him that he owed another quarter for the extra seconds he'd used. The image brought a smile to her face. He really was adorable. And admirable. So he'd bought a dilapidated something on the Cape and was fixing it up. Physical work on the weekends to balance the cerebral work of the week. He was a bright man, indeed.

Several hours later, she was wishing she had some physical work of her own to do. Having finished the crossword puzzle down to the very last word, she was reading through some papers for work. But she felt restless. She wanted to be out doing something, though she didn't have any idea what that something might be. She thought of taking a walk, but the day was gray and not particularly enticing. She thought of calling a friend and going to a movie, but there wasn't one that she desperately wanted to see. She thought of calling a friend, period, but that would mean chatting about personal things, and she wasn't in the mood for that, either.

When Laura Leindecker's daughter called her on the phone, she welcomed the diversion.

"I'm sorry to bother you, Ms Barry, but Mother said you were representing her, and I had to talk with some-one."

"Actually," Faith tried to explain, "your mother and I haven't any formal agreement yet. She was going to take a few days to decide whether she really wants to go ahead with the divorce."

"I think she does," came the answering voice, soft, like her mother's, but more high-pitched. "And I think she should. Especially after what's happened this weekend."

"What is that?"

"He's been here at the house since noon yesterday, and he refuses to leave. The more Mother asks him, the more belligerent he becomes."

"Belligerent?" According to Laura, the man had been charming and humble.

"Yes, belligerent. Please. Let me talk with you. I'm tak-ing a six o'clock flight back to Baltimore tonight, but I could meet you at your office—or anywhere else in Bos-ton before that. I want you to hear my side of the story."

"The divorce," Faith reminded her gently, "is between your parents. Shouldn't your mother be telling me what-ever there is to tell?"

"She's too…timid sometimes. I don't know how much she'll tell. But she's suffering, and I think you should know the facts. They could come in handy when you're planning her case."

Faith couldn't deny the temptation of facts. She knew she'd have to decide whether what she was told was, in-deed, factual, but she felt she owed it to her client to lis-ten. So she gave Beth Leindecker directions to her office and agreed to meet her there at four.

BETH, IT TURNED OUT, was twenty-three, an intern at an ad agency and definitely at odds with her father. "When I arrived home on Friday night, Mother was distraught."

"Did you see or speak with your father that night?"

"No. Mother told him to sleep somewhere else. For all we know, he slept with *her*."

"Do you know who she is?"

"I didn't even know she existed until Mother called on Friday morning!"

Faith wondered whether that call had come before or after Laura's confrontation with her husband. It would be interesting to know how much Beth was egging her on. "Okay. So your father came to the house on Saturday morning."

"Around noon. We couldn't believe he dared show his face there."

"It's still his home."

"But he's not welcome there."

Faith was tempted to point out a few basic legal facts to Beth. Instead, she said, "He must have needed clothes. Grooming things."

"That was what we thought, but he wasn't back for those at all. He was back to stay, he said. He said that the whole thing had gotten out of hand, that Mother had blown it out of proportion. Can you believe that? He admits to cheating on her, then tells her she's blown it out of proportion!"

Faith held up an appeasing hand. In some ways, Beth sounded just like her mother—but with a hotter spark and a shorter fuse. "You mentioned belligerence," she prompted to keep the girl on track.

Beth nodded. "They were arguing back and forth. He was saying that what he did wasn't so awful, and Mother was saying that it was, and I agreed with her."

"You were standing right there in the middle of the fight?"

"I had to. Someone had to protect Mother."

"She couldn't protect herself?"

"Not against him. She's never been able to protect herself against him. He snaps his fingers, and she comes running. It's always been that way."

"Maybe she loves him."

Beth's only response to that was a frown. "She doesn't deserve this hurt. After all these years, she deserves some satisfaction."

"What kind of satisfaction did you have in mind?" Faith asked, genuinely curious.

"He ought to be banned from stepping foot in that house or coming near my mother. She's had a lifetime of his harassment."

"Harassment." Faith echoed the word. It didn't fit with the image Laura had painted of her husband any more than belligerence did. "Harassment by omission, as in emotional neglect?"

"For years it was that. Now it's physical. He started throwing things."

Faith grew more alert. "What kinds of things?"

"The mail, first. Letters and magazines that were on the table in the front hall. Then towels that were piled on the stairs. Then flowers that were on a table at the top of the stairs. Then books, big books from the nightstand."

"The argument worked its way to their bedroom?"

"He followed her there. She kept yelling at him, telling him to stay away, but he followed her there."

"Did he hit her at any point?"

"No."

"At any point, did he raise a hand to strike her?"

"No," Beth said, and Faith sensed a reluctance in the

denial. Beth was clearly eager to think the worst of her father.

"He was just throwing things around. Anything bigger than a book?"

"He kicked the cushion off the chaise lounge. It went halfway across the room."

"Did he aim it at her?"

"No."

"Did he aim anything directly at her?"

"No. But you're missing the point," Beth insisted. "He was throwing things. She could have been hit."

Faith was quiet for several minutes, trying to put what Beth was saying in some kind of perspective, enough to decide whether there was any cause for immediate concern. "That was yesterday afternoon. I take it he's calmed down since then."

"He's still there. She wants him out."

Does she, or do you? Faith was wondering. "Has he calmed down?"

"Yes. But he's still angry. He could act up again at any time." Beth looked truly frustrated. "For the first time in her life, my mother is standing up to him. At least, she's trying to. But if someone doesn't give her a boost, she's going to fall right back on him. I think you should give her that boost, Ms Barry."

Faith didn't like the sound of that at all, and it wasn't because she lacked the courage for it. "Morally, I'm obliged to see if the marriage can be salvaged. I can't urge your mother to push for a divorce. It has to be her decision. If she gives it fair thought, decides that there's no hope for the marriage and that divorce is the only solution, I'll help her. I'm not sure what else I can do. I'll call her, if that will make you feel better. I'll ask how she feels about his being around. There are many couples who live together right up to the point of signing a legal separation agreement. It's sometimes simpler that way. Then again, if your mother is being physically threatened, that's another story."

"She is."

"I'll ask her about it," Faith said, and rose from her desk. "In the meantime, I think you'd be best not goading her on. Be supportive. But remember that this is between your parents. You're grown and out of the house. They have to come to terms with what they want from each other for the next however many years."

Beth took up her overnight case and started for the door. "I think mother needs a court order to keep him out of the house."

"Be supportive, Beth, not inflammatory."

"She needs someone to light a fire under her."

"Do you hate your father that much?"

"I don't hate him."

"Then why are you so eager to get him out of the house?"

"He needs to be taught a lesson. He's had everything his way for so long. It's fine and dandy for him to be delightfully pleasant when he's pulling all the strings. Let someone else pull the strings and he starts throwing things the way he did Saturday. That was an awakening, let me tell you."

"That he has a temper?"

"I'll say."

"Maybe it's a healthy outlet. After all, he was objecting to his wife's kicking him out of the house. Maybe he really wants to be there with her."

"He just wants his way."

"Maybe," Faith conceded, then smiled and squeezed the younger woman's shoulder. "Have a safe flight back to Baltimore. And remember, stay cool. Your parents are going to have to work this out themselves."

"Will you call my mother?"

"As soon as you're on your way."

But she'd barely seen Beth to the elevator and returned to her office when Laura called her. "Is Beth still there? I know she was going to meet you. Has she left?"

"Just a minute ago. Is there a problem?"

"She forgot her gray outfit, the two-piece wool she wore in on Friday. She was too warm in it then, but the weather's getting colder and she'll want it." She sighed. "It's no wonder she forgot it. She was in such a stir while she was here."

"Has she always had trouble getting along with her father?"

"Always. I've been the buffer for years. She feels that he's been unduly stingy with her."

"With money?"

"Money, time, himself. He said it would be too easy to spoil her, and he didn't want that. God forbid he should make things easy for her. When she graduated from college, she wanted to work for him, but he told her she had to work somewhere else. 'Earn her stripes' was the expression he used. What kind of father would make his daughter do that?"

"Many have."

"It was very selfish of him. But I suppose that's nothing new," Laura concluded sadly.

Faith heard the sadness. She didn't hear any sort of panic. "Beth was concerned for your physical safety. Are you all right?"

"I'm fine. Bruce is being difficult, of course. He insists on staying here. When I tell him to leave, he gets furious."

"Do you feel that you're in danger?"

"I don't know what he's going to do next. I've never seen him like this."

"Has he threatened you in any way? Forced you in any physical sense?"

"No. But one of us has to leave this house, and it isn't going to be me. *He* can leave."

"It sounds as if he won't. We can try for a restraining order, but it may be premature." While Faith was the first one to want to protect a client from physical harm, she sensed that the threat in this case was more speculative than real. Bruce had no history of violence. The court would see that. "I'd recommend that you take advantage of his presence and talk with him."

"Talk? What for? I can't trust what he says. Not anymore. Besides, it's a waste of time. I want a divorce."

"I understand that, Mrs. Leindecker, but—"

"I want a divorce. Are you going to represent me?"

"Let's discuss that on Tuesday."

"This is Sunday. My feelings won't change in two days."

"Where emotions are concerned, a lot can happen in two days."

"Not in my case. I want a divorce, and the sooner we get started, the sooner that man will see what he's done."

Divorce for the purpose of revenge was one of the things Faith least liked. It was childish, blind and often ugly. It also tended to overshadow any pluses that might have existed in a marriage. Gut instinct told her that this marriage had pluses aplenty. What she needed was time to see if those pluses could possibly reassert themselves.

"Tuesday, Laura. We'll talk again on Tuesday."

It took another minute, but she finally convinced Laura to hold off any action until then. Hanging up the phone at last, she quickly gathered her things together and left the office. She wasn't as easily able to leave behind thoughts of the case. It bothered her. Clearly, emotions were flying high in the Leindecker home. But a divorce based solely on emotional factors was the most painful for all involved, including the lawyers. Granted, any divorce stirred emotions. At some point, though, practicality and reason had to come into play. It could happen in court. Or before. Faith far preferred the latter.

Letting herself into her apartment, she had a sudden urge to phone Sawyer. She had a good excuse. Her client had called her in fear; Faith was sharing that fear with the lawyer who might, with a call to his client, be able to help.

But Sawyer wasn't home. He'd called her from the Cape—she didn't even know where on the Cape. And he'd called from a pay phone, which meant that the dilapidated something he'd bought didn't have one of its own.

Just for the hell of it, she tried his number in Boston. After ten rings without an answer, she hung up. She told herself that that was okay, that she really didn't have to speak with him, that Laura Leindecker was perfectly safe. But an hour later, she tried again, and then again an hour after that. It was ten o'clock before she finally reached him.

5

"HI, SAWYER, it's me."

She was the last person he'd expected to hear from, still he recognized her voice at once. "Faith?"

"Uh-huh. I've been trying you. You must have just come home."

"There was an accident on the Sagamore Bridge that backed traffic up for miles. I thought it was late enough in the season for the crowds to be gone, but I sat in the middle of a jam for three hours."

She knew how frustrating that could be and would have felt sorry for him if she weren't so envious that he'd been at the Cape in the first place. "Tell me again what you were doing down there."

"I bought a place this summer. It's in East Dennis, an old broken-down thing. But it's on a lake, and it has potential. The land is gorgeous. I figured I could fix up the place myself. I'm an experienced man when it comes to repairs."

The way he drawled it made her smile. "The house in Cambridge?"

"Yeah. Then it was physical therapy more than anything. I suppose it's still that. The physical exercise is different from what I do at work all week. But it's also mentally therapeutic. Gets out the cobwebs, if you know what I mean." He wasn't sure she did. He wasn't sure she'd been thinking of him as much as he'd been thinking of her. They'd agreed to go back to business as usual. But he was having trouble doing that. Maybe the fact that she'd called him meant she was having trouble with it, too.

"Tell me about this place," she said. "How much land do you have?"

"Three acres."

"So you don't see your neighbors?"

"Nope. All I see is trees. And water. And rabbits and raccoons and geese. It's such a total change from everything I have up here—including the house. I mean, we're talking old and worn and crumbly."

"Sounds like you might want to tear it down and start over from scratch."

That thought had occurred to him. "The problem is I'm already committed. The deeper in I get, the more I find that needs to be done, but the more I've done, the less I want to ditch the whole thing." He paused. "Am I making any sense?"

"Lots of it," she said. "You've committed yourself to a course of action. You've come too far to turn back."

"Oh, I'm not sure *too* far," he drawled. "I'm still debating."

"But you keep going back, and you keep doing work, and you keep getting deeper involved."

"Like I say, it's therapeutic."

"Which means that if you finally decide to ditch the project, you'll still have gotten something out of it."

"That's one way of looking at it. You're good at rationalizing, Faith."

"Sometimes," she said. She was thinking of what they'd done with each other on Friday night. She couldn't rationalize it away so easily. Nor, much as she tried, could she forget it for long. But that was beside the point. "I have to ask your opinion on something, Sawyer."

"Shoot."

"Bruce Leindecker. Do you know him well?"

"Well enough," he answered more cautiously. "We've been passing acquaintances for several years."

"Do you think he's prone to violence?"

Sawyer didn't think so, but he wasn't about to say anything until he knew what had happened. Bruce was his client; there were certain privileges to respect. "Why do you ask?"

"I had conversations today with both his wife and his daughter. Apparently there was an ugly scene yesterday. Things were thrown around the room a little."

"By my client?" he asked, then saw no harm in rebutting it. "That surprises me. To my knowledge, he's never been a violent man."

"Are you sure?"

"I said 'to my knowledge.' Maybe the guy's been beating up women on the sly, but nothing's ever come out about it, and with a visible guy like Bruce, you'd think it would."

"Nothing ever came out about the affair he was having."

"One woman. One affair. It had been going on for two or three months. No more."

That was the first Faith had heard of Bruce's side of the story, and while it was interesting, it wasn't surprising. Bruce's story was just that—Bruce's story. And it was Sawyer's job to relate it as told. "So he says."

"I believe him. And I do believe that he wouldn't hurt a woman. Unless those two are driving him mad."

"Sawyer..."

"They may be."

That wasn't Faith's immediate worry. "Beth was concerned for her mother's safety. I take it you don't think she has cause?"

"No, I don't."

"You sound sure."

"I feel sure."

"I'm glad one of us does. I'd feel horrible if I decided to let it go and then my client was batted around. But you say you know your client fairly well. I'm trusting you on this, Sawyer."

"I'm glad you can still trust me on something."

She was a minute in responding. "What do you mean?"

"After Friday night. I'm glad you still trust me a little."

"Of course, I trust you. I've always trusted you. Trust was never an issue."

But Sawyer saw it differently. "You trusted me to take care of you, and I didn't."

"Take care of me?"

"Protect you. I was thinking about this most of the day, and it's really bothering me. If you'd been with someone you trusted less on Friday night, you wouldn't have had half as much to drink. But you trusted me not to take advantage of you, so you may have been more lax than usual. Not only did I let us get carried away enough to make love, but I didn't think a thing about birth control. So now you're sitting there worrying that you're pregnant, because you have a successful career, and we all know that successful careers and babies don't mix."

Faith was astonished. "You spent most of today thinking about this?"

"While I was hammering away on the roof."

"I don't believe it, Sawyer." She took a breath. "Sawyer, do you know what year this is?"

"Of course I do."

"Then you'll know that these aren't the forties, or fifties, or even the seventies. Women have come a long way. Now, I know you don't like to think so—I know that, Sawyer, because much as I love you, you're a throwback to the heyday of male chauvinism. But really, we're not the pretty, dumb, helpless little things we used to be."

"I never said that, Faith—"

"But you imply it. I thought we agreed that on some level we both knew what we were doing Friday night. *You* were the one who said that first, and you're right. So I take at least half of the responsibility. And as far as a baby goes, I'm not sitting here worrying, because just as you said, there isn't a thing I can do until I know one way or the other, and even if I *am* pregnant, I have options! Honestly, Sawyer, these aren't the Dark Ages. I won't be sentenced to wear a scarlet letter on my breast. And I won't have to give up my practice. For your information, babies and careers are mixing better and better all the time." She stopped talking, but before he could say a word, she had another thought. This one riled her. "Ahhh. You're worried you'll have to marry me if I'm pregnant."

"That's not—"

"Save your breath, bud," she argued, suddenly and inexplicably furious. "I wasn't born yesterday, and that goes for experiencing marriage as well as understanding the male mind. I've been married once and it didn't work out. I'm not in a rush to go near it again, and I don't care if there *is* a baby involved. So you can sleep free of worry. No matter what happens, you won't be trapped." She slammed the receiver down hard.

Her hand was still pressing on the phone when it rang.

White-knuckled, she picked it up. "Leave it, Sawyer. You've said enough for one night." She hung up again.

This time when the phone rang, she lifted the handset, but dropped it right back without even putting it to her ear. Before it could ring again, she took it off the hook.

Angrily she stalked across the living room, stood for a minute at the window with her arms pressed tightly across her breasts, then stalked back and headed for the bedroom. She wasn't quite sure what had gotten out of hand, but something had. All she'd done was to call him in concern over her client. It had been a professional call, that was all.

Storming back through the apartment, she put the phone back on its hook and dialed Sawyer's number. The instant she heard his gruff hello, she said in her most confident and business-like tone, "From what the Leindecker women have told me, we don't yet have grounds for a restraining order, but that may change. Please advise your client that if he continues to torment his wife, he'll give us those grounds." She hung up before Sawyer could get in a word.

SAWYER WAS LIVID. Sitting in the dark in his apartment that night, he couldn't remember ever being quite so angry with anyone as he was with Faith. He'd known she had an emotional bent, but he hadn't dreamed that she'd be so quick to fly off the handle at remarks as innocent as the ones he'd made.

Good Lord, she knew he was old-fashioned when it came to traditional male-female values. She'd told him so dozens of times. She'd *ribbed* him about it, which meant that she didn't think it was all bad. He certainly didn't. He liked to think he was honest and responsible. And chivalrous. Those were good things. They showed respect for a woman, and he certainly respected Faith. He might be furious with her, but he respected her—respected and trusted her, which was why he'd marry her in a minute if she was pregnant, and he'd do it happily. He wasn't committed to life as a single. Granted, it was nice to be free of Joanna's smothering, but freedom brought loneliness. Besides, Faith wasn't a smotherer.

God forbid!

She wasn't a smotherer, but she sure as hell was stubborn and hotheaded and...passionate. Ah, yes, she was that. Just as there had been fire in her voice tonight, there had been fire in her body Friday night. He couldn't forget it. His body wouldn't let him. Those same flashes of memory he'd seen through a haze on Saturday morning came to him now, only the haze had cleared.

He saw her as she'd come from the bedroom after she'd changed, wearing an over-size sweatshirt that hid her body, and slim jeans that didn't. He saw the way she'd smiled up at him, her sandy hair covering her forehead in bangs, framing her face in a gentle bob that ended an inch below her chin. He saw hazel eyes that weren't spectacular in and of themselves, but that reflected what was inside, in turn intelligence, mischief, curiosity, enthusiasm and desire. He saw a small, straight nose and lips that were as whimsical as her firm chin wasn't.

Then he saw her naked in the night light, a vision that made his body harden. Her breasts were full, larger than he'd thought, though perhaps firm was the word, he decided. Her waist was slim, her hips flaring just enough to brand her a woman in ways that boyishly slim models couldn't be branded. And inside—inside she was hot and moist, welcoming, generous and demanding.

He wanted her, and he wanted her badly. One night—

half-zonked, but obviously not zonked enough—and he was in physical pain. Hadn't he ever seen it coming? Over and over he asked himself that question, but he wasn't able to come up with an answer. He'd known Faith for over ten years, yet things that seemed so clear to him now—such as her sex appeal and his response to it—simply hadn't occurred to him before. He'd viewed her as a friend, seeing only what was appropriate for a friend to see, overlooking the rest.

He couldn't see her that way anymore. That point of view had been lost beneath two bodies writhing on Faith's carpet Friday night. No longer could he view her only as a friend. After tonight, he wondered if she'd let him see her even as that. She was angry because she thought he was worried she'd hook him into marriage. Well, *he* was angry because she *thought* that! But she hadn't let him say a word, and that was the most infuriating part of it, as far as he was concerned. He didn't like being cut off. He didn't like being silenced when he had something to say. And he particularly didn't like being silenced by a woman.

That was why, shortly before ten the next morning, he barreled through the door of Faith's suite, tipped a finger from his forehead to Loni as he swept past, went into Faith's office and swung the door shut behind him.

She was on the phone, but the stormy look on his face wasn't to be ignored. Nor was the way he planted his hands apart on the outside edge of her desk and, leaning forward, waited. Speedily and with as much finesse as she could manage, she got off the phone. The instant the instrument was out of her hand, he opened fire.

"Don't ever do that to me again, Faith. I'm not a stupid man, and I don't say stupid things. If you have an accusation to make, make it and let me rebut it. That's the way things are done in this world. Nothing gets accomplished when a person makes an accusation and then turns and runs away."

"I didn't run away."

"Figuratively you did. You thought you knew what I was thinking and you didn't like it, so you flipped out, then you hung up on me—four times—without letting me explain myself. That was rude, Faith. *Rude.* What's the matter? Were you afraid to hear what I had to say?"

"Of course not."

"I think you were. I think you knew that I'd come out smelling like a rose, because I wasn't thinking about marriage or being trapped. I wasn't thinking about myself when I talked about the chance of a baby, only you. You're the one whose body would be affected, and you can argue until you're blue in the face, but that's a fact, Faith. As far as conception goes, my body does its thing in seconds, then it's done, while yours is just beginning, so you're the one who'll bear the brunt of a pregnancy."

"I know the facts of life."

"I'm glad to hear that, because you obviously don't know the facts of friendship. A friend doesn't desert a friend when she's in trouble. Even if there wasn't the slightest chance that I was the one who got you into trouble, I'd still be concerned. Okay, so we share the blame for what happened. I'll buy that. But I still feel guilty. I still feel I should have been more responsible." He rushed on when she opened her mouth. "And it doesn't have a goddamned thing to do with selfishness. I was thinking of you. I still am. I'm concerned for you as a friend. And lover."

"Sawyer—"

"I'm concerned, Faith. But you don't want to think that. You want to be angry with me."

"Why would I want that?"

"So that you don't have to think of being attracted to me. You want to think of last Friday night as a mistake, because maybe you've thought about it a lot, and you're feeling things you don't want to."

"Like attraction?" She tried to make light of it. "You're a *friend*, Sawyer. You've said it a million times. We were tipsy."

He leaned closer. His voice grew deeper, sounding alternately vehement and sensual. "We were aroused. We did it to each other, Faith. If you're honest with yourself, you'll admit that."

"We were tipsy."

Very slowly he straightened. The muscle in his jaw flexed. His eyes never left her face as he came around the desk.

"What are you doing, Sawyer?"

"Making my point."

"What's that supposed to mean?" She tried to sound curious rather than nervous, still she backed up a little in her chair. He was very tall, dark and imposing in his navy suit with his eyes so intent.

"I think we have a problem. I think we stumbled onto something Friday night that's not going to go away."

"Look, Sawyer, if it's the thing about a baby that's got you worried—"

"I don't give a damn about that." He bent over, putting his hands on the arms of her chair. "It's the other."

"What other?"

"The attraction."

"There *isn't* any attraction. I *told* you." She flattened a hand on his shirt to hold him off. "Don't, Sawyer. This is very unprofessional. It's criminal. It's...assault."

His face hovered over hers. "No assault."

"Please," she begged, breathing shallowly. "Leave now. Loni's sitting right out there. If I have to scream—"

"No scream. You know damn well that I won't hurt you."

"I don't want this, Sawyer. I don't want this. Please. Sawyer, this isn't *you*—"

His mouth took hers, and she was right. There was none of the teasing, none of the sampling, none of the gentleness he'd shown her on Friday night. His kiss contained the hunger that had been building since then, a hunger that he'd tried to ignore himself until he'd realized the futility of it.

Faith tried to turn her head, but he thrust a hand into her hair and held her still. When she tried to push him away, he took one of her hands, drew her right out of the chair and against him, where she was effectively immobilized. She even tried to keep her mouth closed and rigid, but she was no match for his persistence. The firm stroking of his lips was powerful; they kneaded the resistance from hers as though it had never been, then rewarded her pliancy with the kind of kiss she hadn't believed existed. It was wet and warm, unbelievably erotic. She was shaking inside, sagging weakly against him by the time he raised his head.

Unable to stand, she sank back into her chair. She knew Sawyer had allowed it, or he'd still have her clamped against him, but she wasn't about to thank him.

"Well?" he demanded. His voice was hoarse.

It was a minute before she could say anything. Then, eyes downcast, she whispered, "You've made your point."

"I didn't catch that."

"You caught it."

"Look at me and repeat it."

"What for? So your victory will be complete?"

He caught her chin and turned her face up. "No victory. I'm feeling as frustrated now as you are, but you're right, I made my point."

"And you're happy?"

"Fat chance. I have to be in court at eleven, then again at two on separate cases. I've got clients coming in at four and five-thirty. I have to prepare a motion that's due tomorrow. Somewhere in the middle, I'll have to return half a dozen phone calls and call Bruce Leindecker to discuss the issue of violence. So I'm frustrated as hell, but I can't do a thing about it. Happy? Not by a long shot."

Turning, he thundered from her office with nearly the same air of belligerence that had carried him in in the first place.

SAWYER DIDN'T LIKE starting days off that way. When he did, they invariably went downhill, and this day was no exception. The court appearance at eleven was forfeited when his client didn't show, and the one at two resulted in a continuance. He couldn't get a bead on the motion he had to prepare, because the phone kept ringing even after he'd returned the obligatory calls. The client who came in at four reported that he had inadvertently destroyed a piece of exculpatory evidence, and the client who was scheduled for five-thirty called to say he'd be an hour late.

So Sawyer called Bruce Leindecker and received an earful the likes of which he wasn't prepared for.

"The woman's crazy," Bruce claimed in a voice that lacked its customary composure. "Something's happened to her. After being utterly stoic for twenty-four years, she's suddenly turned violent."

"Violent?" That was a new twist. "Your wife?"

"Yes. I walked into the house on Saturday. I was prepared to sit down with her and try to explain why I did what I did, but she wouldn't listen. She kept cutting me off, telling me how cruel I am and how she's given me the best years of her life. I couldn't get a word in edgewise, but I kept trying, and that made her even more angry. So she started throwing things."

Sawyer knew all too well about trying to get a word in edgewise. He also knew how successfully an irate woman could prevent it. He didn't know about throwing things, though. "*She* was throwing things?"

"A cup and saucer that we'd bought in Ireland, a vase filled with flowers, the engraved picture frame that I'd given her for our twentieth anniversary. She went berserk!"

"Did she hit you?"

"No, but not for lack of trying. She's a lousy shot. Never could do anything athletic. She broke her arm when we were playing tennis in the Bahamas, fell off a donkey when we were touring the Grand Canyon, tripped and broke her ankle on the steps of the Louvre when we were in Paris. Athletic? Hah! She couldn't hit me with her eyes closed."

Bruce's irritation was real, still Sawyer sensed a ghost of indulgence beneath it. "But she kept trying?"

"Over and over, and our daughter stood there cheering her on." The indulgence vanished. "Beth is ticked off at me because I wouldn't give her a job. Well, hell, she was in the bottom third of her graduating class, not because she didn't have the brains, but because she didn't want to study. Is this a good recommendation, I ask you? And did I treat her any different from her brother? No, sir. I wouldn't give him a job, either. It's unhealthy for children to train in their father's business. Far better that they train somewhere else then come back with fresh ideas. But she wanted the easy way out. She figured she could have her cake and eat it too—have a job like a career woman, but still be able to play like her mother does."

Sawyer cleared his throat. "What does her mother—your wife—do, exactly?"

"Shop. Play cards. Meet friends for lunch."

"Has she ever done any work for you?"

"In the early days she did some typing and filing, but once the business started to grow, she retired. She comes into the office once a year to do the Christmas party, which is just fine. She doesn't have a mind for business. She does throw a good party, though. She gets the best people and she makes sure that they don't rob us blind. Caterers do that, you know. Especially with corporate clients. Laura is wise to things like that."

"It's a good quality for the wife of a man in your position."

As though only then realizing what he'd said, Bruce compensated by turning gruff. "The wife of a man in my position should know not to make a scene in the office about his indiscretions. She should know not to run to a lawyer the first chance she gets. And she should know not to bar him from his own home. I put up with that for one night, but that was it. I have never been, nor am I now a violent man, but when my wife unfairly cuts me off, when she won't even let me explain myself, I refuse to sit idly by and take it."

Sawyer could identify with that, too. Faith had frustrated him nearly beyond belief by repeatedly hanging up on him. The frustration had built and built through the night, so that by the time he'd stormed into her office that morning, he was harboring feelings that had bordered on the violent. "What, exactly, did you do?" he asked Bruce, as curious as he was wary.

"I lost my temper, knocked a few things on the floor, but they were harmless things," he added quickly, "like letters and magazines and folded laundry. She leaves the laundry on the stairs every day. It's the most annoying thing. She finally carries it up before she goes to bed, but in the meantime it sits there staring at me."

Sawyer wouldn't mind laundry staring at him as long as it was clean and had been made so by someone other than himself. Of all the chores he'd come into since his divorce, doing laundry was the worst. "Be grateful she does it for you."

"She doesn't. The laundress does. But the laundress doesn't go upstairs. Only the cleaning girl does that, and you can't expect the cleaning girl to be putting personal things away, Laura says. I suppose she has a point. My laundry is always clean when I need it, so I really can't complain." His voice hardened. "I can complain about other things, though. The problem is that I haven't. I've kept my mouth shut too long. So now when I open it to her for the first time, she feels threatened. Well, she should!"

Sawyer would have raised an arm and shouted, "Right on!" if it hadn't been for the one point his client was conveniently forgetting. The marriage, for all its faults, had endured for twenty-four years until Bruce had cheated on his wife. Sawyer wasn't condemning him for it. That wasn't his job. His job was to best advise and represent Bruce in any divorce action that might be taken, and since misbehavior now could become a factor later, caution seemed the way to go.

"What I want you to do," he said, "is to cool it a little. If she's threatened because you're speaking up to her at home for the first time, that's one thing. But if the threat becomes physical, or she *perceives* it as being physical, that's another."

Bruce was indignant. "I wouldn't touch her. I'm not that kind of man."

"I know, but sometimes when men are provoked they do things they wouldn't normally do. It sounds to me like your wife is provoking you these days."

"That's an understatement."

"It also sounds like you've got a real communication problem."

"Maybe," Bruce admitted.

"Are you determined to stay at the house?"

"Yes. At least until she listens to my side of the story."

Sawyer paused, then asked slowly, "Do you want this divorce?" As things stood the Friday before when they'd last spoken, Bruce had been ready to file papers. He'd been angry, of course, mostly at the way his wife had confronted him, and he'd been frightened by Laura's hiring Faith, which was why he'd been so quick to put Sawyer on retainer. Apparently either the anger and fear had faded, or simply shifted in focus.

Good businessman that he was, Bruce said, "I'm making no decisions yet."

"Do you think you can salvage the marriage?"

"I don't know. She's furious. I've never seen her furious before."

"You've never cheated on her before. That does something to a woman."

"I suppose."

"Look, I'm not making judgments. I don't pretend to know what your marriage was like or what caused the affair at the Four Seasons. You should know, though, and if you don't, you'd better try to find out. Communication is the key. I can mediate things, but only to a point. Have you considered going to a counselor?"

"I haven't had time to consider much of anything. I'm too busy trying to make sure she doesn't have the locks on the house changed while I'm at work."

"Would she do that?"

"If she does, I'll put a stop on her charge cards."

"Did you tell her that?"

"Yes, sir."

"Have you told her you're not sure you want a divorce?"

"I told her I'd fight her. I didn't say whether I was talking about the divorce itself or a settlement. I just wanted her to know that I won't be a pansy anymore when it comes to her. If she wants to fight, I'll show her how it's done."

"Be cautious. I can't advise that enough. Be cautious." He hesitated. "One last thought. The affair—is it really over?"

"It's over."

"So if your wife were to hire a private investigator, he wouldn't find you anywhere you shouldn't be?"

"No, sir."

"That's good. There's no need to rile her up any more than she already is. Legally you have every right to stay at the house, but while you're doing it, try to give her some breathing space. Let her calm down a little. Maybe then you'll be able to talk."

LONG AFTER Sawyer hung up the phone he thought about that advice. It applied to Faith and him, he knew. Their relationship had taken several dramatic twists in less than three days, and in the process emotions had been stirred. Those emotions had to simmer a bit, then settle.

Maybe, he mused, he and Faith would be best not seeing each other for a few days.

It was an ironic thought. He hadn't seen Faith for *weeks* before last Friday. Their paths just hadn't crossed often lately. Yet they were best of friends. When they were together, they picked up right where they had left off. They were thoroughly compatible.

They'd always been so. He thought back to the times they'd spent together during law school, where they'd met, and then after, when they'd been establishing themselves in the legal world. They'd always been close, regardless of how frequently or infrequently they saw each other. There was one big difference between those earlier times and now, of course. They'd felt safe then, unthreatened by each other because they were married to other people.

Now they were free, which was certainly why they'd allowed Friday night to happen. But he wasn't sorry it had. He'd done his share of socializing since he and Joanna were divorced, and Faith was head and shoulders above those other women. Sure, it had been a shock waking up in her bed. It had been a shock realizing the way their making love had happened. And it was going to necessitate a rethinking of their relationship. But he wasn't convinced their becoming more than friends was so terrible.

The problem was to convince Faith of that.

6

FAITH SPENT THE WEEK trying to convince herself that Sawyer was nothing but a good friend, a fellow lawyer with whom she just happened to share a case, and a one-time lover. The last caused her the most problem, because much as she tried she couldn't forget the way he'd kissed her. Not when he was making love to her on the rug in the urban nightlight. But when he'd kissed her in her office in the bold light of morning.

He hadn't been drunk then, not even tipsy. There had been nothing to blur his judgment, still he'd kissed her like a lover, and she'd responded. Worse, the response hadn't ended when he'd walked out the door. It had burrowed deep inside, making her restless ever since.

He'd made his point, all right. She was attracted to him—which was just fine, she told herself. Just because a woman was attracted to a man didn't mean there had to be a heavy relationship. She didn't want a heavy relationship. She'd been through the disillusionment of one that had petered out, scattering hopes and dreams to the wind. Now she was enjoying her freedom, and if there were times when she thought of such things as having a family, she reminded herself that she had time. She was only thirty-three. Not over the hill quite yet.

Still her thoughts kept returning to Sawyer and that kiss. It had been, without a doubt, the most exciting kiss she'd ever received. As conservative as he looked on the outside, that kiss had been wild and unconstrained, and he hadn't apologized for it—not when he'd given it, nor in the hours after.

Hours stretched into days, and she didn't hear from him. She was alert when she passed through the lobby of the office building they shared, when she walked through the nearby streets, even when she was in the courthouse, but she didn't catch sight of him once.

Finally Friday morning, she had what she felt was a legitimate reason to call. She reached him at the office on the second try, just as he returned from an appointment.

"Hi, Sawyer." She sounded calm, despite the acceleration of her pulse. She wasn't sure how she'd be received.

"Faith!" He shrugged out of his trenchcoat, only mildly winded from the dash through the rain and up the stairs. "I just got in."

"I'm sorry to bother you."

"No bother." He was inordinately pleased that she'd called, inordinately pleased that she sounded amiable, given the way they'd last parted. "Is everything okay?"

On one hand, it was. His tone of voice, enthusiastic but with that last bit of concern, was the Sawyer she knew and loved. She felt back on stable ground, at least where he was concerned.

On the other hand, there was no stable ground at her client's house. "Laura Leindecker just called. Her husband's gone. After sticking to her like glue all week, he just...disappeared. You haven't by chance heard from him, have you?"

Sawyer frowned. "Not since Monday. When was the last time she saw him?"

"Yesterday morning. He didn't come back to the house last night."

"I'd have thought she'd be pleased. She wanted him out."

"She's worried. It may be habit, still she's worried."

Tossing his trenchcoat aside, he dropped into his chair. "Are you sure the word isn't suspicious?" he asked, but in a curious way, rather than a snide one. "Maybe she's thinking he's with another woman."

Faith had wondered about that, had even dared ask it. Laura had been uneasy with the question. "It would be impossible for her not to be suspicious. She found that note. He admitted to being unfaithful. A basic trust was destroyed then." She paused, trying to hone in on her instincts and convey them to one who might help. "Laura wants to be able to say that he's with another woman, but I think her worry goes deeper. I think she's genuinely concerned."

"Has she called the office?"

"She was embarrassed to do it herself, so she had her cleaning girl do it. He wasn't there. His secretary said he was out for the day."

"Maybe he's away on business."

"He didn't pack any things. I thought maybe he'd contacted you, but if he hasn't—"

"Let me make a few calls." Sawyer had already flipped through the pink slips that were sitting on his desk. None had to do with Bruce Leindecker. "I may be able to push the right buttons and get some information. Will you be in the office for a little while?"

"I won't go anywhere until you call back. Thanks, Sawyer."

As she quietly hung up the phone, she realized that she felt better than she had all week. She liked having Sawyer on her side. He'd been there for so many years, an able resource person, a shoulder to lean on. Strange that their doing something as intimate as making love should pit them against each other—and it had done that, more so than the Leindecker case. If she was lucky, maybe the Leindecker case would be the thing to get them back on the track of being friends. He had certainly been the old, dependable, agreeable, helpful Sawyer a minute ago.

He was all of those things when he called back half an hour later. "Bruce is fine. He's with their son, Tim, in Longmeadow."

Faith let out a soft breath. "Laura will be relieved. She'll also be furious. Why didn't he tell her where he was going?"

"He didn't know where he was going until he got there. He's pretty upset about all this. Wasn't sure Laura would give a damn."

"Of course, she gives a damn. They've been married for twenty-four years."

"Apparently she's been cursing that fact in no uncertain terms all week."

"He's been in her hair all week."

"So he figured he'd give her a break. He needed one, too."

"Maybe Tim will be a calming force."

Sawyer would have liked that, but the brief time he'd spent talking with Tim on the phone wasn't reassuring. "I...wouldn't count on it."

"Uh-oh," Faith said. "What's Tim's gripe?"

"He got married last year. Laura doesn't like his wife. Doesn't think she's good enough. There are some hard feelings, I guess."

"You guess," Faith murmured. The Leindecker case, like many of the other divorces she'd handled, was beginning to sound like a soap opera. But she was being paid to consider each new plot twist. "I guess I'd better call Laura and tell her Bruce is all right. Did he say when he'll be home?"

"When I asked, he got a little annoyed. He said that he's too old to be reporting in, and anyway, she kicked him out, he says. I told him to remember that she was worried. Maybe you could tell her to bear with him."

"I think I can do that," Faith said and reflected on the discussion. Laura swore that she wanted a divorce, which was why Faith had accepted a retainer. But there were times when Faith wondered. "Are we negotiating a divorce here, or mediating a marital squabble? I mean, I'm all for encouraging reconciliation, but I'm a lawyer, not a therapist."

"Mmm. It gets tedious sometimes."

"Do you ever want out?" she asked, thinking in broader terms.

"Lots of times. That's why divorce work is only a small part of my practice. What about you? You do it more often than me."

"I don't like the tedium either. But there's probably less of it in the cases I do. Mostly I represent women, and women are the underdogs in most divorce proceedings nowadays."

"Is Laura Leindecker an underdog?"

"I'm...not quite sure. I'm not quite sure about lots of things relating to this case."

"Ditto," Sawyer said, but he was more interested in other things about which he wasn't quite sure. "I'm heading down to the Cape first thing in the morning. Want to come?"

It was a minute before Faith adjusted to the shift in gears, and even then, the invitation had popped out so suddenly that she couldn't take it seriously. "Uh, thanks, Sawyer, but I've got a million things to do tomorrow."

"Do them today."

"I'm working today."

"Tonight. Do your million things tonight. Come with me tomorrow." His voice was deep and earnest.

"You're serious," she said, realizing it just then.

"Of course, I'm serious. Did you doubt it?"

"I...yes. It seemed like such an unpremeditated suggestion."

"It was, but it's a good one. I want you to see the house."

Faith wanted to see it, too. She also wanted to spend time with Sawyer, who was nicer to be with than just about anyone she knew. She'd have agreed to go in a minute—if it hadn't been for the Friday night before. Thanks to that night, something more than friendship existed between them. She'd spent far too much time thinking about that something than she cared to admit. It had haunted her—the flash of his large hand molding her breast, the wetness of his mouth on her belly, the piercing strength of him as he filled her from the inside out. The haunting made her weak in the knees, and weak in the knees translated into weak in resolve, and without resolve, she didn't trust herself.

"I don't know, Sawyer," she said so softly that her message came across loud and clear.

"Nothing has to happen," he assured her in a voice that was every bit as quiet, but far more sure. "There's nothing remotely seductive or romantic about the place. It's old and broken-down. I'm reshingling the roof. I work the whole time I'm there, and when I'm done working, I'm tired."

He was trying to paint an unappealing picture, she knew, but he failed. The image of Sawyer Bell on the roof doing physical labor was enticing. "So if you're working all the time, what will I do?"

"Look around and decide whether you think I ought to torch the place."

"You can't torch it, Sawyer. Besides, my looking around won't take long. What do I do when I'm done with that?"

"Strip paint from the moldings around the fireplace."

"You'd put me to work?"

"If you're bored. It's good therapy. We agreed on that, remember?"

She remembered, but that didn't alter the fact that if she went to the Cape with him, they'd be together for an extended period of time. A body could only work so long. When it was done working, it could get into mischief.

"I don't know," she said again. This time her voice was softened by a blend of wistfulness and apprehension. "You'll want to stay overnight."

Sawyer hesitated for just a minute. "Yes." He knew what she was thinking. "Nothing has to happen, Faith. We can spend the day working, then go out to dinner and catch a movie or something."

"Where would we sleep?"

"Wherever you want."

"Where do you usually sleep?"

"In a sleeping bag on the floor. But that doesn't mean you have to do it. The floor is warped. It's worse than sleeping on bare ground. It's fine for me, but I wouldn't expect you to rough it that way."

"I'm not fragile."

"You're used to comfort."

"That doesn't mean I can't live without it for a night. I'm not made of fluff."

"But you're a woman."

"So?"

"So your body doesn't conform as well to the floor as mine does. You have curves, Faith. My body is straighter and harder than yours."

For the space of a breath, Faith didn't speak. Then she murmured, "That's what worries me," and it was Sawyer's turn to be silent.

Finally he said quietly, "I want to be with you this weekend, and it doesn't have to be a sexual thing. It can be purely platonic. We'll be friends like we've always been. We won't do anything you don't want to do."

"That's what worries me," she repeated, and Sawyer understood.

"You don't trust yourself?" He hoped it was true. It wasn't that he was a sadist, just that he'd been aroused and aching too often that week. He wanted to think Faith had been, too.

"I'm not sure. I keep thinking about last Friday night and asking why I didn't stop what was happening. I guess—" she rushed on before he could remind her of the wine they'd drunk "—I'm not convinced I was out of it. I remember too many things too clearly."

Sawyer had been asking himself similar questions all week, but he wasn't about to discuss them now. If he could get Faith away with him, they'd have plenty of time to talk. "We won't have anything to drink this weekend. Nothing but coffee. Come with me, Faith. It'll be good for both of us."

"I don't want to make love."

"Then we won't."

"What if I ask for it?"

"Then we will."

"But I don't want to." She straightened in her chair.

"Okay, Sawyer, I'll go down to the Cape with you on one condition. You have to keep things under control. I'm telling you now that I don't want to make love. It's your responsibility to make sure we don't, regardless of what I say when we're down there."

"That's absurd."

"I won't be able to relax with you unless you agree."

Sawyer brushed at the moisture breaking out over his lip. "That's just as absurd as the other. What if you find that you do want it? What if you're relaxed but making love will relax you even more? What if the pain of *not* making love is driving you crazy? What if you're begging me for it? Christ, Faith, I'm not a saint!"

"Then I won't go."

"I'll be a saint."

She had to smile at the speed of his turnaround. But before she could comment on it, he grumbled, "I wonder if this is what Leindecker's been going through all these years. A man thinks he's in control, then a woman gives him an ultimatum and he crumbles."

"Don't crumble. I'm counting on you to be strong. That's your forte, Sawyer. You're a big, strong male. Much stronger than me—isn't that how the chauvinist credo reads?"

"Cute, Faith."

"But I'm serious, at least about your being strong. You are, and I'm trusting you." She paused. "Do you still want to go, or is the invitation rescinded?"

"We're going," he grumbled. "I'll pick you up at six tomorrow morning."

"*Six*. You didn't say anything about—"

"Six. Be ready, or I'm leaving without you."

Before Faith could argue, she was staring at the phone, which was dead in her hand. Replacing it in its cradle, she sat back in her chair, linked her fingers, pressed them to her mouth and wondered whether she was making a mistake. She'd given in to temptation, and though Sawyer had promised to save her from it—and though she trusted him to do just that—there was more to temptation than just sex.

Being with Sawyer, spending the entire weekend with him was a treat she couldn't pass up. She didn't have anything pressing to do over the weekend, and even if she had she couldn't think of anything that would appeal to her more than being with him.

Besides, she needed a weekend away.

Besides, she wouldn't mind stripping the moldings by the fireplace.

Besides, she liked the spontaneity of the whole thing.

So she was going. Feeling slightly scattered, even a little light-headed, she dropped her hands from her mouth and looked down to her desk to see what she had to do before she went home. It was a minute before she could make any sense of the papers strewn before her. They were the rough notes for a talk on family law she was delivering to a law school class the following Wednesday night, and she wanted it to be good. She wanted to teach her own full-term course one day; for that reason alone she had to impress both her students and whatever faculty members might be listening in.

But she wasn't in the mood for concentration just then, so she gathered the papers up, thinking to work on them at home that night. Taking a file from her cabinet, she set it with the papers, then, wiping her palms on her skirt, looked around the office for anything else she'd need.

Almost absently, she glanced at her watch and realized that it was only three o'clock. She couldn't leave for the day. Loni hadn't left. It was far too early—unless she had a court appearance or some other kind of appointment, which she didn't. So she sat back down in her chair and reached for the papers she'd so neatly piled together. She opened to the page she'd been reading, but ten minutes of staring at it without comprehending a word convinced her that it was best saved for another time.

Straightening the papers again, she slid them into her briefcase. Then she sat back, crossed her legs, took a pad of paper onto her lap and began to make a list of calls she wanted to make on Monday in reference to a client whose custody hearing was approaching. She had four names and numbers listed when, with a start, she realized that she hadn't called Laura Leindecker back.

Cursing her distraction, she immediately phoned the woman and passed on the information Sawyer had given her. Laura was relieved, then annoyed.

"Where does that leave me?" she asked. "Am I supposed to sit around all weekend and wait for him to come home?"

"What would you normally do?"

"Sit around all weekend and wait for him to come home. But I'm tired of doing that."

"Where will you go?"

"Out."

"What will you do?"

"Shop."

"Oh. Okay." Faith took a breath. "May I make a suggestion?"

"Please do."

"I think that perhaps you should start thinking about what you want from this divorce in terms of the division of property. Once we formally file papers, we'll get into those kinds of negotiations. It would help if you think about them now."

It was a new tack. Until then, Faith had focused on whether or not Laura wanted the divorce. From the start, Laura had insisted that she did, still Faith knew that the decision had been ruled by anger and hurt, far more than reason. Faith suspected that once Laura turned her thoughts to the specifics of getting divorced and *being* divorced, she might decide it wasn't what she wanted at all.

"I'll think about it," Laura said, but a bit defensively. "He'll fight me. He said he would."

"He doesn't want the divorce?"

"He *must* want it. After all, he's the one who found me so inadequate that he had to go looking for satisfaction with another woman."

Hearing Laura's hurt so bluntly expressed, Faith hurt for her in turn. "Have you asked him why he did that?" she asked gently.

Laura answered in an uneasy tone. "Went to another woman? I think it's obvious."

"Not necessarily. There are reasons why men do things, and being women, we don't always understand. It helps to ask sometimes."

"I can't. It would be too humiliating."

"It may not be as humiliating as you think. It may be that what your husband did had to do with him and something he's going through right now. It may have had little to do with you." She paused. When Laura didn't argue, she said, "Talk with him—if not about the affair, then about the divorce. And remember, stay calm. The calmer you are, the more you'll get from him. If he's determined to fight you, that's something we'll just have to face, but for now, the calmer you are, the better."

STAY CALM. STAY CALM. Those words became a litany in Faith's mind through the rest of that day. Each time she thought of going away with Sawyer, her stomach started to jump. She wasn't sure if it was excitement or nervousness, and she didn't stop to analyze which. She simply repeated the litany in her mind and went about doing everything she had to do to free herself up for Saturday and Sunday.

Actually, if it hadn't been for that jumping stomach, she'd never have made it out of bed when her alarm rang at five-thirty Saturday morning. She hadn't been able to fall asleep until after one, which meant that she was sleeping soundly when the alarm went off. It was pitch-black outside, still night in her book, but the instant she realized why she was getting up so early, her body came to life.

Quickly she showered, dried her hair and applied the lightest possible sheen of makeup. After pulling on a pair of jeans and a comfortable sweater, she put a change of clothes into an overnight bag, along with whatever else she decided she'd need for a rustic sleepover. She was zipping the bag when the doorbell rang.

Sawyer looked stern, dark and tired. She was certain something awful had happened to him, but when she asked, he merely shrugged. "I couldn't sleep." He straightened from the doorjamb which had been bearing the brunt of his weight. "Actually that's a lie. I purposely kept myself awake most of the night so that I'd be too tired to do anything tonight."

Faith closed her eyes to his self-mocking look. "Oh, Sawyer."

"You said it was my responsibility, so I'm making good on it." He reached for her bag. "Is this it?"

"We're only going overnight."

"But overnight usually means three changes of clothes,

two jackets, boots, sneakers and flats, a makeup case, a hair dryer, a curling iron, a vacuum cleaner—"

Faith swept past him into the hall, tugged him out by the arm and slammed the door. She didn't say another word until he'd tucked her into the passenger's seat of his racy black Porsche. "Some car," she breathed, running a hand lightly over the butter-soft leather covering the seat. "Is it new?"

Sawyer took a deep breath. He knew he was being a pill, but he couldn't seem to help himself. He'd stayed up most of the night thinking of Faith, so not only was he tired, but his body was tight. It hadn't helped that he'd slept through his alarm. He'd had time for nothing but a record-fast shower. What he needed was coffee and fresh air.

"I got it six months ago," he said as he rolled down his window. "Usually I rent a pickup when I drive to the Cape. I need the space in back for tools and stuff."

"Why didn't you this time?"

"I wanted to impress you with the Porsche."

Studying his profile, she saw that he wasn't joking. She didn't know whether to yell at him or be pleased. In lieu of either, she said, "I'm impressed. But what are you going to do when you need the space for tools and stuff?"

"I won't this trip. Everything I need is already at the house." He shot her a quick glance, the first softened one since he'd arrived. "Did you have any trouble getting up?"

His glance warmed her. Still, she wasn't about to say that she'd jumped right out of bed in anticipation of seeing him, so she shrugged. "It'd be nice if the sun came up."

"It's coming," he said, and once they cruised their way free of the city buildings, she could see that it was. A faint strip of lavender lay on the eastern horizon with promise of daylight. She found that reassuring. When things were dark, the confines of the car were more intimate, and intimacy wasn't something she wanted to encourage.

They headed south on the expressway. Not long after they'd left the city, Sawyer took a short exit and pulled in at a coffee shop. "Black with one sugar?"

"Good memory."

"I'll be back."

Several minutes later he returned with two large coffees, a bag of donuts and more napkins than they'd use in a year. "Are you stocking up for the house?" she teased.

Sawyer didn't answer until he'd taken several healthy swallows of coffee. The fresh air had helped when it came to mellowing his mood; he was relying on caffeine to do the rest. "They're for the car. If something spills, I want to be able to clean it up."

Faith knew how things were between a man and his car. "Ahhh," she breathed in understanding, then pulled a honey-dipped donut from the bag and took a bite.

Sawyer demolished three in the time it took her to eat one. "I'm getting a refill of coffee. Want one?"

"No, thanks. This is fine."

He left the car, returned with a fresh cup of coffee, tore the cover enough to allow him to drink, then started the engine and returned to the road.

"How long will it take to get there?" she asked.

"An hour and a half. There won't be any traffic this time of day."

"I wonder why not," she murmured, but teasingly. With donuts filling her stomach and the warm smell of coffee filling the car, she was beginning to relax. Sawyer was a good driver. The car was a beauty. The dawning day was clear and bright. At that moment she was very glad she'd come.

The feeling was every bit as strong when Sawyer finally turned the Porsche off the main road onto the private one that wove through his property. Framed on either side by broad-leaved trees and shrubs, it narrowed, turned from hardtop to gravel and grew bumpy. He swore and slowed the Porsche to a crawl.

"Don't worry about me," Faith said, trying not to smile as she looked at him. "I don't mind the bumps." When he didn't answer, she gave in and laughed.

"What's so funny?"

"You. You look like you're in agony."

"I am."

"You're worried about the car. Don't be, Sawyer. It'll survive. What are shock absorbers for, anyway?" Returning her gaze to the front window, she couldn't contain her surprise. "Sawyer?"

He was pulling up at a most unusual structure. Turning off the engine, he curved both hands over the top of the steering wheel. "This is it."

She let out her breath in a thoroughly confused, "Ahhh."

"What do you think?"

"I think...that you're right. The setting is great. The land is gorgeous, lush even this late in the season. Are those apple trees over there? But where's the lake? You said you were on a lake." She opened the door of the car and climbed out. "Is it behind the...house?" She took off in that direction, but she hadn't gone more than three steps into the soft grass when Sawyer caught her hand.

"You don't like it," he said.

"I think it's great."

"I'm not talking about the land. We both know that's great. But what about the house?"

She forced herself to focus on the building. It was tall, round and covered with aged bricks. "It looks like a water tower."

"That's what it is."

"But you called it a house."

"If a house is defined as a place to live in, this is a house. Come on. I want you to see the inside."

Faith allowed herself to be led to a doorway that looked as though it might crumble on the spot. The doorjamb was rotted and hanging off on one side. It was a miracle that the door stayed shut.

Not only did it stay shut, but it wouldn't open—at least, not until Sawyer pushed hard.

Inside, all was dark. Sawyer seemed to know what was where, though, because within seconds he produced a hurricane lamp and lit it. Holding it aloft, he guided her into the center of the room.

Cautiously, staying close enough to him to feel the reassuring warmth of his body, Faith looked around. The room was larger than she'd expected and empty save for Sawyer's roofing material piled to one side and a network of pipes that snaked up its walls. Those walls were of the same exposed brick as the exterior, and looked nearly as weathered. The floor was concrete, dirty and cracked. There wasn't a window in sight.

"This place is spooky," she whispered.

"But it has promise." Still holding her hand, he led her forward.

They were nearly on top of the far wall before she made out a door. Pushing it open, Sawyer led her into an annex that she hadn't been able to see from outside. It was rectangular, narrower than the water tower but deeper, and had windows, wallpapered walls, planked floors and a fireplace.

While it wasn't Versailles, it was a decided improvement on the water tower. She let out a breath. "Better. Much better."

Extinguishing the hurricane lamp, Sawyer set it aside. He took a long tube from the painted mantel above the fireplace, tipped out its contents and unrolled what were clearly an architect's plans for the renovation of the place. Spreading the plans on the floor, he began to explain them to her.

By the time he was done, Faith was sitting cross-legged beside him feeling the fool for her shortsightedness. "You're right," she admitted. "It does have promise. Once windows are cut in the water tower and a sleeping loft is built above the living room, it'll be completely different."

Sawyer looked around the annex. "Once the door is widened and this place is gutted and rebuilt with modern kitchen and bathing facilities, it'll be even *more* different. I agree, it's pretty depressing right now. But there was something about it that appealed to me right away— maybe its isolation, or the woods or the lake, or the uniqueness of the whole thing. I guess that was it. The uniqueness." He gave Faith a smile that melted whatever chill may have seeped into her from the innards of the tower. "Who else do you know who can say that he lives in a converted water tower?"

"Not a soul." She looked back at the plans and grinned. "Not a soul. Unique is the word, all right."

"So you think I should go ahead with it?"

Her grin lingered when she raised her eyes to his. "Definitely. I think it's a super project."

"Don't think I should torch it?"

"You can't. Brick won't burn."

Other things could, though, and Faith suddenly grew aware of them—Sawyer's brown eyes darker than they'd been but warmer, heating her cheeks, her mind, her blood. She could do without that kind of burning, too.

Scrambling to her feet, she brushed off the seat of her pants. "Are we working?"

"We're working."

"Let's get to it, then. From the looks of those plans, there's plenty to do."

7

SAWYER DIDN'T PLAN to do all the work himself. He would have liked to, but he knew his limitations. For starters, time was a factor. At the rate of two weekends a month, it would take him years to make the place livable. He wanted to be able to enjoy it before that. And then there was the matter of skill. He was a lawyer, not a carpenter or a mason or a millworker. He knew how to reshingle a roof, how to refinish floors, how to miter moldings, even how to install cabinets, but when it came to carving windows through brick, wiring an electrical system, designing a heating system and installing new plumbing, he was willing to yield to the experts.

He told Faith as much when they took a break for lunch, which consisted of burgers at a diner on the way into town. "There's no point in doing it if it isn't done right. I don't want to end up with something that will blow apart when the first coastal storm hits."

Faith had spent a good part of the morning in and out of the water tower, first relaying shingles up to Sawyer, then trying to familiarize herself with the tower so she wouldn't shiver each time she walked in. Putting a jacket over her sweater helped beat the chill; she wasn't quite as successful fighting the heeby-jeebies.

"That water tower would withstand an assault by Attila the Hun," she maintained in a wry tone of voice.

Sawyer grinned. "Solid, huh?"

His grin was filled with pride, but it wasn't pride that suffused Faith's insides with a now familiar heat. It was the grin itself, a slash of lips and teeth that was a little curious, a little daring, a little wicked and very, very masculine. And the grin came often. With the drive behind them, with Sawyer fully awake, with the worst of his frustration expended on the roof, he was in the best of moods.

As far as Faith was concerned, that was dangerous. Each time he grinned, she felt tiny prickles of awareness march through her belly. She tried to think back to the days when he grinned and she enjoyed it in an innocent way, but those days seemed an eon ago. She wasn't sure she was ever again going to be able to see Sawyer's grin without melting a little inside.

The water tower, she supposed, was in apt counterpoint to what she was feeling. "Very solid," she confirmed.

His grin relaxed when he took a large bite of his sandwich, but all that did was to shift her awareness from his mouth to his other features. Though he'd washed up before they left the house, he still had the rugged look of a workman. Part of it was due, she was sure, to the gray athletic T-shirt he wore under a faded flannel shirt, jeans that were old, worn and thin, and work boots. The other part was due to the muss of his dark hair, the ruddy color on his cheeks, the size and sinewed strength of his hands, and the power of his features, which seemed, here in the country, more exposed than usual.

Faith needed a diversion. "How did you find the tower? Had you been looking for land down here?"

"Not exactly," he said, but he, too, was distracted. The look in her eyes just then had been full of the kind of appreciation that men dreamed of receiving from lovely women. She fought it; he could see how she deliberately brought herself back, but for several minutes she'd been swept up by something over which she had little control.

That was a good sign, he decided. Faith had a thing about control. She was a harsh taskmaster when it came to ruling herself. It would do her good to lose control once in a while.

As long as he didn't. He'd promised her.

Clearing his throat, he finished his burger off in a bite. When it had gone the way of both its predecessor and a large order of fries, he said, "I got lost, actually. I was visiting friends who were renting a place down here, and I got the directions screwed up. I wound up at the water tower, and it intrigued me."

"Did you know it was for sale?"

"Not then. I finally managed to get where I was supposed to go, and I went back to Boston at the end of the day, but I kept thinking about the tower. It looked abandoned. So I made a few calls, found out that the whole parcel of land was for sale and came down the next weekend to look again."

Faith remembered some of the discussions she'd had with Sawyer way back when. "You always wanted a vacation place. You used to talk about finding something in northern Maine."

"Mmm. Joanna hated that idea. She may have been as maternal as they came, but Earth Mother she wasn't. The thought of being too far from civilization frightened her."

"She'd have liked it down here. You're isolated, but you're not."

"Her loss."

"Your gain. It's really a super place, Sawyer."

He raised two fingers to the waitress and called for coffee. "It'll be even more super when it's done. It won't ever be big, but the way the architect has it planned, there'll be room for everything I want. It'll be a year-round escape." Putting his weight on his elbows, he met her gaze with a look that was frank and unguarded. "I've wanted something like this for years. I wanted it when I was a kid, only my parents couldn't afford their own house, let alone a vacation place. I wanted it when Joanna and I first married, only I didn't have the money then, either. Joanna was the one who bought the house in Cambridge. I was getting benefits from Uncle Sam, and that helped a lot when I was in school, but even when I finally graduated, it was a while before I hit the upper brackets."

The waitress came with their coffee. Sawyer handed Faith a packet of sugar, took two for himself and two thimbles of cream, and focused on the mocha-colored brew as he stirred it. "By the time I had enough in the bank to think about a second home, Joanna and I were on the skids. I felt badly about that. She deserved more of the fruits of her labor than she got. I didn't take care of her very well, at least not during our marriage."

Faith had to smile, but it was a smile made soft by understanding and admiration. Sawyer was, indeed, a throwback to the days where men took care of women. She didn't find it offensive just then, though. As he talked so quietly and honestly, she saw him for the protective and caring man that he was. Joanna, with her need to protect rather than be protected, to care for rather than be cared for, couldn't appreciate him.

Faith could. The thought surprised her, because she saw herself as a thoroughly independent woman, but at that moment, away from the city and her thoroughly independent world, she found the idea of being protected and cared for strangely appealing.

"Does Joanna know what she gave up?" she heard herself ask.

If there was a compliment inherent in the question, Sawyer missed it. He was shifting his coffee cup in its saucer, studying each turn. "She didn't give up so much. When I was in school, I studied most of the time. When I got a job, I worked most of the time. I wasn't much of a companion for her. I think she was as relieved as I was when we finally called it quits."

"Who handled the divorce?"

"Me. It was an easy thing. We agreed on the property settlement. I gave most everything and then some. She'd earned it."

"You are a good man."

He looked up at her. "I like to think I'm a fair one. The marriage wasn't going anywhere, but Joanna had invested a great deal of time and effort in me. Largely thanks to her, I was healthy and productive. She deserved a good settlement. I wasn't about to rob her of it just because I knew I could get away with it in court." He paused, frowned. "Why is it we always end up talking about the past?"

"Because it's part of us. You went through a lot with Joanna. Just because the marriage is over doesn't mean you forget her."

"Is it the same with you and Jack?"

"I don't know," Faith said. She shifted her gaze to the counter, but she was oblivious to the people perched on leather-covered stools at the bar. "Jack and I didn't go through anything like you and Joanna did. He was just there. I went about my life, he went about his. It was an increasingly uninteresting relationship."

"Was it interesting when you first met him?"

Sitting back in the booth, she looked down at her hands. "I'm not sure."

"Did you love him?"

"I guess so."

"You weren't sure?"

Faith raised her head and spoke in her own defense. "I had to do something. I was fresh out of college, just starting law school, and it seemed that everywhere I turned, someone was telling me that if I didn't marry soon, I never would. They said that once I became a career woman I wouldn't have time for anything else. They said that if I was successful, I'd become so threatening to men that none of them would come close." Her words stopped. She shrugged. The ghost of a smile touched her lips and was gone. "I guess I bought it all."

"Who was doing the selling?"

She didn't answer at first. Disloyalty wasn't something she took pride in, and this time there was no wine to blunt the effect. But Sawyer was waiting for an honest answer—Sawyer, whom she trusted. "My family."

Studying her face, he saw a vulnerability that was entirely new. Gently he said, "I've never heard you talk about your family before."

"I try not to."

"You don't get along?"

"Oh, we get along just fine, as long as we don't discuss anything more weighty than the price of eggs."

"They don't live nearby, do they?" He was sure he'd have known if they did, principally because Faith would have been more involved with them.

"They're in Oregon."

"And you're on the opposite coast. By design?"

She pursed her lips, thought for a minute, gave a single slow nod.

"Safer that way?"

"You got it. My parents are very conventional people, and I'm not criticizing that. But I'm not conventional by their standards, and they do criticize me. I go back to visit once a year. That's enough."

"They must be proud of your work."

"They know nothing about it, other than that I'm a lawyer. For all of their interest in that, I could be a toll collector on the turnpike. I've tried to tell them about what I do. I've described some of the more interesting cases I've handled, but as soon as I stop for a breath, they're asking me whether or not I'm dating."

"Did they like Jack?"

"Jack was a husband. That pleased them. But then the questions started coming about babies, and when I told them I wasn't ready to have kids, that set them off. They always found something cutting to say. I've never fit into the mold of what they think a woman should be." Faith chewed on the inside of her lip for a minute. Slowly she released it and in a small voice said, "It hurts sometimes, y'know?"

Sawyer could see that hurt clear as day on her face. It was all he could do not to take her in his arms and soothe her, but he wasn't sure she'd want that. She took pride in being independent and strong. Then again, he wondered whether it was all pride or whether there wasn't a little defensiveness involved. Was she independent and strong because she wanted to be or because that was the only way she could manage on her own? And she was alone. He saw it now as he'd never seen it before. He wanted to soothe her for that, too, but he wasn't sure she'd want that, either.

Before he had a chance to do anything, she sighed. "So, anyway, Jack wasn't the most significant part of my life. He was just a physical presence while I went ahead and did what I would have done if I'd never married him. Sad, isn't it? It was a wasted relationship. I'm glad for his sake that he got out of it. He deserves more."

Sawyer wasn't so sure about that. In his book, Jack had had a gem in his hand and had dropped it. For his lack of care, he'd gotten what he deserved. "What about you? Don't you deserve more? I knew Jack. He was a nice guy, but he wasn't right for you. You were way ahead of him in most every way. He didn't satisfy you. He didn't challenge you. He didn't do anything for you that you couldn't do for yourself. So don't *you* deserve more?"

"I have my career."

"And what else?"

"Maybe that's enough."

"Is it?"

"More coffee, folks?" the waitress asked.

They swung their heads in her direction, startled by the interruption. Sawyer was the first to recover. "Uh, no. I'm fine. Faith?"

She shook her head.

"Just the check," Sawyer quietly told the waitress. When she tore it from the pad and put it on the table, he took it up in his hand. But he didn't look at it. His thoughts were elsewhere. "You sell yourself short, Faith. Maybe we both do. I say that Joanna is better off without me. You say that Jack is better off without you. Well, what about us? Don't we deserve excitement and happiness and fulfillment?" He opened his free hand to ward off an argument. "Yes, I know we get satisfaction from our work. But is it enough?"

Faith let the peripheral conversation, the occasional

laugh or cough, the clatter of china on china fill in where she had no words. At last, she murmured, "I don't know."

He let out a breath. "It's ironic, when you think of it." Not that he had. He usually took life pretty much as it came, without deep thought to the future. "The satisfaction we get from our work was probably what did in our marriages. So now that our marriages are done in, is work enough?" He paused, held her sober-eyed gaze, shrugged. "I don't know the answer, either."

"That's a relief. It makes me feel a little less inadequate." She reached for the check.

"Don't you dare," he growled.

Carefully she retrieved her hand and tucked it in her lap. She heard the voice of command, and while there were times when she felt compelled to exert herself, this wasn't one of them. Paying for lunch at a diner wasn't going to bankrupt either one of them. Somehow it seemed foolish to argue over the bill.

Walking back to the car, he dropped an arm around her shoulder. It was a deliberately casual gesture. "You're a good girl, Faith."

She tipped her head up against his arm and gave him a pert smile, which seemed the least a good girl could do. It also told him that she wasn't grappling with heavy questions such as the one he'd posed. There was a time and a place for everything. Being away for the weekend with Sawyer had its own challenges without the pressure of intense philosophical thought. Time enough to brood about her future in the future.

They made several stops on the way back to the house—one to pick up a sleeping bag for Faith to match the one Sawyer already had, another to pick up a cooler and juice, milk and cheese for snacks, a third to pick up nails, scrapers and sandpaper. But rather than going right back to work, they took a walk. Sawyer wanted to show Faith the lay of the land, and she didn't argue. She loved the outdoors. Well beyond being a break from the city, walking through Sawyer's sun-speckled acres was a treat.

The land was beautiful. It rolled gently from one copse to the next, a world of greenery touched by the occasional crimson or gold. Though it was October, fall was reluctant in coming, as though it knew that a special something would be lost once the trees were bare. As those trees stood, a light breeze stirred their leaves. The same breeze lifted Faith's hair to her cheeks and dusted Sawyer's over his forehead. The continuity was satisfying.

The lakefront was broad and peaceful, perfect for skipping stones and imagining the delights of swimming on warmer days. There was even a dock, decaying to be sure but sturdy enough to hold Sawyer and, when she finally dared join him, Faith. For a long while they sat there, enjoying the silence of the afternoon. Neither of them thought to disturb it with words.

Faith was content. Sitting beside Sawyer on the broken-down dock, she felt she was privy to a moment out of time. She'd left her responsibilities behind in Boston. Her sole job was to...be. On impulse, she lay back on the dock with her hands as a pillow and closed her eyes to the sun. Its warmth was gentle, safe, lulling. Giving in to the soft smile that begged for release, she basked in the serenity of the day.

Looking down at her, Sawyer broke into a smile of his own. Her pleasure pleased him. He'd wanted her to like his place, and she did. She hadn't spoken as they walked, but he could tell from the look on her face that she was enjoying herself.

She might not have. He felt that he knew her well, still the focus of that knowledge was the career they shared. When it came to things beyond the law, his experience with her was more limited. For all he knew, she might have hated the house, hated the architect's plans, hated the rustic, uncultured look of the land. She might have hated the thought of sleeping in a sleeping bag on the floor in front of a fire, but when he'd pointed to a motel they'd passed, she'd given a firm shake of her head. Possibly she was out to make the point that she wasn't as soft as he thought, but if so, there wasn't a chance in hell that she'd win. Looking at her, all stretched out on the dock in her soft sweater and soft jeans, with her soft curves shaping both, he was more aware than ever of her femininity.

As was his body. The longer he looked at her, the faster his heart beat, and the faster his heart beat, the warmer his blood flowed. Somewhere in the middle of that, desire began to gather into a tight knot in his groin.

Moving to ease the knot before it grew painful, he pushed himself to his feet. The dock gave an ominous creak and an even more ominous wobble. He held his breath.

Faith raised her head to look up at him through the shade cast over her body by his. "Back to work?"

"Very carefully," he advised. He gave her a hand up, keeping the movement as smooth as possible, and waited until she'd left the dock before following her. By the time he was by her side, walking back through the tall grasses toward the house, he was in control once again.

His control lasted through the afternoon, but that was easy. He spent most of the time on the cone-shaped roof of the water tower, hammering away at the cedar shingles that had to be spaced just so, to prevent seepage of rain or snow. Yes, it was physical labor, but it demanded a certain amount of concentration from a roofer with his very limited experience. When he finally descended the ladder for the last time, it was with a sense of satisfaction in what he'd done...and a slight apprehension about the evening that lay before him.

For the first time, he wondered whether he'd been wise to invite Faith to stay overnight. Whenever he looked at her, even more when he came close, he felt the same quickening in his body. Sometimes it was in the area of the heart, sometimes in his hands, which itched to touch her, sometimes lower, where the ache was primal.

But he'd promised her that he would be the guardian of her virtue for the night, and he was determined to keep that promise.

Faith was counting on him for that, so she could relax and enjoy herself without having to exert a great deal of constraint. She worked some as Sawyer suggested, scraping and sanding chipped paint from the molding that framed the fireplace, the doors and the annex windows. But she was ready to take breaks at the slightest excuse, whether that was to convey a cold drink to the roof, to wander out in the meadow and chart the gradual descent of the sun or to sit on the grass and watch Sawyer at work.

She was impressed. He was surefooted and able as he carefully placed and hammered down each shingle. He'd long since tossed aside his flannel shirt, leaving him in the gray T-shirt that moved more easily with his shoulders and arms. As he built up a sweat, the shirt grew darker in patches. She was impressed by that, too, but in a different way.

Sitting on the grass with her arms around her knees, she wondered once again why she'd never noticed how virile he was. It seemed hard to believe that what she could drool over now had been before her many times before, and she hadn't appreciated it. Of course, she'd never before seen Sawyer in this kind of physical context, and besides, she couldn't have exactly drooled over him with Jack and Joanna in attendance. Still, she might have privately thought certain things, yet she hadn't. In that sense, she was impressed with herself.

When she married Jack, she had vowed to be faithful. She'd kept that vow. On occasion, she wondered if Jack had. She'd found nothing incriminating—not that she'd been looking—but there had certainly been nothing comparable to the note Laura Leindecker had discovered. Indeed, there had been times toward the end when Faith had almost wished Jack *would* have an affair, if only to make something happen. As it turned out, that hadn't been necessary. Emotional attrition finally took its toll.

So now, freed of the moral obligation of being true to Jack, she was seeing Sawyer in a different light. He turned her on. She was still appalled that they'd made love the way they had that Friday night, but she'd given up denying that the attraction was there. It existed, and it was strong. If she hadn't known it before this weekend, she couldn't miss it now. The question was where it would lead. Granted there was still the possibility that she was pregnant, but she didn't put much stock in that. She wasn't sure why—maybe gut instinct, or the romantic notion that when she conceived a child she'd know at the moment it happened—but she fully expected to get her period in another week. So that left the future very much open where she and Sawyer were concerned.

Where did she want it to go? She didn't know. And she didn't want to think about it. Thinking about it made her uneasy. She wasn't sure why, but it did. So she gathered herself up and went back to work inside until Sawyer called it a day.

"Hungry?" he asked as he leaned over the large sink on the wall of the annex that served as a kitchen. The bathroom sink was miniscule, something he was going to have to remedy.

Faith leaned against the most distant wall, watching him wash up. It was torture. He'd taken off the T-shirt and was sluicing water over his head and upper body with little concern for what splashed on the floor. Wet and gleaming, the sinewed twists at his arms and shoulders stood out well.

She took a shaky breath. "Uh-huh. I'm hungry."

"We could have dinner, then see a movie. There's usually something decent playing in Hyannis."

Faith wondered whether decent meant PG. She hoped so. She wasn't sure she could make it through an R-rated film without gnawing on Sawyer's neck. "That sounds good," she said, a little breathless.

Sawyer toweled himself off, reached for a clean T-shirt and pulled it on as quickly as he could. A sweater went over that, then he turned to her. "All set?"

With a nod, she led the way out through the tower, which was faintly lit now by the deep gold of the low-lying sun. Sensing there was a danger in lingering too long there, she hurried on.

DINNER WAS AN ENJOYABLE interlude before the movie, which turned out to have nothing to do with sex, for which Sawyer was eternally grateful. He didn't need the power of suggestion. His mind was providing plenty of that, and what his mind didn't respond to, his body did.

The air had cooled by the time they left the movie, and

by the time they returned to the house, that cool air had seeped in through the uninsulated walls of the annex.

"Last chance," Sawyer warned. He was on the verge of lighting a fire, holding split logs in each hand. "I can still drive you to a motel."

Faith wore a jacket over her sweater, and though she could feel the night air through the layers, she wasn't about to seek a more cushy shelter. "Don't be silly. This is fine."

"It'll get colder before it gets warmer."

"So light the fire. If that's not enough, I'll crawl into my sleeping bag, and if that's not enough, I'll turn on your car and sleep there."

"You will not."

She laughed. "Just kidding. Go on. Light the fire." She was feeling high without having had a thing to drink. But that was Sawyer's problem. He'd agreed to see that nothing happened.

Sawyer set the logs on the grate, added a third and some kindling, then lit a match. The kindling took off instantly, the logs a few minutes later. Soon the flames were leaping high, sending off a welcome heat.

He sat back several feet from the flames and watched them in silence.

"A penny for your thoughts," Faith said softly as she scooted on her bottom across the floor until she sat at right angles to him. That way she could see both the fire and his face.

"I don't think you want to hear."

"Sure I do."

He remained quiet, though, debating the pros and cons of being honest. His decision came only after he'd dared a quick look at her. Lit by the fire, her features were warm and beckoning, making mockery of the promise he'd made. He desperately wanted to touch her, even if only in the innocent way he might have done two weeks, a month, a year ago. It occurred to him that his best hope of not touching her was to be perfectly honest about his needs.

"I'm thinking," he said in a voice that was low and a little gritty, "that I should be tired. I was up at six. I didn't get much sleep last night. I worked hard for a good part of the day. I had a huge dinner, and that movie was boring as hell. I should be ready to go to sleep. But I'm not."

"Maybe you're overtired."

"That's not the problem." Slowly and more deliberately this time, he shifted his gaze to hers. "I want you, Faith. I know I promised not to touch you, but I'm jumping around inside. Call it restlessness or whatever, but I want you."

She hadn't expected him to be so blunt. For a minute, she wondered whether he was simply trying to shock her. But he wasn't that kind of man. He didn't do things for effect unless he was in the courtroom, and he wasn't there now. The courtroom, the law, Boston were all far, far away. It was just the two of them sitting before a fire in his broken-down house on the Cape. Things were more raw here, unpadded, free of the city's gloss. That knowledge was what made the look in his eyes so stunning. It was a look of need that burned deep, and it wasn't for show.

Unable to handle the intensity of what she saw, she turned her eyes toward the fire. "I don't want that."

"I know. But I can't help it, Faith. I look at you, and it happens."

She could feel it happening to her, too. Their isolation, the fire, his physical nearness, the deep sound of his voice—those things would have done it alone, even if she hadn't seen the hunger in his eyes. "You said it wouldn't. I only came on that condition."

"And it won't. But you asked what I was thinking. So I told you."

He stopped talking, and for a time nothing broke the stillness but the crackle of the fire. Faith studied the flames, following them until they disappeared into the fireplace shaft, but if there was a pattern to their dance, she couldn't find it.

"Why is this happening, Sawyer?"

"This thing between us?" He snorted. "Because I'm a man and you're a woman."

"But we've been those things for a long time, now, and nothing happened before."

"It couldn't before."

"It could have. It's been over a year since Jack and I split and nearly as long for you and Joanna. We've seen each other several times since then, and nothing happened. Why now? Is it all because we had too much to drink last Friday night?"

"That may have started it," Sawyer conceded. He'd given the matter a lot of thought that week, mostly during the night when he'd lain awake while his body ached for what it couldn't have. "But the attraction—or the potential for it—must have been there a lot longer. We just didn't allow it to surface. That's all."

"Then you weren't aware of wanting me before that?"

"I didn't think about it. I didn't think of you in terms of sex. I thought you were pretty and sexy, but you were a friend. First you were married, and then when you were free, you were still a lawyer. A *lady* lawyer."

"Then my parents were right. I scare people away."

"That's not what I meant. I meant that you were a colleague of mine, and I took care to view you as one.

Women have worked twice as hard to establish themselves as lawyers. Men have to work twice as hard to *see* them as lawyers instead of women." He considered her concern. "I can see where you might be intimidating to some men. You're attractive, vocal and successful. But so am I. So you don't threaten me in that way."

"Maybe it would be better if I did," she mused. Her tone was bittersweet, her expression sad.

Sawyer pulled himself up straighter. "Why do you say that?" When, after a hesitation, she simply shrugged, he reached over and turned her face to his. "Tell me why. What's so awful about our being involved with each other?"

"Nothing's so awful about it," she said, raising her chin to free it from his fingers. "I'm just not sure I want to be involved with anyone right now."

"You enjoy being alone? Are you a loner at heart? Was Jack's presence that much of a strain that you don't want anyone else in your life?"

"It wasn't a strain. It was just…disappointing."

"That's an enlightening comment."

She searched his eyes for mockery and saw none. "What do you mean?"

"The only way you could have found your marriage to Jack disappointing was if you'd had hopes for something better." His voice gentled. "We hope for what we want, Faith. What was it you wanted when you got married?"

She dropped her eyes. "I don't know."

"Sure you do. You just don't want to talk about it. Maybe you don't want to *think* about it, but maybe it's time you do."

"Why?" she asked, annoyed as she raised her head. Sawyer was putting her on the defensive, and she was prepared to fight.

He didn't blink. "Because if you're pregnant, you'll have to think about it. You'll have to think about lots of things you might not want to." He paused, watched the fight fade from her face, lifted his hand and stroked her cheek. "Have you thought about being pregnant?"

She swallowed. Still, her voice came out a shadow of it-self. "I'm trying not to. I don't think I am."

"Would you want to be?"

"I don't know."

He ran his thumb along her jaw and spoke very qui-etly. "Yes or no. Would you want it?"

"I don't *know*," she insisted.

"Don't you want to be a mother?"

"Yes, but I'm not sure I want it *now*."

He dropped his hand to his lap. "Did you want it with Jack?"

"I used birth control when I was with Jack."

It was an evasive answer, but he let it ride. "Did Jack want it?"

"Sure." She took a breath, a lot easier now that he'd dropped his hand. She had trouble thinking when he touched her. "Babies went along with marriage, and he wanted it all. We used to argue a lot. I kept telling him the timing was wrong. It would have been hard for me to have a baby while I was in law school, and the law firm wasn't wild about the idea of maternity leaves, and then when I went out on my own, I had the full responsibility of a practice on my shoulders. I tried to explain to Jack that the timing was wrong then, too."

Sawyer wasn't buying into the bad timing theory. "You told me there were ways to do it. When we talked about it last week, you said that a woman can have a ca-reer and a baby."

"She can."

"But you didn't have a baby with Jack."

"I didn't *want* one with Jack!" Faith cried, then stopped short and hung her head. She took one deep breath, then another. The truth hurt, still it slipped from her tongue. "It wasn't the timing. It was him. If I'd had his baby, I'd have been locked to him, and early on I knew that wasn't right. By the time I graduated from law school, I think I knew Jack and I didn't have a future. And what my own instinct didn't tell me, my exposure to family law did. Kids don't make a marriage right. They don't make a bad marriage better. They may hold two people together who'd otherwise have split, but it's doubtful whether those people are happy, and if they're not, it's tough on the kids." She studied the fire in the hopes that it might soothe her guilt. "So that's it. I didn't want a baby with Jack."

"Would you want one with me?"

Her eyes shot to his. His features were golden and strong, but his look was cautious and, in that, vulnerable. She wanted to lie. She wanted to say that she didn't want a baby with anyone, but it wasn't true. For his openness, he deserved the truth.

"If I were to have a baby," she said in a near-whisper, "I'd want it with you."

A shudder ran through him. He sucked in an audible breath, closed his eyes for a minute, tried to get a rein on the flare of desire that accompanied the shudder.

Watching him, Faith was confused. "You want a baby?" she asked in that same near-whisper, then went on in a fuller voice. "If you wanted a baby, why didn't you have one with Joanna? She would have been a wonderful mother."

It wasn't the thought of a baby that made him shudder, as much as the thought of Faith having his. But he couldn't say that. It was too soon, even for him. He took several slow, deliberately calming breaths. "I could say that the timing wasn't right for us, either. Money was an issue. I didn't want a baby until I could afford to raise it with all the things I never had." But he'd never pictured a baby with Joanna's face the way he did now with Faith's. Nor had he ever before been shot through with desire at the thought of impregnating a woman.

He didn't say a word of that, yet his expression was telling. "Don't look at me that way," she begged. She felt it, too, the desire, and it made her uneasy. "Don't hope for it, please, Sawyer? You'll be disappointed."

But he didn't think that was possible. He didn't think Faith could disappoint him even if it turned out that there was no baby. She was incredibly bright and soft and vulnerable, and she wasn't half as sure of herself as she let the world believe. *He* knew she could be the best lawyer, the best wife, the best mother in the world. He also knew she could be the best lover, and though he'd made her a promise that he intended to keep, he wasn't averse to lobbying for his cause.

Coming up on his knees, he took her face in his hands, lowered his head and began his crusade.

8

"No, Sawyer—" Faith whispered, but the last of the sound was taken by his mouth. She flattened a palm on his chest. Within seconds, it was clutching a handful of his sweater, because seconds were all it took for her to feel as though the earth were being swept from under her. His mouth was hot velvet, stroking hers inside and out. His silken tongue found dark, hidden depths to plunder. His large hands held her head in a vise that was gentle but unyielding.

The first touch isn't much more than a token. It's kind of like a hello. The words echoed in Sawyer's mind, but they held no relevance. He and Faith had been exchanging tokens all day, looks and glances that were as expressive as any kiss. Same for hellos. He felt as though they'd been through hours of foreplay. Light tokens and gentle hellos were beyond him now.

That didn't mean he was rough. He could never be rough with Faith. She was too much of a woman for that, and besides, a good deal of his pleasure depended on hers. If she'd been quiescent beneath his hungry mouth, he'd have pulled back. But she was responding to his kiss, opening her mouth, offering her tongue, and while she wasn't aggressive about it, he didn't want that, either. Time enough for aggression once they were familiar lovers. For now, he liked taking the lead. It fed a very masculine need, and the fact that Faith didn't cut down that need as being macho or vain or archaic turned him on all the more.

If she was dynamite professionally because she knew when to stand firm, she was dynamite personally because she knew when to give. Even now, she was offering him the slender column of her neck, the graceful curve of her shoulders, the fullness of her breasts, which continued to surprise and please him. She was offering him her breath in short, wispy gasps, and the occasional tiny sound of excitement that slipped unselfconsciously from her throat.

She was offering him herself, and she'd warned him of that. She'd made him promise to be the one in control even when she wasn't. With a low groan, he dragged his mouth from hers. Slower to follow were his hands, which were splayed just under her breasts and didn't want to leave the warmth they'd found there. He forced them to. Sitting back on his heels, he brought them to his thighs and spread them there, and while the hardness of his limbs was nowhere near as appealing as Faith's warmth, they were something solid to hold.

"Disappoint me? Ahhh, Faith." His voice was hoarse, his broad chest working hard to still the thudding of his heart. "You couldn't disappoint me. Not in a million years. It keeps getting better. Incredibly. Better."

Faith was too stunned to say much for a minute. When she came to her senses, she was aware of wanting another kiss, of wanting much more than that. Need was snaking through her, coiling at certain spots, hurting. In a self-protective gesture, she wrapped her arms tightly around her middle, and though the tightness countered the hurt some, it did nothing for the chill of being out of Sawyer's arms. Groping for the sleeping bag that lay not far away, she pulled at its strings, artlessly unrolled it and dragged it around her shoulders.

It was a shield, protecting her from the intensity of his dark brown eyes. She still felt exposed, but that was her own doing and she sensed it was inevitable. Sawyer got to her. He touched her in places no man had ever touched before, and she let him do it.

"I think," she said in a slow, wavering breath, "that we need to put up a fence between us, something we can't see through."

Sawyer's lean mouth turned at the whimsy. "It wouldn't do any good. I'd know you were there, and I'd want you just the same."

Despite the intimacies they'd shared, the words were strange coming from him, Faith thought. Over the years he'd complimented her, said she was gorgeous and sexy and that he loved her, and she'd said similar words to him, but all in the good-natured way of friends. She couldn't get used to the idea that the joking was done, that the words and thoughts and feelings were for real.

"It's so strong," she whispered mostly to herself, then raised her eyes to his. "Why is that? Is it because we've been without?" She caught herself. "I mean, I've been without. Maybe you haven't."

He twisted to reach for another log and one-handedly added it to the flames. As he watched it settle in and catch fire, he said, "It's not that. I've been with two women since Joanna, each for a night and neither one of them was particularly necessary or memorable."

"Why did you go with them? Was it just for the physical release?"

"Honestly?" He looked at her quickly, then looked back at the fire. It was easier to say something he wasn't proud of when he didn't have to risk seeing disappointment in her eyes. "I did it because I thought that was what I should be doing. I was a single man again. Right and left, friends were slapping me on the back, winking, making ribald jokes, speculating on how good I was probably getting it. It wasn't that I'd sleep with a woman because someone else expected me to, but after a little while, I guess the expectation became my own. I was beginning to think something was wrong with me because I wasn't panting after everything in skirts."

A self-deprecating smile tugged at the corners of his mouth. He drew up a knee and rested his forearm across it. "I used to do that. Way back, before Joanna, before Nam. I pretty much screwed my way through high school. I figured that I'd make up sexually for what I didn't have mentally. When it came to getting the girls, I was way ahead of the guys who drove around in their little red Corvettes." His smile vanished, his pose lost its indolence, and his voice dropped into a chasm of pain. "Then came the war. Once I took that hit, I wasn't thinking of sex. I was thinking of surviving. And when I realized that I would, I began thinking about life itself and the gift that it was. I began thinking that I owed it to someone upstairs to do something more than take a cheerleader under the stands during halftime." He took a deep breath. "Just about then I met Joanna at the VA hospital. Maybe because of where and why we met, sex was never one of our big priorities."

Though he'd intimated as much before, Faith had trouble reconciling the potently masculine man before her with a relationship weak in sex. "Did you ever cheat on her?"

"No."

"Did you ever want to?"

"No. Even after I was well, I had other things on my

mind besides sex. I guess that's how it's been ever since. I have a comfortable life. My work is exciting. I convinced myself that if there was a right woman for me, she'd come along and I'd want her, and until that happened, I wasn't going to spend the goods just for the sake of the spending." He thought back to all he'd said. "So yes, I've been without, but no, that's not why it's so strong between us."

Faith wanted to find a reason. She wanted to put a label on the need she felt so that it wouldn't be quite so frightening. "Maybe it's because of last Friday night. We'd been drinking. Our inhibitions were down. Maybe that set off the need for sex, and maybe it's the memory of that that's turning us on now."

He doubted that. "If it was so, why would I get horny just thinking about what's under your sweater?"

"Because you remember Friday night. You remember feeling satisfaction. It's the memory that gets you horny."

He shook his dark head slowly.

She tried again. "If it hadn't been for last Friday night, we'd still just be friends. We'd be laughing and joking the way we always have. We wouldn't be seeing each other in any kind of sexual way."

"Maybe. Maybe not."

"What is *that* supposed to mean?" she asked, irritated that he wasn't grasping onto her suggestions.

His gaze was direct. He wasn't any more eager to see something negative in her eyes now than he'd been a little while ago, but he felt strongly that she should know how serious he was. "I think last Friday night was the catalyst for something that's very right."

"You're saying that it was inevitable? Come on, Sawyer."

That wasn't what he'd been saying at all, but the fact

that she'd come up with it was telling. It made a statement as to the direction of her own thoughts, and she could deny them until she was blue in the face, but he wouldn't believe her.

"I think that if last Friday night hadn't happened, we might well have gone on forever and ever not knowing any better about what could be between us. But it did happen, and I think it happened *because* there's something between us. We could have stopped, Faith. We weren't that far gone that we couldn't have stopped if there'd been something so wrong with what we were doing. If we hadn't wanted it, we would have stopped. If the potential wasn't there, if we weren't attracted to each other, if we didn't *like* each other, we'd never have made love, no matter how much wine we'd had."

She was listening. She didn't rush to argue with what he'd said. That gave him the courage to go a step further. "It's not just sex. It's a lot more than that. We share a profession. We know each other, respect each other. We have fun together—we said that a whole lot on Friday night, and it's true. We've always had fun together. So now we desire each other, too, and that takes the relationship to a different level. It's the next step in the progression." He took a slightly shaky breath. "I think we have the potential for a really deep thing here."

Faith sat very still for several minutes. With a swallow, she tore her eyes from his and focused on the fire, but that didn't seem enough of a diversion. So she took the sleeping bag from around her shoulders, unzipped the top and shimmied inside. Moments later she was sitting cross-legged inside the thing, enveloped by it, looking at the fire again.

"Faith?"

"I'm a little cold."

That wasn't what he wanted to know. "Talk to me, Faith."

But it was a minute before she did, and during that time she cursed herself as a fool for not running to the nearest motel, locking the door and burrowing in a large, lonesome bed. Then again, she wasn't a runner—at least she'd never been before—and she didn't like the way she was doing it now. She wondered if it was time she faced some of the things that had been hovering at the edges of her mind since Sawyer had made her his.

Her voice was small, muffled by the sleeping bag she hugged to her throat. "I don't want to be involved in a really deep thing."

He caught both her words and a thread of timidity so uncharacteristic that his insides clenched. Faith was a woman of strength. He couldn't fathom the cause of her timidity, didn't like it, resented it. "Why not?"

"I'm not ready for it."

"You're thirty-three."

"I'm not ready."

"Because of what you went through with Jack?"

She didn't answer.

"Faith?"

"I don't know."

"Talk to me. Tell me what you're feeling. Did your marriage to Jack leave a bad taste in your mouth?"

She thought for a minute. "Not really."

The pause worried him. He wondered whether there was more to the story of her marriage than anyone knew. "Did he hurt you?"

"Hurt me? As in beat? Of course not."

Still her voice lacked its normal zing. She sounded distant, confused, as though something had indeed happened and she was just now trying to figure it out.

"What is it?" he coaxed, letting his voice tell her that he wanted to help. He was still a friend. No matter what else ever happened, he was still a friend.

Her eyes flicked from the fire to his, and the concern she found there tore at her. "Nothing. Really. My marriage was innocuous." But she paused, disturbed, and focused blindly on the floor. "It was disappointing. I've told you that. It was just a big fat zero."

"Better a zero than hell, I'd say."

She didn't smile. "I'm not sure. It's healthier sometimes to fight than to do nothing at all. At least that shows *some* kind of feeling. But there wasn't any between Jack and me. Not for a long time."

"And that bothered you."

"Yes, it bothered me. It wasn't the way marriage was supposed to be. It wasn't the way *I* wanted marriage to be."

"How was that?"

"Close. Warm. Fun. Satisfying. Supportive. I wanted my husband to be my best friend, but he wasn't. We were roommates. Period."

Sawyer was watching her closely, but he couldn't read anything more on her face than she was saying. "So you were wrong for each other. We all make mistakes. God only knows I did. And our clients? Mistakes all the time. So your marriage didn't work out. That's no reason to punish yourself by spending the rest of your life alone."

"I'm not punishing myself."

"What would you call it?"

"Making sure I don't make the same mistake twice."

"That's crazy, Faith. I'm not like Jack."

Abundantly aware of that as she looked at him, she caught in a breath. "That's the problem."

He didn't make the connection. "What do you mean?"

"You're more vibrant than Jack. You're more fun, handsome, ambitious, interesting, sexy. You're more of just about everything. But I'm still the same."

He stared at her in confusion before muttering, "I still don't get it."

"You're *special*, Sawyer," she cried, then stopped when her throat grew tight. Dropping her eyes, she tried to regain her composure.

It was while she sat cocooned to her ears in the shiny blue sleeping bag with her eyes downcast that Sawyer began to understand.

"Babe?" When she didn't look up, he came forward, dug her chin from the slinky folds of the bag and tipped up her face. "You're afraid you can't make it in a deep relationship?"

She tried to look away, but he wouldn't allow it.

"Is that it, Faith?" He couldn't believe it. "Is *that* what you took away from your marriage to Jack?"

She swallowed the knot in her throat, but no sooner had she done that when her eyes filled with tears. Trying to maintain what little dignity she had left, she looked straight at him and said in a soft, wrenching voice, "I think the world of you, Sawyer. If I were to pick the one man I like and respect most, I'd pick you. I don't think I could bear it if we got into something deep and then it died."

What her tears started, her words finished. A tight fist closed around Sawyer's heart. "So you'd rather not try at all? Faith, that doesn't make sense!"

"It does to me. I'm the one who has to live with myself knowing that I've failed at something important."

"Is that what you've been doing for the past year? I thought you were fine after the divorce."

"I was. I was relieved to be free. But that didn't mean I

didn't feel guilty about not making it work. Now, here *you* are, and suddenly the stakes are higher. You're more special than Jack any day."

Sawyer wasn't sure he believed that, but the fact that Faith did made the clenching around his heart ease into a gently kneading caress. Without another thought to what she might or might not want, he drew her, sleeping bag and all, to his chest. He pressed her cheek to his throat, where he could feel the velvet of her skin, while the long arm he coiled around her lower back anchored her to him.

"Y'know," he began softly, "for a bright lady, you can be damned dumb at times. Did it ever occur to you that I'd have an active role in whatever relationship we have? If I'm so special, would I really let it fail?"

She didn't answer. She was too comfortable being held in his arms, listening to the indulgent caress of his deep voice.

"Did it ever occur to you that you and I have a hell of a lot more going for us than you and Jack ever had? We're mature. We're established. We have money. We're both lawyers, and we're good friends. So now we're lovers. I think that sounds pretty nice."

"It sounds scary," was her muffled reply.

"Not scary, because we're not making a life-or-death commitment. We're just going with the flow."

"What flow?"

Closing his eyes, he tightened his arms around her and drew in a shuddering breath. "The one through my veins that says I need you."

"I don't want you to need me."

"Too late. It's done."

"Make it stop."

"I can't. It's too strong."

"But I want to go back to being just friends. It was more fun that way."

"How do you know? You haven't given this way a fair chance."

"I don't want to spoil what we have, Sawyer."

"How about making it better? What would you say to taking what we have and building on it?"

She'd say that it was a dream and that she'd lost dreams in the past. She'd also say that it was a risk. She could lose everything if it didn't work out. "I'm frightened."

Sawyer loosened his hold on her only enough to give him access to her mouth. He kissed her long and deep, offering her a taste of his hunger. It was his way of telling her not only how much he wanted her, but how satisfying she was. By the time he raised his head, her lips were moist and swollen.

He touched her cheek with a trembling finger. "Let's try," he whispered hoarsely. "Let's see how good it can be."

Faith wanted to do that so badly she hurt, still the fear remained. "What if it isn't?" she whispered back.

"Then we'll go back to being friends. We're both adults. We're experienced. We'll know if what we're doing isn't working." His gaze touched each of her features, pale in the fire's light and as fascinating to him as the spiraling tendrils of flame, themselves. "I'm not asking for a commitment. All I'm asking is that you give it a shot. Because I can't *not* do that, Faith. You've given me a taste, and now I want more." He paused and his voice went slack. "But maybe that's *my* problem. Maybe you don't feel the hunger."

"You know I do."

He let out a small breath. "So we share the problem.

We could ignore it, but then we'll always be wanting and wondering. I don't want to live that way, Faith."

Looking up at him, Faith knew that they'd reached a crossroads. She saw it in the virile planes of his face and the quiet demand in his eyes. He'd never make a scene. He wouldn't push her to do something she didn't want to do, but he knew her well. He knew that she wanted him. What he didn't know was whether she had the courage to take him.

It hit her then, suddenly and convincingly, that there was no contest. If she refused him, she'd be disappointing him anyway, and that was the last thing she wanted. She'd take the risk. She had to. Far better to see where the wanting would lead than to live forever with the wondering.

"I don't want to live that way, Faith," he repeated in a pleading whisper.

"I don't, either."

For what seemed an eternity, they looked at each other. Only gradually did they realize that they'd reached an agreement.

"So," she whispered, feeling strangely awkward. "What do we do now?"

"Sit and talk."

His answer pleased her, enough to allow for a glimmer of her usual spunk. "You don't want to just strip and do it?"

"No. I want to sit and talk."

She glanced down at her voluminous cocoon. "Like this?"

His lips twitched. "No. Not like that."

Setting her carefully on the floor, he added another log to the fire. When it caught flame, he turned to his own sleeping bag, unzipped it, opened it wide. Seconds later he had Faith's unzipped, and while she knelt by the fire, he connected the two. Then he sat back on his heels and looked at her. "I want to hear more about your family. Will you tell me?"

She eyed him curiously. "Why?"

"Because I'm interested."

"But I'm not them."

"You were once." He sent her a lopsided grin. "You've clearly evolved into a higher form of the species, but I've always liked history. It was the one subject in school that I paid attention to."

"History was more intriguing than girls?"

"Yeah. Less fickle. More predictable. Longer lasting."

"Does that mean you'll immerse yourself in my history and forget all about me?"

"Not a chance," he said too softly.

A frisson of excitement shot up and down her spine, making her shiver.

He misinterpreted the tiny movement. "You're cold." He tugged the double sleeping bag closer to the fire and held it open. Faith crawled in. He followed and took her easily into his arms. It was a minute before they'd settled comfortably, his body supine, hers angled into it.

She was cautious at first, but her caution didn't stand much of a chance against the feel of his body. It was long and solid, still it accepted her shape with surprising malleability. He was like that, she realized. Strong, yet flexible. That made the step they were taking a little less threatening to her. Gradually, she gave him more of her weight.

Sawyer did his best not to hug her hard in thanks for her trust. And trust was what it was about just then, he knew. She was trusting him to take care with not only her body, but her mind. She'd been hurt by her marriage, and though the hurt had been by default, the pain had been real. Now, curled next to him, she was vulnerable again. He rather liked that thought. He liked feeling responsible for her. The only problem was that he wanted to make love to her there and then, only he'd told her they'd talk.

Closing his eyes, he breathed in the sweet smell of her hair. Between that and the soft feel of her body, the weight of her hand on his chest, the bend of her knee over his, he was in an agony of bliss.

Faith felt something of what he did, but for different reasons. "This is so strange," she whispered.

"How so?"

"Being with you like this. We've known each other for so long. I keep thinking we're doing something we shouldn't be doing."

"We're not."

"You sound sure."

"I am."

She sighed. "Nice, to be so sure."

"You'd be sure, too, if you stopped thinking so much. *Feel* it, Faith. It *feels* right."

It felt more than right to Faith, but what he said was true. She thought too much. She wasn't used to relying on feelings. "I analyze things to death, I guess."

"Which is great for some things. It's one of the reasons you're such a dynamite lawyer. You look at a case from every possible angle before you decide on the best course of action, and you have to, because judges and juries don't decide things by intuition. They need arguments and facts. We don't."

But there were certain facts of which she was becoming increasingly aware, such as the fact that when he spoke his deep voice rippled through her, and the fact that his shoulder was just broad enough and full enough to make a wonderful pillow, and the fact that the scent of warm male after a day's work was surprisingly exciting.

Mostly she was aware of the fact that she wanted him. She might have joked about stripping and doing it, but there must have been a little wishful thinking in the joke. The more she relaxed against him, the more she tightened up inside.

Reflecting her thoughts, Sawyer shifted his lower body.

Faith tipped back her head and looked at him. The new log had brightened the fire, still his expression wasn't easily read. His eyes were dark, his lips firm, but it was only when the flames danced up with a sudden snap and a sizzle that she was able to see tiny lines of tension.

"Don't look at me that way," he whispered, not once taking his eyes from hers. "I'm trying."

"Trying what?"

"Not to take you right now. I said we'd talk."

"Why did you say that?"

"Because I want you to know that what's between us isn't only sex."

Faith knew that. "We've been good friends for a long time. You said it yourself—we had a lot going for us before we ever tried sex."

"Still there's a lot to say. Friends say certain things, lovers say others."

She kept looking at him. She wanted to say that she'd like to experience the lover part again before they got into deep discussions, but that seemed wrong. After all, she'd been the one putting him off.

"Help me, Faith," he growled. "I'm trying, but it's not easy."

But she couldn't look away. She was intrigued by his

features, so carved and commanding, so taut with desire that she had trouble believing she was the cause.

He closed his hand over hers on his chest. "Why do you look so surprised?"

"I...uh..."

He began to move her hand in widening circles. "You don't believe that I want you?"

"I don't believe how much," she said guilelessly.

"Much. Very much." The circles edged lower as a wry grin pulled at his mouth. "And more by the minute." He had her hand at the snap of his jeans, but there the circles ended. After a minute's hesitation, he moved their hands southward to cover the raised ridge of hard flesh that pushed insistently against his fly.

Faith could barely breath. Vague glimpses of that other time, made hazy by the wine she'd had, brought the recollection of heat and length. But this was different. There was no haze, and the reality straining against her palm was far more than a glimpse. Heat, length, thickness, power—she was aware of all of those things as, with agonizing slowness, Sawyer inched her hand over him. When she saw his eyelids drift shut, even more when she heard the low, guttural moan that he couldn't suppress, she realized that the power was hers as well.

Shaping her fingers to better capture his strength in the stroking, she levered herself up and sought his mouth. He gave it to her, along with a wet, deep-seeking kiss that left her dizzy. It also left her far removed from thoughts of sensible discussions. What she was feeling, not only beneath her hand but deep inside her, was strong enough to decide the matter. She and Sawyer were making love then and there. Once they were done, they could talk.

She conveyed her decision to Sawyer by going in for a second kiss. This one was even more involving, and by its end, she was flat on her back with him looming above her.

"Last chance," he said. His low voice vibrated with need. His dark eyes were on fire from within. "Last chance, Faith."

Again she answered without a word, this time flattening both palms on his chest, running them up to his shoulders, then reversing direction and sliding them down over his chest and belly until they met at his burgeoning sex.

He moaned again, again helpless to hold it in, but he wasn't so helpless that he didn't know the import of the moment. Making love with Faith was going to be different this time than it had been before. This time they were stone sober. They knew what they were doing and why. And Sawyer knew that it had to be better than either of them remembered it being, if they were to have a shot at the future. He had to show her that when it came to sex, she was everything he'd ever wanted.

That was actually the easy part, because it was true. He couldn't control the hunger in his mouth when he kissed her, or his need to repeat the kiss from one angle, then another. He couldn't control the depths to which his tongue plunged in its search for hidden droplets of her sweetness. He couldn't control his need to nuzzle her neck, to inhale her scent as though it were life-giving oxygen, to nudge aside the crew neck of her sweater and nibble on her collarbone.

He told her of his pleasure in a myriad of wordless ways—in the smokiness in his eyes when he cupped her breasts, the tremor of his hands when he freed her from her sweater, the eagerness of his breath when he explored her through her bra. Whispered words came when he removed that wisp of lace and nuzzled her swollen flesh. He told her how beautiful she was, how responsive, and he showed her by chafing the pad of his thumb over her nipple until it was puckered and taut, then taking the hardened nub into his mouth and drawing it deeply between his teeth.

By this time she was holding tight to his shoulders, arching toward him, taking short, shallow breaths, and it was easy to go on. He undid her jeans and skinned them from her legs, then smoothed his hands over her panties until they followed. As though he'd been stifled before, when she was finally fully naked he couldn't touch her enough. With broad sweeps of his hands he covered her body from top to bottom. His palms were flatter over her throat, her hips, her legs; his fingers curved around her breasts and lower, on the focus of her womanly heat.

No, showing her how precious she was was the easy part. The hard part was restraining himself. At times he shook all over with the need for penetration. At times his breathing was heavy enough to wake the dead. But he was bound and determined to bring her to a fevered pitch of arousal before offering her the satisfaction they both sought.

She complicated things by moving against him in the most provocative, if innocent, ways. With slow turns and twists, silent yearnings spoke through her body, and then, when the turns and twists grew more frenzied and still didn't give her what she craved, she reached for his clothes. He thought he was safe as long as he was dressed, but she wasn't allowing that. One minute she was writhing in response to the sensuous glide of his fingers inside her, the next she was frantically struggling with his zipper.

"*Now*, Sawyer," she whispered. "Please. Now."

Grasping her wrists, he dragged them up and pinned

them by her shoulders. His mouth closed over hers in a long, hot kiss, but if he thought that by breaking the momentum of touching he'd slow things down, it didn't work. The feel of her body beneath his was incendiary, adding the final spark to what was already glowing and ready to flame.

With a low moan, he left her long enough to tear his sweater and T-shirt over his head and work his pants down. Even before he tossed them aside, Faith's hands were on him.

Ironically that did slow him down. Her touch was too special to ignore, slender hands and curious fingers working their way through the hair on his chest, teasing his nipples, scoring his ribcage. He wanted to savor it, which was another way of telling her how good she made it for him, but when her hands slipped past his navel and found the grooves where his thighs connected with his torso, his resolve snapped. Coming over her, he drew her knees up to flank him and entered her with a single powerful thrust.

She gasped, stunned by the force of the filling, and for an instant Sawyer wondered if he'd hurt her. Her eyes were closed, her face shadowed. He couldn't make out her expression.

"Faith?"

But while he watched, she broke out into a slow smile, a crescent of sunlight in the midst of shadow, telling of the ecstasy she felt. "Don't stop now," came her whispered drawl. The sound was sexy to match the sultriness of her smile, both of which matched the feminine allure of her body, which was gold-tipped in the fire's dancing light.

Sawyer was driven just as much by what was going on in his head as what was happening to his body. He didn't believe that a woman could be as beautiful as Faith was and still be real. He'd set out to pleasure her as she'd never been pleasured before, but it seemed that in approaching his goal, the tables had turned. He'd never had a woman smile up at him like that, as though he were her world and she wanted no other.

He continued to bask in the heat of her smile until his body began to clamor for attention. Then he moved, slowly unsheathing himself, even more slowly and deeply returning to her heart. His breath pulsed against her lips, ragged between kisses. When soft sounds came from her throat, he increased the pressure of his mouth and stroking hands, and when she began to squirm against him, he increased the speed of his thrusts. He took pleasure in her every response, growing hotter and harder until the battle he fought against release seemed doomed. In a last-ditch effort to regain control, he paused, but in that instant, while he held himself as still as his quivering frame would allow, Faith arched into a powerful climax, and he utterly lost himself. Within seconds, bowing his back and pushing deeper than ever inside her, he vaulted into an orgasm of his own.

It was staggering, spasm after spasm of pent-up passion turned loose in her heated body, but Faith felt the powerful pulsations only as a counterpoint to her own shattering release. When the brightest of the starbursts faded, she floated for a time in the limbo between heaven and earth. Only when Sawyer's breathing evened by her ear, when he slid his sweat-slick body to the side and pulled her over to face him did she open her eyes. What she saw in his nearly sent her aloft again. Neither the night or the dying light of the fire could hide the adoration there.

"How do you feel?" he asked in a whisper. He slid one

still-shaky hand into her hair and stroked her scalp through the silken strands until he'd caught the last of his racing breath.

She searched for the words to best express it, but her mind was reeling again, this time from his look. "I feel," she finally managed to whisper back, "as though I've just finished off a magnum."

He grinned at her answer. "A little drunk?"

"A lot drunk."

"A little dizzy."

"A lot dizzy."

"But you didn't have a drop. Neither of us did, and still..."

She shaped a hand to his cheek, less sure with the trailing off of his words. "Still what?"

"Still...I felt like I was taken out of myself...immersed in you...lifted..." He stopped, feeling foolish and more than a little inadequate. "I'm not good with words."

But Faith had heard him in action more than once. "You're incredible with words."

"Not when it comes to something like this. I can talk hard facts and make persuasive arguments, but I'm not a poet."

"You're on your way."

But he shook his head. "I can't describe what it was like, Faith. It would take dozens of elaborate words and silvery phrases."

"Try plain ones."

"I love you."

She hadn't expected those particular words. Her eyes went wide, and for a minute she couldn't breathe, much less speak. Finally, diffusing the moment the only way she could, she tucked a hand against his neck and said softly, casually, "We've always loved each other."

"This is different, Faith. I love you."

"Like I love you."

"Only if you're talking forever." When she didn't have a comeback for that, Sawyer drew her to him. He cradled her head against his chest and the rest of her body fell into place, as though it knew from long experience just where to go. "Too much, too fast?"

After a minute, she murmured, "Mmm."

"Scary?"

"Yes."

"I'll give you time. I won't push. All I ask is that you let me see you." He endured a minute of gut-wrenching silence before prodding. "Will you let me do that?"

It wasn't so much that she'd let him, but that she didn't think she could keep him from it. Besides, it was what she wanted. She was still frightened; she knew she'd fear disappointing him even now, and it would be worse if she agreed to forever. Selfishly, though, she couldn't bar him from her life. She wanted more of him. She wasn't so inexperienced with men that she couldn't tell a good thing when she saw it.

"Faith?"

"Yes," she said, her breath stirring the drying hairs on his chest.

"We'll see each other?"

"Yes."

His body relaxed just that tiny bit, though not completely, because her nearness was stirring his senses. He ran a hand lightly from her shoulders to the small of her back, loving the satiny feel of her skin, which, even aside from his scars, was so different from his. He half-wished it were broad daylight so he could look at her. Strange, but he'd never seen her, really seen her naked.

That wasn't all that was strange. Curving a large hand

over her bottom, he drew her closer. "Funny how things turn out sometimes."

His words registered through the light-headedness she was feeling again. "Hmm?"

"Before, when we started to make love, I wanted to show you how good it could be between us. I wanted to show you that it would be better than the first time, much better. I wanted to show you that you were all I've ever wanted." He paused, buried his face against her neck, breathed in the erotic scent of woman and sex that he found there, made a low sound in his throat. "I don't know how much of that I showed you, but I sure showed myself. You're it, Faith. You're what I want."

Being held so securely in his arms, feeling the strength of his body and its masculine warmth, Faith was just high enough to believe him.

9

THAT BELIEF lasted through the weekend, and understandably so. Sawyer rarely left her side. He got her talking about all the things she didn't want to talk about and many of the things she did, and in both cases he interspersed the discussion with light touches and impulsive kisses. He wasn't fawning, though; his timing was perfect in that way. He knew when to touch, when to sit back and listen, when to ask a question, offer a comment, even tell her she was nuts. And he knew just when to take her in his arms and hold her tightly.

They made love often through Saturday night and then again on Sunday. Faith had never thought of herself as the multiorgasmic type, yet Sawyer brought her to peak after peak. His own stamina—and the multiple releases he, too, found—seemed further proof of his claim of love.

Inevitably, though, they had to return to the city. Faith put off thinking about it until the last possible moment. She felt she was living a dream and didn't want it to end.

Sawyer had no intention of letting that happen. Intent on showing her that things would be just as good between them in the city, he deliberately put off having dinner until they were back. He went with Faith to her place while she showered and changed clothes, then brought her to his while he did the same. Looking distinctly urbanized, they ate at Locke Ober's—again a deliberate move on Sawyer's part, since the restaurant, with its sense of tradition, was symbolic of the Boston they knew professionally.

Nor was he letting her slip away after that. He insisted on staying the night, and while she made token argument, sensing he was prolonging the inevitable, she let herself be convinced.

He didn't make love to her that night. "I've run out of condoms," he teased, and she almost believed him, given the number of times they'd made love. "I think I'll just hold you."

That was just what he did, and in so doing, he touched Faith more deeply than his sex ever had. Tenderly he cradled her against his large body until she'd fallen asleep, and though his hold shifted during the night with the turns both of them made in their sleep, at no point was she aware of being cold or alone.

At dawn's first light, he brought her awake with soft kisses and slow strokings, then proceeded to make love to her until she was crazy with need. No condom was necessary; he had other ways to protect her. When it was over, when she was lying utterly replete in his arms, he gave her a final hug before easing himself from the bed.

She watched him dress, feeling a loss with each part of his body that he covered. Before he left, he came to her. Planting both hands on either side of her pillow, he looked her in the eye.

"I know what you're thinking. You're thinking that we're both going back to work today and everything will be over. You're thinking that I'll sit in my office wondering what the hell the weekend was about. But you're wrong. I'll sit there thinking about you. I'll be wondering what you're doing for lunch and whether I can meet you, or whether I can manage to jimmy my schedule around so I'll bump into you in the courthouse. I'll be wondering what time you're getting home tonight and whether I can see you again." He took a breath. "I'll control myself during the day, Faith. I won't cut into your time. But I want you tonight." He stopped speaking on that declarative note.

Another time, Faith might have objected to his lack of a question—or if not objected to it, at least teased him about it. It was an extraordinarily chauvinistic thing to do, and she was a thoroughly modern woman. Just then, though, she wasn't feeling thoroughly modern. She was feeling reassured by his forcefulness, even turned on by it, though she sensed that the latter had something to do with the spark in his dark brown eyes, the random muss of his hair, the piratical shadow on his firm-drawn jaw. He was a quintessentially virile man, to which her body, still warm and tender from his loving, could attest.

Taking a slightly uneven breath, she said, "How about a study date?"

He got the message. "You have to work."

"I was planning to do lots this weekend, only a randy guy came by and swept me away."

He slanted her a grin. "Randy guy, huh? Yeah, I guess he did get carried away. But he'd do it again in a minute." He paused. "Study date? Is it that, or nothing?"

She nodded.

"Where?" he asked.

"My office. Around seven. We can bring in pizza."

Lowering his head, he fitted his face to the soft curve of her neck. He breathed in her love-warmed scent for a last minute before pulling away. "You've got yourself a date."

"HE SUGGESTED we go on a date," Laura Leindecker told her on the phone later that morning. "Can you believe it?

After being gone all weekend, he wants a date. After twenty-four years of missed dinners and canceled parties and late arrivals home, he wants a date."

Faith wasn't in the mood for adversity. She'd made a successful appearance in court on behalf of a client and was back in her office feeling cautiously optimistic about life in general and Sawyer in particular. She wasn't looking for anything that might upset the moment's balance.

Nor did she think that the idea of a date was so stupid. She'd made one with Sawyer. It was standard practice for a person feeling his or her way in a relationship.

"What did he suggest?" she asked pleasantly.

"Dinner at the L'Espalier. But that's not even my favorite restaurant. He *knows* what my favorite one is—or used to be—only he didn't dare suggest it."

"He was being considerate," Faith reasoned. "He knew how you'd feel. He was respecting your right to feel that way."

Laura wasn't fully convinced. "Maybe." Her voice grew wary. "He says he wants to talk."

"Then you should go. Listen to what he has to say. You'll be safe. He wouldn't dare act up in a restaurant."

"I suppose not." She sounded nervous. "But he's so good with words. He'll convince me of something. I know he will."

Faith tried to be supportive without yielding. "You're a strong woman, Laura. Don't underestimate yourself. You don't have to forget your grievances because he's taking you to dinner. But you do need to talk about what's happened and why."

"He'll tell me about *her*. He'll probably lie."

"Will he?" She let Laura think about that for a minute. "And if you don't want to talk about what's happened, talk about what you *want* to happen. Talk about the future. Talk about getting a divorce. Talk about the division of property. But talk. You have to communicate with each other."

"I don't want to communicate," Laura argued in a soft, pleading voice. "I want to file for a divorce. I want him to know that he can't do what he did to me and get away with it."

"You want to hurt him the way he hurt you, but will that give you what you want? Think about it, Laura. I can file a Complaint for Divorce with the court tomorrow, and a copy of the complaint will be served on your husband. Once that's done, it's a matter of public record, and once that happens, even though you can withdraw the complaint, something changes. Deeper feelings get stirred up. It's harder to go back. That's why you have to be really sure of what you want." She paused. "You're paying me to guide you through a divorce, but my first priority is your well-being. If your well-being is best served by a divorce, fine. If not..."

Her words trailed off, but she'd hit the right button, because Laura did agree to have dinner with her husband. Faith felt as though she'd achieved a minor victory. She would have called Sawyer to tell him if it hadn't seemed improper. It also seemed a little contrived. When push came to shove, she just wanted to hear Sawyer's voice.

It must have been her lucky day, because her wish was granted shortly after lunch when Sawyer stopped in at her office. Wearing a charcoal-gray suit with fine pinstripes running through it, he looked very professional and devastatingly handsome.

The first thing he did was close the door to her office. The second was to come around the desk and give her a kiss that shot professionalism to bits. The third was to drop into a chair and say, "Bruce Leindecker doesn't want the divorce at all. He says he loves his wife, and he says it on no uncertain terms."

Faith was a minute coming down from his kiss and another one focusing in on what he'd said. "He loves his wife."

"That's what he says," Sawyer declared in a satisfied way.

"Interesting," she mused. Her mouth still tingled. She was feeling pleasantly warm inside and decidedly close to Sawyer, which was probably one of the reasons why she tipped her hand. "Laura is still hurt and angry. But I think she loves him, too."

"Has she said that?"

"Lord, no. She says the divorce will teach him a lesson."

"She's being vindictive."

It sounded worse coming from Sawyer. "Not vindictive. She's just venting her anger."

"Maybe she's being too emotional."

"She has a right to be emotional."

"Too emotional? Nothing is accomplished then. Bruce is still trying to talk with her, but she won't listen."

"She will," Faith said with a satisfaction of her own. "He invited her out to dinner. I got her to agree to talk with him then."

Sawyer bobbed a brow in approval. "Good work, Faith. I knew you could do it. There's nothing like a woman to calm down another woman."

"Excuse me?"

"Women understand each other. They know what it's like to be highly emotional, so they can help each other when it happens."

"Uh...Sawyer...that is a gross overgeneralization. Not

all women are emotional. Some never are. And your conclusion isn't even correct. The reason women understand each other is because they have a capacity for understanding and compassion that men just don't have. Laura Leindecker trusts me. That's why I was able to convince her to go to dinner with Bruce."

"And I think it's great. She has to listen to him for a change."

"Sawyer! She's been listening to him for twenty-four years!"

"Maybe she listens, but she sure doesn't hear."

Just as Sawyer was championing his client, so Faith championed hers. "She hears. And for twenty-four years, she's heeded. Laura has been a quiet, obedient, practically subservient wife. She has swallowed her complaints and made a comfortable life for herself. Suddenly she is betrayed. She doesn't trust Bruce the way she used to. Obedience comes harder now."

"Laura Leindecker is a highly emotional woman. She's making this whole thing far more complicated than it has to be."

"He *cheated* on her," Faith cried. "That's what started it all. How does it suddenly become Laura's fault?"

Sawyer sat forward, his eyes dark and intent. "I didn't say it was her fault. I said that she's complicating things. They might have patched up their differences without ever seeing a lawyer if she'd listened in the first place."

"Listened to what?"

"His explanations for why he had the affair."

"And why was that?"

"Because he was curious. A young, attractive woman came on to him. He's reached the age where he's flattered. He also knows dozens of men who've had affairs. He wanted to find out if it was so great."

"That's rubbish, Sawyer! Do you honestly believe him?"

"Yes, I believe him. I don't condone what he did, but I can understand how a man can be driven by curiosity that way."

Faith recalled what he'd told her about the months after his divorce from Joanna. "You weren't married then, Sawyer. You didn't hurt anyone by giving in to curiosity. Bruce did. He hurt Laura deeply. I'm not sure she can ever recover from that."

"Which is an emotional answer if I've ever heard one," he scoffed. "Of course, she'll recover. She'll listen to Bruce. He'll tell her that the affair didn't mean a thing, that he only saw the woman six times and—"

"Six times! If it didn't mean a thing, why did he see her six times? Did it take him six times to satisfy his curiosity, or was it six times before his wife found out? Did he think she *wouldn't* find out? If the affair was so meaningless, why in the *hell* did he leave that note in his coat?" She raised flashing eyes to follow Sawyer, who'd risen and was coming toward her. "Bruce Leindecker was wrong, Sawyer. He betrayed a woman who'd done nothing to deserve it. If he thinks she's going to easily forgive and forget, he's crazy. And so are you if you agree with him."

Curving his hands around the arms of her chair, Sawyer bent at the waist, ducked his head and put his cheek by hers. In a deep voice that gave individual emphasis to each word, he said, "I do not agree with what he did. I think he was wrong in having that affair, and I'd think it even if his wife *had* deserved it. I believe in fidelity, Faith. I always have."

His message took the wind from her sails. Or maybe it was the deep rumble of his voice. Or the warmth of his cheek. Or his clean male scent. Or the looming presence of his body. But the fight went out of her as quickly as it had come. She grabbed his necktie just below its knot and held on.

When he spoke again, she heard a suspicious smile in his voice, "I do love it when you get emotional." He kissed the tip of her ear. "It's a definite strength. A man likes it when a woman shows some fire. It means she cares." He dragged his mouth across her cheek.

"I care about all my clients," she argued, but weakly.

"You care about me. That's what this is about."

"It is?"

"Um-hmm." He nibbled on her jaw. "You want to know that my judgment is sound. You want to be comfortable with the sides I take. You want to be sure that we're playing the game. You don't mind my representing the bad guy as long as I don't buy his cause, particularly in this case. Am I right?"

He was, but she didn't want to say so lest she dislodge his mouth from her lower lip.

"So," he breathed softly, "that's another way I need you in my life. You're my conscience. Without you, my chauvinism is apt to run away with itself."

Having had just about enough of his teasing, Faith tugged him down by the tie for a full-fledged kiss. When it was done, she lingered for a minute with her eyes closed and her lips a breath from his. She could stay that way forever, she knew, but if she did that, Sawyer would be onto her in more ways than one. And she had work to do.

Pushing him away the same way she'd pulled him in, she said, "Go. I have a brief to write."

He headed for the door. "Are we on for seven?"

"We're on."

THEY DIDN'T BRING in pizza after all, but imported corned beef sandwiches from the sub-basement deli in their building. By ten, Faith was nearly falling asleep at her desk.

"I can't imagine why," she quipped, yawning. "You've bored me so that I've done nothing but sleep for the past two nights."

Sawyer laughed and said nothing in his own defense, principally because he intended to keep her awake for part of a third night as well. And she didn't fight him. When they went back to her place and he took her in his arms, she went willingly. She moaned her delight when his mouth refamiliarized itself with her body's nooks and crannies, and when her hunger took a different twist, she even became the aggressor. It was a new role for her. Passion drove her on, but during the brief instances when the newness of it stunned her, Sawyer had ready words of praise and love.

Once she fell asleep that night, Faith was completely out of it. She didn't stir when Sawyer kissed her at dawn, didn't waken when he climbed out of bed and dressed, didn't open an eye when he softly called her name.

He left her a note. It was the first thing she found after she realized she was alone, and it helped in easing her disappointment at finding him gone.

Sweetheart,
You were sleeping so soundly that nothing short of a buffalo stampede would wake you. Not having any buffalos on hand, I tried some kissing and touching, but even that didn't work. So I'm off. I have a committee meeting at six tonight that will probably drag on until nine. I'll call you then.

Love, Sawyer.

Faith lay back down and held the note to her breast for another few minutes while she slowly woke up. Then she climbed from bed and got ready for work. Just before she left, she folded the note and tucked it into a pocket of her briefcase.

That was a tactical error.

Each time she opened or closed the briefcase, which was often on a day filled with appointments outside the office, she stared at the pocket and thought of the note. By late afternoon, she'd taken it out and read it numerous times, had traced the letters of his name with her finger, had even held the folded paper to her cheek as something he'd touched. It was the last time, when she folded the note and tucked it away not in her briefcase but in her bra, that she began to realize the extent of her feelings for Sawyer.

They overwhelmed her. She didn't like that at all, because she felt she was losing control. It wasn't like her to put love letters in her bra, any more than it was like her to wait for the phone to ring, or be disappointed when she woke up alone in bed, or plan her days to free up her nights.

In an appallingly short time, she'd grown dependent on seeing Sawyer. But she'd never been dependent on a man like that before, and she didn't think it was healthy.

That was why, when Sawyer dialed her number at nine-thirty that night, the phone went unanswered. Thinking she might have run out to do a quick errand, he tried again in fifteen minutes, then in fifteen after that. So he ruled out a quick errand. On the vague chance that she was still working, he tried the office number, but the answering service ruled out her presence there.

He decided that she had to be out with friends, and while one part of him thought that was just fine, the other was furious that she hadn't bothered to tell him. A simple phone call would have done it. If he'd been out of the office, she could have left a message. That would have been the considerate thing to do, since she knew he'd be calling.

By eleven, when there was still no answer, he began to worry. So he tossed on a jacket and jogged along the waterfront until he reached Union Wharf. He rang her bell. When that produced no response, he rang it again. And again.

After the fourth or fifth stab, Faith opened the door. The relief he felt was instant, then instantly forgotten in the face of the decidedly disgruntled expression she wore. "What do you think you're doing, Sawyer?" she asked. Though her voice was imperious, her appearance was anything but. She wore a white nightgown that went from her throat to her wrists and toes, and a long white terry wrap robe over that. Her face was clear of makeup. Her hair was brushed back behind her ears.

Sawyer thought she looked tired and more than a little vulnerable. That softened his annoyance, but only a bit. "I was worried," he barked. "I've been trying to reach you for two hours. Why aren't you answering your phone?"

"I was out. I just got back."

"Where did you go?" he demanded.

"I was visiting a friend. Not that it matters. Sawyer, I don't have to report to you."

"You knew I'd be calling. I left you a note this morning and told you that. If you weren't going to be here, you could have let me know. Then I wouldn't have worried."

Her fingers whitened on the doorknob. "You shouldn't have worried anyway. I'm a big girl. I've been taking care of myself for a while now. You should have just assumed that I had other plans, instead of assuming I'd be home waiting for your call."

Sawyer put both hands on his hips and glared at her. "I never assumed you'd be waiting. I assumed you'd be around. I assumed that since it was a work night and you complained about getting no sleep, you'd be tired."

"I am," she declared. "So thank you for coming over, but you can go home now. I'm going to sleep."

She made to close the door, but a well-placed foot stopped its progress, and he slipped inside. "Not without me, you're not." He shut the door behind him.

The determination on his face was so strong that she took a step back. "What do you think you're doing? You can't just barge in here like this!" She lowered her voice to a more controlled tone. "I want you to go home. I want to be alone."

"You don't want that," he said.

"I certainly do."

He shook his head and reached for her, catching her in his arms and holding her there while she protested.

"Let me go, Sawyer."

"Not until you tell me what's bugging you. Was it the note? Was it that I didn't call you during the day? Or stop down to see you? Was it my having to work tonight?"

"No!" She pushed against his chest, but it was an unyielding wall of muscle. "I don't care whether you work or not!"

"Then it was one of the other things."

Still she squirmed. "*No!* You don't have to call me during the day, or stop down to see me. In case you hadn't noticed, I have work to do, too. I have as demanding a career as yours. I don't have time to dally between cases any more than you do. Let me *go*, Sawyer."

Ignoring her cries, he held her tightly. "I'd make the

time to dally with you if I thought you wanted it," he said in a quieter voice that flowed gently by her hair, "but I've been trying to respect your career. I know how hard you work. I know how much your work means to you. And I know how good you are at it. So I'm trying not to get in the way during the day. That was why I left the note. I figured it would carry over to tonight. I need to see you at night, Faith, and if I can't see you, I need to know why. Why didn't you call if you weren't going to be here?" He took a shuddering breath. "I love you, Faith. I know you don't want to hear those words, so I've done my best not to say them, but I do love you. Did you think I wouldn't worry when no one answered the phone after so long?"

The fight had left her with the quieting of his voice, and by the time he was done talking, its gentle, almost pleading tone had done a job on her anger. Closing her eyes, she let herself lean against him. "Oh, Sawyer."

"What?" he asked hoarsely. "What does that mean?"

"It means I don't know."

"Don't know what?"

"What I was thinking. Feeling. Doing."

He stroked her back with large, knowing hands. "Sure you know. You're just not ready to verbalize it. You're tired. You're in a lousy mood. Maybe it's that time of the month."

Tired or not, she probably would have hauled back and socked him if she hadn't heard the teasing in his voice. "That, Sawyer Bell, is the most bigoted thing you've said yet. Men have moods just like women. I have every *right* to be in a lousy mood. I'm not tired. I'm *over*-tired."

Without another word, he moved her under one arm and headed for the bedroom. When she'd taken her robe off and was tucked into bed, he sat by her side. "You're right. You need sleep."

She studied his handsome face. "Are you leaving?"

"You want me to."

"You said you were staying."

"But you'd rather sleep alone."

She darted a glance at the empty side of the bed. "There's room here. I'd hate to send you out in the cold."

"It's not very cold. I can jog back the same way I came."

"Or you can jog back in the morning." She paused, then before she could ask herself what she was doing and why, whispered, "Stay, Sawyer. I want to sleep with you."

Sawyer stayed.

"THE WOMAN WON'T TALK," Bruce Leindecker complained to Sawyer when he called on Wednesday morning. "I took her to dinner, and we sat like two very civilized people. She listened to what I said, but she wouldn't talk."

"She just sat there, mute?" Sawyer asked.

"Not mute, exactly. She offered simple answers to simple questions, but when I asked her to tell me what she felt, she just stared at me. Let me tell you, that stare hurt."

"Did you tell her that?"

"No."

Sawyer rubbed the back of his neck. He was getting a little tired of hand-holding, though he was being paid well to do it. "Maybe you should have."

"Then she'd have done it more. She wants to get back at me. She wants to hurt me like I hurt her. It doesn't seem to matter how much I apologize. She's still angry. Maybe she really does want out."

"Maybe she needs more time."

"Maybe I should just give in and file for divorce myself. If I did that, she'd talk. She'd say she doesn't want the divorce after all and attack me for wanting to dump her." He paused. "Reverse psychology. It's not such a bad idea."

Reverse psychology had worked for Sawyer the night before. As soon as he'd said he was leaving, Faith had changed her mind about wanting him to. He suspected Laura might do the same—and it had nothing to do with a sexist bias, because he used the tactic repeatedly with difficult male clients. No, he suspected Laura might do the same because he was privy to information Faith had passed on. If Laura did love Bruce, she'd protest the divorce as soon as it became a serious consideration.

But gut instinct told him the timing wasn't right for that. "Wait. Just a little longer. Reverse psychology can work, or it can backfire. It would be a tactical error to threaten something and have her call your bluff. Backing down would weaken your position." He debated the alternate courses of action. "You're still living at home, aren't you?"

"Yes."

"Okay. So keep talking to her and keep after her to talk back. Don't be discouraged. She's been badly hurt, and it's the kind of hurt that won't go away with an apology or two."

"But I'm legitimately sorry. She knows that. She knows me."

Sawyer reflected on the things Faith had said. "She may have thought she did once, but she never imagined you'd go off and have an affair. So in addition to being hurt, she's probably afraid to trust you, or her own instincts where you're concerned. You have a long road

ahead, Bruce. This isn't something that a woman can easily forgive and forget." He rocked back in his chair wearing a small, smug smile, thinking that Faith would be
proud of him. He might be a chauvinist, but he wasn't beyond being broadened.

Bruce wasn't as pleased as he was. "From the way you
talk I'd do just as well to toss in the towel now. Are you
saying that I've got to *grovel*?" Sawyer could almost hear
him straightening in his seat and donning his executive
front. "I won't do that, Sawyer. I may love the woman,
but *no* woman—or man, for that matter—runs me into
the ground like that. I'm not without pride. If she pushes
me too far, I'll give her a divorce with pleasure."

"I doubt it will come to that. Just give her time."

Bruce agreed to do that, and Sawyer hung up the
phone. His first thought was to call Faith, but he meant
what he'd said about disturbing her. It wasn't as if something momentous had happened with the case. And besides, they had a date for lunch.

That gave him the excuse he needed. Lifting the phone,
he dialed her number. When she came on, he said, "Was
that twelve-thirty or one? What did we finally decide?"
Their plans had been a little muddled in Sawyer's dash to
throw on his clothes and get out the door in time to jog
home, shave, shower, dress and make an eight o'clock
breakfast meeting.

"One," she said softly.

"Ahhh. Okay. That's great." He paused. "Everything
going all right?"

"Fine. Busy." But she didn't hang up.

"Great. Hey, listen, I'm sorry to bother you, but I just
wasn't sure and I didn't want one of us waiting."

"You're no bother."

"Maybe I should have run downstairs, just poked my head in and asked you in person."

"*That* would have bothered me."

"Why that?"

"Because you're a distraction any way you come, but seeing you in the flesh is the worst."

"Is that a compliment or a complaint?"

"You figure it out," she said with a smile in her voice. "You can tell me what you decide at lunch. Goodbye, Sawyer."

HAVING LUNCH with Sawyer was a different experience because for the first time, eating at a local restaurant that they both frequented separately, they were seen together. The place was packed with acquaintances and colleagues, most of whom probably assumed they were discussing matters of law.

Faith knew the truth, though. This wasn't a legal lunch but a social one. She enjoyed being with Sawyer. She also enjoyed being *seen* with him, and that bothered her a little. Professionally, she had her own identity. She wasn't out to get respect riding on another lawyer's coattails. She earned her own respect.

No, the pride she felt didn't have to do with her image as a lawyer. It had to do with her image as a woman, and that was what bothered her. She felt more feminine when she was with Sawyer. She felt that people would *see* her as being more feminine, and it surprised her that she cared. But she did care, which meant that she had much more to lose if the relationship ended.

More and more, it seemed, she was growing dependent on Sawyer. He was in her mind whenever her mind wasn't occupied with work. She was quickly coming to expect that she would see him for dinner and then spend the night with him. She feared she'd be crushed if he decided he needed a night alone.

She thought of being the first to do it, of telling Sawyer herself that she couldn't see him that night and sticking to it this time. If she was the one who rejected him, it wouldn't hurt so much, she figured. The problem with the figuring was that she really wanted to see him. Making excuses would be a bit like biting off her nose to spite her face.

On and off through Wednesday afternoon, she wallowed in a state of indecision. Then Laura Leindecker called.

"My husband won't leave me alone," she cried. "We have to do something. I'm not sure how much more of this I can take."

Faith was beginning to feel like Dear Abby, and she didn't think she cared for the role. "What's he doing?"

"He is waging a campaign to win me over. First it was dinner, then breakfast. He's calling me from the office three or four times a day wanting to know how I am and what I'm doing. This is very strange for a man who absented himself from my life for so many years."

"He loves you."

"He's scared."

"Scared of losing you."

"Scared of losing the house or the Mercedes or the millions he'll have to settle on me."

"From what I understand, he's got more than enough to go around."

"But he's making me crazy with his constant attention. It's gotten so that I feel guilty going *shopping* because he can't reach me in the stores."

Taking a breath in a bid for patience, Faith said, "Maybe if you gave him a little encouragement, he wouldn't feel that he has to work so hard to convince you of his devotion."

"I don't want his devotion!"

"I thought you did. I thought that was what this was all about. You were complaining that he was never around."

"He wasn't," Laura cried, "but I got used to that. I structured my life so that I had things to do, and I have even more things to do now that the children are grown. But they're women's things, like luncheons and bridge club and garden club, and Bruce is going to be in the way."

Faith sighed. Much as she tried to respect Laura's dilemma, she was tiring of the game. "What is it you want?"

"I want things to be the way they were! I want Bruce to go his way and me go my way, and when he's not on a business trip or tied up late at the office, we can see each other. Maybe I do want him to be devoted, but I don't want to be smothered."

"And you really don't want a divorce."

"No, I don't want a divorce."

"Do you love him?"

"I've loved him for so long that I wouldn't know how *not* to love him."

"Have you told him that?"

"How can I? It's the only lever I have left."

The phone line was silent for a minute. Then, slowly and quietly, Faith said, "Please, Laura, please talk to him. Tell him what you've just told me. He doesn't want a divorce any more than you do. There's nothing wrong with your marriage that some good heart-to-hearts won't fix. Tell him how you feel. Not just the surface things, but deep down inside."

"That won't work," Laura said sadly. "We've never been able to talk that way with each other."

"Maybe it's time you started."

"But I can't trust him. I did once, and look where it got me."

"He made a mistake. He knows that and regrets it." Faith sighed. "Either you give him another chance, or we file papers tomorrow. You have to decide one way or the other, Laura. It isn't fair to you, it isn't fair to Bruce, and it isn't fair to Sawyer and me. We're lawyers. It's our job to push for reconciliation, but we can't lead you through that the way we'd be able to lead you through court. We're not trained to be marriage counselors. You have to decide which you want."

Laura made a small, bewildered sound. "Why do *I* have to make the decision?"

"Because," Faith said with sudden insight, "you're the one with the power."

10

THROUGH THE REST of the day, Faith thought a lot about women and power. They underestimated themselves, she decided. Too often they bought society's line and associated men with the power, and maybe that was true in the business sphere, but not necessarily in the personal, more emotional one. Laura Leindecker was in an enviable position. She knew what she wanted, could reach out and take it if she decided to, and in that sense she held her husband in the palm of her hand.

Sawyer wasn't one to be held in any woman's palm, and Faith wouldn't have it any other way. Still, there were times when she wished he wasn't so sure of himself and his feelings. Then she wouldn't feel so weak by comparison.

Such was her line of thinking that night at his place, which was where he took her after work, and while she watched him grill steaks and toss a salad, she felt increasingly powerless. Her relationship with him seemed to be barreling forward, and as it went, she had less and less control over it.

There were three possible reasons for that, she decided. The first was that Sawyer was right, that the relationship had lain dormant for years and now, under newly favorable circumstances, was ripe for the growing. In that case, the relationship itself, the male-female dynamics were controlling Sawyer and her.

The second possibility was that Sawyer was the one in control, that he was the force behind the onrush of their relationship. He was more aggressive than she was. He was the one making sure that they spent every free minute together, and it was at his insistence that they were sleeping together every night.

She didn't fight him very hard, which raised the third possibility. She wondered if it was simply her own *lack* of control where Sawyer was concerned that was letting things snowball. Because they were snowballing. The more she was with Sawyer, the more she enjoyed being with him, and the more she had visions—fleeting, granted, but nonetheless vivid—of being with him forever.

She might have felt a semblance of power if Sawyer was running around trying to please her. But he wasn't. He knew what he wanted, which just happened to be what she wanted. He was perfectly at ease, perfectly comfortable, perfectly happy doing things that were satisfying for them both.

He was also attuned to the tiny crease that showed up between her eyes from time to time, and whenever he saw it, he immediately and deliberately filled her mind with different thoughts. Still, the issue of who she was as a woman, whether she was an active or a passive one, whether she had any real power, shadowed her. Long after they returned to her condo, after they'd made sweet, sexy love, she lay awake thinking about it. Each time she came near to an understanding, Sawyer would do something in his sleep—tug her closer, kiss her, whisper her name—and the issues became muddied again.

She knew one thing. He did love her.

She knew another thing. She did love him.

What she didn't know was whether she was the type of

woman who could sustain a relationship like that, and whether she could bear it if she wasn't.

Thursday morning came too soon. She'd found no answers to her questions and she'd had far too little sleep. It was an easy matter to keep her eyes closed while Sawyer dressed, but it was harder to ignore him when, as was becoming his habit, he came to sit beside her before he left.

"Plans for today?" he asked, smiling at her sleepy look.

"I don't know," she mumbled flatly.

"Uh-oh. You're tired."

"Mmph."

"And cranky. Should I let you get into the office and call you there?"

"Mmm."

Without another word, he bent his head and placed a chaste kiss at the corner of her mouth, then left.

Because he'd read her so well, she was in an even worse mood, and because she was in an even worse mood, she felt even weaker, which made her more angry. She stomped out of bed, went into the bathroom and slammed the door.

Then she found that she'd gotten her period.

"GOOD MORNING," came Sawyer's deep voice on the phone shortly after she'd arrived at the office.

"Hi, Sawyer," she said in a no-nonsense, businesslike way.

He got the hint. "You're busy."

"Very."

"Can I see you later?"

"Uh, I don't know." She flipped through her desk calendar—unnecessarily since the day's appointments faced her on a single page. "I have one meeting after another."

"Lunch?"

"With the mayor."

"I'm impressed."

"Don't be. It's business."

"Then I'm jealous."

"No need. It's me and six other women."

"Sounds kinky."

She sighed.

"Okay," he conceded. "I'll call you later."

HE TRIED HER at two o'clock, but she hadn't returned from lunch. He tried her again at three, but she'd returned and left again. When he tried her at five, she was with a client. So he left a message for her to call him when she was free.

She called him at six-thirty, and her tone was anything but encouraging. "Sorry I've missed you. It's been one of those days."

"You sound tired."

"I am. I think I'll go home and go to bed."

There was no mistaking the lack of an invitation. But then, Sawyer had had a premonition all day. "Is something bothering you?"

"I just said it. I'm tired."

"Beside that."

"What could be wrong?"

You could be uptight about us. You could be feeling crowded. You could be missing your freedom. "I don't know. You tell me."

"I'm tired, Sawyer."

"But if I said that I'd go home with you and work while you sleep, you'd say no, wouldn't you?"

It was only a minute before she said, "Yes."

"You want to be alone. Why?"

"Because I want to sleep."

"You wouldn't sleep better if I was there?"

She heard his gentle teasing, but she was determined to resist its lure. "That's an egotistical question if ever there was one."

"I sleep better with you than I do alone."

"Sure. Sex is a powerful sleeping pill."

He abandoned gentle teasing. "Even when we don't make love, I sleep better when you're with me. What's wrong, Faith? What's eating you?"

"I'm tired."

"Talk to me. Tell me what it is."

"I'm tired."

"Tired of me?"

"Tired, period. I need sleep. Alone."

He listened to what she was saying and tried to read between the lines, and though he could imagine what the problem was, if she wouldn't talk, they couldn't work it out. He debated pushing her, but the idea that she might be legitimately tired kept him from it. He figured he could give her a little time.

"Okay," he said. "You go on home and get your sleep. I'll call you in the morning."

"I'll be in court in the morning."

"Then I'll call you before court."

"No. I'll be with my client before court."

"Then I'll call you after court."

"I don't know when I'll be back."

"I'll keep trying," he said, less indulgently now. "You're being crabby, Faith, and I don't think it has anything to do with being tired. It has to do with us, but unless you tell me what it is, I can't do anything about it."

He was pushing her, just as he'd told himself he wouldn't do moments before, but he was helpless to stop. "There may be times when you'd like to turn back the clock and make things between us the way that they used to be, but you can't do that. I can't do it. I don't *want* to do it. So we'll talk. If not now, later." He meant every word he was saying, and then some. "You're running, Faith. But I run faster. I'll always catch up. Remember that."

He hung up the phone before Faith could tell him how dumb what he'd said was. And it was just as well. The more she thought about it, the more she realized that it hadn't been such a dumb thing to say at all. Sawyer had an advantage over her that had nothing to do with physical size or strength. It had to do with determination. He knew what he wanted, and he wasn't letting it get away.

She was flattered. More than that, she was gratified. More than that, she was touched and touched deeply—so much so that at times during Thursday night, she felt herself on the verge of tears. She was frightened. She wanted Sawyer, but didn't want to want him, and she was terrified of losing him. She was alternately confused and frustrated and angry.

By Friday morning, she was feeling totally washed out. At some point during the night, her mind had pulled a temporary blank and allowed her to sleep, but it hadn't been enough. The light of day illuminated all the things she preferred to have left hidden in the dark.

Grateful to have something to fully occupy her mind, she met with her client at eight, then went to court. By eleven-thirty she was back at her desk, and though she hadn't come up with an answer to the Sawyer dilemma, she found herself willing the phone to ring. He said he'd call. When he didn't, she felt angry—not so much at him, but at herself for being disappointed.

Being disappointed was her lot in life, she decided in a fit of self-pity as she threw papers and files into her briefcase and headed for the law library to work. If she wasn't in the office, she reasoned, she wouldn't be there to hear the phone not ring, which was some improvement on the disillusionment of waiting and wishing.

Sawyer found her at the library. It was nearly four, and neither the dimming light of day nor the heavily shaded lamp on the table could hide his irritation. Slipping into the wooden armchair beside her, one of eight at the long mahogany table, he leaned close and whispered, "Where in the hell have you been? I've been looking all over for you."

"I've been here," she whispered back. She didn't know whether to be pleased that he'd found her or not. Her heart didn't wait for her to decide; it was beating faster than it had moments before.

"Why wouldn't Loni tell me?"

"Because she didn't know. I said I was going out. I didn't want to be disturbed."

Sheltered by knitted brows, Sawyer's eyes skipped toward the two other men at the table. Though they seemed engrossed in their own work, he carefully kept his whisper low. "Well, you're going to be disturbed. We have to talk, and we have to talk now."

"I'm working now."

But he was already closing the books she'd been using. "We'll go to Timothy's. It's right around the corner. We can take a quiet booth at the back."

"Timothy's is a bar."

"So a drink might do you good."

"I don't drink."

"It might loosen up your tongue."

"I don't need a drink to loosen my tongue. I don't want to talk."

"Come on, Faith. You're pulling a Laura Leindecker, and what was it you told her? That she had to share her feelings with Bruce?"

"They're married. We're not."

"Through no fault of mine. I'd have asked you last weekend and seen the deed over and done by now if it had been up to me."

"Well, it's not." Her whisper took on a panicky edge. "Sawyer, what are you doing?"

He was gathering her papers together and stuffing them none too neatly into her briefcase. "We're getting out of here."

"I'm not leaving."

"If you don't," he said, pausing in his work to lean extra close, "I'll give you a slow...wet...deep...kiss."

Faith could hardly breathe. Sawyer's nearness was bad enough, but when his breath fanned her ear and his words heated her insides, her resolve was more fragile than ever. Still she clung to it.

Grabbing her papers from Sawyer's hands, she put them into the briefcase herself. "You'll give me no such thing. I'm going back to the office." Snapping her briefcase shut, she stood.

He was right beside her when she left the table. Before she could go far, he closed a hand around her arm. "You're coming with me."

"No way." Her voice remained a forced whisper. "It's over, Sawyer. I've made up my mind. I apologize for having led you along, but this relationship isn't for me. It's too time-consuming. Too distracting. Too demanding. I can't possibly be what you want, and I'm exhausted trying." With the carpeted room left behind, her heels beat a rapid tattoo on the floor.

"It's the fighting that's exhausting you," Sawyer declared. Though they no longer had to whisper, he kept his voice low. That didn't blunt its urgency. "Give in. Let it happen. Say you love me."

They trotted down the broad marble stairs, nodding to a judge coming up, but not pausing. When they burst through the large double doors and hit the street, Faith tried to turn in the direction of her office. Sawyer firmly propelled her the opposite way.

"Sawyer, I can't," she cried. "I have work to do."

"Work will wait. This won't."

"What's the big rush?"

He strode on holding her arm, his dark eyes straight ahead. "Yesterday was unbearable. Last night was even worse. I won't let things go on like this. I spent years watching my marriage fizzle, and I didn't fight because I didn't care, but I care about this. You say it's over. I don't believe that. If you want to convince me, you'll have to do it now."

"I just did," she argued. "This relationship is too much for me to handle."

"Bullshit."

"Say what you want, but it's true."

"You were handling it just fine at the start of the week," he argued, generating anger to cover up the unsettled feeling in the pit of his stomach. "Nothing's changed since then, except that you started getting *scared* that you couldn't handle it. So you decided not to try. That is *cowardly*, Faith, *cowardly*!"

"So I'm a coward. That's as good a reason as any why it won't work."

They reached Timothy's. Sawyer kept his hand in firm

possession of her arm while he drew her through the door. "Two of whatever's on tap," he called to the bartender as he swept down the long bar to a booth near the back. It was the only free one. The bar was filling up with happy-hour patrons. The noise of their chatter didn't bother him, any more than the dimness of the place did. Both provided a certain privacy.

When he'd successfully nudged Faith into the booth, he slid in opposite her. Without preamble, he pierced her with vibrant brown eyes and picked up where they'd left off. "What you're doing is totally out of character. You weren't meant to be a coward, Faith. Professionally, you're one of the bravest women I know. You've taken on cases that other lawyers have refused, and you've won. You've taken on Boston's staid legal community and done more for family law than any other lawyer in years. And you haven't done so badly personally, either. You stuck with Jack because you believed in marriage, and when it became obvious that it wouldn't work, you had the courage to let go."

She sputtered out a laugh. "That's a contrived way of looking at it. I *failed* in my marriage. I stuck with it because I *didn't* have the courage to let go. I only got out when it became obvious that there was nothing left. It didn't take courage at that point."

Sawyer wanted to scream in frustration. He didn't understand why she had to be so hard on herself. "Why do you insist on seeing the worst? Why do you choose the most pessimistic view of what happened? There were positive things in your marriage. I saw them." He gave a small, impatient shake of his head. "But I don't want to talk about your marriage to Jack. That's over and done. I want to talk about us."

Resting her head against the wood back of the booth,

Faith eyed him forlornly. "Nothing's changed. Back when we were at the Cape, I told you my worries. They're the same."

"You're afraid you'll disappoint me."

"And myself."

"Monday, Tuesday and Wednesday—were you disappointed?"

She thought back to the warmth in which he'd kept her cocooned, and she couldn't lie. "No. I wasn't disappointed then."

"Because you enjoyed what we did. You enjoyed being together."

She nodded. "But I grew dependent on that, and I don't like being dependent."

"So you tried to put me off. That's why you wouldn't see me yesterday or last night."

She tried to defend herself. "Things between us have gotten too intense too fast. We need to cool off."

"But we won't. Out of sight doesn't mean out of mind." He spared only a moment's glance at the frothy steins the bartender brought. "I thought about you all last night. Can you honestly say you didn't think about me?"

"No. I thought about you."

"And you decided that since you like me so much, you shouldn't see me so much. You don't want to become too dependent on me—or have me become too dependent on you. You don't want to be disappointed if something goes wrong." Arms on the table flanking his untouched beer, he leaned forward. "That is *convoluted logic*. It's like saying that a lamp makes reading a breeze, but you'll sit in the dark so you won't come to rely on the lamp in case the bulb blows. Well, hell, if the bulb blows, you get another. Things can be repaired. So can relationships, if they mean enough to you."

Eyes holding hers, he sat back. "The Leindeckers are together again. I got a call from Bruce after lunch telling me that they've kissed and made up."

That was news to Faith. "Really?" she asked cautiously.

He nodded.

"I haven't heard anything about it from Laura."

"Because you've been incommunicado since lunchtime. She called. Loni told me."

In the brief respite from her own troubles, Faith allowed a small smile. "They're forgetting about the divorce?"

"They're going to try to work things out. Bruce was extremely grateful to us. Especially to you. Laura told him that you kept pushing for a reconciliation. You kept telling her to talk with him and tell him how she felt." He paused, wondering if she was getting the point, deducing from the unenlightened look on her face that she wasn't, deciding to make it himself. "How can you preach that and not do it yourself?"

Her eyes widened. "I *am* talking to you. You know how I feel."

"You wouldn't talk with me yesterday, and, no, I don't really know how you feel. You've never said whether you love me or not."

"I have, too. I've told you I love you dozens of time."

"As a friend."

She swallowed. Closing her eyes for a minute, she thought of those warm, wonderful times when she lay in his arms. "And as a lover," she said, sending him an unknowingly adoring look. "I could never respond to you the way I do, or do the things I do to you if I didn't love you."

For the first time since he'd found her at the library, Sawyer experienced a faint lightening in the area of his heart. Again, he leaned forward, this time beseechingly. "Then give it a try, Faith. Don't fight it. Don't ruin the present by worrying about the future." When he saw the skepticism on her face, he hurried on. "Listen, I don't know what the future holds. None of us do. Life doesn't come with a road map telling exactly what turn to take when in order to get to a prescribed destination." That thought gave him pause. "Where do you want to go? Do you know? Supposing you were to look ahead ten or twenty years, what do you see yourself doing, being?"

"I see myself as a successful lawyer."

"What else?"

"I don't now."

"What do you mean, you don't know? What do you *dream*?"

"I don't know."

"You do, but you won't say. You *are* as bad as Laura Leindecker."

"And you're like Bruce. You won't leave me alone. Why not, Sawyer? That's all I'm asking, just to be left alone. Is it so difficult to do?"

Straightening his shoulders, Sawyer took a different tack. Keeping his voice low, he said, "Okay. I could leave you alone. I could let you go back to the kind of life where work is basically all there is. I could let you bury yourself in the law. I could disappear from your life. Does that sound better?"

It sounded devastating, but she didn't say it.

He went on. "We could do what we did for years, bump into each other at conferences or seminars or political fundraisers. Maybe we'll even have another chance to work with each other. We could meet by accident on the street once in a while, date other people, sleep with other—"

"I don't want that."

"What?"

"To sleep with other people. I don't want it."

"You don't want to do it yourself, or you don't want *me* to do it?"

Her eyes blazed. "Both. Either."

"But you don't want to sleep with me."

She didn't answer.

Her lack of response stirred Sawyer's frustration, which in turn made his voice sound harsh. "What do you want, Faith? Beyond a career, what do you want? There must be other things. You're a woman capable of warmth and love. Don't you want an outlet for those?"

She stared at him. Oh, she knew the answer to that one, but she was afraid, so afraid to give it, and Sawyer knew that.

"Why is it so *hard*?" he asked. "You always used to talk to me. You used to tell me everything. Why can't you now?"

"Because things have changed between us!"

"We're more involved."

"Yes."

"So we should be sharing even more." He reached his limit. If she wouldn't say it, he would. "Damn it, Faith, I want it all! I want you as my law partner, my wife and the mother of my kids, and I think that if you can be honest with yourself and with me, you'd admit that you want those things, too."

Hearing him put it all into words was nearly more than she could bear. "I do," she cried softly, "but it's a dream.

That's all. A dream. Life has ways of taking unwanted twists. I've seen it happen time and again. We hope for things, and when they don't happen, disillusionment sets in. I'd be devastated if that happened with us."

"It won't. We love each other. We have so much going for each other."

"But I'm a lawyer," she said, and tears began to gather on her lower lids. "I'm a lousy cook and a lousy cleaner, and I wouldn't know how to change a diaper if my life depended on it."

"So you'll learn. We'll learn."

"But I'm not even pregnant!" she cried and, feeling an awesome ache, she scrambled out of the booth and ran toward the front of the bar.

Swearing, Sawyer tossed several bills on the table to pay for the beer they hadn't touched, and took off after her. He caught up half a block from the bar. Snagging her by the wrist, he hustled her into the nearest doorway, out of the line of rush-hour foot traffic. His hands went flat against the granite on either side of her shoulders. His large body prevented her escape.

"When did you get it?" he demanded, furious enough to momentarily overlook the tears streaking down her cheeks. "Your period. When did you get it?"

"Yesterday morning."

"And that's when the trouble started." It suddenly made sense. "You figured I'd be disappointed that you weren't pregnant."

"*I* was disappointed," she cried. "That was bad enough."

"Because you wanted to have my baby," he said. The gentleness that hit him then, the heart-wrenching care dissolved whatever anger he'd felt. His hands left the granite, slipped around her back and drew her snugly against him. "Ahhh, Faith. I do love you. You have to be one of the most bullheaded women I've ever met in my life, but I do love you."

"I wanted to be pregnant."

He recalled the way she'd talked when they'd first discussed the possibility, and knew she was telling the truth. "Why didn't you tell me? I wouldn't have had to bother with—"

"I couldn't tell you. I didn't know how you felt."

"You could have asked."

"But then I'd have *known* how you felt."

"Mmm, that makes sense."

"It does. If you hadn't wanted a baby, and it turned out I was pregnant, you'd have been disappointed. Same thing if you'd wanted a baby, and I *wasn't* pregnant. So I was better not knowing."

He tucked his head lower against hers. "You're never better not knowing, Faith. And you're never better keeping things to yourself. A relationship is about sharing. You know that. You've counseled any number of clients on it, most recently Laura Leindecker. So if you can tell them to communicate, why can't you do it yourself?"

"Because I'm emotionally involved, and when I'm emotionally involved I can't think straight!"

"You've got that right, at least. As far as the rest goes, you're out in left field."

"See? I'm a disappointment already."

"Did I say that?"

"You were thinking it."

"No, ma'am. I was thinking that I love it when you're out in left field, because it gives me a chance to play hero. It feeds the macho in me."

She groaned, but the sound was barely muffled by his

coat when he pulled back, took her hand and started off. She had to trot to keep up. "Where are we going?"

"Somewhere."

"Obviously. Sawyer, I can't go anywhere," she cried as the breeze dashed the tears from her cheeks. "I have work to do."

He didn't miss a step as they turned onto Beacon Street. His hand kept hers well in its grip. "Y'know, I'll bet you didn't give Jack half this much trouble when you agreed to marry him."

"I didn't give him any trouble, and I haven't agreed to marry *you*."

"I'll bet you just smiled and said yes, when there were dozens and dozens of reasons why the marriage wouldn't work."

"I was young and stupid. So was Jack. We wanted marriage more than we wanted each other."

"And the irony of it is," Sawyer went on as though she hadn't spoken, "that here we are with dozens and dozens of reasons why a marriage between us *will* work, and you're driving both of us crazy dreaming up problems."

"I'm not dreaming them up!"

"Some people do that, y'know. They can't bear the thought of happiness so they throw stumbling blocks in their own way." Pulling Faith faster to cross Tremont Street before the light turned, he yelled, "Taxi!" The cab that had just dropped off a customer and was starting to pull away from the curb stopped. Too involved in defending herself to question him, Faith slid in at Sawyer's urging and resumed the discussion the minute he joined her.

"I *do* want to be happy. I've never deliberately thrown stumbling blocks in the way of that."

"No?" To the waiting cabbie, he said, "Copley Place."

"Copley Place?" Faith echoed. "Sawyer, I have to work." But the cab was already on its way, as were her thoughts. "I'm being cautious, that's all, and there's nothing wrong with it. I've already flunked out of one relationship. Every day I see the tattered remains of other relationships. I'm thinking of *you*, Sawyer."

"Okay," he said in a lower voice, "think of me." With the creak of aged vinyl, he shifted on the seat to face her. "Think of how much I want you, not only today and tomorrow but for all the tomorrows after that. Think of how much I want to work with you and travel with you and finish the place at the Cape with you and have kids with you—" When she looked stricken by the last, he hurried on. "Not right away. I'm glad you're not pregnant. I want you to myself for a while. Besides, if you were pregnant, you'd think that was why I wanted to get married, when it's not."

"I haven't agreed to *any*—"

The rest of her protest was lost in the kiss Sawyer gave her. It was a sweet kiss, powerful in that sweetness. It said he loved her, loved her even when she was being difficult. That was very much what he was thinking, and when—after trying the kiss from several different angles simply because her lips were so pliant—he finally lifted his mouth from hers, he felt the theme worth discussion.

"You can't disappoint me, Faith," he said. His face was inches from hers. Almost reverently he held her chin in the notch of his hand. "You can't *possibly* disappoint me. You're one of the best lawyers around. Whether you win or lose a case, you give it your all, which is more than most do and as much as any client can ask. As a wife, you'll be smashing, and I don't give a damn whether you're a lousy cook—"

"I'm lousy at it because I hate doing it," she blurted

out. She was having trouble thinking with the taste of him lingering on her lips and his face so close and his voice so gentle, but she had to speak up. She feared it might be her last chance. He was so near and dear. Her resolve was slipping. "What kind of wife hates to cook?"

"The kind who has a full-time job outside the home and doesn't have the time or energy to spend working over a stove. And there's nothing wrong with that. I don't expect you to be superwoman. If we need a cook, we'll hire one. Same thing for when babies come. I may be traditional about some things, but I'll never ask you to stop working unless that's what you want. Besides, you said it yourself—babies and careers are mixing better and better these days."

"I don't know anything about mothering."

"Neither do I. So we'll learn. There are books all over the place, and classes." He brushed the tip of his finger by the corner of her eye as he visually devoured her features, then went on in a voice that was even lower and slightly rough, "And as a lover, you're more than any man could imagine. No woman has ever turned me on like you do. No woman has ever done to me what you do." He took in a short, sharp breath. "The other night...what you did...where your mouth was and your hands..."

He didn't have to finish. Faith remembered the moment well. She'd shocked herself, not only with what she'd done but with the pleasure she'd taken in the doing. A soft, sexy smile stole over her lips. "Liked that, did ya?"

"Yeah," he whispered. "I liked it."

"I've never tried it before. So, it worked?"

"Oh, yeah." Even in memory it was working, but the

jolting of the cab through the traffic was a reminder of where he was. "You're dynamite, Faith."

She liked the sound of that. "But what happens when I get older? Will I still be dynamite when my hair is gray and my breasts sag and I have cellulite on my thighs?"

"By that time, I'll be bald and paunchy and my eyesight may be so lousy that I won't be able to see the cellulite on your thighs."

"You'll never be bald and paunchy."

"How about my eyesight? Will you love me even if I can't see straight?"

"Of course I will. What kind of dumb question is that?"

"The same kind *you're* asking," he said and gave her a minute to realize it before saying, "There are two points here, m'dear. The first is that you're dynamite to me because of who you are, not what you look like. The second," and he sobered, "is that none of us knows what the future holds. We have to look at what we have now and decide whether we think it's strong enough and positive enough to make us happy today and optimistic about tomorrow." He lowered his voice again, this time in urgent coaxing. "Come on, babe. You know we can make it. Stop fighting. Give it a chance."

But before she could respond one way or the other, the cab pulled up at the Marriott Hotel. Without so much as a look at the meter, Sawyer stuffed a ten-dollar bill into the cabbie's outstretched hand, opened the door and pulled Faith out. Keeping her close by his side, he entered the hotel at a broad stride.

"What are we doing here, Sawyer?"

"You'll see."

They were passing through the lobby, and for a minute Faith thought he was going to take a room on the forty-fifth floor and make wild, passionate love to her over-looking Boston. It was a romantic idea, and it wasn't beyond him at all, she knew. When they passed the registration desk without stopping, she wondered if he'd taken a room in advance. "That was a presumptuous thing to do," she murmured, half-flattered, half-annoyed.

"What was?"

"Booking a room without even knowing whether I'd come. You assumed I'd cave in, didn't you? Beth Leindecker said her mother always did that. Bruce snapped his fingers, and she came running."

"I should only be so lucky," Sawyer said under his breath, then added, bemused, "I didn't book a room." Sure enough, they passed the bank of elevators and headed toward the escalator that led to the mall level.

"Oh." She frowned. "Then what are we doing here?"

"Going shopping. Watch your step. Hold on. That's it."

"Sawyer, I've been on an escalator before. But why are we going shopping? And why here? Prices are exorbitant here. I have to warn you, I'm almost as lousy a shopper as I am a cook."

"I don't believe that. You always look spectacular."

"Sure, because I'm drawn to the most expensive item on the rack. It happens every time, like there's some kind of radar flowing between the price tag and my head without my seeing a thing."

"That's fine. Price is no object. I want the best." Fingers laced through hers, he drew her off the escalator, toward the first store on the left.

"The best what?"

"Diamond ring."

Her eyes widened as they passed through Tiffany's

vaulted portals. She tugged back on her hand and whispered loudly, "What are we *doing* here, Sawyer?"

Her tug didn't faze him. He strode right along. "Buying you an engagement ring. I want all the bozos in Boston to know that you're taken."

"But we're not engaged."

"We certainly are." He produced a dashing smile for the woman behind the counter. "We'd like to look at engagement rings—something substantial, maybe with a few little stones on the side—sapphires, rubies, whatever goes with diamonds—you know what I'm talking about."

The saleswoman certainly did. She had carefully removed several spectacular possibilities from the showcase and placed them on a bed of navy velvet before Faith could find her tongue.

"Sawyer," she murmured out of the side of her mouth, unable to take her eyes from the rings, "uh, Sawyer, I think we should talk."

Leaning close, he said in the same side-mouth murmur, "Definitely. What do you think? I think the blue stones look a little cold next to the diamond. I like the green, the emeralds. They go with your eyes."

"My eyes are hazel."

He looked into them. "They look green to me. Maybe it's what you're wearing." He dropped a quick glance at the long pleated skirt, sweater and blazer she wore, a blend of solids and plaids in plum and moss. "Super outfit," he mouthed. His eyes glowed in appreciation.

Cheeks growing pink, Faith tore her gaze from his and forced it back to the rings. "I can't accept one of these."

"Why not?" He put his mouth by her ear and whispered, "I love you. I'll always love you. I'll love you until the sun sets in the east, until the rivers run dry, until

Santa gets stuck in a chimney in Winnemucca, Nevada—"

"They're too elaborate." She looked beseechingly at the saleswoman. "Haven't you got something a little simpler?"

Sawyer started to argue, but before he could do much more than tell her she deserved the best, the saleswoman produced two rings that stilled his tongue. Both held single stones, one round, one pear-shaped.

"Ahhh," Faith breathed in awe. Smiling, she carefully lifted the pear-shaped ring from the velvet. "This is more like it."

"Don't you want something a little more showy?"

"You're the one who wants something showy. It's the old macho pride." She continued to hold the ring, spellbound by its sparkle. "This is special. Simple but exquisite."

He had to agree that it was, still he'd envisioned something different. "Maybe we should look at something with more than one diamond." He turned to the saleswoman. "How about it? Something with one big stone and two little ones on the sides? Maybe with diamonds all the way around?"

Faith was still admiring the pear-shaped diamond when the saleswoman added two other rings to those already out. Faith didn't like either as much as the one she still held in her hand. "They're too busy. If a stone is beautiful, it should stand on its own." She took a soft breath. "I like the solitaire."

"You're worried that the others are too expensive, but I'm telling you, Faith, money isn't an object here. If I can't splurge on the woman I love, who *can* I splurge on?"

"Sir?" the saleswoman spoke up a bit nervously. "About the ring your fiancée is holding—it's the finest quality diamond we carry." She cleared her throat. "Given that and its shape and size, I'm afraid it's the most expensive one I've shown you."

Quickly but carefully, Faith set the ring down. "I should have known," she muttered. "I do it every time."

But Sawyer was lifting it, taking her left hand, slipping the ring on her third finger. It fit perfectly. "Simple and exquisite." He grinned. "We'll take it."

"We can't take it," Faith whispered, but the sharpness she'd wanted to put into the whisper fell prey to the beauty of the ring on her finger—that, and the contrast of Sawyer's long, lean hand holding hers. "We...I...can't."

"You can," he said softly, and something in his tone brought her eyes to his. They were dark and intent, filled with love and a kind of bare-hearted expectancy that made Faith tremble. "You can," he whispered. "You can do it, Faith. You have the power to reach out and try, and that's all I'll ever ask of you. Reach out and try. Give it your best shot. Nothing's a given in life, but there's so much hope in this. I want it. You want it. Together we'll make it work." Her eyes went wider, as though he'd said a magic word, but her lips remained pressed close together. "What do you say? Wanna give it a try?"

She wanted that more than anything, and in that moment she realized the extraordinary power she did have. She had the power to bring Sawyer happiness—and the power to find it herself. Yes, there was a risk. The stakes were frightfully high. But the alternative? Standing there, looking up into Sawyer's face as she could quite contentedly do for years and years, she knew that the alternative was no alternative at all.

Words eluded her, but words weren't needed. Her answer came in a short nod, a soft smile, the tears that filled her eyes and the arms that went around his neck. When he slid his own arms around her and crushed her to him, she felt a joy she'd never known. She also felt a confidence she'd never expected.

He was right. Together they'd make it work.

IT TAKES A REBEL

Stephanie Bond

This book is dedicated to my editor, Brenda Chin,
who "gets it" and challenges me
to be a better writer.

1

"JACK, ARE YOU LISTENING?"

Jack Stillman jerked his attention back to his brother's voice on the phone. "Hmm? Sure, bro."

"I'm counting on you," Derek said in that patronizing big-brother tone that Jack hated.

He rolled his eyes, leaned back in his desk chair, and propped his feet on the corner of the desk. "Stop worrying, I can handle things until you get back."

"I'm not worried about your ability," Derek said dryly. "It's your dedication that keeps me up at night."

Jack frowned. "Your new bride should be the only thing keeping you up at night."

Derek chuckled in a way that told Jack he hadn't spent *every* minute of his honeymoon worrying about the ad agency. "Just remember—"

"I *know*, bro, I know. The gal from the IRS office will be by this afternoon, the phone bill needs to be paid, and I have an appointment with Al Tremont tomorrow morning at ten. I have everything under control."

"Since we need to make a good impression on this IRS agent, you might not want to call her 'gal.'"

He sighed, loath to spend the afternoon with some dried-up hag who wanted to scrutinize his W-4's.

"Is the office straightened up?" Derek asked.

Jack glanced at the pizza box sitting on his desk from yesterday, and the cartons of leftover Chinese from the day before. On the other side of the room that housed both his and Derek's desks, the floor-to-ceiling bookshelf had collapsed, the timing of the mishap probably hastened by his overuse of the mini-basketball hoop on the side, he conceded. Twice he'd thought about straightening the mountain of reference books and papers on the floor, then changed his mind. And he hadn't gotten around to sorting the mail in the two weeks since Derek had left. He raised the lid on the pizza box and lifted the remaining stone-cold slice to his mouth for a bite. "The place looks peachy," he said through a mouthful of rubbery cheese.

"Good. Then tell me you dressed up."

Jack looked down at one of the short sleeve floral shirts he'd acquired during his extended vacation in Florida, then opened his top drawer and withdrew a black and white striped tie from the wad of spares he kept there for emergencies. "Tie and everything," he said, flipping up the collar of his shirt and fashioning a loose Windsor knot.

"And you got a haircut?"

He ran his hand through his dark shaggy hair and grunted what he hoped passed for affirmation.

Derek sighed in relief, so he must have sounded convincing. "And you have ideas drawn up for Tremont?"

Jack shot a look in the direction of his sketch pad, then flicked a chunk of pepperoni from the blank top sheet. "Some of my best work ever."

"Great. What did you come up with?"

"Uh, I'll call you and go over the presentation when I get everything back from the printer."

"You're the artist," Derek said with a little laugh. "I'm nervous about you meeting with the IRS woman, but I have to admit, I'm sure you'll do a good job with Tremont. This account could put us in the big league, you know."

Jack winced and rubbed his stomach. Guilt and cold pizza did not mix. "I know, Derek, I won't let you down." He checked the clock on Derek's desk—he'd lost his own watch in a poker game in Kissimmee—and straightened. The IRS gal would arrive in another hour. "Listen, bro, gotta run."

"Call me on my cell phone if the agent has questions you can't answer."

"Sure thing. Give Janine a kiss for me, and make it French, okay?" He hung up before Derek could reprimand him, bit off another chunk of pizza, then winged it toward the overflowing trash can. After wiping his hands on his cut-off denim shorts, he pushed himself to his feet with an aggrieved sigh. Might as well get the darn bookshelf fixed.

He stretched tall into a mighty yawn, then padded barefoot to the closet they used as a supply room. He'd have time to slide into his deck shoes before the broad got there. Jack shook his head at the neat shelves, the bins of miscellaneous office supplies and the various tools. His brother had inherited their mother's penchant for order, while he had inherited their father's tendency toward turmoil.

God rest his father's sweet soul, the old man was still doing them favors. Paul Stillman, ever the generous spirit, had once stopped on New Circle Road to assist a motorist, only to discover the man was none other than Alexander Tremont, owner of the Tremont department store chain. Tremont had been on his way to a meeting at his flagship store in Lexington, Kentucky, and their father had given him a lift. When the two men hit it off, Tremont had promised the Stillman & Sons agency a chance at his business once his contract with a high-powered agency had run its course.

Last week, Al Tremont's secretary had phoned to keep his promise. Saddened to learn of their father's passing, Tremont nonetheless set an appointment to discuss ideas for a new ad campaign. Derek had been ecstatic when Jack told him, and considered cutting short his honeymoon, but Jack had assured him he could handle the presentation.

And he *could* handle the presentation, he told himself. He'd already performed some rudimentary research by calling acquaintances to ask what the hell the store sold. He still had nearly twenty-four hours until the Tremont appointment, and he always did his best work under pressure. If history repeated itself, his most creative ideas would strike him around three o'clock tomorrow morning.

He pulled down a tool belt and strapped it low around his hips. Begrudgingly, he lifted the stepladder to his shoulder—might as well change the two expired overhead lightbulbs while he was at it.

Upon closer inspection, the bookshelf was in worse shape than he'd thought. He ended up reinforcing the brace under each shelf and tightening every screw that held the piece together. Once the unit was stabilized, he positioned it against the wall, then knelt to start replacing the heap of books, binders and periodicals.

Two minutes into the pile, between volumes of advertising trade magazines, he stumbled across an old friend—the 1997 *Playboy* "Southern College Coeds" issue. A dog-eared page took him directly to the University of Kentucky offerings. Wow, still impressive. And by chance, he'd spotted the blonde in the cropped T-shirt at the next football game he'd attended. What was her name? Jack peered more closely. Oh, yeah—Sissy. He and Sissy had shared some good times.

"Excuse me."

At the sound of a woman's voice, Jack jerked his head up and slapped the magazine closed. In the doorway of their disheveled office stood the most drop-dead gorgeous woman he'd ever had the pleasure of setting his eyes upon. His body leapt in unadulterated admiration. The woman was...tight. Tight black hair bound away from her face. Tight skin over sharp cheekbones and a perfect nose. Tight set of her mouth and chin. Tight tailored pale blue suit that hugged every curve of her long body. Tight look from her haughty blue eyes. Tight grip on the black briefcase she held.

To say the IRS rep didn't look anything like what he'd expected was an understatement of laughable proportions. "Yes?" He adopted a charming expression. His mind raced ahead to the drinks, the dinner, the bed they were destined to share.

"I'm looking for Mr. Stillman."

Oh, and a husky voice, too. He'd surely died and gone to heaven. "You found him," he said, then tossed the magazine to the floor and walked toward her.

"You're Derek Stillman?" she asked, not hiding her surprise.

"No, I'm his brother, Jack, the better looking one." He grinned. "Derek is out of town, but I've been expecting you."

"Oh?" she asked, scanning the contents of the office. "You know who I am?"

"Sure," he said cheerfully. "Derek and I were just discussing the meeting on the phone."

Suddenly he realized the unkempt appearance of their office might run in their favor—the woman could certainly see they weren't hiding income. He laughed and gestured around. "As you can see, we're not exactly the cream of the advertising agencies." He made a rueful noise. "A month ago we were on the verge of bankruptcy, and now we're just hanging on by the skin of our ass—um, teeth, so this shouldn't take long."

"Indeed," she said, her enunciation clipped. "I believe I've seen enough." She turned as if to leave.

He panicked. "Wait—what about our appointment?"

"Consider it canceled."

Jack nearly whooped with relief—Derek would be ecstatic that the audit had been dismissed, but he wasn't about to let this creature just walk out of his life.

"You don't have to be so hasty," he drawled, strolling closer. "There's a silver lining to every cloud." When she turned back, he angled his head at her and gave her his most devilish grin. "How about dinner?"

One thin jet eyebrow shot up. "With you?"

He winked. "I grill a mean steak."

Her smile was, of course, tight. "I'm a vegetarian."

Jack blanched. He'd heard of vegetarians, but he'd never met one. "Well, I grill a mean...head of cabbage. What do you say?"

Her eyes narrowed. "I say 'no.' Goodbye, Mr. Stillman."

"Wait," he said, trotting after her into the reception area, where they kept a desk, a phone and an extinct computer for appearances. The two weeks' worth of mail nearly obscured the top of the dummy desk.

She turned again, her mouth pursed, her gaze chilly.

He spread his hands. "At least give me your card so I can prove to my brother that you were here." He'd call her and eventually wear her down—he always did.

The black-haired beauty hesitated, then withdrew a

gold business card holder, extracted a card, and flicked it down on the corner of the reception desk. She opened the door and exited to the hall. Jack caught the door and stuck out his head to watch her walk away. Head up, her stride was long, and she never looked back as she disappeared around the corner.

Jack whistled low and under his breath. "Tight little behind, too." Spirits high, he turned back to the door and laughed aloud. The Stillman & Sons Advertising Agency sign on the outside of the door dangled crookedly by a thin chain. He'd been meaning to fix that, too, but the disrepair had undoubtedly been a bonus. He couldn't wait to call Derek, and he couldn't wait to call the mystery woman. He loved a gal who played hard to get.

Jack lifted his arm and patted himself heartily on the back. Derek was always complaining that he didn't pull his weight around the office, but from what he could see, running the place was a pure cinch. The auditor was practically in his pocket; in fact—he cracked his knuckles with one sweeping motion—maybe he'd be able to negotiate some sort of tax-free status between the sheets. He grinned—when he was hot, he was red-hot. Closing his eyes, he could practically feel the imprint of Tremont's handshake tomorrow as they agreed on a deal even more lucrative than his brother could have imagined. Humming in anticipation, Jack walked back into the messy reception area and picked up the card the smoky siren had left.

Then he nearly swallowed his smooth tongue.

Alexandria Tremont, Director of Marketing & Sales, Tremont Enterprises.

WHEN ALEX REACHED the parking lot, she was still marveling over the sheer audacity of Jack Stillman. She

swung into her sedan, banged the door closed, and
scoffed as she turned over the key in the ignition. The
man was a joke, and a lame one at that. She wheeled out
of the parking lot that was as shoddy as the so-called professional office buildings around it, making a wild guess
as to the owner of the dusty black motorcycle sitting at a
cocky angle.

She hesitated for half a heartbeat, tempted to lower the
rag top of her white convertible on this sunny fall day,
then decided she didn't want to have to bother with re-
doing her hair when she returned to the office. Funny,
but she hadn't driven with the top down nearly as much
as she thought she might when she'd bought the car on
impulse last spring. Lately she'd been regretting her
splurge; what had once sounded fun now seemed rather
silly.

Alex dodged a pothole, then eased into side street traffic and headed for the bypass, her foot depressing the gas
a little harder as the image of Jack Stillman's smug face
rose in her mind. The nerve of the man, making a pass at
her! Her cheeks warmed at the memory of his raking
gaze, as if he were entitled or something, the cad.

The bronzed bum hadn't even bothered to put his best
foot forward—or even don shoes for that matter—to impress a potentially huge customer. If there was one thing
she resented, it was a man with an attitude who had absolutely nothing to back it up, and Jack Stillman appeared to be the poster boy for arrogance. He'd obviously mistaken her for the kind of woman who would be
swayed by his stray-dog good looks. The scoundrel undoubtedly planned to shmooze her and her father with
good-old-boy charm—a southern staple she'd come to
despise during her rise through the ranks of the family
business.

Her father had insisted, and rightfully so, that she start on the sales floor as a teenager and learn the business from the bottom up. Over the past fifteen years, she'd worked doubly hard to overcome the stigma of being the boss's daughter. Even her own father had resisted moving her into management, even though she knew the business inside out by the time most kids were finishing college. She'd reached the level of director two years ago, and was now in the running for the position of vice president of sales and marketing recently vacated by a retiree. The competition was stiff, but her record had been exemplary, and the new vice president would be announced any day. Her father would be so proud if the board of directors chose her.

Then, perhaps, Al would be forced to recognize her contribution to the company, to stop interfering with her duties and decisions. This situation with the Stillman & Sons agency was a perfect example. The vice presidential duties had been split among the four sales directors for the time being, and though the responsibility of choosing a new advertising agency had been assigned to her, her father seemed determined to give their considerable business to the doubtful Stillman & Sons agency because of a from-the-hip promise he'd made to a Good Samaritan. The man had since passed away, but Al wouldn't hear of 'going back on his word.'

And now they were left to deal with a derelict son who read *Playboy* at the office and fancied himself a ladies' man. Alex sighed. She really didn't need the hassle.

She lifted the lid to a compartment on her armrest, removed her cellular phone, and punched in the number for her father's private line.

Her father answered after a half ring. "This is Al," he barked.

"It's Alex," she said. "Is this a bad time?"

"Never for you, Alex," he murmured, his voice softening. Despite his flaws, she really loved him. "What's up, my dear?"

"I just left the Stillman & Sons advertising agency."

"I thought the agency was sending someone here tomorrow morning."

The questioning tone in her father's voice made her squirm. "I, um, had some time and decided to pay them a courtesy visit."

"And?"

There it was again—that tone. "And they're not in our league, Dad." She winced at her slip because she preferred not to address him personally when they discussed business.

"What makes you say that?"

"The place is a mess, and Jack Stillman wasn't much better—raggedy, unclean, the man even asked me out." As if she would even *consider* going out with the buffoon.

"Can't fault his taste."

She rolled her eyes at his chuckle. "Stillman & Sons is a low-class operation."

"Did you see their portfolio?"

Alex balked. "It hardly seemed worth the trouble."

"Well, I have it on good faith that the agency is small, but good. I want to see what they have to offer. You're forgetting, Alex, *we* used to be the underdog."

Alex bit back her argument, knowing she couldn't change his mind when he was in such a mood. In fact, she was starting to worry that the reason she'd been chosen for this assignment was so her father could pull the strings without appearing to. "Okay," she conceded. "The appointment stands. I'll see you at ten in the morning."

"Have a nice day, sweetheart. By the way, Gloria wants you to come over for dinner soon."

She wrinkled her nose at the mention of her father's wife—the woman was dim *and* dull—then mouthed some vague response before saying goodbye. Alex disconnected the call, feeling torn, as usual, after talking to her father. Was it so wrong to want his love *and* his respect?

But as she replaced the phone, she suddenly realized she didn't have a thing to worry about where the meeting was concerned. Jack Stillman would swagger in tomorrow looking like a wasted tourist and even her honorbound father would recognize the absurdity of working with the down-and-out agency.

Alex smiled and lifted her chin. With Jack Stillman's unwitting 'help' tomorrow morning, she'd be able to kill two birds with one stone: Her father would be forced to consider the reputable St. Louis advertising firm she was advocating, which also meant he would be forced to admit that she was right. And since the episode would unfold in the presence of various VIP's, her chance for the vice presidency would undoubtedly improve.

With a new outlook, she laughed aloud, mentally thanking the disreputable-looking advertising man for being in the wrong place at the right time. Her dear mother had once said that every event in this seemingly disjointed world actually happened for a reason. Apparently her mother's theory even extended to her unpleasant encounter with the repulsive Jack Stillman.

2

"DEREK'S GOING TO KILL ME." Jack held his head in his hands, fighting some kind of weird swirling sensation in his stomach. And his heart was racing as if he'd just run for a ninety-nine-yard touchdown. "He's absolutely going to kill me."

"In that case, I hope you have cash."

He glanced up to the open doorway. A plump fiftyish black woman stood dressed in white pants and shirt, wearing a lopsided red paper hat that read "Tony's." "You the stromboli sandwich with extra cheese?" she asked, her hand on one hip.

Jack nodded miserably, thinking even food wouldn't help his mood today.

"That'll be six dollars and forty cents." She dropped the sack on the desk unceremoniously and wiggled her fingers in his direction. Her fingernails were at least two inches long. And bright yellow.

With a heavy sigh, he pushed himself to his feet and removed his wallet. He counted eight one dollar bills into her hand, then added another when she lifted a winged eyebrow.

"You the handyman around here?" She nodded toward his tool belt as she stuffed the money into a fanny pack around her waist.

"Sort of," he mumbled. "This is my company...and my brother's."

"The murderer?"

Jack frowned. "Hmm?"

Her head jutted forward. "The man who's going to kill you—is he your brother?"

"Oh. Yeah."

"Why?"

"Why what?"

Her eyes rolled upward, and she spoke as if to a child. "Why is he going to kill you?"

Irritated by the woman's nosiness, he scowled. "It's a long story."

"Lucky for you," she said, revealing remarkably white teeth and surprising dimples. "You're my last delivery."

She had a pleasant way about her, he conceded, kind of...motherly. The woman was only trying to be nice, and what could it hurt to unload on a stranger? He shrugged, indifferent to her interest. "I'm supposed to be running this place while my brother is gone, but I f—" He swallowed at the disapproving look the woman shot him. "I mean, I messed up royally."

"How's that?"

He quirked his mouth from side to side. "A woman IRS agent was supposed to stop by, so when this gal showed up a while ago, I assumed she was here for the review."

"And?"

"And instead she was here about a huge account I'm supposed to pitch tomorrow—Tremont's department stores."

"And?"

"*And*, let's just say I downplayed the success of the business a tad—not the impression I was aiming for."

"So, who was she?" She leaned against the desk and

studied her nails, obviously unaware of the significance of doing business with the southern retail chain.

"Alexandria Tremont. She must be related to the man who owns the place—"

"Daughter."

Jack stopped. "You know her?"

The woman ran a finger along the desk, then blew a quarter-inch of accumulated dust into the air. "I know *of* her. My son works in menswear at their store on Webster Avenue. Says that Tremont miss is a real go-getter."

"More like a real ball buster," he muttered to himself.

"Uh-huh, and not too bad to look at, if I recall."

"A little too skinny, if you ask me."

"And single, I think my boy said."

"No wonder—she's as cold as a freaking statue."

Her eyes didn't miss a thing, bouncing from an unturned calendar to a lopsided lamp shade to the silent computer. "Uh-huh. She's rich, too, I'll bet, and re-f-i-i-i-ned, with a royal shine."

He smirked, remembering that on top of everything else, Princess Tremont had caught him ogling a naughty magazine. "Well, she wasn't *that* impressive."

She glanced at his bare feet and lifted a long yellow nail. "As opposed to you?"

Jack frowned. "I don't make a habit of trying to impress people."

The woman crossed her arms over her matronly bosom. "You married?"

"No."

"Now there's a surprise."

"But my brother is," he added, as if Derek's goodness could atone for his own sins. "In fact, he's away on his honeymoon."

She sniffed. "When's he due back, your brother?"

"In another two weeks." Jack rubbed his temples as he picked up his earlier train of thought. "And Derek will kill me when he hears I've bungled this opportunity with Tremont."

The woman leaned over and walked her fingers through the mail pile, then harrumphed. "First, he'd have to find you in all this mess. Where's your office manager?"

"We don't have one."

"I'll take it," she said matter-of-factly, plucking her paper hat from her head and dropping it into the trash can.

Jack blinked. "Take what?"

"The job," she said, her voice indignant. "You get back to whatever it was you were fixing—I hope it was the sign on the door—and I'll get things organized in here."

"But there isn't a position—" The phone rang, cutting him off.

The woman yanked it up. "Stillman and Sons, how can I help you?"

She had spunk, he conceded. And a decent telephone voice.

"The overdue invoice for Lamberly Printing?"

She glanced at him, and he shook his head in a definite "no." The company simply didn't have the money.

"A check will be cut this afternoon," she sang.

Incredulous, Jack could only stare when she hung up the phone. Then he spat out, "We can't afford to pay that invoice!"

"I said a check will be cut, I didn't say for how much."

Jack pursed his mouth—not bad.

She picked up the greasy bag of food and shoved it into his hand. "Looks like you're having a working lunch." Dismissing him, she turned back to the mound of mail and began to toss junk letters into the trash.

He gaped. "Wait a minute. Who the devil *are* you?"

Without glancing up, she said, "Tuesday Humphrey, your new office manager."

He wondered if the woman was unstable, but her eyes were intelligent, and her hands efficient. Exasperated, Jack lifted his arms. "But we're not hiring an office manager!"

"I know," she said calmly. "Because the position has been filled."

The phone rang again, and she snapped it up. "Stillman and Sons, how can I help you?" Her voice smiled. "Mr. Stillman is in a client meeting, but just a moment, and I'll check." She covered the mouthpiece. "Alexandria Tremont's secretary confirming your appointment at the Tremont headquarters at ten in the morning."

Jack squinted. "But she just *canceled* the appointment."

Tuesday uncovered the mouthpiece. "It was Mr. Stillman's understanding that the appointment was canceled. No? Hold, please, while I see if his schedule will still allow him to attend."

She covered the phone. "It's back on—are you in?"

He nodded, his shoulders sagging in relief.

Tuesday uncovered the mouthpiece. "Yes, ma'am, please tell Ms. Tremont that Mr. Stillman is looking forward to a productive meeting. Thank you for calling." She hung up the phone and returned to her sorting task. "Guess you still have a chance to impress the Tremonts."

"Guess so," he said, his mind racing.

"Well, get moving." She snapped her fingers twice. "We both have a heap of work to do."

Jack hesitated. "An IRS agent is supposed to come by."

"You already told me, remember?" She flung a water sports equipment catalogue into the trash.

His hand shot out in a futile attempt to retrieve the catalogue—he could use a new water ski vest. But at the challenging expression on Tuesday's face, he emitted a resigned sigh. The crazy woman couldn't do more damage to their business or reputation than he had. They had no money to steal, no trade secrets to pilfer, no client list to filch. And at least he wouldn't have to answer the damn phone. "Knock yourself out," he said, splaying his hands. "But I can't pay you."

He stepped into the hall and closed the front door behind him to tackle the lopsided sign first. Within a few moments he'd rehung the smooth plaque of walnut upon which their father had painstakingly lettered and gilded the words "Stillman & Sons Advertising Agency" nearly twenty-five years ago. Without warning, grief billowed in his chest as his father's easy grin rose in his mind.

At his wife's encouragement, Paul Stillman had abandoned his modest home studio to become an entrepreneur when the boys were pre-teens. Jack had viewed the move as an act of treason against his father's natural calling. He'd admired his father's independence, his ability to adequately, if not luxuriously, provide for the family with the lively paintings he sold to local designers and businesses. He hadn't wanted to see his father saddled with overhead and commuting and sixty-hour work weeks, but his father said the earning potential was better, and he owed their mother a retirement fund.

Indeed, his father had set aside a nice nest egg doing graphic artwork and ad plans for small- to medium-size businesses in Lexington, and later, mail order catalogs. Stillman & Sons had been a true family business—their mother ran the office, Derek had cut his accounting teeth on the books. Even Jack had pitched in on occasion, brainstorming with his father on the more creative projects, although the business itself had held—and still held—an unpleasant association for him. He banged down the hammer, connecting with his thumb instead of the nail head, then cursed and sucked away some of the pain.

He'd watched the stress of the agency take its toll on his otherwise carefree father. His hair had seemed to gray overnight, and worry lines had plowed deep into his forehead. His paintbrush and easel had languished, and little by little, Paul Stillman's zest for root beer and whistling and people-watching had drained away.

Oh, his father had remained easygoing enough, but his good cheer seemed forced, and he'd stopped visiting the local art galleries, once a favorite getaway for him and his younger, more creative son. Jack missed those outings and he blamed the family business for taking his father away from him. At thirty-four, he recognized those feelings as childish, but he stubbornly clung to them nonetheless. From his perspective, responsibility sucked the life out of a man and left him with less to offer the very people he was trying to provide for.

Jack pulled a bandanna handkerchief from his back pocket and slowly wiped dust from the plaque. Frowning wryly, he scrubbed especially hard on the ending *s* in "Sons," half hoping the letter would disappear. If truth be known, Derek was the son who deserved the agency—Jack wasn't sure why his brother vehemently insisted he remain a partner.

Predictably, Derek had joined the agency full time when he graduated college, and the family expected nothing less of Jack. Instead, two years later he'd skipped his own graduation ceremony and hitchhiked to New Orleans where he'd put his two degrees—art and international business—to use by becoming the premiere artisan in Blue Willie's infamous tattoo parlor just off Bourbon Street. By some stroke of divine luck, Jack had decided to return to Kentucky two years ago only weeks before a heart attack had claimed his father.

And except for a few "sabbaticals" here and there, he'd remained in Kentucky to help Derek run the agency, which had lapsed into a slow decline after their father had died. Their mother had turned to traveling with her sister, and Derek...well, Derek had turned into a tyrant— although, Jack conceded, he himself hadn't been the model business partner. An unpleasant feeling ballooned in his chest, but he'd always refused to waste time on useless emotions like guilt, remorse, love, or hate. Funny, but all kinds of strange sensations seemed to be rolling around in his empty stomach this morning. It was as if Alexandria Tremont had set the tone for the day. Jack kneaded the tight spot just below his breastbone. The sooner he ate that sandwich, the better.

Swinging open the door, he was startled by a cheerful humming sound. He'd nearly forgotten about the self-proclaimed new office manager. Poor lady—she was probably bored and neglected by her son, looking for some way to kill time. Wonder what Derek would say?

Oh, what the hell, Derek had left *him* in charge, hadn't he?

To her credit, Tuesday had performed small miracles in the few minutes he'd been in the hallway—the mail lay in three neat piles, and the desk and bookshelves fairly gleamed. She had found a radio and tuned in a local light-rock station, which provided the background for her spirited humming.

"Two phone messages," she said, handing him pink slips of paper. "Bill collectors, both of them. I told them our accounting staff was preparing for an audit, and bought you a few days."

Jack grinned. "Great."

"Just a few days," she warned, as she moved around the room, cleaning with what he recognized as his favorite tie-dyed T-shirt, which he'd been looking for. She stopped long enough to shake her finger at him. "So you'd better not blow that meeting tomorrow, young man."

Properly chastised by a virtual stranger, he lifted his hands and escaped into the back office to finish the bookshelf. He tested the unit's sturdiness and methodically replaced the books, but his mind wasn't on the task at hand.

Jack simply couldn't shake the memory of Alexandria Tremont standing there appraising him with her cool, disapproving eyes, her nose conveniently tweaked upward by nature to spare her the trouble of having to lift it when she spoke. He'd seen that look before, the sneer that branded him a loser by people who didn't know that he could have been a hotshot executive had he simply chosen to be. At the meeting tomorrow he'd just have to show the uppity woman that he could hold his own among her kind.

Then he was angry at himself for wanting to impress anyone, much less Alexandria Tremont. He smoothed his ruffled pride by reasoning he was doing it for Derek and for the good of the agency, but anger fueled his energy. By the time he'd returned the books to the shelves and replaced the two lightbulbs, Jack felt that strange prickly feeling again, that alien sensation.

Apprehension? Jack inhaled deeply, but the tightness in his chest didn't diminish. Could be. Derek had certainly complained enough about being apprehensive over one thing or another—perhaps this roiling nausea was why his brother kept a bottle of Pepto-Bismol in his desk and in the glove compartment of his ultraconservative car.

Jack stooped to retrieve a can of beer from his desk drawer, but froze when he heard raised voices from the front office. The IRS agent? He slipped into his shoes, removed the tool belt, and jogged to the front, but his feet faltered when he saw that Tuesday had a suited man pinned facedown on the desk, one arm behind him. The man's face was a mask of pain.

"Tuesday!" Jack bellowed. "What the devil are you doing?" He reached for her hands and pried them loose from the visitor's arm, despite her protests.

"I'm trying to help the poor man," she insisted, resisting Jack. "He said his back was hurting, so I gave him an adjustment."

"This maniac popped a bone in my neck," the red-faced man yelped. "She probably crippled me!"

When at last he righted the man to a seated position, Jack shoved his hands on his hips and glared at Tuesday while introducing himself to the stranger. "I'm Jack Stillman, and I apologize, Mr.—?"

"Stripling," the smallish man chirped, straightening his tie. "Marion Stripling, IRS."

Jack closed his eyes. *Marion*—no wonder Derek had told him to expect a female. "I apologize, Mr. Stripling, for this woman's—" he shot her a lethal look "—complete lapse in judgment. Truthfully, I don't even know her myself."

The man looked incredulous. "What, did she just wander in off the street?"

"Something like that," Jack mumbled.

"What kind of a loony bin operation are you running here?"

"One that's losing money," Jack assured him. "Mr.

Stripling, this way back to my desk, please. I need to have a word with my *office manager*."

The man scowled in Tuesday's direction, then picked up his briefcase and fled in the direction Jack indicated.

Jack turned back to Tuesday. "Well?"

She maintained a haughty position. "My late husband was a chiropractor. When Mr. Stripling told me he'd been delayed because of back pain, I was simply trying to help."

His eyes widened. "By holding him down against his will and popping a bone in his neck?"

She wagged a finger in the air, her hip cocked to one side. "You'll see, he'll be thanking me."

"*You'll* see, he'll be *suing* me!" Jack sputtered, then held his temples, at a loss what to do next.

The phone rang, and she jerked it up. "Stillman and Sons, Lexington's number one advertising agency. How can I help you? Yes, hold please." She covered the mouthpiece, then smiled sweetly and held the phone in Jack's direction. "It's your brother."

3

ALEX STRETCHED HIGH to relieve the pressure of bending over the desk in her apartment for the past hour, then reached for the crystal goblet of white wine she'd been nursing since arriving home from her typical twelve-hour day. Using her stockinged foot, she levered the chair around to stare over the lights of downtown Lexington. It was another in a string of unusually warm October evenings. On impulse, she'd opened the sliding glass door leading to her balcony to dilute the stale air in her condo. The fresh breeze and the view revived her.

The University of Kentucky was having some kind of sports function because the streets leading to campus were choked. Not particularly fond of sports, she nonetheless recognized the huge economic advantage of having a popular college athletic program in town: athletics attracted attention for the university, swelling the student population, and college students remained the strongest buying group for the local Tremont department stores.

Alex swallowed a mouthful of chardonnay, thinking she should attend a college game of some sort with her father, a bona fide sports nut, just to see what all the fuss was about. On the other hand, Heath would undoubtedly take her in grand style if she wanted to go, even though he wasn't much of a sports buff either.

Heath Reddinger had been scrupulously accommodating to both her and her father since joining the senior management of Tremont's as Chief Financial Officer. She had liked him immediately—he was handsome, intelligent and sensitive. Her father, on the other hand, had never taken to Heath, although Al appreciated his contribution to the company, and had nodded in acquiescence when she and Heath had become engaged two months ago. Alex smiled as she fingered the diamond solitaire he'd given her. Heath was hard-working, predictable and fairly low-maintenance. She appreciated men with nice, neat edges.

Her smile faded when the face of Jack Stillman appeared to taunt her. The unkempt man was a loose cannon. She knew instinctively he was just the kind of man who could stir her father to rebellion. But she was determined to work with the St. Louis ad firm who could put Tremont's on the same page as Roark's and Tofelson's— two southeastern chains with toeholds in Louisville which, according to a survey she'd commissioned in her position as Director of Marketing and Sales, were ranked higher than Tremont's in perception of quality and style. In layman's terms, the other stores were deemed more classy than Tremont's. But the St. Louis ad agency could change all that. Just last year, they'd taken an unknown soft drink into the sales stratosphere with an award-winning campaign.

Her phone rang, rousing her. Heath's name appeared on the caller ID screen, so she picked up the cordless extension, along with her goblet of wine and headed toward the kitchen. "Hello."

"Hi, honey."

She stopped to straighten a pillow on the sofa—living in an open loft apartment meant everything had to be in its place. "Hi. Did you get my message?"

"Yes. Do you want me to come over?"

They hadn't slept together in weeks, but she simply wasn't up to his lengthy, methodical foreplay rituals tonight, not with work issues weighing on her mind. "I'm really tired, and my day is packed tomorrow."

"Oh, okay." Agreeable, as always. "By the way, Al asked me to sit in on the morning meeting with the local ad agency. I hope that's okay with you."

She'd suspected as much—her father was gathering supporters, and he knew Heath was anxious to gain his favor. Alex pursed her mouth, weighing her response. "That's why I called, although I personally think the meeting will be a waste of time. I paid the agency a surprise visit today and the owner is a Neanderthal."

"Hmm. Did you tell your father?"

"Sure, but he insists on going through with this charade because of a promise he made to the former owner of the agency."

"Well." Heath hesitated, always a little nervous when she disagreed with her father. "I guess it'll be a short meeting."

"Uh-huh," she agreed as she moved into the tiny blue and chrome kitchen nook situated in a corner. "I'm sure you'll agree with me wholeheartedly once you meet this character." She recorked the wine bottle and returned it to a shelf in the refrigerator door. "We'll have to stick together to convince Daddy that we need to elevate the quality of the firms we do business with. You know—being judged by the company we keep, and all that jazz."

"Okay," he agreed, but he sounded as if he were sitting on a fence row, casting glances on either side.

She tore off a paper towel and wiped a ring of moisture gathered on the tile counter where the bottle had sat. "Maybe we can have dinner tomorrow night."

"Great! I'll make reservations at Gerrard's."

Her favorite—Heath was such a gentleman. For a few seconds, she reconsidered having him come over, then decided guiltily that she needed the sleep more than the physical attention. "Gerrard's sounds wonderful. I'll talk to you tomorrow."

After disconnecting the call, Alex removed the pins from her hair and sighed, feeling restless and antsy for some reason she couldn't quite put her finger on. She grabbed a magazine and her half-full glass, then fell into her white overstuffed chair-and-a-half and propped her feet on the matching ottoman. With the pull of a delicate chain, she turned on a Tiffany-style floor lamp and fingered the large porcelain bead at the end of the chain, studying the intricate design she had memorized long ago.

The lamp had been a moving-in gift from her mother when Alex had first bought the spacious loft condo. She wasn't sure which one of them was more excited with the find, but then her mother had passed away suddenly, before they'd had a chance to decorate the unique space together. Alex knew it sounded corny, but when she sat under the lamp, she felt as if her mother's spirit glowed all around her. She sipped from her glass, and idly fingered the pages of the magazine, subconsciously absorbing the latest styles, colors and accessories. The store carried that line of coats...that line of separates...that line of belts.

Jack Stillman...Jack Stillman. Alex laid her head back and frowned at the antique tin ceiling she'd painted a luminous pewter. Why did his name tickle the back of her memory? Perhaps it was just one of those names...

A frenzied knock on her door interrupted her thoughts. She knew who it was even before she pushed herself to her feet and padded across the white wood floor, but she checked the peephole just in case. Lana Martina, friend, fool, and neighbor, peered back at her, her arched white eyebrows high and promising.

Alex's spirits lifted instantly—Lana was a full-fledged, flat-out, certified nut who just happened to have taken a liking to quiet, scholarly Alex while they were in high school. Within the halls of their private Catholic school, Lana was a walking scandal, her pleated skirt always a little too short, her polished nails always a little too long. But her incredible intellect had kept the nuns at bay. In fact, Alex had met her on the debate team, and while the girls couldn't have come from more different backgrounds, they had formed a lasting friendship.

Alex swung open the door, smiling when she saw Lana held two pint-sized cartons of ready-to-spread cake frosting. "Mocha cocoa with artificial flavoring?" her friend asked, reading from the labels. "Or fantasy fudge with lots of nasty preservatives?"

"Fantasy fudge," Alex said, standing aside to allow Lana in. Her friend was as slim as a mannequin, but her personality needed as much room as possible.

"I brought utensils," Lana said, holding up two silver dessert spoons. "It's such a pain to get chocolate out from under your fingernails."

Alex took the proffered spoon and carton of icing, then followed Lana to the sitting area. Having performed this ritual countless times, they assumed their respective corners of the comfy red couch, Alex's feet curled beneath her, Lana sitting cross-legged.

"Nice silver," Alex observed, studying the intricate pattern on the end of the heavy spoon.

"It belongs to Vile Vicki." Lana ripped the foil covering off the top of her carton.

"You *stole* her silver?"

"Borrowed," Lana corrected, dipping in her spoon and shoveling in a mound of chocolate big enough to choke two men. "She's such a witch," she said thickly.

Alex smiled, then spooned in a less impressive amount of the creamy fudge icing, allowing the sweet, chocolaty flavor to melt over her tongue before she responded. "She can't be that bad."

"You don't live with her," Lana insisted. "The woman is simply the most self-absorbed, tedious, annoying female I've ever met."

"There's Gloria the Gold Digger," Alex said, pointing her spoon.

"At least she was smart enough to marry your father."

"True," Alex conceded with a sigh. Hopes that she and her father would become closer after her mother died had been dashed by Gloria Bickum Georgeson Abrams. The woman had brought a disposable pan of the most hideous macaroni salad to their home after her mother's funeral, and had been underfoot ever since.

"I swear, Alex, I'm going to kill her."

"Gloria?"

"No, Vicki. Do you know what she did?"

"I can't guess."

"Guess."

"I can't."

"Sure you can."

Alex sighed. "Borrowed your suede coat again?"

"She *ruined* it. No, worse."

"Forgot to pay a bill?"

"I had to flash the cable man so he wouldn't cut us off. But it's worse."

"What?"

"Guess."

"Lana—"

"She's dating Bill Friar."

Alex swallowed. "Oh." Lana was the most popular, outgoing woman she knew, and her looks were extraordinary, if offbeat—classic bone structure and violet-colored eyes allowed her to pull off spiky bleach-white hair. But Lexington men did not stand in line for eccentric-looking women with an I.Q. that put her on the Mensa mailing list. Bill Friar had seemed to be the exception—at first. Then the big phony had broken her friend's big heart.

"Yeah, 'oh,' is right." Lana shoveled in another huge bite. "She has the nerve to rub it in my face."

Alex felt a pang for her friend. "Are they getting serious?"

"No, she's dating a dozen other guys. She only went out with him to get back at me."

"How did she know you and Bill were once an item?"

Lana stirred the spoon aimlessly, her eyebrows drawn together. "She read my diary."

Alex sucked on her spoon, her eyes wide. "She didn't."

"She did and, just watch, I'm going to get her back."

"Why don't you just find another roommate?"

"We both signed the lease, so I'm stuck for another eight months, but after that, I'm outta there. Meanwhile," Lana said, holding up the ornate spoon, "I'm going to borrow *her* things for a while. These are her earrings, too."

Alex leaned forward to get a better look at the copper spheres. "Nice."

"Aren't they? So what's new with you?" Lana asked, fully vented and ready to listen. "I phoned you this morning for lunch, but your secretary said you were out."

"I was running an errand on the east side."

"Eww. Why?"

Alex took another slow bite before answering. "Ever hear of a guy named Jack Stillman?"

Her friend blinked. "Sure. Hotshot receiver for UK when we were freshmen. Don't you remember?"

Alex worked her mouth from side to side. "Maybe, maybe not."

"Great looking, big man on campus, dated the varsity *and* the junior varsity cheerleading squads."

"He sounds pretty forgettable."

Lana laughed. "He had a perfect record his senior year—never once dropped the ball. Of course I'm not surprised you don't remember. You practically slept at the store back then to impress Daddy, not that things have changed much in fifteen years." Her smile was teasing. "You really need to get out more, Alex."

"Heath and I go out."

"That tree? *Please.* My blow up doll Harry is more exciting."

Alex had heard Lana's lukewarm opinion on Heath too many times to let the comment bother her. So he wasn't Mr. Excitement—she didn't mind. "To each her own."

Lana put away another glob of empty calories. "I suppose. Why the questions about Jack Stillman?"

"He owns an ad agency in town and he's pitching to us in the morning."

"Well, I guess he grew up after all."

"I wouldn't go that far," Alex said dryly. "This morning I dropped in to check out his operation and had the displeasure of meeting the man."

Lana leaned forward, poised for gossip. "Is he still gorgeous?"

"I couldn't tell under that heavy layer of male chauvinism."

Her friend frowned, then her mouth fell open. "He got under your skin, didn't he?"

Alex squirmed against the suddenly uncomfortable overstuffed goose down cushions. "Not in the way you're implying."

Lana whooped. "Oh, yeah, under like a syringe."

She sighed, exasperated. "Lana, believe me, the man is no one I would remotely want to work with."

"So, who's talking about work?"

Alex rolled her eyes. "Or anything else. He's a player if I've ever seen one, and the man doesn't exactly scream success, if you know what I mean."

Lana made a sympathetic sound. "Too bad. He used to be hot."

"I believe he still operates under that delusion."

"So you don't think he'll get your business?"

"Not if I can help it."

"Well, let me know how it goes," Lana said, standing and stretching into a yawn.

Alex frowned. "You have to go already?"

"Four-thirty comes mighty early."

"When are you going to buy that coffee shop?"

"Maybe when I acquire a taste for the dreadful stuff," her friend said with a grimace. "I still keep a stash of Earl Grey under the counter. I'm busy tomorrow, but let's have lunch the day after and you can let me know how it goes with Jack the Attack."

"Jack the Attack?"

Lana nodded toward the wall of bookshelves. "Check your college yearbook, bookworm. Goodnight."

"Here's your spoon."

Lana grinned. "Keep it."

Alex was still laughing when the door closed behind
her friend, but sobered when Jack Stillman's face rose in
her mind to taunt her. The man was shaping up to be
more of a potential threat than she'd imagined. She
walked over to a laden bookshelf and removed the yearbook for her freshman year of college. Within seconds,
she located the sports section and, as Lana had said, it
seemed that Jack Stillman had been the man of the hour.
Although UK was renowned for all of its team sports
programs, Jack the Attack had been heralded for single-
handedly taking his football team to a prestigious post-
season bowl game, and winning it.

Page after page showed Jack in various midmotion
poses: catching the football, running past opponents,
crossing into the end zone. The last page featured Jack in
his mud-stained uniform, arm in arm with a casually
dressed man who was a taller, wider version of himself,
behind whose unsuspecting head Jack was holding up
two fingers in the universal "jackass" symbol. Twenty-
two-year-old Jack had the same killer grin, the same mischievous eyes, with piles of dark, unruly hair in a hope-
lessly dated style. Alex smirked as she mentally
compared the boy in the picture to the man she'd met this
morning. Too bad he was such a cliché—a washed-up
jock still chasing pom-poms.

Alex snapped the book closed. The ex-football star angle worried her. Her father was already aware of it, she
was sure, and the fact that he hadn't taken the time to en-
lighten her probably meant he would bend over backward to work with Stillman just to be able to tell the guys
at the club about the man's athletic accomplishments.

Anger burned the walls of her stomach, anger about
the old boy's network, anger toward men who shirked
their duties but advanced to high-ranking corporate po-

sitions because they had a low golf handicap and could sweat with male executives in the sauna. Subtle discrimination occurred within Tremont's, although she was working judiciously to address disparity within the sales and marketing division. And subtle discrimination occurred within her own family. Had she been a son, an athlete, she was certain her father would have showered her with attention, would have fostered her career more aggressively. She ached for the closeness that she'd once shared with her mother, but that seemed so out of reach with her father.

She blinked back tears, feeling very alone in the big, high-ceilinged apartment. Fatigue pulled at her shoulders, but the sugar she'd ingested pumped through her system. She needed sleep, but her bed, custom made of copper tubing and covered with a crisp white duvet, looked sterile and cold in the far corner of the rectangular-shaped loft.

Alex located her glass of wine and finished it while standing at the sink. Knowing the ritual of preparing for bed sometimes helped her insomnia, she moved toward the bedroom corner to undress. After draping the pale blue suit over a chrome valet, she dropped her matching underwear into a lacy laundry bag. From the back of her armoire, she withdrew a nappy, yellow cotton robe of her mother's and wrapped it around her. After removing her makeup with more vehemence than necessary, she walked past her bed and returned to the comfy chair she'd abandoned when Lana arrived, covering her legs with a lightweight afghan.

But she lay awake long after she'd extinguished her mother's light, straining with unexplainable loneliness and frustration, stewing over unjust conditions she might never be able to change. Right or wrong, she channeled her hostility toward the one person who, at the moment, best epitomized life's arbitrary inequities: Jack Stillman. Clod-hopping his way through life and having the Tremont business laid at his feet because he was a man and a former sports celebrity simply wasn't fair.

Remembering Lana's words, Alex set her jaw in determination. Perfect record be damned. The infamous "Jack the Attack" Stillman had already dropped the ball—he just didn't know it yet.

4

"*DON'T DROP THE BALL, JACK.*"

Derek's words from much earlier in the workday reverberated in his head. In the middle of the crisis with the IRS guy, Jack had somehow explained away Tuesday's presence—later he'd given her a fifty dollar bill and told her not to come back—and he managed to convince Derek that he had everything under control, including the Tremont's presentation.

Jack swore, then tore yet another sheet from his newsprint drawing pad, wadded it into a ball, and tossed it over his shoulder with enough force to risk dislocating his elbow. His muse had truly abandoned him this time. Three-thirty in the morning, with no revelation in sight. Forget the printer—this presentation would have to consist of raw drawings and hand-lettering.

If he ever came up with an idea, that is.

"Think, man, think," he muttered, tapping his charcoal pencil on the end of the desk, conjuring up key words to spark his imagination. *Clothes, style, fashion, home decor.* He needed a catchy phrase to convince people to shop at Tremont's.

Shop till you drop at Tremont's spot.

If you got the money, honey, we got the goods.

Spend a lot of dough at Tremont's sto'.

Okay, so he was really rusty, but at least it was a start. He sketched out a few unremarkable ideas, but a heavy stone of dread settled in his stomach—this was not the best stuff that had ever come out of his pencil. The tight little bow of Alexandria Tremont's disapproving mouth had dogged him all evening. The woman obviously didn't expect much and, despite his efforts to the contrary, that was exactly what he was going to deliver. Dammit, he hated wanting to impress her...not that it mattered now.

Pouring himself another cup of coffee from a battered thermos, he raked a hand over his stubbly face and leaned back in his chair. Jack winced as the strong, bitter brew hit his taste buds at the same time a bitter truth hit his gut: He was washed up. Being at the top of his game—no matter what the arena—used to come so easily, and now he was struggling for mere mediocrity.

His college football career had been a joyous four-year ride of accolades, trophies and popularity—a young man's dream that afforded him unbelievable perks, including as many beautiful women as he could handle, and enough good memories to last a lifetime. But for all his local celebrity and natural talent, he hadn't even considered going pro, partly because he didn't want to put his body through the paces, and partly because he'd simply wanted to do more with his life, to strike out and experience new settings, new people. And frankly, he'd always hated doing what was expected of him, whether it meant playing pro football or working for the family ad agency. Until now, he hadn't realized how much he missed striving for something beyond having enough beer to wash down the native food of wherever he happened to be.

But inexplicably, the yearning that had lodged in his stomach the previous day had permeated other vital organs until he could feel it, see it, breathe it—the need to achieve. The need to make something out of nothing. The need to prove to others that he could hack it in any environment. The need to prove to himself that he still had his edge. And, he admitted with the kind of brutal honesty that comes to a man in the wee hours of the morning, Alexandria Tremont played a startling role in his reawakening. Just the thought of the challenge in her ice-blue eyes brought long dormant feelings of aspiration zooming to the surface. He hadn't felt this alive since he was carried off the football field on the shoulders of his teammates for the last time. He wanted this win so badly, he could taste her—er, it.

The rush of adrenaline continued to feed his brain, which churned until the light of early dawn seeped through the windows. Jack discarded idea after idea, but he refused to give up hope that something fantastic would occur to him.

Around seven, and with little to show for his sleepless night, Jack heard a scratching sound on the front door. He went to investigate, stapler in hand for lack of a better weapon. To his abject consternation, Tuesday opened the door and marched inside, flipping on lights as she went. She wore an attractive flowered skirt and a modest blouse. "Morning," she sang.

"How'd you get in?" he demanded.

She held up a Tremont's department store credit card, of all things. "I jiggled the lock—this is no Fort Knox, sonny. You're here early."

"I didn't leave," he said, scowling. "And I thought I told you not to come back."

"You were having a bad day," she said cheerfully. "So I thought I'd give you another chance." She leaned toward him and grimaced. "Oooh, you don't look so good."

"I know."

"Did you finish the presentation?"

"Yes."

"Is it good?"

"No."

She sighed, a sorrowful noise. "Well, you'll have to wow them with charm, I suppose." She squinted, angling her head. "What were you planning to wear?"

He looked down at his disheveled beach clothes and shrugged. "I hadn't thought about it, but I'm sure I can rustle up a sport coat."

Tuesday grunted and picked up the phone. "What are you, about a forty-four long?"

He shrugged again, then nodded. "As best as I can remember."

She looked him up and down. "Six-three?"

Again, he nodded.

"Size twelve shoe?"

"Thirteen if I can get them. Why?"

Tuesday waved her hand in a shooing motion. "Go take a shower and shave that hairy face. Hurry, and yell for me when you're finished."

Jack wasn't sure if he was simply too tired to argue, or just glad to have someone tell him what to do. The Tremont's account was lost now anyway—he would merely go through the motions for Derek's sake.

He retreated to the bathroom in the back, grateful for the shower the landlord had thought to build. Shaving had never been a favorite chore, and it took some time to clear the dark scruff from his jaw. He checked in the cabinet on the wall, and sure enough, Derek had left a couple pairs of underwear, along with a pair of faded jeans and a few T-shirts. Derek was more thick-bodied than he, but the underwear would work. Jack had barely snapped the waistband in place when an impatient knock sounded at the door.

"You through in there?"

"Give me a second," he called, then wrapped a towel around his waist before opening the door.

Tuesday strode in, carrying a comb and a pair of scissors.

"Oh, no," Jack said, shaking his head. "You're *not* cutting my hair."

"Oh, yes," she said, motioning for him to sit on the commode lid. "That woolliness has to come off. Come on, now, don't argue."

He stubbornly crossed his arms and remained standing.

She pointed the scissors at him. "Don't make me climb up there. Do you want to blow this chance completely?"

Jack sighed and shook his head.

"Then sit."

He sat. And she cut. And cut and cut and cut.

Cringing at the mounds of dark hair accumulating on the floor around him, Jack pleaded, "Gee, at least leave me enough to comb."

She stepped back, made a few final snips, then nodded and whipped off the towel protecting his shoulders. "There, you look human again." Tuesday exited the bathroom with purpose.

Half afraid to look in the mirror, Jack did so one eye at a time. Damn. He pursed his mouth and lifted a hand to his sheared head. It was short, but it didn't look half bad. He turned sideways and ran a hand over the back of his neck. "Long time, no see," he murmured. He leaned over the sink and wet his short hair, then combed it back. "Hello, ears."

"Here you go, handsome."

Tuesday was back, this time holding a vinyl suit bag.

"Suit, shirt, cuff links, tie, socks, belt and shoes, size twelve—your toes'll be pinched just a mite."

Jack's eyes widened. "Where did you get this stuff?"

"My son, Reggie," she said. "Remember, he works for Tremont's?"

"Oh, right," he said. "Menswear?"

She nodded. "Natty dresser, my Reggie." She handed him the bag. "Clothes make the man, you know."

Touched, Jack reached for the bag, then stopped and stared at her. "Tuesday, you're a genius."

She gave him a dismissive wave. "I know that, son. What took you so long to catch on?"

Jack unzipped the bag, his mind jumping ahead to his blank sketch pad. He had about an hour to get a new idea down on paper.

"Tuesday, I'm going to be cutting it close. Will you call me a taxi?" A trip across town on his motorcycle might compromise the condition of his portfolio, he realized.

"I did. It'll be here at a quarter to ten," she said, then turned and closed the door.

Jack grinned at his own reflection, suddenly feeling young again. He was back, and good wasn't a big enough word to express how he felt. He felt...he felt...*energized.* And lucky. And teeming with fiery anticipation at the look on the ice princess's face when he walked through the door.

"Look out, Ms. Alexandria Tremont," he murmured. "Ready or not, here I come."

THE FAVORITE PART of Alex's day was walking through the various departments of Tremont's before the doors opened to the public. This morning, she acknowledged, the routine also served to soothe her anxiety about the impending advertising meeting. Actually, she felt a little sorry for Jack Stillman—the clueless man was in way over his swollen head. But regardless of her opinion of him and his agency, she honestly didn't enjoy watching people make fools of themselves. Alex sighed and sipped coffee from a stoneware mug. Hopefully the meeting would be mercifully short.

Her mood considerably lighter this morning than the previous evening, the store seemed exceptionally pleasing: the sweep of formal gowns on so-slim mannequins, the musky blend of popular perfumes, the neat stacks of thick towels on cherry tables, the flash of silver tea sets. In the past decade, Tremont's had made the subtle move from a discount department store to a more upscale shopping experience for the upper-middle class of Lexington and the surrounding area. Alex liked to believe her sales and marketing policies of pushing retail boundaries had something to do with the transformation.

She stopped to compliment Carla, one of the most senior salesclerks who always arrived at her station in the jewelry department early enough to give the glass counter an extra swipe, then Alex moved toward the stairs by way of menswear. A tall well-dressed youth was tagging slacks for alterations, his hands moving swiftly. Alex's mind raced as she tried to recall his name—she'd seen it at the top of the commission lists often enough. Ronnie? No, Reggie.

"Good morning, Reggie."

He jerked up his head and dropped the pants he held. "G-good morning, Ms. Tremont," he said as he hurriedly knelt to retrieve the clothes. "Sorry, I'm clumsy today."

Alex dipped to help him. "Nonsense." But she did squint at his dark head that was tilted down. She'd spoken to the young man several times and she'd never known him to be nervous, yet his hands were practically shaking. "Is everything all right, Reggie?"

"Hmm? Oh, yes, ma'am. Just fine." But he made only fleeting eye contact as he straightened.

"Good." Alex stood and brushed off the behavior with a smile, then rescued a navy and gray barber-pole striped tie in danger of falling from a display table. "Are the new ties selling well?"

Glancing at the tie she'd smoothed, he swallowed, sending his Adam's apple dancing. "Yes, ma'am. Especially the C-Coakley line."

"My personal favorite," she said, pleased that the line of ties her father had gruffly pronounced as "damnably expensive" were selling well despite the admittedly steep price tags. "Keep up the good work, Reggie."

Her chunky-heeled black leather pumps felt nice and solid against the polished marble floor as she walked toward the stairs. The stairs themselves, although a mainstay in her casual exercise program, were a bit of a test today in her shorter than usual skirt—black crepe with no slit. She climbed the four flights of stairs slowly to prevent perspiration from gathering on the paper thin indigo blouse beneath the black jacket. Near the top, she checked her watch. Nine-thirty. Just enough time to grab another cup of coffee and sift through the previous week's sales figures. Might as well head for the conference room early and claim a good vantage point. Things could get interesting, and she wanted a view.

Her secretary Tess, an efficient and animated young woman who studied fashion merchandising at night, was holding out the sales reports before Alex even reached the woman's desk.

"Thanks, Tess."

"You look tired."

So much for her new under-eye concealer. "I guess I need more caffeine."

"Let me get your coffee, Ms. Tremont." Despite Alex's numerous requests for Tess to call her by her first name, her secretary insisted on addressing her formally. Before Alex could protest, Tess had relieved her of the stoneware mug and refilled it with black Irish roast from a coffeemaker on a credenza. "Do you have anything for me to add to your agenda today?"

"No," Alex said, inclining her head in thanks as she took the mug. "Just be on the lookout for a Mr. Jack Stillman for the ten o'clock meeting, and show him to the boardroom, please."

"How will I know him?" Tess asked, her green eyes wide and interested.

Alex bit back a smirk. Her pretty secretary was a bit of a flirt, and always perked up when a man came around. Shaggy Jack Stillman was probably right up her alley, too. "Believe me, you can't miss him." She shook her head good-naturedly as she walked down the hall to the executive conference room, nodding good morning to a half-dozen peers and subordinates as she went. Tess ran through men like most women ran through panty hose.

Alex frowned down at her own durable black hose. Funny, she hadn't bought a new pair in ages.

At the door to the conference room, she hesitated only a second before stepping inside. In her opinion, these four walls encompassed the most unappealing space in the entire five-story building. Alex had attempted to overhaul the depressing room many times, but she'd finally tired of butting heads with her father, who insisted the conference room be left as is. *As is*, however, was an oppressive collection of dark, clubby wood bookshelves studded with sports paraphernalia. A thoroughly masculine domain, the three darkly paneled walls adorned with gaping fish frozen into curling leaps, and worse, two antlered deer heads. Alex felt nauseous every time she looked at the poor creatures.

The furniture wasn't much better, the bulky chairs so unwieldy she could barely move them in and out from the broad-legged table. She chose the chair at the head of the table, farthest from the door. After setting down her coffee cup and the reports, she crossed the gloomy room to open the window blinds on the outside wall. As far as she was concerned, the sole good feature of the room was the view.

Rolling hills of pasture land and forests provided a backdrop for the modest Lexington skyline. The fiery October hues threw the white board fences encircling distant grazing land into stark relief. The flying hooves of two yearlings sprinting across a slanted field reminded her that fall horse racing season at Keeneland started in a couple of days. Alex smiled, momentarily distracted, and experienced a rush of gratitude to be living in such a beautiful area.

Winding, tree-lined roads led residents into the downtown area, a myriad of old tobacco warehouses, new office buildings, slender town houses and fountained courtyards. Brick, stone, metal, concrete, glass, water, one- and two-way streets—all these elements combined to create the casual, eclectic cityscape that embodied Lexington: part urban, part rural, totally accommodating.

Tremont's flagship store and administrative offices occupied a five-story building on Webster Avenue just a few blocks from the center of downtown, and walking distance from Alex's loft apartment. They had managed to compete with the malls by building an adjacent parking structure and, at her persistent urging, by developing a food court on the entire first floor of the building, including a sidewalk café that had become very popular with the business lunch crowd and the Junior League. As a result, gift shops and service businesses had popped up all around them.

Alex sipped her coffee, feeling very much like a proud parent admiring her offspring. She had contributed to the growth of Tremont's, and Tremont's played a vital role in the downtown economy. Long after she was gone, Tremont's would be a living, breathing entity, a legacy of her father's and her own and her children's impact on the city and the state. The knowledge pleased her immensely.

As she stared down at the street, a red taxicab pulled alongside the opposite sidewalk, and a man alighted. Bound for the financial building two doors down, she suspected, then she squinted to study the man in the distance as he leaned inside to pay the driver. He certainly looked the part of a money man—commanding figure, dark hair, proper suit. Her tongue poked deep into her cheek. And he wasn't a bad-looking fellow, either.

"What's so interesting?"

She dropped the blind, turned, and conjured up a smile for Heath Reddinger, who looked fair and fit and smart in his navy pinstripe suit and tortoiseshell-rimmed glasses. "Just people-watching."

His forehead furrowed. "Alex, you look tired. I thought you were going to bed early last night."

"I did," she said, telling herself she should feel flattered by his concern rather than faintly annoyed. "I'm fine, really."

Heath glanced back toward the door to ensure they were alone. They both agreed not to flaunt their relationship during work hours. "I'm sorry, but I have to cancel dinner tonight," he said. "I just discovered I'm needed in Cincinnati. I'm leaving this afternoon."

"For how long?" She'd been looking forward to a relaxing evening together, and to the sea bass at Gerrard's.

"No more than a couple of days, I think."

Alex frowned. "A problem with our bank?"

Heath sipped his creamed coffee before he answered. "No problem, just an issue. Can I get a rain check on dinner?"

She nodded, respectful of Heath's dedication to her father's company.

Heath reached forward and smoothed a finger back from her temple. "Maybe we should plan a long weekend away when I get back, hmm?"

A light rapping on the door accompanied by Tess clearing her throat diverted Alex's attention over Heath's shoulder. The flash of irritation that her secretary had been privy to the intimate gesture and conversation was quickly replaced by her puzzlement at the tall gentleman standing next to a beaming Tess. A memory cord stirred at the base of Alex's brain, and she realized the dark-headed visitor was the same man she'd watched climb out of the taxi on the street below. A salesman, of course. What else would a man as handsome as he be doing for a living? Riveting dark eyes, tanned, planed features, immaculate suit. No wonder Tess looked like she'd been plugged into an electrical transformer. Alex grudgingly indulged in a twinge of appreciation of her own—the man was...noteworthy.

Alex stepped around Heath. "Yes, Tess?"

"Mr. Stillman is here."

Alex blinked, wondering why Tess had announced Stillman's arrival before introducing the salesman. Her gaze darted to the man, and one side of his mouth curved upward. Confusion flooded her.

"Good morning, Ms. Tremont," the man said in a hauntingly familiar voice.

5

A FULL FIFTEEN SECONDS passed before Alex made the connection that this...paragon...was the same wild-eyed, bushy-headed, scruffy-faced irreverent vagrant she'd spoken to yesterday. Her jaw loosened a bit, and her mind raced, trying to reconcile the two images.

Meanwhile, Jack Stillman seemed to be enjoying every minute of her discomfort. His dark eyes—brown? green?—alight with the barest hint of amusement, never left her face. Her heart pumped wildly, sending hot apprehension to her limbs while alarms sounded in her ears. His full-fledged grin catapulted his unnerving energy across the space between them to wrap around her. Alex resisted the pull, leaning into the conference room table until the hard edge bit into the front of her thighs. This man was dangerous, and she would do well to keep her distance, and to keep her wits about her.

"Good morning, Mr. Stillman," she replied coolly, then gestured toward the opposite end of the table. "Won't you have a seat?" Getting the man off his feet would give her the slightest advantage.

Instead of answering, he strode toward Heath and extended his hand. "Jack Stillman of the Stillman & Sons Agency."

Heath introduced himself, and Alex could have kicked herself for her gaffe. The men shook hands, although the set of Heath's chin emanated a certain wariness. Bobby

Warner, a fellow sales director and her prime competition for the vice presidency walked in with his signature swagger, then gaped at Jack.

"You're not the Jack Stillman who played for UK in the early eighties?"

Jack dimpled. "Guilty."

Behind them, Alex rolled her eyes.

"I'll never forget that sixty-six-yard touchdown against Tennessee in eighty-four," Bobby said, stepping back to feign a catch while Alex stared. She could count on her colleagues to overlook Jack Stillman's exaggerated celebrity and do what was best for the company... couldn't she?

To her relief, several other associates entered the room—the public relations director, another sales director, two vice presidents and a couple of marketing assistants—chatting among themselves. She left the introductions to Bobby, who seemed disturbingly chummy with Jack Stillman after only three and a half minutes. The group body language concerned her. The men leaned toward him, hands in pockets, athletically wide-legged— even Rudy Claven, who hadn't missed being a woman by much, and was teased mercilessly by the company softball team for "throwing like a girl." And the four women in the room seemed to hang on to every detail as Bobby ingratiatingly expanded on Jack's scoffing I'm-not-a-legend preamble.

Ugh.

Alex pretended to mingle as they waited for her father, but instead studied Jack from beneath her lashes, part of her marveling over his physical transformation, all of her wary to the point of nervous tension. He panned his audience to include everyone in a glory-days anecdote he'd probably recounted a thousand times, and his gaze seemed to linger on her longer than necessary.

Men were like cats, she observed, pretending to study her watch. The more you ignored them, the more they wanted your attention. She forced herself not to listen to Jack Stillman's words, although his baritone was impossible to shut out. Someone had found a photo of the '85 UK football team among the cluttered bookshelves, and there he was, Jack pointed out as everyone crowded around, then launched into a story about the fellow who sat next to him. Within seconds, everyone was laughing.

Oh, brother. Alex took a deep gulp of coffee and scalded her tongue. "Dammit!"

Her expletive coincided with a lull in the laughter and seemed to reverberate from the dark walls. Everyone turned to stare, including Jack, whose eyes danced with amusement as she ran her tender tongue against the roof of her mouth. She had the strongest urge to stick it out at him.

"Problem, my dear?" her father asked, strolling into the room with all the casual ease of a man who owned the floors, walls and ceilings. At last everyone fell away from Jack Stillman and headed toward the table, scrupulously avoiding the chair opposite Alex, reserved for her father, of course.

"No," she said somewhat thickly, walking around the table. "Allow me to introduce Mr. St—"

"*Jack Stillman*," her father cut in, pumping the visitor's hand, his broad face creasing in a grin reserved only for the most privileged. "*Jack the Attack.*"

Alex wanted to heave.

"It's a pleasure to meet you, Mr. Tremont," Jack said, looking duly humbled.

"Aren't you in top form," her father said. "Nice suit, son. One of ours, I do believe."

Jack nodded and smoothed the sleeve of his charcoal-gray suit. "Your private label."

She'd been so distracted by the change in his appearance, she hadn't noticed he was wearing one of the most expensive suits they carried. Brownnoser.

"Nice tie, too," her father continued with an appraising nod.

Over his crisply starched white shirt, Jack was sporting a tie identical to the gray and navy barber-pole striped one she'd fingered earlier this morning, one in the line her father had scoffed at, but suddenly thought was "nice."

Her father turned to the assembled group and beamed while clapping Jack on the back. "He wears our clothes. The man is talented *and* smart."

They obliged with a round of laughter while Alex fumed. As far as she was concerned, the man was a fraud, and his presentation would undoubtedly reflect his ineptitude. After all, clothes did *not* make the man.

"Shall we start the meeting?" she asked over the din, irritated when Jack sat next to her father. Darn it, she should have separated them, she realized too late. Luckily Tess arrived with the presentation easel, so Alex directed her to set it up on her end of the room. Her secretary loitered, casting sideways glances at Jack Stillman until Alex cleared her throat meaningfully.

Once the door closed, Alex took a deep breath. "Okay, everyone, let's get this over wi—" She stopped abruptly, feeling a flush creep up her neck as surprised looks darted her way. Alex hesitated, half afraid her father would jump to his feet and assume control of the meeting. But his face was remarkably placid.

"I mean, let's begin," she amended smoothly. "As you know, Tremont Enterprises is looking for a new advertising agency to take the company into the millennium." Pausing for effect, she tried to inject just the right amount of doubt into her tone. "Mr. Jack Stillman of the Stillman & Sons Agency is here today to convince us that his small, family-owned business can handle an account the size of Tremont's."

At the tightening of his jaw, she saw her veiled barb had hit home. "Mr. Stillman, perhaps you can tell us more about yourself and your company." As she took her seat, Alex gave him a tight smile that said she would reveal him at the earliest convenience for the con man he was. "After all," she added, "not everyone was treated to the, um, *enlightening* reception I received yesterday."

His smile was sublime as he stood and launched into a brief background of his family business, including his and his brother's degrees from UK, and the recent addition of a large regional natural food manufacturer to their client list. Distinctly unimpressed, Alex was hiding a yawn behind her hand when he looked her way. "But I'm glad you brought up your visit to my office, Ms. Tremont, because it dovetails perfectly into my presentation for today."

She realized he was waiting for a response, so she obliged with as little interest as possible. "Oh?"

Jack's mouth twitched as his gaze bore into her. "You see...my plan worked perfectly."

As his words sunk in, Alex sobered with a sense of impending doom. "What plan would that be?"

He stroked his chin thoughtfully as he walked around her father's chair. She caught a glint of silver in his hair when he stepped through a shaft of sunlight. "What was your impression of me yesterday, Ms. Tremont?"

The dark walls of the room suddenly seemed closer, and the hairs at the nape of her exposed neck tingled. "The truth?"

His eyes glittered. "Absolutely."

Alex pursed her lips. How could she best put into words that she found him to be a very base individual who might be more at home digging a ditch and ogling female pedestrians than playing at running a business? Studying his smooth, too-confident face, she decided that Jack Stillman needed to be taken down a notch. Or three. "Frankly, I found you to be rather odious."

Eyebrows shot high around the table, accompanied by sharp gasps and a titter or two. "Alex!" her father admonished, but she didn't break eye contact with Jack. This was personal.

Her opponent's smile was patient. "Why?"

In her peripheral vision, she saw heads pivot back and forth between them, but as far as Alex was concerned, she and Jack were the only two people in the room. An invisible tunnel connected them across the table. She felt an alarming draw to her energy, as if the space wasn't big enough for the both of them. With effort, she matched his smile. "You mean other than the fact that you were rude and boorish?"

Bodies shifted.

He spread his large hands. "My apologies if you were offended, but I believe you were reacting to something other than my words."

"Such as?" she asked dryly.

"My appearance?"

Alex blinked, but didn't reply.

"In fact," Jack said, walking around the table toward her. "You didn't recognize me when I arrived today, did you, Ms. Tremont?"

Irritated, she crossed her arms. "You do look quite different, Mr. Stillman."

He turned to address everyone else. "Just so you'll know, when Ms. Tremont came by yesterday, I was wearing cut-off shorts, a Hawaiian shirt and a tool belt."

What was he up to? "You forgot the bad tie and the fact that you were barefoot," she supplied, shoving her shoulders back into the stiff chair. Chuckles circled the table, but she remained stoic.

"Ah, you *are* observant." He graced her with a charming smile, then gestured to himself, sweeping his hand down his torso as he walked closer still. "Would you say my appearance today is an improvement?"

Hot anger shot through her, and her eyes traveled the length of him as if they had a mind of their own. Standing almost within touching distance, Jack Stillman was one gorgeously put together man, but she wasn't about to give him undue credit for lucking into a favorable gene pool. "Anything would be an improvement."

His answer was a devilish grin of concession, which drew more light laughter from the table.

Alex didn't appreciate being put in the hot seat—especially when she'd planned to be roasting Jack Stillman right about now. "Mr. Stillman, I assume you have a point?"

"Ah," he said, raising a finger and lifting the portfolio he'd leaned against the wall, then placing it on the easel. "My point is that a certain old saying has credence." With a flick of his wrist, he unsnapped the little strap that held together the worn leather portfolio, and Alex stifled a scoff. A large hand-painted color poster showed a man in a football uniform throwing a pass, cheering fans behind him.

Jack lowered the panel to reveal another poster showing the same man wearing chinos and a casual shirt flipping burgers on a grill, a couple of admiring women standing nearby with umbrella'd drinks. The next poster showed the man in a suit carrying a briefcase and checking his watch as he hurried somewhere, again with a couple of female onlookers. The fourth poster showed the now shirtless man reclining in bed, wearing boxer shorts, a woman's hand resting on his shoulder. Her midsection stirred at the intimacy of the moment translated by the simplicity of the picture. She guessed he'd shown great restraint in not depicting *two* women's hands.

Her eyes strayed to Jack, unnerved that he seemed to be gauging her reaction. She kept her expression passive, and glanced away, not about to reveal that the picture conjured up images of Jack Stillman himself reclining in bed with a lover. She banished the disturbing thought and forbade herself from making such appalling slips in the future.

"My point, one that Ms. Tremont can attest to, is—" he encompassed the room with a tantalizing smile and flipped down the poster to reveal a slogan in neat black block letters "—Tremont's. Because clothes *do* make the man."

Alex thought her head might explode on the spot.

JACK HOPED NO ONE could hear his heart thrashing in his chest—the scheme of putting a creative spin on yesterday's fiasco was risky, but he had nothing to lose. It was fourth down with long yardage, and he'd been scrambling to find a seam in the end zone. The deadly look Alexandria Tremont gave him, however, was akin to taking the pigskin right between the eyes. Now his only hope was to escape the game without further injury. He eyed the distance between her and him, versus him and the door—could he make it?

The room crackled with expectant silence, then Al Tremont suddenly burst out laughing, clapping his fleshy hands. "I *like* it."

Jack exhaled the breath he'd been holding as the others, as if awaiting their boss's cue, began to hum and nod their approval. Heath Reddinger seemed noncommittal, but from what he had observed when he'd followed the secretary into the room, Reddinger and the fetching Alexandria were involved romantically. The thought stirred a different kind of competitive urge in Jack's stomach. Now Reddinger darted looks toward his ladylove, waiting for a glance of...permission? Poor sap.

Apparently Alexandria wasn't influenced by her father's favorable opinion. "Excuse me," she said in a crisp tone as she swept her gaze over her colleagues. "Excuse me!"

Jack suspected if she'd had a gavel within reach, she would have banged the table top, but everyone fell silent and gave her their attention.

She pressed her lips together, as if gathering her composure, then spoke, her voice rich and controlled. "Frankly, I think the ad is a bit sexist. After all, our typical shopper is *female*, and we can't afford to alienate her."

"We wouldn't be alienating her," Jack said, speaking as if he were already part of the Tremont's team. He withdrew a television commercial storyboard of a woman shopping in the men's department. "Instead we'd be saying, 'Come into Tremont's and outfit your man in style.'"

Outfit your man? She narrowed her eyes at him. "I repeat for the benefit of the hard-of-hearing, I think the idea is sexist, and if I were the customer, I would be offended."

Jack felt perversely compelled to provoke her, although he wasn't sure why. "But you, Ms. Tremont, are not the typical female customer." Reciting from memory the demographics hastily gathered from Reggie over the taxi driver's cell phone, he said, "Correct me if I'm wrong, but I believe the typical customer is both younger *and* married."

He had hit a nerve—maybe two.

While Alexandria turned a becoming shade of crimson, Al Tremont laughed again, slapping his knee. "He's got you there, Alex."

Alex. The name suited her, Jack decided, then he plunged ahead. "She is also less educated and less successful," he added, hoping to placate her, although from the set of her mouth, he hadn't. "But she spends a disproportionate amount of her disposable income on clothing. I think we can entice her to spend even more of her own money—" he grinned "—or someone else's—"

More laughter sounded, accompanied by nods.

"—buying clothes for her man."

"Clothes for her man?" Alex's tone was heavy with disdain. "Mr. Stillman, that thinking smacks of chauvinism."

"Maybe," he conceded. "But how are menswear sales?"

"We don't divulge sales figures to outsiders."

"Menswear sales are lousy," Al Tremont offered.

"But improving," Alex insisted, gripping the edge of the table and shooting her father a withering glance.

"I assume profit margins are higher for men's clothing to compensate for the lower volume," Jack continued, trying to smooth the brewing disagreement between father and daughter. "So it makes sense to target an underselling, high-margin department. Present a campaign specifically designed to bring women into the store to shop for the men in their lives, and they're sure to wander into other departments."

"We could put cross-promotional materials for women's wear, children's and housewares in the men's department," one of the young women offered.

Jack remembered she was an assistant in marketing. "Great idea," he said, and was rewarded with a blushing, shy grin. "Coax them into other departments after they've finished shopping in menswear."

Side conversations erupted around the table. Jack could see the idea catching and spreading. Alex sat rigidly in her chair, eyeing her associates.

"Mr. Stillman, do you have any experience in producing television commercials?" Heath Reddinger asked, restoring the room to relative quiet.

Good old Heath—offering a bit of disguised resistance for Alex's sake. "No," he admitted. "But I do have a relationship with a local producer, who does top-notch work." A chance glance at Alexandria revealed her too-blue eyes had rolled upward, so he directed the rest of his remarks to her father.

"I recommend that you contract a male model exclusively for Tremont's, then flood the media with his image."

Tremont was nodding. "I like it—simple, straightforward, smart."

Alexandria cleared her throat noisily. "It's not the level of sophistication I had in mind for the store. I wanted to spotlight our women's designer clothing, our fine jewelry, cosmetics—"

"Alex," her father cut in, his face stern. "I think we

should take Jack's proposal under serious consideration."

"Perhaps," she returned across the table, her own expression firm, "we should ask *Jack* to leave the room so we can discuss the pros and cons among ourselves."

Jack moved toward the door, but Al Tremont held up his hand. "Stay, son. I just need to know how much all this is going to cost."

"Father," Alex said, rising, her eyes wide. "This matter is far too important to be decided unilaterally in mere minutes. Remember, we have other agencies to interview, and besides, the entire marketing team should convene and discuss—"

"Alex," her father said abruptly, his mouth set in a frown, his double chin shaking, "I've made up my mind, and it's the Stillman agency I want!"

Although the words were music to his ears, Jack was aware of awkwardness vibrating between the walls, and for a moment, he felt a pang of sympathy for Alexandria. The man did seem to be a bit overbearing, and Jack was curious to see how she would respond.

"Father, a word with you outside?" To her credit, her tone was sweet, but he detected a slight tremor. She marched toward the door and exited, head high, leaving the door ajar. Jack and everyone else shifted their glance toward Al Tremont, who sighed heavily, then pushed himself to his feet and followed her, muttering under his breath.

ALEX PACED IN THE HALLWAY, shaking with a level of anger she hadn't experienced since discovering her father was going to marry Gloria the Gold Digger scarcely a year after her precious mother's death. How dare he undermine the authority he'd given her mere weeks ago!

And in front of colleagues and other vice presidents, no less—not to mention that abominable Jack Stillman. *Clothes do make the man.* How lame. Thoughts of what she would do if her father didn't follow her were cut short by his appearance.

"Alex, what is the meaning of this?"

She crossed her arms. "I was going to ask you the same thing. The last time I looked, choosing an advertising agency fell under my area of responsibility." Gesturing toward the conference room, she said, "I can't believe you would just hand over our account to that inept man!"

"Imagine," her father murmured, a nostalgic smile on his broad face. "Jack the Attack working for me."

Incredulous, Alex's mouth worked up and down in alarm. He was dismissing her opinion on this critical matter? "Dad, surely you're not willing to jeopardize our advertising campaign, possibly our entire holiday sales season, simply to hire that has-been jock?"

He clasped her hand between his two. "Alex, dear, the man is talented, and he has a catchy idea that the rest of the staff likes."

"They're just humoring you."

"Then I wish you would, too," he said, adopting a heart-melting smile.

"Dad—"

"Alex, do this one thing for me. Work with Jack Stillman to get this campaign off the ground and let's see where it goes."

"But the timing...it's so risky—"

"And sometimes it takes a rebel to shake things up," he said, then looked contrite. "Sweetheart, I'm sorry I raised my voice in there, but I think you had your mind made up before the man even walked in."

"Dad, if you could have seen him yesterday—"

"And now we know why he looked the way he did, to make a point."

Alex scoffed. "That's impossible—he had no idea I was dropping by. On top of everything else, the man's a pathological liar."

"I like the boy, and my gut tells me this is the right thing to do, but it won't work unless you get on board."

"Oh, you need me now?" She hated the hurt she couldn't seem to keep out of her voice.

His smile was indulgent. "Of course, sweetheart. I won't offer Stillman the contract unless you agree to monitor the campaign."

A warm, fuzzy feeling lodged beneath her heart, and she smiled in spite of their disagreement. How she loved this man—her mentor, her hero. She couldn't dispute the fact that his business judgment was *usually* sound, although she had an ominous feeling about this particular decision.

"In fact—" he winked "—taking on this kind of project will prove what a team player you are, my dear."

The vice presidency—was he dangling his endorsement in front of her? Alex sank her teeth into her lower lip.

"What do you say?" he asked, squeezing her hand. "Help me keep my promise to Jack's father. I have a feeling their business could use a life preserver."

"More like a crash cart," she observed dryly.

"So you'll do it? For me?"

The last vestiges of her anger dissolved and she nodded, amenable to a compromise. "But only for two weeks. If the focus group doesn't like what Jack Stillman comes up with, then we cut ties with him and interview the St. Louis firm."

Her father beamed. "That's my girl." With his hand on her waist, he steered her back in the direction of the boardroom. Alex felt buoyed, willing to accept full credit for his good cheer.

Resigned to the unpalatable task before her, Alex inhaled deeply and followed him back into the room, aware of the anxious glances from the table. Al walked up to stand beside Jack, pulling Alex close to him on the other side. Behind her father's shoulders, she caught Jack Stillman's mocking gaze and wondered how she'd keep from socking him over the next fourteen days.

"I'm happy to report," her father said, his eyes shining, "that Alex and I have reached a compromise to give Mr. Stillman the opportunity to impress us, and I'm sure that, just like on the football field, Jack won't let us down."

Jack inclined his head to acknowledge the smattering of polite applause. "I'll do my best, sir."

Two weeks, Alex told herself, forcing a smile to her lips. She could walk on hot coals for two weeks if she had to. And it wasn't like they'd have to be together every minute—after all, Jack wouldn't be involved in *every* aspect of the project. He would simply hand off his ideas to the photographer and the producer of the commercials, for instance. She could take it from there. Yes...things weren't so bad.

"In fact," her father continued, his face animated. "I just had an inspiration! Who needs to look for a male model when we have Jack the Attack?"

Alex's stomach vaulted. "What?"

"What?" Jack asked at the same time.

"Why, it's perfect," Al continued, gesturing to Jack with both hands as if he were presenting a refrigerator to a studio audience. "*Jack* will be the spokesman for Tremont's. He'll be the star of our commercials!"

He clapped Jack hard on the back, but Alex was the one who felt as if her heartbeat needed a jump start. *Jack Stillman*, the Tremont's spokesman? She opened her mouth to scream no, but her voice had fled—apparently to join her father's good sense.

And her father had eyes only for Jack. Puffed up with pride, he beamed at his new recruit. "How about it, son?" Al turned and gestured to some invisible horizon, his thumb and forefinger indicating a name in lights. "Just imagine, when people see 'Tremont's,' they'll think of 'Jack the Attack.'"

Alex's vision blurred. She mumbled something about an important conference call and walked out of the room as calmly as her knocking knees would allow. Her father was so preoccupied with his find, he'd never miss her. On the way to her office, mind reeling, she somehow managed to snag her panty hose on a rattan wastebasket.

Great. On top of everything else, now she had to buy new panty hose.

TUESDAY LAUGHED, her eyes wide. "You went over there flying by the seat of borrowed pants, and came back with the account *and* the starring role?"

Jack shrugged and loosened his tie. "The old man was so excited, I had no choice but to say yes."

"What's your brother going to say about you modeling?"

He frowned. "It's *not* modeling."

She quirked an eyebrow. "You going to put on their clothes and let people point a camera at you?"

He jammed his hands on his hips, ready to argue, then sighed and nodded.

"Sounds like modeling to me. You must have impressed them with the new you. How did Ms. Tremont react?"

"Not well," he admitted. In fact, the one dim spot of the day had been when he'd looked up from shaking Al Tremont's hand to find that Alex had disappeared. She had a prior appointment, her father had explained unconvincingly, then assured Jack he'd be seeing a lot of Alex in the next few days since she would serve as his liaison to the company. The news had stirred his stomach oddly. He'd wanted to speak to her, to extend an olive branch before he left, but Al had dismissed his daughter's reaction.

"She had her heart set on a fancy shmancy advertising

outfit in St. Louis," he'd said. "Give her a few hours for the news to sink in, then call her to set up a time when the two of you can get together. I won't lie to you, son—she's a handful, but she's as smart as a whip. You're going to have to suck up a little to win her over, but I'm sure you can handle it." With that, Al, Heath Reddinger and Bobby Warner had whisked him off to an early and extended lunch.

At first, retelling football stories had been amusing, but after ninety minutes of constant prodding by Tremont and Warner, the enjoyment had worn mighty thin for Jack, and, he suspected, for Reddinger. Between the jokes, he had tried to glean as much business information as possible from the trio, but the sole kernel of interesting data was an overheard comment that Alexandria was left holding a dinner reservation for two at Gerrard's while Reddinger left town to handle a banking issue.

Jack had studied the men throughout the meal and concluded that Al Tremont was a risk-taker with enough wisdom to attract talented people—Jack liked him—that Bobby Warner was a quick study with enough wisdom to attract debate—Jack respected him—and that Heath Reddinger was a yes-man with enough wisdom to attract the boss's daughter—Jack *dis*liked him.

It was the sort of dislike one man felt for another man who had something the first man strongly thought the second man didn't deserve. Not that the first man *wanted* the something he thought the second man didn't deserve, it was just that the first man possessed an innate sense of justice.

"She didn't take it well at all," he repeated, half to himself.

Tuesday waved her hand. "She'll get used to having you around. Might be good for the both of you."

Jack frowned. "What's that supposed to mean?"

"Grown folk have to learn to get along with people they don't like."

"I never said I didn't like her."

"I was talking about *her* not liking *you.*"

He bristled. "Why wouldn't she like me?"

Tuesday harrumphed. "You think because you put on that fancy suit and got a haircut that the woman can't see through you?"

"You were the one who put me in this getup—under duress, I might add."

She wagged her finger in his direction. "You might have impressed the men, and maybe even the fickle women, but my guess is that after the way you treated Ms. Tremont when she came here, she'll be on her guard. Smart lady, judging by the way you conduct business."

"I got the account, didn't I?"

Tuesday snorted. "Sounds like they want your face more than your advertising talent."

"Gee, thanks for the vote of confidence."

"That's part of my job," she said with a shrug.

"Speaking of *your* job, there isn't one. We can't afford you."

"You can't afford *not* to have me," she replied, lifting both hands.

Frowning, Jack glanced around the front office, not a bit surprised to see that Tuesday had rearranged its contents in a more pleasing manner. A fresh but pungent odor permeated the air. "What's that smell?"

"Paint," she said, nodding toward the yellow walls. "I thought this room could use a pick-me-up."

Jack stared at the clean, bright walls. What color had they been before? "*You* painted?"

Tuesday shrugged. "An apron, a gallon of paint, and a roller—no big deal. Besides, I was bored."

"Where did you get the supplies?" he asked suspiciously.

"Call it a contribution," she said. "I wanted to make this room more comfortable."

"Well, don't get too comfortable," he warned. "There *is* no job."

She sniffed, disregarding him completely.

Jack frowned. "When is Mr. Stripling supposed to arrive?"

She nodded toward the back office. "He's been here for an hour—I gave him another back adjustment and sat him at Derek's desk. He wants to talk to you a-s-a-p about missing quarterly tax payments." Tuesday extended a hand-written note which presumably held the man's instructions.

Jack glared and snatched the piece of paper. "Keep your hands off our auditor! Anything else?"

Tuesday walked around the desk she had made her own, complete with a nameplate—where had *that* come from?—and picked up a handful of pink phone message slips. "Donald Phillips wants you to review new pages to the company's website."

"I don't suppose he said anything about sending us a check," Jack grumbled.

"It arrived today."

"Great. We need to—"

"Pay the phone bill, the electric bill, Lamberly Printing, the post office box rental, Beecher's Office Supplies and three returned check charges from the bank." She smiled and handed him a stack of papers. "Counter-sign the check for deposit, then sign all the checks I filled out."

"I'm not giving you this check to deposit," he declared. "I hardly *know* you."

Without missing a beat, Tuesday picked up her purse and swung it over her shoulder. "I wasn't offering," she said, enunciating each word. "The rest of your phone messages are there for you to read yourself, and envelopes for the bills are already addressed and stamped."

Jack felt a little contrite as she walked toward the door, her hips swaying with attitude. "Where are you going?"

"Home," she tossed over her shoulder. "I'm taking the rest of the afternoon off."

"You don't have a job to take time off *from*," he reminded her grumpily.

"See you tomorrow, model man."

Jack massaged the bridge of his nose, then carried the handful of papers with him to the back office. Mr. Stripling sat at Derek's desk surrounded by files and folders, with a boardlike device strapped to his back, his face arranged in an unpleasant expression.

"Good day, Mr. Stripling."

The man scowled in his direction. "Is it? I hadn't noticed, having been assaulted once again by your office manager and left to sit here all afternoon wracked with unbearable pain."

Jack swallowed a smile at the image of Tuesday pinning the slight man down long enough to crack his neck—again. Hadn't the man seen it coming this time? "I apologize, Mr. Stripling, but that unstable woman does *not* work for us."

"So you've said, and I find the entire situation quite suspect."

Jack flung his arm toward the files the man was delving into. "You'll see—there's no record of having a Tuesday Humphrey on our payroll."

"Which means you've been paying her under the table," Stripling chirped. "A crime in and of itself."

"No—" Jack held up his hand, then stopped. "Forget it," he mumbled, crossing to his own desk where he tossed the stack of bills. "I've got more important things to worry about."

If possible, the man stiffened even more, and his bow tie practically twitched. "More important than the IRS?"

"Yeah," Jack said, falling into his seat. "An irate woman."

"Your office manager?"

"No," he said, picking up the phone to dial Derek. "A different irate woman. I seem to be collecting them."

As the phone rang on the other end, his spirits lifted in anticipation of telling his brother the news about the account, but he debated telling Derek that he had also been asked to be the Tremont's spokesman. He didn't want to give Derek the impression that he might sacrifice the work of the agency to satisfy this spokesman gig. Besides, Tuesday had pricked a concern he'd been harboring since leaving Tremont's—perhaps Al Tremont was more intrigued by the thought of Jack the Attack doing commercials for the department store than the thought of Jack Stillman doing advertising work for the department store.

"Hello, this is Derek."

"Hi, bro. Did I catch you at a bad time?"

"Jack, thank goodness! I've been going crazy waiting to hear from you. How'd the meeting go with Tremont?"

"We got the account."

"That's great!" Derek whooped and lowered the mouthpiece to yell the news to someone else—presumably his wife Janine—then returned. "How long is the contract for?"

"Two weeks."

"Two weeks?" Disappointment filtered his brother's voice. "Is that *all*?"

Rankled, Jack said, "It was the best I could do under the circumstances."

"What circumstances?"

"The decision to go with our agency wasn't unanimous."

"Did Mr. Tremont like the presentation?"

"Yeah, he liked it fine. It was his daughter who had a problem with it, and she's the director of sales and marketing."

"Daughter? What's she like?"

Jack's pulse spiked. "Young and hostile."

Derek emitted a thoughtful sound. "Pretty?"

His shrug was for himself, he supposed. "If you like the white-and-uptight type. I have two weeks to impress her, and if I do, we go back to the negotiating table."

"I'm coming home right away."

Panic gripped him—the last thing he wanted was for Derek to come home and find him making commercials. Two weeks would give him time to get a handle on the details. "Derek, man, don't do that," he said, laughing and forcing a casual tone. "Trust me, I'll have this thing well on its way by the time you get home. Enjoy the rest of your honeymoon."

"Are you sure?"

"Absolutely." He spent the next few minutes describing the concept of the ad campaign, then assured him—ignoring the unfriendly look that Stripling shot his way—that the audit was going smoothly and that the crazy lady who had made herself their office manager was gone. He didn't add "for the day."

"Jack," Derek said, his voice dipping. "I'm proud of you."

Touched and a little shaken, Jack scoffed. "Don't go getting all mushy on me. The business isn't in the bag yet."

"You just have to impress this Tremont lady, huh?"

"Yeah, but she's an uppity princess."

"Single?"

"I didn't ask," Jack hedged, knowing she was single— ergo Reddinger.

"Just be on your best behavior, okay?" Derek pleaded. "Don't try to be starting something."

"That's crazy," Jack protested. "I wouldn't—"

"Yes, you *would*. If you haven't noticed, little brother, you have a way of sabotaging your own success."

Jack sighed. "Relax, she has a boyfriend."

"Ha! Never stopped you before."

"Oh, and this coming from a guy who married the bride-to-be of a friend of his."

Derek grunted. "Steve and I aren't friends."

"Wonder why?"

"Okay, Jack, okay. But I'm telling you—stay away from this woman's bed."

"My contact with Alex Tremont will be limited to her wiping her six-hundred dollar stiletto shoes on my back."

"Promise me."

"Promise you what?"

"Promise me you won't become involved with this woman."

"What? No!"

"Then I'm coming home."

"No!" Jack sighed, then turned his back to the eavesdropping auditor and cupped his hand over the mouthpiece. "Okay."

"Okay, what?"

He rolled his eyes heavenward and lowered his voice even more. "Okay. I promise I won't become involved with...this woman."

"Great. I know I can trust you to keep your word to me, Jack."

Derek's words reverberated in his head long after he hung up the phone. By the time he signed all the outgoing checks and sealed the envelopes, Mr. Stripling was ready to leave. Jack helped him to his car while doing his best to ignore the man's ominous comments about missing forms and late payments. He assured the man they would discuss it later. Then Jack locked the office, rode his motorcycle to the bank to make the deposit, and dropped the bills into a mailbox.

Maneuvering through five o'clock traffic, he acknowledged he hadn't yet called Alex to set up a time to meet with her as her father had suggested. He also acknowledged that just the thought of seeing her again sent the blood rushing to the lower portions of his body. And irritation to nerve endings elsewhere.

He dreaded talking to the woman on the phone, knowing she'd probably resist every opportunity to meet with him. Her father's words came back to him. *You're going to have to suck up a little to win her over, but I'm sure you can handle it.* Jack had never had to suck up to a woman in his life, and Alex Tremont didn't strike him as someone susceptible to sucking up anyway. Dammit, he'd have to be clever, which meant this was going to be a lot of work.

He sighed heavily, then from nowhere an idea popped

into his mind. With growing confidence, Jack smiled and revved toward home, telling himself that just because he was already anticipating seeing Alex again did *not* mean he was going back on his promise to Derek.

7

ALEX KICKED OFF HER SHOES and removed the pins from her hair, lightly massaging her scalp as she finger combed the waves. Taking stock of her physical well-being, she acknowledged wryly that her feet hurt, her back hurt and her hair hurt. On a scale of one to ten for bad days at the office, she gave this day a nine, saving ten for the distinction of being fired.

Noticing the flashing light on her voice recorder, she pushed the play button as she walked past.

"Alex, this is Lana. You have to help me, I'm begging you. Vile Vicki is hip to me borrowing her things to get her back for borrowing *my* things. I need to stash a few valuables at your place until I can off her and dump the body."

Shaking her head at her friend's nonsense, she attempted a laugh, but in light of her abysmal day at the office, the noise came out sounding a bit strangled. After the farce of a meeting to "investigate" Jack Stillman's company as a potential advertising firm, she'd received preliminary reports from a reputable retail research firm that Tremont's was definitely losing sales ground, even worse considering that one of their main competitors was holding steady, and the other was posting significant gains.

What a time to be flushing their advertising dollars down the drain.

Before it slipped her mind, Alex dialed Lana's number—she and Vile Vicki were way beyond sharing a phone number—and left her a message to use the spare key and deposit her valuables in the antique chest she used as a coffee table, adding that Lana simply could not, however, hide Vicki's body in the chest. She hung up, thinking the couch looked extremely inviting, but she needed to eat, and the sole food items in the refrigerator—a jar of pimento olives and the carton of leftover fudge icing—would not suffice.

She also refused to stay in simply because Heath had left town. Irked for no reason she could put her finger on, she paced the perimeter of her apartment, peering out the windows at early dusk, feeling jittery. She sat down at her mother's mahogany baby grand piano showcased in the window of her loft, aching with the need to talk to her mother, to solicit her wisdom.

Life was pulling at her—Heath wanted to set a date, the pressures at the store had grown exponentially, Al wanted her to bond with Gloria while she yearned only for her father's affection. And now this liaison with Jack Stillman that went against her every instinct. The man oozed trouble, and she had the distinct feeling that the situation would become much more complicated before leveling out.

Alex pinged on a key or two with a sad smile—considering the few rusty tunes she could play, turning on the groaning faucet in the bathroom seemed simpler.

Suddenly she brightened, deciding that this evening would be the perfect time to indulge in her long-unfulfilled desire to ride again—to climb onto the back of a horse like when she was a child and bring the animal to a gallop.

She hadn't ridden in over a decade, but lately the longing to lean into the wind and feel her hair whipping her neck had recurred with more frequency. Lana said the urge for unbridled freedom was a by-product of becoming engaged, an explanation which Alex had dismissed. All she knew at the moment was that a therapeutic ride this evening would erase the stubborn image of Jack Stillman's smug, handsome face and her father's grating words, *When people see "Tremont's," they'll think of "Jack the Attack."*

Not the person who bore the name of his store, the person who had devoted her entire life to his business, the person who spent sleepless nights mulling strategies to grow sales, to eke another half percent out of their margins. Not *her*, but Jack Stillman.

She stomped to a bookcase, yanked out the yellow pages, then flipped to the *H*'s, only to be interrupted by a telltale frenzied knock on the door. Loath to answer Lana's certain questions about Jack, she nonetheless recognized the futility of postponing the inevitable. Still holding the phone book, she undid the chain and swung open the door. But the sight of the figure standing in the hallway stunned her into silence.

Holding a black motorcycle helmet beneath his arm, Jack Stillman inclined his dark head, his green-brown eyes dancing. "Good evening."

Her first impulse was to slam the door in his face, but she resisted. "The evening just took a decided turn for the worse," she said wryly. "How did you find my apartment?"

He gestured to her hand. "A brilliant invention, which I see you also utilize—the phone book."

His gaze swept over her, lingering on her loosened hair, traveling down to her stockinged feet. She tingled, and curled under her toes, mortified to be caught so completely off guard by the man she was supposed to "monitor," according to her father. "A gentleman would have called first."

He winked. "Ah, finally we agree on something—I'm not a gentleman."

A threat? A promise? "What are you doing here?" she blurted. Besides looking impossibly handsome, that is. His white cotton shirt, unbuttoned just enough to reveal the top of a snowy undershirt, was tucked into plain-front khaki chinos, belted with a thick black leather belt that matched his low-heeled boots and slightly worn leather jacket. Seasoned, generic clothes that might have come from Goodwill for all she knew, but devastatingly appealing on his lean frame. The split-second observation gave her a jarring glimpse into how the man might come across in a commercial.

He grinned—oh, Lord, a cleft in his chin, too.

"Your father suggested that you and I get together to talk about the ad campaign, and after the meeting today, I thought maybe it would be better if we got together in a more casual setting."

She pursed her lips, warily considering him and his offer. "Such as?"

"Such as Gerrard's?"

Alex blinked.

His laugh was mildly apologetic. "At lunch I overheard your fiancé tell your father that he'd made reservations before he had to leave town unexpectedly."

Funny that neither of the men had mentioned that they'd lunched with him, or for that matter, had invited her along. "How did you know Heath was my fiancé?"

He shrugged, his shoulders eclipsing the light from the hall. "I made an assumption based on the scene your secretary and I walked in on this morning and the rock on your finger."

"Oh." She rubbed her thumb on the underside of the ring, causing it to tilt and flash in the incandescent lighting. Symbolic of everything she wanted—if she married Heath, she could create her own loving family. Even her staid father wouldn't be able to resist the lure of grandchildren.

"Have you two set a date?"

Alex looked up and suddenly wondered if this playboy had children and ex-wives scattered about. He seemed too much of a big kid himself to be a good father, but then again, what did she know about good fathers? "I...I'd rather not discuss my personal business."

"Okay." He scratched at his temple, shifting his weight to his other foot. "So what about dinner—does Gerrard's work for you?"

The man had a lot of nerve assuming she didn't have something better to do like, like, like...where had she been planning to go? Oh, yes—horseback riding. She patted the phone book, glad for an out. "Sorry, I was on the verge of making other plans."

Before she realized his intention, he'd taken the book from her and turned to the page she'd held with her thumb. Her cheeks flamed as he scanned the listings.

"Hmm. Either you're looking to buy a new saddle, or you were planning to go horseback riding."

Feeling all of nine years old, Alex clasped her hands behind her back. "I, uh, was planning to go riding."

He closed the book and angled his head at her. "Well now, if it's a ride you're looking for, I can certainly oblige."

His throaty voice was free of innuendo, but his eyes told her the conversation could veer in any direction she wished to take it. In the course of a heartbeat, all kinds of naughty images galloped through her mind. She swallowed, squashing the imagery. The man was, after all, a professional flirt.

"Oh?" she asked lightly. "Do you own a horse?"

"Horse*power*," he corrected, setting the phone book on a table just inside the door. He patted his helmet. "Nothing like it—wind in your face, sun on your back, hugging the curves."

She almost smiled at the little-boy delight in his voice. The man was nothing if not compelling. His grin lit up his entire face, pushing up his sharp cheekbones, lifting his thick black brows, crimping the corners of his amazing eyes. He had a mischievous look that reminded her of a boy in her first grade class who had always talked her into stunts that resulted in either injury or punishment.

"I'd better not," she murmured, although even the hair on her arms strained toward him. "Besides, the restaurant probably already filled the reservation." In truth, the thought of sharing a meal alone with Jack Stillman unnerved her mightily.

"I checked, and they haven't." As if he sensed her wavering, he leaned forward, stretching his free arm to the other side of the jamb, filling the doorway. She caught a whiff of leather and a cologne unidentifiable to her well-trained nose. "Look, Alex, we got off on the wrong foot, and I'd like the chance to make it up to you."

Her nickname had rolled off his tongue so easily, she almost missed it. The implied familiarity rankled her, reminding her that she had much more at stake in the days ahead than Jack Stillman. A sobering flush warmed her neck. "Mr. Stillman, you assume too much. There's no need to 'make anything up' to me. Our relationship is and will continue to be strictly professional."

He held up one hand and laughed. "Whoa—I think we can both agree that the *only* thing we have in common is being blindsided by your father."

Alex straightened. Why did his corroboration with her statement seem like a thinly veiled insult? "My father tends to be impulsive."

He nodded. "And you take after your mother?"

His offhand reference to her dear mother struck yet another nerve. "I make my own way."

As if he sensed he'd stepped out of bounds, he gave her a rueful smile. "Let's face it, I need your support to make this a successful ad campaign. You and I might disagree on the means to the end, but we both have a vested interest in the end itself—more visibility for Tremont's."

A sliver of victory threaded through her chest as her mental footing returned. "Are you admitting, Mr. Stillman, that you can't do this without me?"

He laughed, a soft snort, then crossed his arms over his broad chest. "What I'm saying," he said, the bass in his voice rumbling in her ears, "is that we need each other."

There it was, that implication of intimacy that sent a chill up her back—not to be mistaken for a *thrill*, of course.

"But that's where we differ," she said with a tight smile. "You see, if *you* fail, then *I* will be proven right—that Stillman's isn't the ad agency for Tremont's."

He nodded, then pulled at his chin. "Except I suspect you're the kind of businesswoman who prefers to, um, *win* fair and square."

"This isn't a contest, Mr. Stillman."

His mouth twitched. "Oh, but isn't it? Father versus daughter?"

Alex swallowed hard, mortified that the stranger could

see straight into her heart. "That's ridiculous. I only want what's best for the business."

She defied the urge to squirm under his probing gaze. Suddenly he smiled again and smacked the helmet in his hand, as if a decision had been reached. "Good, then we want the same thing, which is precisely why we should get started as soon as possible. Dinner is my treat."

She inhaled deeply, contemplating the ramifications of having dinner with this man in a highly public place where she and Heath were known as a couple. Then she realized that Gerrard's would be the most innocent of places for them to dine—no one could accuse them of a clandestine meeting.

"All right," she relented, injecting as much authority into her voice as possible. "But we go Dutch."

His smile wavered, but he nodded. "Wear something warm, night riding can be chilly."

Having a dinner meeting was one thing, but hanging on to this man on the back of his bike? Alex shook her head. "Oh, no—I'm not climbing on that rattletrap motorcycle."

He shrugged. "Okay, if you'd rather I ride with you—"

"I'll meet you there," she said, then banged the door closed and exhaled.

THE WOMAN WAS A LITTLE short on charm, Jack decided as he glanced at the clock over the restaurant bar for the fifth time in as many minutes. He'd considered waiting outside her apartment complex until she emerged, then realized that some states would consider that stalking and, frankly, he didn't want to give Alex the impression that he would sit around waiting for her. With that thought, he sprang up from the barstool and leaned against the bar—he'd *stand* around waiting for her instead.

"Want another?" the bartender asked, pointing to his draft beer.

"No, thanks," Jack said, swirling the remainder of the ale in his glass.

The guy squinted, then his face broke into a wide smile. "Hey, you're Jack Stillman, aren't you?"

"Yeah."

The man stuck out his beefy hand and pumped Jack's. "Wow, this is a pleasure. What have you been doing, man?"

Jack adopted an accommodating expression. "This and that, mostly traveling."

"You back in town for good?"

"Good question." Jack pushed his empty glass forward, loathe to engage in a drawn-out conversation. Where the devil *was* she?

"Are you coaching?"

"Nope."

"Too bad, man. So what *do* you do?"

"My brother and I run an ad agency in town."

"Oh." The man nodded awkwardly, duly unimpressed. "You waiting for a dame?"

"How'd you know?"

"You got that hang-dog look."

He shot him an irritated frown.

"If you're interested," the man said, nodding across the room, "there's a sweet little redhead in the corner who's been trying to get your attention for a half hour."

Intrigued, and nursing a fair amount of spite toward the tardy Alexandria, Jack turned to check out the woman in question, quickly assessing she had all the bare essentials: height, curves and—most importantly—

proximity. He twitched an eyebrow in her direction and was rewarded with a toss of hair and a dazzling smile. The redhead picked up her drink and walked toward him, a deep inhale away from splitting the seams of her faded jeans.

"Howdy," she drawled as she stepped up next to him at the bar.

He nodded a greeting. Knowing he'd never remember her name, he simply didn't ask.

She turned her back to the bar and leaned on her elbows. "You played football for UK, didn't you?"

Jack smirked. "You don't look old enough to have followed my career."

"I'm not. My father has an autographed picture of you in our rec room—it's been there since I was a kid."

Feeling ancient, Jack picked at peanuts from a dish on the bar.

"Buy me a drink?" she asked, pursing her bright pink mouth into a pretty pout.

"Looks like you're still working on that one," he said, nodding toward the frozen pink drink she held that coincidentally matched her binding pink T-shirt.

"I'm always planning ahead," she oozed, and leaned closer as she laughed. At a loss, he manufactured a laugh, too.

"Did I miss something funny?"

Jack jerked around to find Alex standing behind them, her dark eyebrows high. He straightened, feeling ridiculously guilty, and conjured up an innocent smile. "No, just making conversation." He tossed a few bills on the counter, nodded to the redhead, then turned back to Alex. "Ready?"

She nodded, but from the pinched look around her lovely mouth, she was feeling guilty about meeting him...which meant she was capable of bending the rules. He grinned at the prim set of her shoulders as she walked three steps ahead of him all the way to the reservations station.

"What name?" the hostess asked.

"Reddinger," Alex said.

"Stillman," he said at the same time, which garnered a sharp look from his companion. At the hostess's perplexed expression, he added, "There's been a change from Reddinger to Stillman."

Alex shot him a suspicious frown and he winked back. "Right this way."

He fell into step behind Alex as the hostess led the way to their table. She'd bound her hair again into a tight little wad, but had changed to loose, black dress jeans that hugged her hips and a turquoise silk blouse that shimmered under the lights as she walked. More than one man stole a glance as she walked between tables. Jack picked up his pace, his hand hovering near her waist of its own volition.

The hostess stopped at a secluded table for two near the enormous stone fireplace that held a fire, more for appearances than for heat. He beat Alex to her chair by a heartbeat and pulled it out for her.

"Thank you," she said, sounding wary as she allowed him to scoot the seat beneath her.

After handing them a wine list, the hostess disappeared, replaced seconds later by a waiter. "Good evening, Ms. Tremont," he said, a genuine smile on his young face as he unfolded her napkin and draped it over her lap. But when he turned to Jack, he faltered a bit, obviously expecting someone else. So she and Reddinger were regulars, huh?

"Rick, this is Mr. Stillman," Alex supplied. "He's a..."

she glanced over at Jack, making eye contact for two whole seconds "...business associate...of Mr. Reddinger's...and mine."

The waiter eyed him suspiciously, but nodded cordially enough.

"We'll have a bottle of chardonnay," she continued, setting aside the wine list.

"I'll take another beer," Jack said.

Alex eyed him as if he were a barbarian. "Bring a carafe of chardonnay for me," she amended with a small smile.

Once the waiter left, silence enveloped them. Jack attempted to catch her gaze, but it was as if an invisible iron gate had sprung up around her—she sat folded into herself, serene and stunning, as sleek as a cat, a different creature than the woman who had answered the door barefoot, on the verge of going horseback riding. The dichotomy intrigued him. "You look beautiful," he said before he could stop the words.

He got her attention, but she didn't appear particularly pleased. "Mr. Stillman—"

"Jack."

"—let's get down to business, shall we?"

Although he wanted nothing less than to talk about business, he said, "Sure. Where do you propose we begin?" She toyed with her empty wineglass, her engagement ring twinkling under the lights. Reddinger was a very lucky man.

"First things first," she said, leveling her ice-blue gaze at him. "You were lying this morning when you said that my visit to your office fit into some convoluted plan of yours. You had no way of knowing I would be stopping by."

"You can't prove that allegation," he said mildly, leaning his elbows on the table, etiquette be damned. God, she was gorgeous.

She lifted one delicate eyebrow. "I don't trust you."

He lowered his voice. "Are you normally this paranoid?"

One side of her mouth drew back. "Call me prudent."

The woman had lost her sense of humor somewhere between her apartment and the restaurant parking lot. "How about if we call a truce?" he asked, steepling his hands. "Just through dinner. Then we can go back to pecking each other to death if we want to."

She inhaled deeply, then released the breath in a long sigh. "Okay. I suppose the first thing we need to do is figure out how much can be feasibly delivered in the next two weeks."

"I'll follow your lead." *Anywhere you want to take me.* He blinked—where had that thought come from?

She pursed her mouth, and he could see the wheels turning in her pretty head. "I say we meet with the television producer and a photographer as soon as possible to shoot a cluster of spots around the—" she cleared her throat "—slogan."

Jack ignored her slight. "Meanwhile, I can polish the text for the print ads, come up with radio scripts, and shop around for billboard space."

"Then my team and I will coordinate internal promotions to complement the media efforts," she said with resignation in her voice. "We'll do the best we can with what we have to work with."

Jack gave her a wry smile. "You really should put a lid on your excitement."

The corners of her mouth curled up a fraction. "You might have blinded my father with your pseudo-celebrity, Mr. Stillman, but I'm a bit more skeptical. By signing your agency, my staff's work is multiplied. Believe it or not, baby-sitting you for the next two weeks isn't at the top of my wish list."

She leaned forward, offering a glimpse of her cleavage in the silky, button-up blouse. *Speaking of wish lists.* His promise to Derek was forgotten as lust flooded his limbs. He knew he was on shaky ground, but he opened his mouth anyway. "If it's any consolation, you're hands-down the best damn looking baby-sitter I've ever had.

8

SHAKEN DOWN to her sensible loafers, at first she thought she had misheard him. But one look at the raw invitation in Jack's eyes, and she knew she hadn't. How did one respond to such an overt remark? Sure, the feminine part of her was flattered, but the practical part of her was convinced he was playing her. He needed her cooperation, didn't he? The man probably knew only one way to influence women—between the sheets.

She opened her mouth to put him in his place, but the waiter arrived with her wine and his beer, then asked for their dinner order. Alex murmured she would have her usual, and Jack ordered a rare porterhouse steak, barbarian that he was. She capped her agitation and concentrated on steering the conversation back to business, finally pinning him down on a delivery date for the print ads. Within a few minutes, she felt as if she were regaining control.

"Will your brother be contributing to our account?" she asked, taking a larger swallow of wine than was probably wise on her empty stomach.

"Not creatively," Jack said. "Derek is more of a numbers man. And he's out of town for another couple of weeks on his honeymoon." Her expression must have given her away because he smiled and said, "You look surprised."

"I guess I assumed he was like you," she admitted, although she really didn't know what that was.

"You mean footloose and fancy free?"

So he wasn't attached. Alex lifted her glass to her mouth and nodded, more interested in his answer than she cared to reveal.

"He was, up until a couple of months ago. Derek flew to Atlanta to stand in for me as best man at my college buddy's wedding, and ended up falling in love with the bride."

She choked on her wine, coughing and sputtering like an idiot. Jack stood and jerked on her arm as if she were three years old, and as if it would help at all. At last, she waved him away, still tingling where his big warm fingers had touched her. "You mean," she asked hoarsely, "that he stole his friend's fiancée?"

"Well, it's not as sordid as it sounds," he said. "They were trapped together in a hotel room under some kind of strange quarantine, and fell in love. Janine decided to call off the wedding, then a few weeks later, she and Derek reunited and were married."

Alex acknowledged the wine was going to her head because she actually cooed. "That's so romantic."

Jack shrugged, apparently less convinced. "I suppose."

"Is he like you in other ways?" She remembered the two of them in the yearbook, and wondered if they were as close as the picture portrayed.

He laughed and she registered alarming pleasure at the rumbling noise. "The similarity ends at the last name. Derek is serious, uptight, takes the weight of the world on his shoulders. But he's a great guy, and he seems really happy with Janine. She's good for him, I think. He's lightened up quite a bit."

She propped up her chin with her hand and watched him refill her wine glass from the carafe. "Where did they go?"

"Hawaii."

"That's nice," she murmured. She'd always wanted to go to Hawaii, but the timing had never seemed right to be away from the office. And now with the vice presidency on the line...

"A client we recently contracted with, Donald Phillips, has a condo on Maui. He was so pleased with the work Derek did on his account that he gave him the keys for an entire month."

"Honey."

Jack's head jerked up and his eyes widened. "What?"

"Honey," she repeated, reaching for her glass. "Donald Phillips's company makes honey. I went to school with his daughter."

He relaxed, then lifted his beer.

By the time the waiter delivered their food, Alex was feeling so relaxed herself, she was reluctant to indulge in her crab cake salad, and merely picked at it. Jack, on the other hand, dove into his steak and baked potato with such gusto, she had the feeling if he'd been by himself, he would have tucked his napkin into his shirt collar and dispensed with utensils. With no regard to the direction of her thoughts, she silently compared the man sitting across from her to Heath.

Jack Stillman was a man's man, big and angular and earthy, with a presence that would put most people at ease—most people who *liked* him, she clarified quickly. Heath, conversely, was precise and scholarly, with a presence that put most people on their best behavior. Jack had a wildness about him, from the way he talked to the way he carried himself across a room. She wondered if he realized that nearly every woman in the restaurant was captivated by him, sliding sideways glances his way behind reading glasses and dessert menus.

She was starting to think she was the only woman in Lexington who was immune to his good looks and casual charm. Lucky for her, she'd gotten a glimpse of the scoundrel behind the smile before succumbing to his questionable charm. She had Heath, and she had no desire to get mixed up with the likes of Jack Stillman, a confirmed ladies' man, with whom she would also be working. She was warming to the idea of him starring in Tremont's commercials—women found him irresistible, it seemed. But she still didn't trust him. The man was trouble, a rebel if she'd ever seen one, determined to have his way.

She supposed he was the same with women. Swallowing more of the dry wine, she conceded that in another place, another time, she herself might have responded to his allure, his unrefined good looks, his smooth tongue. The mere fact that she was aware of him physically, however, didn't alarm her, because knowledge was power. Subsequently, she made a pact with herself as the meal progressed to keep this man at a distance with whatever emotional tools she had handy—a sharp tongue, a cold shoulder—to preempt such an impossible situation. Who had said the best defense was a good offense? Probably some neurotic single woman afraid of losing herself to a man. Maybe Lana, after the Bill Friar incident.

"Are you sure you feel like driving?" Jack asked an hour later when they emerged from the restaurant.

"I didn't drink much more than you did," she said, giving in to her need to lean on his arm to combat her sudden light-headedness.

"But I ate a full meal," he said. "And I outweigh you by at least a hundred pounds."

She blinked, trying to clear her head. "I'll be fine." She certainly wouldn't drive in this condition, but neither did she want Jack to take her home. She'd wait in her car until he left, then walk back into the restaurant and call a cab.

"Looks like the decision was made for you," Jack said when they approached her car, pointing to a steel device locked onto her rear wheel.

"Oh, no, they booted my car?"

"The city's new alternative to towing," he said, nodding with no apparent concern. "It's saving us thousands in tax dollars."

"Oh, shut up," she snapped, then gestured wildly. "When I pulled in, the guy leaving this spot said it was paid for for the rest of the evening." She groaned, then kicked the device, which sent pain shooting up her leg. "Ow, ow, *ow!*"

"Don't hurt yourself," he said, laughing, which only fueled her ire. While she limped in a circle, Jack pulled out a piece of paper to write down the number on the neon sticker plastered onto her window. "Looks like it's too late to call now, but you'll get it straightened out in the morning, and your car should be safe here overnight. Meanwhile, I'll take you home."

She stopped and straightened. "I...don't like motorcycles."

"Have you ever been on one?"

"No." Motorcycles were too...risky. *Jack* was too risky.

"It's just like riding with the top down on your convertible," Jack cajoled, steering her toward the bike.

Now didn't seem like the time to admit she'd only put the top down a handful of times, twice to get ficus trees home from the nursery. She lifted her index finger when an idea came to her. "I don't have a helmet."

"I have a spare," he said, unlocking a storage box behind the seat.

"But...there isn't enough room for me."

To her dismay, Jack turned her around to peruse her backside, then said, "I think we'll be able to squeeze you on board."

She continued to claim she'd rather call a taxi even as he lowered a helmet to her head. Her bun was a painful obstacle. "Ow!"

He looked amused. "Looks like you might actually have to let your hair down."

In response to his sarcasm, she withdrew two pins and released her hair, tossing it in defiance. Jack stopped suddenly and stared down at her, his expression more serious than she'd seen all evening. He was too close for her to think straight; the man emitted some sort of strange energy field—some kind of chemical, maybe? The perfume counter had reported mixed sales on the new scent that contained animal pheromones. Perhaps they should have tapped Jack Stillman instead of wrestling muskrats for the stuff.

A noisy knot of diners walked by them, breaking the spell, thank goodness. Alex was then beset with a spasm of shivers in the cool night air, although she conceded that Jack's oversize fingers fastening the chin strap of her helmet probably contributed to the gooseflesh. He slipped off his leather jacket and settled it over her shoulders. The silky lining of the heavy coat still resonated with his body heat, giving her insight as to how it might feel to be enveloped in his arms. Alex tried to drive the ludicrous thought from her mind, but his nearness set her reason on tilt, and set her skin on fire.

"Ready?"

She realized that he'd already climbed onto the machine, released the kickstand, and was waiting for her to join him.

Alex swallowed. "What do I do?"

"Left foot on this footpeg, swing right foot over the seat, then get a hand hold."

She managed all of it rather shakily, except for the hand hold. "What do I hang on to?" she asked, nearly panicked when he started the bike engine.

"Me," he tossed over this shoulder, then gunned forward, forcing her to fling her arms around his waist. "Try to enjoy it."

She tried, but she didn't. The bite of the chilly fall wind nipped at her exposed neck and hands. Traffic sounds rang in her ears. She buried her face between his shoulder blades, and the beating of his heart made her feel mortal and small—if they crashed, they'd be killed for sure. And she hadn't planned to die hanging on to a man she didn't even like.

But gradually, she did relax, and finally opened her eyes. Her senses were heightened, her pulse elevated, her awareness of the man she clung to, keen. The fuzzy warmth of security seeped into her chest—Jack wouldn't allow anything to happen to her. The vibration of the motorcycle combined with being jammed up against his body lent a heaviness to the juncture of her thighs, shocking her, but rendering her powerless to resist the sexual energy of the man and the machine. When he wheeled into her driveway and cut the engine, she was too weak to climb off without his support.

"I'll walk you up," he said gruffly, looking around the dimly lit parking lot.

She didn't protest because he seemed to have acquired

a black mood since they'd left the restaurant, and appeared anxious to be rid of her. He probably thought that she was an inconvenience, or that she was a wimp about riding the bike, or that she was keeping him from a rendezvous with that redheaded tart he'd been laughing with at the bar when she arrived. Regardless, she matched his stiff gait and maintained silence until they reached her apartment door. Jack took her keys and unlocked the deadbolt, then gave her an awkward smile as he handed them back to her.

"Thanks for agreeing to meet with me," he said curtly. "I hope this project turns out to be productive for both of us."

Alex looked up, and swallowed hard. The man was gorgeous, for sure, his dark eyes nearly black in the filtered light of the hallway, his short hair appealingly rumpled from his helmet, his cheeks ruddy from the cool wind. She shrugged out of his jacket and handed it to him, self-consciously smoothing her own disheveled hair. "Thanks for the ride home. And I, too, hope this project is productive for both of us."

He didn't move, and neither did she, afraid she would sway into the sexual pull emanating from him. Something was happening here, and although she couldn't put a finger on it, her body seemed to know. His Adam's apple moved. His mouth twitched, as if he were about to open his mouth and...and...

"Goodnight, Alex."

Say goodnight. Relief and something else less identifiable coursed through her, and she reached for the doorknob. "Goodnight, Jack." Heart thudding in her ears, Alex pushed open the door, then froze, a scream dying at the back of her throat.

"What?" He was by her side immediately.

"There!" she shrieked, cowering against him. Across the room, the silhouette of a man stood out clearly against the light pouring in from the windows.

Alex's heart jumped to her throat as Jack thrust her behind him. "Who's there?" he shouted.

The intruder didn't answer, didn't move.

"Go call the police," he barked.

She felt the muscles of his arm bunch beneath her death grip. When she realized he meant to confront the person, fear paralyzed her. He lunged across the room, tackling the dark figure. Jack's grunt reverberated through the room as both men fell to the floor. Horror descended when she heard the sound of a gunshot, and a corresponding groan from Jack.

"Jack!" she screamed. Police forgotten, she lunged for the light switch—she had to help him.

As light spilled into the room, she ran forward, then stopped at the scene before her, her hand to her open mouth. Uncontrollable laughter bubbled out, so intense she had to bend at the waist.

Jack lay sprawled facedown on top of Lana's blow-up doll Harry, who had suffered a blow*out* when he'd been tackled. Jack gingerly turned his head, blinking under the wattage of the row of track lighting running overhead, then pushed himself up, staring down at the doll's half-inflated leering face. "What the hell?"

Alex could only shake her head and laugh harder.

He frowned and lumbered to his feet, feeling his ribcage. "I'm glad you find my pain so amusing."

She sobered a tiny bit, hiding her laughter behind her fist. "Are you injured?"

One side of his mouth pulled back in a wry grin. "Just my pride."

"If it makes you feel better," Alex said, laughing anew

as she walked over to the victim sagging against the floor, the life hissing out of him, "Harry got the brunt of it."

"Harry?"

"Er, Horny Harry, to be exact." She picked up the unfortunate rubber doll, glad his somewhat alarmingly anatomically correct body was covered by a pair of baggy pajamas, although his hard plastic erection was obvious beneath the thin fabric.

Jack pursed his mouth. "And does Reddinger know he has such, um, stiff competition?"

Alex threw him a withering glance. "He's not mine."

His eyebrow quirked upward. "Reddinger, or Harry here?"

He maintained a teasing expression, but she had the strangest feeling he was half-serious. "I was talking about Harry," she said lightly. "My neighbor Lana asked if she could bring some of her things over, but I didn't realize she meant him."

He emitted a low, rolling laugh. "Sounds like a lonely woman."

"It's a long story. Are you sure you're okay?" she asked as she stowed Harry safely in a chair.

He nodded. "On hindsight, I'm glad you didn't call the police."

She wet her lips, suppressing another smile. "Now I know why they call you Jack the Attack."

"Oh, now that's hilarious. And I was beginning to think you didn't have a sense of humor."

Alex warmed, realizing that in the past few hours they had gone from near-enemies to sharing a moment of laughter in her apartment.

"Nice place," he said, his head pivoting. He hesitated a

second longer than necessary when his gaze passed over her bed in the far corner.

Alex ignored the zing of electricity that barbed through her. "Thanks."

"Do you live alone?" His voice held only casual curiosity.

"Yes."

"Then you play?" He nodded toward the baby grand piano.

"Not really. It was my mother's."

"Was?"

"She died a few years ago."

His brow clouded. "I'm sorry. I know how tough it is to lose a parent."

She nodded, unable to speak past the lump of emotion that lodged in her throat at his earnest tone—they did have something in common, she and this rebel.

Silence stretched between them, gazes locked, until he looked past her and gestured to the still-open door, a smile hovering on his handsome face. "Well, I guess I'd better be going."

Alex grasped the back of a bar stool and stood rigid until he walked by, closing her eyes as his energy field passed over her. At last she made her feet move, and she followed him to the door, strangely reluctant to see him leave, yet unable to identify why. "Jack."

He turned around, his hand on the doorjamb. With his back to the light in the hallway, his face was cast in shadows.

Flustered, she gestured toward her tiny galley-style kitchen. "W-would you like a cup of coffee? It's the least I can do for someone willing to brave a prowler on my behalf." Was that her voice squeaking? Was that her heart thumping?

His dark eyes glittered and she thought he was smiling, but couldn't be sure. "You were right earlier about us keeping this relationship strictly professional," he said, "and no matter how much I'd like to stay for, um, *coffee*, I think it would seriously compromise our deal." He touched his hand to his forehead in a mock salute. "But I appreciate the offer, boss, more than you know."

Mortification bled through her veins when she realized he thought she was propositioning him. For the second time that evening, Alex banged the door shut in his face.

9

"AT LEAST HE KNOWS who's in charge," Lana said, forking spinach salad into her mouth.

"Believe me," Alex said, "when he called me 'boss,' it wasn't out of respect." She sneezed into her napkin. "And that damn motorcycle ride gave me a cold. Yesterday was the first sick day I've taken since I had mono when I was eighteen."

"Didn't Jeff Summers have mono about that same time?"

Alex frowned. "So?"

"Ah, so your *last* hell-raising boyfriend made you sick, too."

"Jack Stillman is *not* my boyfriend, Lana. I'm engaged for heaven's sake!" Then she pursed her mouth. "But now that you mention it, he does remind me of Jeff— what a loser he turned out to be."

"So either bad boys are gritty and germ-laden, or they wear down your resistance," Lana teased.

Feeling sour, Alex severed a miniloaf of bread with a small serrated knife then set it back down on the restaurant table. Jack Stillman's words from two nights ago still rang in her ears. "How that man interpreted 'would you like a cup of coffee?' to mean 'would you like to have sex with me?' I'm not sure, but it's indicative of his gutter mind and abounding arrogance."

"Maybe you were giving off signals," Lana said with a shrug.

"That's ridiculous."

Her friend eyed her. "You don't find him attractive?"

She averted her eyes. "Well...I'm not blind. He's nice looking, as much as I can remember." She'd recalled every contour of his face, every expression, at the oddest times over the past couple of days.

"You're blushing."

"I am not."

Her friend laughed. "You know, Alex, the rest of the world entertains a naughty thought once in a while and even *survives*. Lighten up. It's okay to lust after this guy."

Alex scoffed. "Lana, I'm in love with Heath. We're getting married, remember?"

Lana leveled her violet eyes across the table. "So you've set a date?"

She squirmed on the tiny chair. "Not yet, but soon."

After a few seconds of pregnant silence, Lana said, "I just hope you're not settling for Heath because you think it's the right thing to do."

She sighed, a little annoyed with the psychoanalysis. "What's that supposed to mean?"

Lana put down her fork. "Alex, I know you. You miss your mother, and your father is so...distant, it's natural that you would turn to Heath for the security of a warm, fuzzy family."

Alex swallowed the lump of emotion that had formed in her throat. "What's wrong with wanting security and a family?"

"Not a thing. As long as you truly love the man."

"But I do love Heath."

A dreamy expression came over her friend's face. "But does he make you feel *passionate* and *alive*?"

She attempted a laugh. "Lana, passion isn't the glue of a lasting relationship. You were passionate about Bill Friar, and look what a mistake it would have been to marry *him*."

Lana held up her hand, stop-sign fashion. "Right you are. I'll keep my mouth shut."

"Good," Alex said with a smile. Her friend resumed eating, unaware that her words had dredged up worries Alex thought she'd put to rest when Heath had proposed.

Suddenly her friend burst out laughing. "I just wish I'd been there when Jack tackled Harry—oh, that's hysterical." She dabbed at her eyes with her napkin.

Glad for the change in subject, Alex smiled wickedly at the memory of the great Jack humbled. "It was a bright moment in my week. Is Harry repairable?"

"He blew a nut, but with a little duct tape, he'll be as good as new. I'm not sure why men need two of those things anyway. By the way, when will you see your hero again?"

She frowned, uncomfortable talking about Jack Stillman on the heels of discussing her wedding. "We're meeting in less than an hour to select his wardrobe for the commercial shoot."

"Oooh, dressing and undressing—sounds like fun to me."

"Fun? We'll be lucky to find something big enough to accommodate his ego."

Lana wagged her eyebrows. "Do you need an assistant?"

Alex pointed her pinkie across the café table. "It's shameless women like you who keep shameless men like Jack Stillman on a pedestal."

"Yeah, well, it's uptight women like you who keep Metamucil on the shelf."

"I'm trying to be professional about this."

"And it sounds to me like he's abiding by your wishes. After all, he could've stayed for coffee the other night and not have respected you the next morning."

"I offered the man a lousy cup of coffee, and that's *all*."

Lana laughed. "Don't worry, I believe you. You're the only woman I can think of who wouldn't jump his bones at the first chance."

"Why does that sound like an insult?"

"Because you're being way too sensitive. Not to change the subject, but what's the status of your promotion to vice president?"

"Status quo. A decision should be announced any day now."

"I'll keep my fingers crossed for you."

"Thanks."

Lana glanced at her watch. "I hate to run, but I'm meeting with the bank manager this afternoon."

Alex clasped her hands together. "You're buying the coffee shop!"

"*Thinking* about it, that's all."

She grinned, elated for her friend. "Let me know if you need a silent partner."

Lana's bordeaux-colored mouth quirked from side to side. "Thanks, Alex, but I'd rather have your friendship than your money."

"It doesn't have to be an either-or situation—look at me and my dad."

Lana gave her a pointed look.

Alex sighed in concession. "Okay. Just let me know if I can help."

"Thanks. And eyes wide open this afternoon in the dressing room—I expect *firm* details."

"Get out of here."

"Bye."

Alex toyed with the angel hair pasta on her plate a few minutes longer before she abandoned her lunch, troubling thoughts niggling the back of her mind. She'd been outraged at Jack's recognition that she was physically attracted to him, and it was that outrage which had kept her awake at night, she told herself, not the image of his mocking grin, his dancing eyes.

And this infuriating anticipation of seeing Jack again was only because she wanted to get the whole thing over with, this expensive, time-consuming experiment of her father's. And the dressing and undressing part was nothing to be nervous about—she'd worked with plenty of male models. One thing was certain: She would have to take control of the situation early on to maintain the upper hand where Jack Stillman was concerned.

Yes, she decided, reaching for her water glass with a shaky hand, *take control.*

CONSIDERING THE WAY their business-dinner meeting had ended, Jack figured he'd better arrive at the wardrobe meeting at Tremont's early. But as luck would have it, Stripling had questions regarding some of Jack's entertainment expenses incurred the previous year. Since Jack could barely recall the events of the previous *week,* he had problems substantiating the receipts. Jack spent over an hour trying to convince the man that The Golden Pony was a hotbed of business networking opportunities—this while ignoring Tuesday's muttered quotes from the Bible on the evils of the flesh as she flitted around the office taking measurements. For what purpose the woman was measuring, he didn't care to know.

In short, he was late.

"You're late," Alex confirmed when she emerged from her office to meet him, her arms crossed, her red mouth unsmiling.

"Sorry," he said, shaken anew by her beauty. "Problems at the office."

"*Your* problems, not mine. Let's go—my time is money."

And his wasn't, apparently. How did she do that? he wondered. How did she give the impression she was snapping her fingers in time to her rapid little stride. He had to jog to catch up to her, barely making it onto the elevator before the door closed. Sensing her mood, he stepped to the opposite side of the small cubicle and whistled tunelessly while they descended. Not a great lover of perfumes—he refused to stray from Old Spice— he nonetheless appreciated the citrusy fragrance emanating from her rigid body. Very...tasty.

Her hair was tightly bound again. She wore an immaculate pale gray suit with sharp, uncluttered lines and a lemon-yellow blouse peeking through the vee of her buttoned jacket. He'd bet the woman didn't own a single garment with polka dots or ruffles. Ten to one, she slept in that big cold-looking bed of hers in black flannel pajamas with thick socks on her feet. Reddinger didn't seem to be the hot-blooded type.

As if she were reading his mind, her shoulders shook with a shiver as she stared straight ahead.

"Are you cold?"

She sniffed. "I caught pneumonia riding on that death machine of yours the other night."

"Oh, good," he said as the doors slid open. "Something else today that's my fault." He swept his arm toward the opening and gave her a pleasant smile.

Her mouth tightened and she strode out into the men's department as if she owned it. Which she kind of *did*, he acknowledged with a smirk, then followed her, wishing he'd taken more pains dressing this morning. His "proper" attire was negligible to begin with, and the set of barbells in the corner of the Florida guest house he'd shared with Teresa—or was it Tammy?—had expanded his biceps and deltoids to the seams of the polo shirts in his closet. One beige golf shirt had been a passable fit, so he'd tucked it into navy slacks, which weren't bad. But he couldn't find a belt or a pair of non-holey socks, so he skipped both and donned a pair of buttery-soft loafers, which had once been tan-colored, if memory served.

Oh, well, clothes had never been that important to him. Nakedness was just so much more interesting.

"Hi, Reggie," Alex said as she walked up to a sales counter.

He recognized the handsome black youth immediately because of the resemblance of his smile to Tuesday's.

"Hello, Ms. Tremont."

"Mr. Stillman, this is Reggie Humphrey, one of our top sales associates. Reggie, this is—"

"Jack Stillman," Reggie finished, stepping out from behind the counter and extending his hand with a grin. "This is a real pleasure, sir, working with Jack the Attack."

"The pleasure's mine," he said smoothly.

Alex cleared her throat, bouncing a time's-a-wasting glance between them. "Let's get started, shall we? Reggie, would you fetch a tailor?"

The young man nodded, then disappeared. Alex

turned back to him and tapped the notepad she held. "I'll need your sizes, please."

She really was a stunner, he affirmed as he studied her smooth skin, and her luminous eyes, which were aimed straight at him. Darn his promise to Derek—he bet she was a real tigress in bed. Sometimes the bun-packing yuppies were sleepers. "Sizes of which body parts?" He grinned, hoping to cajole a smile out of her.

Instead, her mouth pursed into a tight little bow and fifteen seconds passed before she said through gritted teeth, "Shoulders."

"Forty-four."

She made a note with a gold-tone pen. "Height?"

"Six-three."

"Neck?"

"Sixteen and a half."

"Sleeve?"

"Thirty-six."

"Waist?"

"Same."

"Shoe size?"

"Thirteen, extra wide."

She shook her head, as if disgusted.

"It has its advantages," he felt compelled to inform Miss Unenlightened.

When she glanced up, pink tinged her cheeks, much to his satisfaction. She closed her eyes briefly, then looked back to the notepad. "Inseam?"

"Thirty-six."

Reggie returned, reporting that a tailor would meet them at the dressing rooms.

"Thank you, Reggie. I need you to record the items of clothing as I select them."

Jack squirmed. As *she* selected them?

Reggie produced a rolling clothes rack, and appeared poised to follow her around.

She walked to the suits first, walking her fingers through them. "The brown Twain, the light blue Dion, the olive Tremont's." Alex moved from rack to rack, rattling off colors and labels for slacks, shirts, ties, sweaters, jeans, belts, socks, underwear, shoes and a couple of items he'd never even heard of, all of it conservative and stuffy. She frequently consulted Reggie, whose opinion she seemed to respect.

"Follow me," she said, explaining that a couple of dressing rooms had been set aside for the fitting. He and Reggie traipsed behind her as if carrying the ends of her fur-trimmed robe. Jack did, however, manage to snag a package from an underwear rack as he trotted by. If he had to be subjected to this dress up game, why not shake up Alex a teensy bit?

The dressing room area was a secluded clearing of gleaming gray marble. A love seat faced two changing stalls with louvered three-quarter doors. Jack suspected that special male customers were treated to this private alcove during extensive shopping trips. Alex directed Reggie where to place the rolling clothes rack, then thanked and dismissed him.

Alex consulted the list Reggie had assembled, then without ceremony, transferred a stack of clothing from the rack to his arms. "We'll start with underwear so the tailor can take your precise measurements."

"You don't trust the ones I gave you?"

Her smile was deceptively sweet. "Men have a way of exaggerating in one direction or the other."

He lifted his eyebrows, but her expression was threatening, as if she dared him to make a smart remark. Amused by her solemn demeanor, Jack simply smiled and moved obediently into the dressing room. The louvered door covered him from shoulders to knees, allowing him to watch Alex watch him beneath her lashes as he removed his shirt. Masculine pride welled in his chest as he tossed his shirt on a bench. Twenty-two was a distant memory, but thanks to good genes and occasional exercise, he'd been able to maintain a decent physique.

"Did you get your car released?" he asked.

She sneezed into a handkerchief, then nodded. "Yes, in exchange for ninety-five dollars."

He whistled low. "You should have let me buy your dinner." When she didn't answer, he added, "Next time." Again, she didn't answer. Shrugging, Jack removed the black thong underwear from the package he'd nabbed and proceeded to stuff himself into the scrap of Lycra. Damn, men actually wore these things? A jock strap was more comfortable. After much adjusting, he stepped back to appraise his bulging reflection. Not half bad for a has-been.

He glanced over the door to where Alex sat in the middle of the love seat, legs crossed primly, expression humorless. "Mr. Stillman, I don't have all day, and you still have a lot of clothes to try on."

Incredibly, his body leapt at the sound of her chiding voice—he'd never been turned on before by a scolding. He sucked in a breath through his teeth and said, "Coming." Chuckling at his own word choice, he stepped out, adopting a most innocent look on his face.

AT THE SOUND OF THE DOOR clicking open, Alex looked up...and the pen slipped out of her suddenly loose hand. At first glance, she feared he was naked, then realized with no small amount of relief that his privates were covered by a minuscule amount of stretchy black fabric. He stood before her, hands on hips, legs shoulder-width apart. His bronze body was finely corded and accented with patches of dark hair on his chest, stomach and thighs. He had the physique of an athlete, all right—any athlete. Long-limbed and so finely put together, his body seemed tuned for any type of physical activity. Sexual awareness zipped through her, warming her erogenous zones.

At last, she dragged her gaze from him and pretended to study the list Reggie had assembled. "I...don't recall seeing that particular...garment...on the list." Was that her voice, high and breathless?

"They were on the pile," he said simply. His shrug displaced all kinds of muscle. "This modeling stuff is new to me—am I supposed to turn around or something?"

On treacherous ground, Alex swallowed, striving to calm her jumping pulse, the desire that had pooled low in her stomach. Perhaps if she didn't have to look him in the eye... "That...would be fine."

He turned to stand with his back to her, his legs wide apart. The skinny strap of the thong left nothing to the imagination, and why should it, she asked herself, when the reality was so impressive? The sole flaw on his body, if it could be called a flaw, was a black tattoo high on his right shoulder, a pair of wings about the size of a silver dollar. The lower regions of her body thrummed outrageously at the sight of those wings, given movement and texture by the bumpy muscle beneath his smooth skin.

"You...can turn back around now," she said, struggling for composure. In hindsight, she should have started with suits. Where the devil was that tailor?

He didn't move, except to lift a hand to scratch his temple. "Gee, boss, I don't think turning around would be such a great idea at the moment."

The meaning of his words sunk in, sending heat to her thighs. Then she heard footsteps on the other side of the privacy screen and breathed a sigh of relief that the tailor had arrived.

"Hello, my dear—oh!"

Alex turned just in time to see her father's eyes widen as his gaze landed on nearly nude Jack. Worse, Heath walked in behind her father and adopted a similar expression. Her heart jumped to her throat and she jumped to her feet when she realized how compromising the situation looked. "Father, Heath—what an unexpected surprise." She hugged the clipboard to her chest and pasted on a serious expression.

Jack looked over his shoulder and lifted his hand in greeting, but otherwise didn't move a muscle. "How's it going, Mr. T? Reddinger?"

"Fine, Jack," her father said, his voice laced with amusement as he gave her a questioning look. Heath just continued to look from her to Jack. Or rather, from her to Jack's backside.

Wanting to disappear, she instead conjured up a sublime smile for Heath. "Wh-when did you get back in town?"

"Not long ago," he replied absently.

"And not soon enough," her father muttered for her ears only.

She frowned at him and shook her head in warning.

"Heath and I were both looking for you, my dear," her father said in a louder voice. "Tess told us where to find you."

She was going to fire that woman. "Jack and I were just starting to choose his wardrobe for the photo shoot and the commercial."

"Let's try to keep the censors off our back, shall we?" Al said cheerfully.

"Father," she said, exasperated. "We're waiting for the tailor."

"When he gets here," her father said, peering around Jack, then clapping him on the back, "let him know our boy is a left-handed dresser."

Alex closed her eyes briefly, her cheeks flaming.

"Alex," Heath said. "May I see you outside?"

"Of course," she said, unreasonably nervous, but delighted for an excuse to flee the preposterous scene.

Once they stepped around the corner, Heath scanned the area, then grabbed her hand, pulled her into an alcove, and kissed her soundly. Surprised at his uncharacteristic behavior at work, Alex laughed and drew back, hiding her unexplainable irritation. "What's this all about?"

"I missed you," he said, his gaze intent. "And I guess it did something to me when I saw you with a half-dressed man."

She scoffed, feeling prickly. "That's ridiculous. I can barely stand the man."

"Good," he said, giving her a crooked grin. "I'm sorry I missed our dinner at Gerrard's."

Alex fidgeted, reluctant to admit she'd used their reservation, even sat at their *table*, with the man she could barely stand. Heath wouldn't understand the circumstances, she reasoned—Jack giving her a ride home, then tackling a would-be attacker in her apartment. It all sounded too...intimate.

Anxious to spend time with Heath and erase the memory of Jack, she smoothed his jacket lapel and tilted her face up at him. "How about us taking the afternoon off tomorrow and using my father's box at Keeneland for opening day at the races?"

Heath smiled. "Terrific. I'll pick you up at your apartment at noon."

Alex exhaled in relief—just the two of them. By the time she got through this disconcerting afternoon, she'd be ready for a day without the presence of "Jack the Attack" Stillman.

"Whew," Jack said to Reggie upon emerging from the dressing room. "Am I ever glad *that* is over." The binding thong had been nothing compared to the torture of behaving himself around Alex all afternoon while she pulled and poked at his clothing, suggesting alterations that the tailor marked with a gazillion little razor-sharp pins. "That tailor missed his calling in acupuncture."

Reggie laughed good-naturedly. "When my mom told me you were going to be the new spokesman for Tremont's, I was hoping I'd have the chance to work with you, sir."

"Call me Jack. 'Sir' makes me feel like I'm a hundred years old." Jack leaned one arm on the counter. "Listen, Reggie, speaking of your mother, is she, uh—"

"Unstable?" the young man asked with a grin.

"Well, the thought had crossed my mind."

"To be honest, all of us kids have just gotten used to her eccentricity. She travels around the country, stays with one of us for a while, then moves on to another."

"How many siblings do you have?"

"Nine."

"Wow. No wonder she acts like a general."

"Yep, she's a go-getter. If it makes you feel any better, though, she's a smart lady."

"Yeah, well, no offense, but I think I have too many smart ladies in my life right now." He looked around.

"Ms. Tremont left."

"Probably went to let the air out of my tires," he muttered.

Reggie laughed. "She said she was going to accessories to buy a new hat for tomorrow."

"Tomorrow?"

"Opening day at Keeneland. Said she and Mr. Reddinger are using her father's box seats."

Jack always wondered who sat in the expensive box seats, and now he knew. Personally, he thought the cheap seats had the best access to the betting windows, but then again, the people in the boxes attended the horse races mostly to socialize, to see and be seen, not to wager their beer money on the trifecta.

"Sounds fun, doesn't it?" Reggie asked, his voice wistful.

"It'll probably rain," Jack said sourly, then thanked Reggie for his help and moved toward the escalator. He wasn't sure why the thought of Alex spending the day with Reddinger bothered him so much—they were a couple before he came on the scene and probably would be long after his stint with Tremont's ended. Nursing an increasing bad mood, he stepped onto the down escalator only to see Al Tremont on the opposite escalator, being carried up.

"Jack, I was hoping you hadn't left," the beaming man called, turning as they passed. "I forgot to ask you earlier if you would join me tomorrow in my box at Keeneland for opening day."

Jack's ill humor vanished. He cupped his hands around his mouth so his voice would travel across the distance widening between them. "Thanks—I'll be there!"

10

TUESDAY WAGGED HER FINGER. "With work coming out of your big ears, you're going to spend the afternoon at the racetrack?"

"It's business," Jack insisted.

"So if your brother calls, I can tell him where you are?"

He balked. "That might not be prudent."

She put one hand on her hip, arm akimbo, and nodded. "Mmm-hmm. I thought so."

Jack gave her his most charming grin. "But I feel lucky. In fact, I'm planning to win enough money to get new equipment for the office." He gestured around, then stopped and squinted. Several vines and ferns, plus two palm trees accented shelves and corners in the front office. "Where did all the plants come from?"

"I have a green thumb," she said, then handed him a stack of papers. "Sign, lick and mail."

"Tuesday." Jack ran his hand down the length of his face. "There is no job! I can't pay you for working here."

"Five dollars," she said, pulling out a file drawer. Rows of new color-coded hanging files swayed gently.

"What?"

"Put five dollars on the daily double for me, horses two and five." She turned a placid smile in his direction. "And that'll be my pay for the first two weeks."

"What if it doesn't come in?"

She shrugged. "Life is a gamble."

Jack pursed his mouth—he could live with that. He walked through the doorway into the back office where the auditor still claimed Derek's desk. "How's it going, Mr. Stripling?"

The man scowled. "If you must know, terribly." His voice and hands were shaking, and the boardlike device was still strapped to his back by a cord around his waist and chest.

Jack poured himself a cup of coffee from the little refreshment center Tuesday had established on a sturdy table she'd confiscated from the supply room—coffeemaker, tea bags, creamer, sugar and fresh minibagels every morning. He'd considered hinting for jelly donuts, but decided not to push his luck. Her one rule had been not to touch the single china cup and saucer sitting nearby—it had been her mother's and was to be used only in emergencies, she instructed. Jack wasn't exactly sure what kind of an emergency would require fine china, but he hadn't argued. He lifted his mug in the other man's direction. "More receipt problems?"

"No, not more receipt problems," the man snapped. "Unbeknownst to me, your office manager has been plying my tea with some repulsive concoction of dried leaves—she's probably trying to poison me."

"Tuesday," Jack yelled, stirring cream into his coffee. "Are you trying to poison Mr. Stripling?"

"No," she yelled back.

Jack took a bite out of a blueberry bagel and shrugged. "You heard her."

Stripling's face reddened to a deep crimson. "I'm on the verge of convulsions here."

Tuesday appeared and sashayed by, rolling her eyes as she headed toward the bathroom. "It's called energy, tax man. That's what ginseng does for a body."

Jack dropped into his chair, chewing. When the door closed behind her, he said, "So that's what she's on."

"*Mr.* Stillman," Stripling croaked, his eyes bulging. "This will not look good in my report."

"Yeah, well, life's a bitch." Jack unfolded the paper and snapped it open to the day's racing form. "You play the ponies?"

"I most certainly do not."

He made a sympathetic sound. "Too bad. Races five and eight have great-looking long shots."

After a stretch of silence, Mr. Stripling cleared his throat, then offered, "My father was a groom for Spectacular Wish."

He flicked down the corner of the paper. "No kidding?"

The little man shifted in his chair, his expression slightly less unpleasant. "I do not kid."

"Then you *have* to place a bet, because the third horse in the eighth race is the granddaughter of Spectacular Wish."

He had the man's attention. "Through mare or sire?"

"Sire."

"Maiden race?"

"Yep."

"What are the odds?"

"Sixty to one."

"Let me see that form," the man said, and stood up with amazing agility for a man bound to a board.

"Lovely hat," Heath said with a smile.

Alex touched the wide brim of her chocolate-colored straw hat. "You don't think it's too big?"

"No. I think it's very chic."

"We're pushing these for fall, so I thought I'd advertise." She stepped back to allow him inside her apartment. "You look nice yourself."

He wore classic horseman colors: hunter green slacks and a tan shirt, with a navy-and-green-plaid cotton sweater tied around his neck. "Thanks," he said, looking boyish as he gave the bridge of his small glasses a nudge.

"Just give me a minute to change my purse." Alex agonized between two purses, finally settling on a brown leather tote to go with her cream-colored water-silk dress, fitted through the torso, but with a long flowing skirt. At the last minute, she tossed a brown leopard-print scarf around her shoulders.

"Jacket?" Heath asked.

"No, I—" Alex looked up and stopped, staring at the black leather coat Heath held by the collar. *Jack's* coat. Oh, no. "Wh-where did you find that?" she asked, stalling.

Mouth pursed, he nodded to a table behind the door. "Under there."

"Really? It...must be one of the things Lana dropped off." She smiled wide—convincingly, she hoped.

"It's a man's coat."

Her smile dissolved. "Well, she's been stealing things lately—it's all very weird." Alex looked at her watch and gasped. "Oh, fudge. Look. We'd better get going if we don't want to miss the first race." With one motion, Alex yanked the coat out of his hand and tossed it over a chair. "You know how bad parking can be." She steered Heath back into the hallway and closed the door behind her.

And Heath, bless his trusting heart, didn't ask another question about the jacket. Just to make sure, she chattered the entire drive about news and nonsense, since all the work-related topics that came to mind seemed to lead back to Jack: The vacated vice presidency...proving herself by taking on difficult tasks...the Jack Stillman project. Sliding sales...a new ad campaign...the Jack Stillman project.

"It's crowded all right," Heath noted as they waited in a long line of cars to access the preferred parking area. "I'll drop you off, then park and meet you at our seats."

"Okay," she agreed, feeling a bit guilty. She didn't mind the walk, but she did want to minimize the chance of the mysterious leather jacket coming up again. Once inside, the crowd noise and the excitement would alleviate conversation for the most part. She gave him a loving smile before she alighted and closed the door to his black Mercedes. As he pulled away, Alex berated herself for not simply telling Heath the truth. After all, her evening with Jack had been purely innocent, hadn't it?

Hadn't it?

She sighed inwardly as she merged with the crowd of people moving through the admission gates. The Keeneland facility was a rambling two-story stone structure that housed covered walkways, spectator grandstands, restaurants, and window after window for placing bets. Horse racing appealed to all walks of life—retirees looking for a day of inexpensive entertainment, college kids looking for an excuse to party, professionals looking for a network, dyed-in-the-wool horse people looking for a reputation, and hard-core gamblers looking for this month's rent. Most people dressed up, and many women wore hats, as was tradition. As far as people-watching venues were concerned, Keeneland was one of the finest.

Alex loved it here. Just walking past the paddock area where the horses exercised was thrilling—the sight of the colorful silks, the pungent odor of groomed horseflesh, the whinnying of eager mounts. All of it sent the blood rushing through her veins, as if she were a teensy part of the centuries-old legacy.

But the best moment came after climbing the stairs to the stands and walking out for the first breathless view of the track. Awesome. The enormous ring of freshly raked black earth was lined with a fence on both sides, and skirted by lush grass and beautifully manicured shrubbery that spelled out "Keeneland" in enormous letters. As large as a movie screen, the black tote board sat on the inner ring of grass, already flashing jockey changes and entry scratches. The entire scene hummed and was poignant enough to make a person want to burst out singing "My Old Kentucky Home."

Her spirits lifted with every step as she made her way toward the box seats in the milling crowd. Alex held on to her hat and tilted her face to the sun—she was spending a gorgeous day with the man who cared most about her, and Jack Stillman was far, far away.

"Well, if it isn't a small world."

Alex froze, unwilling to believe the familiar voice behind her belonged to the person she thought it did.

"I said, *if it isn't a small world.*"

Keeping a firm hold on her hat, Alex whirled. She gaped at Jack Stillman lounging in her father's box, clad in faded jeans and a pale blue denim shirt, with his black booted feet crossed at the ankles and propped on the little half wall that separated their four seats from the adjacent box. Small binoculars hung around his neck.

She marched closer and gasped, "What are you doing here?"

"Drinking a beer," he said, lifting the half-empty plastic cup.

"I mean, what are you doing *here*, in our box?"

He grinned behind black sunglasses. "Your dad invited me."

Her heart pounded at the thought of sharing such a small space with him and—good Lord—with him *and* Heath for several hours. "Why?"

Unfazed by her obvious disapproval, he shrugged. "Because he likes me, I suppose."

Exasperated, she closed her eyes and took a deep breath. "Where *is* my father?"

"I haven't seen him, he told me to meet him here." He peered around her. "Is your boyfriend with you?"

Alex gritted her teeth, then said, "Yes, Heath is with me, and this seating arrangement simply will not work."

"Why not?" He looked at the chair wedged next to his and the two close behind him. "Four seats, four people." He lifted his sunglasses and squinted up at her. "You might have to lose that lampshade on your head, though."

Her mouth fell open. "You insufferable—"

Jack stood abruptly, balancing his beer with one hand, waving with the other. "Hey, Mr. T!"

Alex blew out a long, shaky breath, fisting her hands to resist strangling Jack, then turned to offer her father a welcoming smile.

"Jack! And Alex—what a delightful surprise!"

She leaned forward to kiss her father's cheek, but her hat poked him in the eye.

"Goodness, my dear, that thing is dangerous."

"I'm sorry," she murmured, shooting a murderous look toward Jack who hid his smile behind a drink from his cup. "I should have asked if you were using the box today. With Gloria the Gold—" She stopped, bit her tongue, then continued, "I mean, with Gloria out of town, I just assumed it would be okay if Heath and I came."

"But it is," her father said cheerfully. "This is a family box, Alex, you know that. We'll have a wonderful time, all of us." He put one arm around her shoulders, and one arm around Jack's, pulling them into him. "And with Jack being our company spokesman, he's practically family."

JACK GRINNED AT AL—the man was immensely likable. And he respected him for his down-to-earth attitude despite his accomplishments and wealth. He realized suddenly how this man and his own father had formed a bond during their brief encounter. Paul Stillman, like Jack, would have responded to Al Tremont's magnanimous outlook, and Al surely reacted to his father's spirit of generosity. In fact, Al reminded him a bit of his father—not so much in looks as in personality. The kinship was comforting.

He glanced from Al's glowing face to Alex, who glared at him beneath the brim of her ridiculous hat with an almost palpable dislike. Did he imagine it, or did she pull closer to her father? Puzzled, Jack withdrew from Al's casual embrace, and excused himself to collect drinks for the group. While standing in line at the concession stand on the top level, he mulled his observation. Was it possible that Alex was *jealous* of her father's time and attention?

From his vantage point behind and above the stands, he watched Alex with her father, studying their body language. They were still standing, as was most of the crowd since thirty minutes remained until the first race. Alex seemed to find excuses to touch him—straightening the collar of his golf shirt, reaching up to smooth a strand of his sparse white hair.

Al appeared to tolerate her ministrations, but not much more. In fact, he seemed more absorbed in his racing form than in the elegant woman next to him who so obviously adored him. Jack frowned as Reddinger emerged from the crowd to join them. Al shook his hand, but kept Reddinger at arm's length. The man leaned close to Alex and angled his head as if to kiss her, but the hat got in the way.

Jack smiled.

He paid for four beers and four bowls of thick, dark burgoo stew, then elbowed his way back to the seats. "Lunch is served," he said, nodding hello to Reddinger, who nodded back with a distinctly unfriendly look.

"Ahh," Al Tremont said. "I've been craving burgoo since I last had it at the spring races." He collected a bowl and a cup of beer, then settled into one of the two front chairs. Jack looked back and forth between the happy couple. "There's enough here for everyone, and my arms are getting a little tired."

"Um, we don't eat red meat," Reddinger said, wrinkling his nose as his hand snaked around Alex's waist. The man looked like a prep school class president. He probably owned a pink sport coat.

"More for us," Al chirped, having already put a dent in his first portion of the stew thick with a dozen kinds of meat, including wild game.

Jack smiled back at Reddinger and Alex, then nodded toward the beer. "Do you beatniks eat hops and barley?"

"Actually, we prefer mint juleps," Reddinger said.

Naturally.

"Ah, have a beer," Al said, waving away their resistance. "You two don't know how to have a good time."

Jack struggled to hide his mirth as the pair frowned, then dutifully retrieved their cups of beer. He started to claim the seat next to Al, but the older man held up his hand.

"Jack, I need to discuss a few matters with Heath. Would you mind if he sat with me?"

"Not at all, sir." He exchanged tight smiles with Alex and Reddinger, then dropped into the seat behind Al and proceeded to eat. The couple stood around, shifting from foot to foot and murmuring for a couple of minutes before Reddinger sat down next to Al. Within a few minutes, the men had their heads together.

Alex stood a few steps away in the grandstand aisle, apparently unaware that the sun turned the thin dress she wore into a virtual peep show. Jack settled back in his chair to enjoy the view of her slender silhouette, the curve of her breasts bound up in a thin-strapped bra, the line of her hip skimmed by high-cut panties. Damn, with her long graceful neck and delicate limbs, the woman could easily be mistaken for a ballet dancer instead of a ball-buster. He took a long sip of cool beer and swallowed hard.

"Jack, we're going to place our bets," Al said, standing. "Want to come?"

Jack tore his gaze from Alex. "No, thanks, I'm covered for the first two races."

"Alex?"

She shook her head, and with the shade of her huge hat, nearly caused an eclipse of the sun. "I'd rather not fight the crowd."

"I'll place a bet for you," Heath said, and she smiled her thanks.

Jack frowned as the men turned and climbed up the concrete steps toward the covered top level where most of the betting windows were located. As much as Jack wanted to keep ogling her, he was even more compelled to bring her closer. "You going to stand all day?"

The only indication that she'd heard him was a slight lift of her chin. Then, holding the cup of beer as if it were swill, she stepped inside the box, moved her folding padded chair as far away from Jack's as possible—a full two inches—and sat down primly.

Jack watched with his tongue in his cheek as she looked for a place to set her unwieldy shoulder bag and a place to position her expensively clad feet. After a few minutes of shifting, adjusting, and fidgeting, she fell still, staring straight ahead, her shoulders shoved back against the metal chair.

"Comfortable?" he asked.

She turned her head and the brim of her hat poked him in the eye.

"Ow!"

"I'm sorry," she said, jerking back and spilling most of her beer on her dress. "Oh, dammit!" She jumped up and held the wet fabric of her skirt away from her. With his lap full of unclaimed food, Jack could only lean forward and dab at the wetness on her thigh with a handful of napkins.

"Stop it!" she snapped, swatting at his hand. When she realized that people around them were staring, she sat down, morosely holding the half-full cup of beer.

"Why don't you drink it before you drown yourself?"

She shot him a sideways glare, then lifted the cup to her tight little mouth and took a tentative sip. "You left your coat at my apartment," she said, her voice accusing.

"I figured as much," he said. "I kept forgetting to ask if you found it."

"*Heath* found it."

"Oh." He smiled into his beer, then spooned in the last mouthful of burgoo and chewed slowly. "Got you in trouble, did I?"

"No!" She turned her head and her hat poked him in the eye again.

"Ow!" Jack covered his watery eye and glowered at her with the other one.

She winced. "I'm sorry!"

Jack set down his trash, then politely said, "Excuse me." He stood and with both hands, lifted the hat from her dark head and flung it across the top of the crowd down toward the infield, where the more rowdy patrons gathered in a sea of moving color.

"Hey!" she shouted, staring open-mouthed as the hat sailed on the air like a big, brown Frisbee, finally hooking onto the head of a humongous man, who promptly ripped it off and winged it farther down the line, like a beach ball in a sports stadium.

Her eyes widened to dangerous proportions, and her face flushed fuchsia. Sputtering, she glared at Jack. "That hat cost three hundred dollars!"

He whistled low as he settled back in his chair and retrieved his beer. "Looks like you're going to have to win big today to recoup that loss."

"Me? You mean *you!*" She stood and stared down at him until he'd taken two more deep drinks of beer. Her arms, shoulders, and fisted hands began to shake. "I...you...I'm going to tell—"

"Your daddy? Or your boyfriend?" he asked, half expecting the woman to tackle him, and fully expecting to like it.

"You are so immature," she hissed.

"Mr. Stillman?"

Jack turned to see a red-haired man standing near him,

holding an impressive looking camera and wearing what looked to be some kind of press pass. "Yes?"

"My name is Majeris—I'm the sports anchor for the local PBC affiliate. Sammy Richardson told me to look you up while I was here covering opening day. Said you'd just signed on as a spokesman for a local business, and that I might get a sound bite for tonight's broadcast."

Jack rose and extended his hand. "Nice to meet you."

"Pleasure's mine, sir. You're a legend around the sports desk."

Smiling, Jack said, "That's nice to hear, especially since I've been out of the game for so long. But I'm back in town, running an advertising firm with my brother, Derek—he also played football for UK—and there's a possibility I might become the spokesman for Tremont's department store." He grinned and extended his arm to include Alex, who, besides wearing a dazed expression, sported a wet, stained dress and hat-flattened hair. "Meet my lovely boss, Ms. Alexandria Tremont."

Majeris lifted his camera and shot a half-dozen pictures of the two of them before Alex could even blink.

11

ALEX FINALLY RECOVERED enough to ask the reporter, "Excuse me, but who did you say told you about Mr. Stillman?" Tremont's had not yet issued a press release announcing the name of their new spokesman—Alex had wanted to wait until the end of the two weeks, in the highly likely event that Jack would not work out.

"Sammy Richardson."

"Sammy is producing the commercial spots," Jack supplied. "We spoke this morning to set up studio time for Monday. I figured the station would be sending out someone to cover opening race day, so I thought why not get a headstart on publicity?"

She manufactured a smile, thinking that throwing Jack under the pounding hooves of the horses as they raced by would surely make the eleven o'clock news. "Yes, why not?" she parroted, finger combing her hair in an attempt to counter the effects of her now-missing hat. "Mr. Majeris, you may report a *rumor* that Jack Stillman will be signed by Tremont's, but our public relations department will supply your station with a press release in due time."

The man nodded curtly. "A couple more pictures, Jack?" He shot Alex a guilty glance, then added, "Of Jack alone?"

Tingling with indignance, Alex stepped back while the young man shot several photos in succession with Jack grinning into the lens. Then Jack signed an autograph for the young man who asked that he sign "Jack the Attack." And either several spectators had already recognized Jack or the reporter's camera had tipped them off, because before Majeris could leave, a knot of people had gathered for autographs. He worked the crowd like a pro, flirting and signing his name with a flourish.

Alex drained her half cup of beer, then sat down when the alcohol bypassed her empty stomach and zoomed straight to her head. He was a good-looking man, she admitted miserably, an opinion that was mirrored in the eyes of the women trying to get close to him. The denim shirt he wore accentuated his dark hair and his ruggedness. But she remembered too well that he looked just as good in a designer suit. And even better in black thong underwear. Extremely vexed, she acknowledged that her father's choice to make Jack the store spokesman might not have been as faulty as she had first presumed.

God, how she hated being wrong. And in front of her father, no less.

By the time his fan club had dissipated, Alex had even ventured to taste a spoonful of the dark stew he had bought—which wasn't half bad—and she was contemplating going to the ladies room to remove her pale, sheer panty hose. Why keep up the pretense of dignity? She sighed as her beautiful hat, torn, dusty and misshapen, skipped and bumped its way across the infield far below.

"It didn't suit you anyway," Jack murmured as he reclaimed his seat. "You look better in a motorcycle helmet."

"I'll let the milliners know they're missing out on a trend," she said wryly, not about to let on that his words made her heart skip a beat.

"I predict we have the winners," her father announced as he and Heath returned, tickets in hand.

Heath smiled as he handed her a ticket. "I picked horse number six for you, sweetheart, because the silks are red, and I know it's your favorite color."

Next to her, Jack snorted softly.

Alex squirmed. "Thanks." She shot an irritated glance toward Jack. "Which horse did you bet on?"

His mouth twitched at the corner. "Let's just say that red isn't my favorite color." When Heath and her father sat in the front seats, he added under his breath, "I prefer flesh tones."

She tried not to react, but the man was so outrageous, she couldn't help shaking her head in exasperation.

"I think I see the beginning of a smile," he whispered.

"You're mistaken," she whispered back, determined to keep her mirth under wraps. Jack simply mustn't know how much his nearness affected her.

The tote board ticked down to five minutes until the first race, and the mounted entries were led onto the track by calmer lead horses with their own riders. The crowd hummed louder in anticipation as the horses performed their customary walk down the homestretch of the track, then turned and walked back to the starting line. The jockeys lifted their crops toward the grandstands, churning the spectators into a higher froth.

"Alex," Heath shouted over the din. "Is that *your* hat?" He pointed, his eyebrows high, toward the swollen infield, where the weary hat was still being bandied about.

"Yes," she replied dully, refusing to look at Jack. "It...got away from me."

The starting gate was pulled across the track by a small tractor, and the nail-biting task of loading the horses into the gate was begun. Alex had seen more than one horse and rider injured during this most dangerous part of the race. As was customary, the second the last horse was safely inside, the front gates slammed open, and the horses shot forward.

Alex gave in to the tangible excitement, impossible to ignore as the horses stretched forward until their bodies were almost horizontal. The crowd in the grandstand jumped to their feet in waves. The noise was thunderous as everyone shouted for their chosen mount and the nimble-tongued announcer belted the names of the front runners at every turn. Less than a minute later, the race was over. Horses number two, one and seven came in to win, place and show, and a quick glance at the program revealed the odds on at least two of the entries had been long. Much to her dismay, the number six horse carrying the red-silked jockey not only crossed the finish line last, but way, way behind with a lazy, playful trot that had the audience laughing.

Alex ripped her ticket in half to the tune of Jack's chuckle.

"I only had the show horse," her father said, turning around.

"Nothing for me," Heath said.

Everyone looked to Jack, who seemed remarkably calm.

"Well?" Alex prompted.

His shrug was casual. "I hit the exacta."

Alex glanced at the tote board just as the payout for the exacta—choosing the win and place horses—flashed on the screen. A two dollar bet returned three hundred and fifty dollars, and she suspected that Jack's bet had been more than two dollars.

Her father whooped and Heath pursed his mouth.

Alex simply smiled and murmured, "At least you can afford to buy me a new hat."

He didn't answer, simply relaxed in his chair to study the day's racing form, punctuated, she noted, with mysterious notes in the margins, and dotted with curious circles and boxes in various colors.

"Some kind of foolproof system of yours?" she asked, squinting under the glare of the sun.

He handed her his sunglasses, and feeling stubbornly deserving, she took them. "My system isn't quite as scientific as picking the horse based on the jockey's silks," he said, one side of his mouth drawn back.

Scientific or not, his system seemed to work because by the end of the third race, he'd racked up more winning tickets. Her father had hit a couple of payoffs himself, but she and Heath had nothing to show for their hit-and-miss guessing.

"What do you have in the fourth race?" she asked, waving off Heath's offer to place her bet.

"This one's tough," Jack admitted, shaking his head. "The favorites are so strong, they're bound to win and place, but they'll only pay out a pittance."

"So?" She leaned over, watching his finger move over the form as he pointed out subtleties in bloodline, jockeys and race length. He had nice hands, she observed, her mouth going strangely dry. Large and square-palmed, long, blunt-tipped fingers, good for catching footballs, she supposed. With a flash of revelation, she realized how Tremont's new fine jewelry department could be showcased in the commercials in a way that would appeal to women—she could put a wedding ring on him. But as quickly as the idea occurred to her, she tabled it, struck by the feeling that a wedding ring on Jack Stillman's finger seemed so unnatural that it might come across to the audience as being unbelievable.

"What's wrong?" he asked, scrutinizing his hands.

She shook her head, embarrassed. "Um, nothing. I was just thinking that you must miss playing football."

"Why would you say that?"

Alex shrugged. "It's your identity, isn't it? Jack the Attack?"

Jack nodded, then stood abruptly and mumbled that he needed to place another bet. Perplexed, she turned to watch him climb up the concrete steps of the grandstand, noticing hers wasn't the only pair of feminine eyes following him. And her chest filled with unreasonable satisfaction that he was with her today.

Well, not really with *her*, since he'd come as her father's guest.

A cell phone rang, causing Alex, Heath and her father all to reach for their personal devices.

"It's mine," Heath said, flipping up his phone's antenna and pressing his hand against his opposite ear.

Alex took the opportunity to tell her father about Jack's "plant" with the local sports reporter. "I don't like it, Dad. I thought we agreed he would prove himself first— two weeks, one of which is almost gone, I might add."

"We did."

"Yet he's acting as if he's already a permanent fixture at Tremont's. He didn't even run that little stunt by me first!"

"But you know any publicity is good publicity as long as they spell the name of the store correctly."

"Dad, he's a loose cannon."

"Which means," her father said mildly, "that it's up to you to keep tabs on him."

"But—"

"Honey, like I said before, Jack Stillman is a rebel, and I think he's just what we need around Tremont's to shake everything up a bit. In fact—" he tilted his head and gave her a gently curious look "—if I didn't know better, I'd say Jack had *you* shaken up."

Alex swallowed hard, telling herself not to overreact, yet stunned since her father had never before broached the subject of her personal life. "But you *do* know better," she corrected in a calm tone that belied her panic. Was her attraction to Jack so transparent that even her *father* could tell? She searched his blue eyes, so like her own, looking for comfort, trying to relay her confusion over the men in her life.

Al wet his lips and looked as if he might say something, then was interrupted by Heath flipping his phone closed.

"I hate to do this to you, Alex," Heath said, "but I'm needed at the office."

"What?"

"I'm sorry, sweetheart, but I didn't give my secretary enough notice to clear my afternoon calendar, and one of my appointments was already on a plane to Lexington when she called to reschedule."

She stood and sighed. "Well, if it can't be helped."

"There's no reason for you to leave," Heath said quickly. "I'm sure your father will be glad to take you home."

Alex looked to her father, who nodded confirmation.

"Okay," she relented, thinking that the day hadn't turned out anything like she'd planned. Still, she could have fun with her father and perhaps start to chip away at the wall erected between them by neglect and indifference. They both were to blame, she realized, studying her father's noble profile—she hadn't exactly extended herself since Gloria had come onto the scene. She vowed to make more of an effort to draw her father closer to her. And when she was a vice president, they'd be working closer together, too.

Heath distracted her from her musings with a quick kiss, and her father left to place a bet on the next race. Alex sat down, feeling restless and warm with the sun bearing down. Since her hat was no longer making the rounds, she imagined it dying a slow, painful death under the feet of tipsy spectators. Her ire rose just thinking about it.

"Shade, milady?"

She looked up to see Jack twirling, of all things, a cream-colored ruffled parasol.

His smile highlighted the cleft in his chin. "I'd hate to be responsible for freckles on that upturned nose of yours."

Despite his backhanded compliment, the picture he presented was simply too incongruous to keep a straight face. "Feeling guilty, are you?"

"Feeling generous," he corrected with a grin as he stepped into the box and slid the frilly umbrella into the hole behind their seats provided for the boxholders who wished to buy the pricey souvenirs. "Since I cashed in on the last race, and since it's down to just the two of us—" Jack stopped when she placed her hand on his arm—not an unwelcome gesture, just surprising.

"What do you mean 'down to just the two of us'?"

Jack pointed over his shoulder with his thumb. "I saw Al upstairs. He said he and Reddinger had to leave, and asked if I would see you home." He watched the emotions play over her face with a sinking realization. "You didn't know?"

She shook her head. "Don't worry, I'll call Heath to come back and pick me up when his meeting is over."

And he'd actually thought she'd agreed to—perhaps even wanted to—spend the rest of the afternoon with him, hence the ridiculous umbrella. "Suit yourself," he said with a mild shrug, not about to admit his acute disappointment, and not sure if he understood his own reaction. Regardless, considering how close he'd come to kissing the woman—and more—the last time he'd taken her home, her alternate plan seemed wise. His promise to Derek ran through his head as if on continuous play. Determined to get his mind off the leggy beauty sitting next to him, he turned his attention to the leggy beauties on the racetrack.

Except his task proved to be harder than he expected, mostly because Alex showed more curiosity in his picks and the reasons behind them. Despite his resolve, he liked having answers to questions she asked—for once. As her interest grew, she placed a couple of bets based on his recommendations, and when their long shot horse came in to place in the next race, she grabbed his arm and jumped up and down. Impulsively, Jack whirled her around and lowered a quick kiss on the cheek. Her eyes widened, but before she could chastise him, he grabbed her hand and pulled her up the steps to collect her payout. Jack blamed his pounding heart on the quick ascent. Derek was right, he conceded—he knew the woman was dangerous, yet he couldn't seem to help himself.

For her part, Alex quietly cashed in her winning ticket, then excused herself to the ladies' room. When she rejoined him at their seats a few minutes later, warning bells sounded in his head because she handed him a beer, and held one of her own. Plus, to his consternation, she'd shed her panty hose somewhere along the way, which gave him even more bare skin to endure. Jack took a long sip of the beer, then held the cool cup to his cheek. Best to steer the conversation back to business as soon as possible.

"I heard you're in the running for a vice presidency."

"Who told you that?"

"Your secretary."

"I should have guessed. The woman's in love with you, you know." She rolled her eyes.

Jack laughed. "So is it true?"

"About the vice presidency? Yes, I'm in the running, along with a few colleagues and a couple of external candidates."

"Who will make the decision?"

"The final call is the board of directors', although they'll probably take the recommendation of the members of senior management and my father."

"Sounds like you're a shoe in," he said carefully. She shook her head and he wondered if she knew how lovely she was—cheeks flushed, the wind picking up the ends of her hair. Her profile was classically tilted, a masterpiece that made his fingers itch for a stick of waxy pastels, or a vine of drawing charcoal to get the lines down on paper. He hadn't drawn anything for his own pleasure in years.

"I won't get favorable treatment simply because of my last name," she said. "In fact, my father is so concerned about nepotism, sometimes I think he errs in the other direction." She looked over at him with a rueful smile. "Sorry, you probably think that sounds like sour grapes."

"No." He wasn't inclined to criticize the one insightful tidbit she'd offered him into her personal and professional life.

"I'm actually very grateful for having the chance to learn from my father. He's a brilliant retailer who somehow seems to stay ahead of the trends even though he hasn't bought a new suit in ten years."

Jack smiled. "A great observer of the human condition."

She nodded, then took a small sip of her beer. "Although I can't say I always agree with him."

He lifted his cup for a drink. "Like his decision to hire me, for instance?"

She sighed. "Jack, you and I both know that *my* father hired you because of a spontaneous promise he made to *your* father, and because of your notoriety. Can you see why I'm a little skeptical? I've seen your office, remember. I know how limited your resources are. If I weren't concerned, I wouldn't be fulfilling my responsibility to the company."

Jack felt a stab of remorse for not stopping to consider the awkward position Alex must be in—follow her father, or follow her conscience. For the first time in his life, he wished he was successful by conventional standards, successful enough to give Alex confidence in his ability. Funny, but she was the only person—definitely the only woman—who hadn't taken him at face value. He was going to have to earn her trust, and respect. The fact that he was the cause of the little crease in her brow caused his gut to clench. "Alex," he said quietly, "I realize you have no reason to believe me, but I won't let you down."

She studied him for a few seconds, then tilted her head, a smile playing on her full lips. "I'm not certain, but I think I like this side of you."

Jack's pulse kicked up. "What side is that?"

"The almost-serious, professional side."

Did a more beautiful pair of eyes exist in the world? He

gestured toward her, head to toe. "I think I like this side of you."

Her thin, arched eyebrows rose. "What side is that?"

He grinned. "The beer-drinking, bare-legged gambler."

She blushed, then looked back to the track. "Which proves," she said, her voice featherlight, but deadly serious, "that anyone can playact for a few hours, but at the end of the day, we are who we are."

The bell announcing the start of the next race sounded, and her attention was diverted to the running of the maiden race that featured the granddaughter of Spectacular Wish. She leapt to her feet, cheering their underachiever on to victory. Jack was so distracted watching her and reveling in the elated hug she gave him afterward, he almost forgot to be glad for the chunk of change he'd just won. If he didn't know better, he'd have sworn that a subtle shift in their relationship had occurred during their abbreviated conversation.

Whatever the cause, Alex did seem more relaxed as the last couple of races were run. "It's much better when you're winning," she said, her eyes as bright as a child's as he removed the parasol in begrudged preparation to leave. The crowd, mostly losers for the day, had begun to dissipate much earlier in order to avoid the rush of exiting traffic. Suddenly her mouthed rounded to an O. "I forgot to call Heath!"

Jack closed his fingers around her wrist as she delved into her purse, presumably for her cellular phone. "I'll drive you—I need to pick up my jacket anyway." He told himself it was a good reason to put himself in an otherwise risky situation of being alone with Alex at her place. She stared down at his hand, and he reluctantly released her.

But she didn't retrieve her phone.

Instead, she struck out ahead of him, parasol twirling over her shoulder, and tossed back, "You're pretty confident for a man who destroyed my new hat."

Thoughts of hurrying to catch up with her were dismissed when he caught sight of her curvy sway. This was one woman he wouldn't mind walking a few steps behind for the rest of his—er, for a while. "Like I said, it didn't suit you."

"I know," she said, her voice sarcastic. "I look much better in a motorcycle helmet, my eyes squeezed shut, and holding on for dear life."

"Well," he drawled, loving the way the soft, long skirt of her dress floated up as she walked, revealing the backs of her knees and the curve of her calves. "I'm partial to that 'holding on for dear life' part." He nearly plowed into the back of her when she stopped abruptly to give him a pointed look.

"Okay," Jack pulled a snowy handkerchief from his back pocket and waved it in surrender. "I'll behave."

She shook her head, but he'd seen her look much more angry. Unbelievably buoyed, Jack steered her in the direction of his bike, parked on a knoll inaccessible by most vehicles. He withdrew his extra helmet and helped her strap it on snugly, tucking strands of dark lush hair beneath the face edge. Her skin was velvety smooth beneath his knuckles.

"You must have lots of passengers if you carry an extra helmet," she remarked.

He shrugged, poking at a stubborn strand next to her eye. "I suppose."

"Any passengers who are more, um, *regular* than others?"

Jack stopped his ministrations, but she was studying

her fingernails. Was she asking what he thought she was asking? "Just one," he said, giving her chin strap a final tug. "In fact, I bought the helmet for her."

"Oh."

Jack pulled on his own helmet, threw his leg over the seat, then lifted the kickstand with an upward jerk and forward roll. He reached back to flip down the footpegs, then braced for her to climb on.

Alex frowned down at her dress. "This is going to be awkward."

He grinned. "I promise not to look." With fingers crossed on the handlebar grips, he turned his gaze forward—to take in the entire show in the side mirror. Between the unwieldy lowered parasol she held under her arm, the big purse, and her voluminous skirt, she was quite the performer. And her pale-colored panties, it seemed, were trimmed with scalloped lace. He stifled a groan as she settled in behind him, sitting as stiffly as one of her store mannequins.

He started the engine, then said, "Relax." Rolling his shoulders, he reveled in the feeling of her breasts pressed against him.

She did relax, a millimeter or two, as he maneuvered through the traffic at a leisurely pace. When they came to a stop in a line of exiting traffic, Alex lifted her head and looked around.

"Are you comfortable?" he asked.

She nodded, and after a few minutes, she cleared her throat. "This, um, regular passenger of yours—she must be very important if she warrants her own helmet."

"She is," Jack assured her. "But then Mom has always been pretty close to my heart." He winked at her in the side mirror, boosted by her unexpected smile. On impulse, he covered her hand curled around his waist with his own, instantly struck by the softness of her skin and his desire to entwine their fingers. "Hold on for dear life," he warned in his most ominous voice, then begrudgingly released her hand and accelerated, cutting out of the traffic and threading the bike toward Versailles Road.

He took the long way to Alex's downtown apartment, telling himself in the beginning he was avoiding the worst of the traffic, but finally admitting to himself that he was prolonging their ride for his own selfish purposes, relishing the feel of her slender body melded to his. When his roundabout route came to an end in her parking lot, he was already looking forward to Monday—not because he would be filming the commercials, but because he would be seeing Alex again.

The knowledge spooked him so much, he could barely help her undo her helmet. "Before long, you'll be a pro," he teased, then realized he was implying that she would be riding with him again...and often.

She blinked those beautiful blue eyes, while running her fingers through her loose hair. "Is this motorcycle your only transportation?"

"Yep. If the weather is bad, I usually borrow my brother's car." He smiled down at her, caught up in her beauty shining in the light of early dusk. Yet his reference to his brother reminded him of his promise. "I'll just walk you up, grab my jacket, and be on my way."

He followed her through the stairwell and up three flights to her apartment, this time keeping his gaze squarely on the back of her head. When Alex unlocked her door and walked inside, he hung back, thinking the hallway was the safest spot in the vicinity. Alex obliged by returning quickly with his jacket dangling from her long-fingered hand.

"Thanks," he said, taking the jacket, but suddenly unable to move. "I guess I'll see you Monday at the studio."

She nodded.

Ordering his feet to retreat, Jack said, "Have a nice evening."

"Jack."

"Yeah?"

"Thanks for...a fun day."

"See," he said, reaching forward to brush that same stubborn strand of silky dark hair from her flushed cheek. "You *can* have fun if you let yourself." He'd been trying to get Alex to loosen up, but now he realized his resistance was far more secure when fending off her barbed tongue, rather than wondering how it tasted.

Before he had time to change his mind, he cupped his hand around the back of her neck and lowered his mouth to hers for a quick kiss that turned exploratory as soon as his mouth met hers. A day's worth of teasing and restraint poured into the kiss. Knowing it might well be his only one, Jack foraged her mouth thoroughly, savoring the sweetness of her flavor. His body, already keen for her, vaulted to painful awareness of her proximity. When she moaned into his mouth, he pulled her against him, divulging how much she excited him.

When a noise sounded behind him in the hall, Jack lifted his head to see remorse flash in Alex's eyes as her gaze darted to the person walking toward them, humming.

"Oh!" A tall woman with spiky white hair stopped short, her eyes round as she eyed them both. "Pardon me, I...I...never mind." She turned on her platform heels and disappeared around the corner at a pace somewhere between a jog and a sprint.

He looked back to Alex, his eyebrows high, his lips stinging, his erection straining.

"My n-neighbor," she explained, pulling back and touching her mouth absently. Her chest rose and fell quickly and a frown marred her forehead. "Jack, about what just happened—"

At her agonized tone, he held up his hand and plastered a glib smile on his face. "A little friendly curiosity—now satisfied."

A myriad of emotions played over her face, then she appeared immensely relieved. "Right. Well...thanks again for the ride home. Good night."

Wringing his jacket, he stared at her closed door for several seconds, wondering what might have ensued without the appearance of Alex's neighbor. Nothing wise, he was certain. As he retraced his steps to his bike, Alex's earlier words came back to him.

Anyone can playact for a few hours, but at the end of the day, we are who we are. Amen to that, Jack thought, grateful for the interruption. And he couldn't imagine two people at farther ends of the spectrum than he and Alexandria Tremont: She was a purebred, he was a mongrel. She was the princess, he was the pea.

He scratched his temple as he straddled the seat. Funny, but he couldn't remember ever wanting to be anything other than what he was. Until now.

Jack glanced up at the white and yellow lights emanating from Alex's windows, spilling over the black wrought iron rail of her balcony. With the onset of darkness, the warm lights glowed like a beacon. What the devil was this woman doing to him?

12

STILL SHAKEN from the intensity of Jack's kiss, Alex disrobed in a daze, then stepped under a warm shower, figuring she had about ten minutes before Lana returned demanding details, although her neighbor would be mightily disappointed since Alex herself wasn't even sure what had happened. She leaned her head back and allowed the warm water to run over her body—nice, but a poor substitute for a man's hands.

Jack's hands, she realized with dismay, wondering if her startling attraction to him had something to do with her somewhat stale relationship with Heath. Using a bar of raspberry scented soap, she lathered her body with a rich layer of suds, luxuriating in the aroma.

The kiss had simply...happened. What had he said? *A little friendly curiosity—now satisfied.* She frowned as she rinsed her hair. It certainly hadn't taken him long to decide she wasn't worth the trouble.

She emerged from the soothing spray reluctantly, and dressed slowly in cotton leggings and an oversized T-shirt that she knotted at her waist.

After all, a girl had feelings.

Opting to let her hair dry naturally, she crossed to the kitchen and opened the refrigerator door on the off chance that a veggie pizza from Malone's had materialized in her absence. It hadn't.

Obviously she wasn't as hot as the women he was used to...having.

Morose, she stuck her finger into the carton of fudge icing for an unhealthy gob of the stuff, and sucked it off as she wandered around the apartment feeling restless and prickly. She turned on the television and flicked through the channels before switching it off again. She considered calling Heath, but for some reason she resisted, stubbornly clinging to the electrical awareness she'd experienced when Jack kissed her. Wise or not, the desire still swimming in her stomach felt good. Exhilarating. Had Heath's kisses ever made her feel so disoriented and foolhardy? Surely she would have remembered this, this, this *bizarre* jittery sensation.

Alex dropped into her favorite chair and leaned her head back with a sigh, hugging a pillow to her chest. So she lusted for the man—so schlep her into the same category as every other woman who crossed his wayward path. With a wry smile she acknowledged that as much as she liked to think she pursued lofty, esoteric goals, she wasn't above base passion.

What a blow to realize that sex, not commerce, made the world go around.

But what a relief to know that she was capable of the kind of desire that Lana espoused.

Right on cue, the rapid knock on her door announced the arrival of her friend. Anxious to unload her new revelation, despite the ribbing she knew she was due, Alex abandoned the pillow, padded to the door, then swung it open.

But her pulse spiked when Jack's broad shadow fell across her doorway, swallowing her. He stood, hands at his sides, legs wide, head slightly bowed, his face obscured in the darkness. Her throat tightened, squeezing off her ability to talk as reasons for him returning raced through her mind. He was having engine trouble. He wanted to discuss Monday's shoot. He wanted to grab a bite to eat somewhere. He needed directions.

"I came back to finish what we started."

Or he'd come back to finish what they'd started. She swallowed as the raw longing in his voice cut through her. It was crazy, the way her body responded to the magnetism emanating from him. Crazy and wonderfully overwhelming, and worthy of exploration. Before she could process a rational thought, Alex stepped forward, looped her arms around his neck, and pulled his mouth down to hers. His gladdened groan sent a wake-up call to every nerve in her body, and his arms moved fluidly to encircle her waist. His lips were hungry, hard, urgent. His body was taut for her, and the knowledge sent moisture to the juncture of her thighs.

Reaching lower to cup her bottom, he lifted her off her feet and carried her inside. He kicked the door closed behind them. She lost track of time and their direction, but was gratified sometime later to feel the softness of her bed at her back. Her thighs opened to accommodate him as he stretched atop her. He pressed her deep into the covers, his body alive with movement—his mouth devouring hers, his hands beneath her, pulling her hips against his hardness.

His blatant desire for her fueled the destruction of her own inhibitions. Alex summoned the energy to push at the leather jacket around his shoulders, forcing him to shift and shed the garment. His gaze locked with hers, his eyes heavy-lidded and glazed, his open lips transferring air in and out of his lungs with heavy gasps. She moved in a liquid haze, carried along by a tide of passion. With one quick jerk, the snaps on the front of his denim shirt were freed, laying his chest bare to her seeking fingers. In another second, the shirt was gone. She scarcely had time to register the corded beauty of his upper body before he tugged the knot of her shirt loose and shimmied the thin material over her head to bare her to the waist as well.

After a glance of appreciation that warmed her, he fell upon her, his palms closing around her breasts, coning the tips for his seeking mouth. Alex cried aloud when he suckled her, reveling in the brush of his chest hair against her skin. He drew her flesh deep into his hot mouth, his moan vibrating against her sensitive nipple. Nearly blind with wanting him, Alex threaded her fingers through his hair and urged him to draw harder. At her insistence, his tending escalated from gentle laving to little bites that left her twitching. Slowly, he kissed a trail to her waistband, then pushed himself to his feet, rolling her thin pants down her legs as he stood.

Jack was so worked up at the thought of making love to Alex that he nearly came at the sight of her nudity, a jolt to his already electrified system. She was breathtaking—long-limbed and toned, with high, jutting breasts, and a slender waist that gave way to a generous swell of hip and taut thighs. Gritting his teeth for control, he leaned forward, grasped her by the waist, and pulled her to the edge of the bed, loving the contrast of her dark hair splayed against the white comforter, loving more that the tall bed was just the right height for him to make love to her in a most enjoyable position.

With little urging, she opened her knees, revealing the glistening pink petals of her womanhood, sending her musky scent to torment him further. With rapidly vanishing restraint, he stood between her knees, probing her with careful fingers, readying her for his body until her moans and undulations became too much to endure. Feeling like a schoolboy in his haste, Jack fumbled with the front of his pants. It was as if his body had never done this before, a reaction that triggered a small alarm in the recesses of his blood-deprived brain. At last he freed his raging erection, which answered her mewling call with a few drops of oozing lubrication. Never before had he been tempted to skip a condom, which in and of itself sobered him enough to slow down for a heartbeat. Fishing in his back pocket for his wallet, he prayed he'd replaced the last one he'd used, because only a word of refusal from Alex could stop him now, protection or no.

His knees practically buckled with relief when he found one, and he set a record rolling it on. A split second of guilt barbed through him for not at least removing his jeans, but Alex already had him so close to the brink, he didn't want to risk taking the time. And if truth be known, he wanted her so badly, he couldn't bear the thought of another delay. Trembling with anticipation, he pulled her knees to his waist and pushed the tip of his erection against her wetness. Her leg muscles tensed and a moan tore from her lips as he thrust inside her unbelievably tight channel, setting his jaw for maximum restraint against the torrent of fire that consumed him.

He moved cautiously, filling her and retreating with climbing desire. Jack was struck by the erotic sight of her, arms wide, hands fisted in the white comforter, back arched, breasts high, mouth moving with alternate coos and gasps. Her vocal responses bolstered his confidence that he was stimulating her in the way she wanted, and carried his own climax close to the surface. He coaxed her to his plane, drawing her legs up to rest against his shoulders, kissing her ankles as he thrust deeper and deeper and murmuring how incredible she felt wrapped around him. Escalation of the noises emerging from her throat alerted him that she was nearing climax, driving him to thrust harder and faster while tensing to contain his own release.

From her body's state of disarray, Alex sensed the approaching orgasm would surpass her previous experiences, but she wasn't prepared for the mind-numbing, muscle-stealing explosion of euphoria that broke over her body in waves. Shameless in her abandon, she cried out his name, bucking against the steel rod of his flesh imbedded in her. She had just started to descend to Earth when Jack's body went rigid and he growled his release against her leg. Alex reveled in the light pressure of his teeth, the hot blasts of his ragged breath on her skin.

He was magnificent in the dim lighting, the toned planes of his stomach contracting and relaxing in quick spasms. She was fascinated by the juncture of their bodies, which seemed almost surreal. His jeans rode just low enough on his lean hips to allow his body access to hers, a sharp contrast to her complete nakedness. As cool air hit her body, Alex began to feel exposed, and whispers of remorse nudged at her. She moved to disengage their bodies, eliciting a clutching groan from Jack. He held her to him while controlling his careful withdrawal, a satisfied smile on his handsome face.

Alex eased back onto the pillows at the head of her bed, her body singing with completion, humming with unimagined indulgence. She clung to the sensation of their mutual pleasure, postponing the inevitable regret.

Jack, on the other hand, seemed undaunted by their indiscretion. He pulled away the sheet when she attempted to cover herself, and kissed her breasts leisurely. "You are so incredibly beautiful," he whispered against her skin, evoking another wave of desire through her body.

Within the space of a heartbeat, he drew her back into the tantalizing languor of his embrace, nuzzling her neck, kissing her thoroughly before rolling over to lie next to her. His sigh fanned her temple.

"I didn't mean for this to happen," he said, "but I'd be lying if I said I hadn't thought about it since the first time we met."

Alex closed her eyes, berating herself. She'd imagined a budding emotional connection between them today, when they'd really only shared a few laughs, a few drinks, and a few looks. He'd wanted to sleep with her from the beginning, so he'd behaved accordingly. Yes, they'd developed a rapport. Yes, they'd had fun. Yes, they were physically compatible. But she'd been so desperate for that elusive...soul mate...that she'd conjured up feelings between them that simply didn't exist. Darn Lana and all her talk about passion.

"Are you sleeping?" he whispered.

"No," she managed to say. "Just thinking."

"Hey, don't get too deep on me," he teased. "Is your bathroom close by?"

A stone of comprehension fell to the bottom of her stomach. Speechless, she gestured toward the door, her vision blurred with tears as she watched him cross to the bathroom, his pants still undone.

When the door closed, she covered her face with her hands. What had she done? Spread her legs for Jack Stillman, a man she neither liked nor respected, and someone she'd have to work with for at least the next several days. She moved jerkily from the bed to yank on her discarded clothing, biting back a sob when her ring caught on her T-shirt. With a shaky hand, she hung Jack's shirt from a bedpost, then hastily smoothed the telltale wrinkles from the white comforter.

If only the episode could be so easily erased from her mind, she acknowledged with a trembling sigh. She'd never been loose with her body, had never handed over the precious commodity of herself without a level of emotional commitment from her partner. So why now, why Jack Stillman? Sure, he was handsome, but Lexington had its share of nice-looking men.

Alex sank her teeth into her lower lip. *Heath.* Oh, no, what had she done?

When the bathroom door opened, she nearly jumped out of her skin. Jack emerged wearing a smile, the fly of his jeans still zipped, but unbuttoned. Sex appeal rolled off the man's naked torso, necessitating the need to turn her back. At the sound of his approaching footsteps, she realized that he still wore his riding boots, just another reminder that their encounter had been quick and dirty.

"I'm hungry," he murmured into her ear from behind, his arms snaking around her middle.

"I'm not," she said distinctly, unlocking his hands and walking out of his embrace.

"What's this?"

She inhaled deeply, then turned to face him, arms folded over her breasts, which still tingled from his touch. "What's what?"

He frowned, hands on lean hips. "This attitude."

Alex swallowed, terrified that he looked so good to her, even after their hurried sex. The episode was obviously nothing unusual for him—he probably knocked on doors and wound up in strange beds all the time. A man like Jack would never understand what a monumental mistake their few minutes together represented to her. Keeping her voice level, she said, "You need to fasten your pants and leave, Jack."

One eyebrow arrowed up. "That's it? Fasten my pants and leave?" His voice was low, but tinged with anger.

His response fueled her defenses, causing her to lash out. "So sorry if most of your conquests provide more than one round."

His mouth tightened, but otherwise, he didn't move.

The longer the silence stretched between them, the more unsure Alex was of her ability to resist him again. The man had a way of mastering a room and the people in it. She had thought herself immune to his uncanny charisma, but had never been so wrong. Unable to break eye contact with him, Alex watched him walk toward her, seemingly in slow motion. With his every step her resolve crumbled, and with a sinking dread, she realized where they were once again headed.

A knock on her door halted his progress, and she sighed with relief. Lana to the rescue. Alex turned to the door and called, "Lana, I'm a little busy right now."

"Alex," Heath said, and the sound of his voice sent terror to her heart.

She turned wide eyes toward Jack, who seemed almost...amused? Gesturing wildly, she hissed, "You have to get out of here!"

"Why?" he whispered. "I locked the door—just don't let him in."

"He has a key," she whispered back, her heart thudding in her ears. Heath did not deserve to find another man in her apartment. Louder, she called, "Give me a minute and I'll be right there." Desperate, she ran to retrieve Jack's shirt. "You have to hide!"

He caught his shirt and shrugged into it, then fastened his jeans. "I will *not* hide just because you can't admit the truth to your boyfriend."

Alex stopped, facing him. "And what truth would that be?"

"That he obviously doesn't satisfy you."

Her face flamed in the face of her wantonness. "I love Heath," she said calmly.

"Oh, you *love* him? Well, your loyalty is staggering."

His sarcasm stung her like a slap. She imagined all kinds of scenes if Heath and Jack squared off in her apartment, Jack gloating, Heath the cuckold. She hated herself, and she hated Jack Stillman. "If you have a decent bone in your body, you won't do this," Alex managed to say.

"I'll just use my key," Heath announced, and she closed her eyes, tensing for a confrontation. She opened her eyes at the sound of a door sliding open, just in time to see the blue of Jack's shirt disappearing over the railing of her balcony. The sheer curtains billowed inside the apartment, dancing on the breeze. Before she could react, Heath opened the door, and she wheeled to give him a smile she snatched from thin air.

He gave her a quick embrace, but all Alex could think was that the aroma of another man's lovemaking lingered on her body. "Enjoying the balcony?" Heath asked, nodding toward the open door.

"Um, no, not exactly," Alex said, slipping out of his arms and crossing to the open door. "The insects are so bad, you know." She slid the door closed, just in time to muffle the low rumble of a motorcycle starting. At least the cad hadn't broken his neck, she thought with a tiny rush of relief.

"Your bug zapper isn't working?" Heath asked behind her.

"Not on this particular pest," she murmured to the glass door, watching the single taillight disappear at a breathtaking speed.

"OKAY, ALEX, I have a fifteen minute break, so you'd better talk fast." Lana set a mug of steaming coffee in front of Alex and plopped down in the opposite café chair.

"Who says I have something to talk *about?*" Alex was already reconsidering her impulse to stop by to see her friend before putting in a few hours at the office on a Saturday morning.

Lana looked toward the ceiling. "I'm assuming this impromptu visit has something to do with the grinding fullbody kiss you shared with Jack the Attack last night, followed by his subsequent return, then Heath's appearance, and my next door neighbor's shrieking phone call that some man was scaling down the fire escape ladder from your apartment."

Stunned, Alex swallowed a huge mouthful of coffee. "I didn't realize I was under surveillance."

"Our cable was finally cut off, and the traffic in and out of your apartment was more interesting than watching static."

"Gee, thanks."

"Just be glad I was able to talk Mrs. Standish out of calling the police," Lana said. "Holy hickey—is that a *bite* mark on your leg?"

Choking on the coffee she sucked down her windpipe, Alex's gaze flew to the area between her ankle and calf, the pink imprint of Jack's perfect teeth clearly visible on her bare leg below the hem on her long floral skirt. She hadn't noticed it this morning, but then again, she wasn't accustomed to checking her body for telltale love bites, either. Alex quickly crossed her legs at the knee, tucking the offensive mark out of sight. "I, um...I, um..."

"You're blushing again," her friend said with a whoop. "So, was he as fantastic a lover as he was rumored to be in college?"

Alex massaged her temples, wondering if she should unload her grievous mistake on her friend or let it fester inside her until she ruptured from guilt. Finally, she sighed and nodded morosely.

Lana squealed. "I knew it! The best you've ever had?"

Her dignity long gone, she winced and nodded again.

Another squeal. "How *romantic*—your lover sneaking down the fire escape as your fiancé walks through the front door!"

"Lana, it wasn't romantic, it was lunacy. It was deceitful. Heath is a decent man who deserves better." She stared into the depths of her coffee, wishing she'd been thinking as clearly last night as she was this morning.

Her friend was studying her with those disconcerting violet eyes. "Oh, my God. You're falling for Jack Stillman, aren't you?"

Alex's eyes bulged from her aching head. "You can't be serious. I don't even *like* Jack Stillman."

"Disdain keeps a relationship interesting. Look at my folks."

"Lana, for heaven's sake, there's no 'relationship' here. The man is a playboy, heavy emphasis on the 'boy.'"

"He looked full-grown from my vantage point."

She scoffed. "He probably went home and carved a notch in the post of his waterbed."

Lana lifted a pale eyebrow. "Just one notch?"

Alex rolled her eyes. "Yeeeeees."

"Did you tell Heath?"

"No."

"Good—take this one to your grave."

"Considering I almost had a stroke last night when Heath showed up, I nearly *did* take it to my grave. He only stayed long enough to have a drink, but I was an absolute nervous wreck by the time he left." She exhaled noisily. "I should have told him last night. Instead I was awake all night, wallowing in guilt."

"Alex, you're too uptight. You and Heath aren't married yet, you know."

"But we're supposed to be setting a date soon!"

"Life is all about timing, girlfriend."

Alex frowned, reluctant to unleash that particular line of thinking.

Lana tilted her head. "Hmm—loose hair, pink cheeks, bright eyes. If you ask me, depravity suits you."

"You know, if you don't buy this coffee shop, you really should consider counseling."

"Me, be a counselor?"

"No, I meant you should *see* a counselor."

"Oh, very funny. You know, a black widow spider also turns hostile after good sex."

Alex stuck her tongue out at her friend.

"So, when will you see him again?"

"Who?"

"Jack!"

Alex sighed, certain there was no more miserable, sinful person walking the streets. "Monday. I'm supervising a combination commercial and photo shoot. I don't have the slightest idea what I'll say when I see him."

"I wouldn't worry about it. Men tend not to obsess over illicit sex. They save their energy for bigger things

like professional wrestling...and eating foods that end in
o."

"Well, I'm sure you're right about one thing," Alex observed wryly. "Jack Stillman hasn't lost a wink of sleep
over our little encounter."

JACK YAWNED for the umpteenth time, cursing the insomnia brought on by wondering if Reddinger stayed at
Alex's apartment last night. More than the lost sleep,
though, he simply hated the feeling of helplessness and
frustration, and that he was letting it get to him. After all,
he'd only known the woman for a few days. If it didn't
bother her to cheat on her boyfriend, why should it
bother him?

He banged his fist on his desk. Because, dammit, it had
taken all his nerve to go back to her apartment and risk
making a fool out of himself. He'd hoped she felt the
chemistry between them that had his senses on a tilt, but
he couldn't be sure. He couldn't read this woman—she
was different than the females he was accustomed to.
Cold, hot, smart, gorgeous, engaged, sexy, engaged, passionate. Engaged.

He resented like hell sneaking over her balcony like a
blasted criminal while blankety-blank Reddinger
marched in the freaking front door like a bloody king.
And it stuck in his craw to realize that what had been a
fairly relevant experience for him had been little more
than a tumble to Alex.

You need to fasten your pants and leave, Jack.

At the memory of her words, he muttered a few more
choice words of his own into his thick, cold coffee. He'd
never been asked to leave a woman's place before, except
by the occasional rankled boyfriend or brother or father.
He'd made the mistake of thinking that because their

passion had been electric for him, that it had been for Alex, too. Apparently, that wasn't the case.

He should have taken more time with her, he thought, chastising himself. Been more gentle, more—he grimaced—sensitive. But the woman had him so worked up, it was a miracle he'd lasted as long as he did. He'd told himself that he would take his time when they made love again, which would have been before morning if he'd had his way. Alex wasn't the kind of woman a man could sample—he wanted his fill of her, and it irked him like the dickens that she didn't share his sentiments.

Jack stopped and frowned. Sentiments? Bad choice of words.

When another yawn overtook him, he stood to limp around his desk on the ankle he'd sprained when he dropped from the end of the fire escape ladder. He sighed, running his hand down his face. At least the office was blessedly quiet. Tuesday, thankfully, believed in weekends off from her non-paying job. And Stripling the Fed definitely wouldn't be bothering him on a Saturday. So he was determined to finish several drawings today for the Tremont's account and a few other odds and ends—if he could stay awake.

When the phone rang, he was tempted to let it go, then, buoyed by the slim chance that Alex might be trying to reach him, he yanked up the receiver. "Stillman & Sons Agency, Jack speaking."

"Well, I *don't* believe it," his brother Derek said. "You in the office on a Saturday."

Jack winced, not in the mood to hear from his brother—Derek was having all the sex he could withstand with a woman he cared about.

Not that he actually *cared* about Alex, Jack reminded himself.

"Are you there, Jack?"

"Yeah, I'm here." Naturally, he didn't want anything bad to happen to the woman, but that wasn't the same as *caring* about her.

"You don't sound so good, bro. Late night?"

"Not particularly. Just a little tired." Because if getting naked with Alexandria Tremont was foolish, *caring* about her would be just plain stupid.

"How's the Tremont account going?"

"I'm working on it now. Thought I'd put in a few hours, before going to the football game with old man Tremont this afternoon." Because the poor man who lost himself in those blue eyes of hers was doomed to a life of servitude.

"I'm impressed. In the office on a Saturday and shmoozing the client, too. If I didn't know better, Jack, I'd say you were...working."

"I see marriage has turned you into a comedian," Jack remarked dryly. Although a life of servitude between the thighs of the exquisite Alexandria held a certain amount of appeal.

"So, have you managed to wow the boss's daughter—what's her name?"

"Alexandria. And I wouldn't exactly use the word 'wow' yet." Although, dammit, if he could just convince her to give him another chance between the sheets, he'd rock her world.

"You'll do all right if you can keep your libido under control."

Jack frowned, realizing that, once again, Derek was right. He'd probably blown his only chance to win over Alex by dragging her to bed like a Neanderthal. Once Reddinger and her father found out, they'd kick him off the account for sure. Then he straightened with a revelation.

What if she'd set him up? How convenient that good ol' Reddinger had shown up last night when he did. Maybe she'd concocted the entire scheme to get rid of Jack and secure the other firm she'd wanted to work with all along. He gulped. And as much as Al Tremont liked him, he might draw the line at Jack the Attack diddling his precious daughter. In fact, if Derek wanted to kill him for bedding Ms. Tremont, he might have to stand in line.

"Jack," Derek said. "You *are* keeping your word to not get involved with this woman, aren't you?"

Remorse washed over him that he'd jeopardized the acccount, and worse, that he'd imagined Alexandria *wanted* him. "Derek, we're not involved," he said thickly. Alex had made that much perfectly clear, hadn't she? *You need to fasten your pants and leave, Jack.*

Now that he looked back on the episode, he felt downright used. Like a...a...a piece of meat.

"Well, that's a relief," Derek said. "Promise me you'll be on your best behavior."

"Yeah, I promise." A rather *large* piece of meat, but meat nonetheless.

"Anything else going on I should know about?"

"Um, no, not a thing." Jack leaned down to massage his throbbing ankle. He didn't have the time or energy to launch into the office problems, plus he didn't want to wreck the rest of Derek's honeymoon. "How's Hawaii?"

"Great," Derek said. "What little we've seen of it."

"Bad weather?"

"No, good sex. I figure we can buy a postcard book or something at the airport when we leave."

Jack chuckled. "Janine has really loosened you up, man."

"Yeah, it's amazing how a woman can change you."

When an image of Alex's face flashed in his mind, Jack suddenly sobered. "That's assuming a man needs to be changed."

"Yeah, well, we're not all perfect like you, Jack. Hey, I have to go—Janine just yelled for me."

"And you jump when she calls?"

"Like a randy kangaroo," Derek said cheerfully. "You just wait, man, a woman's going to come along someday and blindside you, too."

Jack frowned and hung up the phone. He didn't begrudge his brother happiness—God knew he deserved it. But he'd become one of those I-found-the-meaning-of-life-and-you-need-it-too-brotha-and-sista married people. No, thanks.

Pure resolve drove him to finish the drawings in record time, which he tucked into a portfolio. Since he was picking up Al at his office, he'd stop on the way and make color copies to leave on Alex's desk so she'd have them before the photo and commercial shoot on Monday. The drawings were good and maybe they would prevent his ass from being fired, if his suspicions regarding Alex's wiles were confirmed.

Jack sighed, mentally kicking himself with every step through the parking lot. He'd find out soon enough, he supposed.

"Send the tray of rings to my office as soon as possible, please." Alex hung up the phone and made a check mark on the inventory of items she was gathering for the shoot on Monday. At this rate, she'd need a van to get Jack's wardrobe and props to the studio. She sat at her desk, too restless and distracted by the events of the previous evening to address anything but the most superficial items on her to-do list.

Snatches of their hurried lovemaking flashed through her mind, unbidden. If she closed her eyes, she could still feel his hands on her, could still feel their bodies joined. But when she opened her eyes, all she could feel was the blanket of guilt settling over her head. She wasn't sure what had come over her last night when Jack had returned to her door, but so far she had ruled out common sense, rationality and coherence.

Leaning forward on her elbows, Alex pressed her fingers to her temples and admitted the awful truth. *She had wanted him.* Blame it on being thrown off balance by his sudden appearance at the racetrack, blame it on the disappointment of Heath leaving early, blame it on the proximity to Jack the rest of the afternoon, blame it on the weather, but she had wanted him in the most base way a woman could want a man. Worse, she wanted him again.

At the short rap on her door, Alex turned, relieved at the sight of her father standing in the doorway. They had the whole afternoon together, just the two of them—just the tonic she needed to put Jack Stillman out of her mind. "Are you ready to leave for the gallery?" she asked, reaching for her purse, then hesitated at the sight of his rather casual clothing.

"Alex, dear, I'm sorry. I left you a message at your apartment this morning, but you must have already left. Would you mind if I take a rain check on the gallery showing?"

Disappointment barbed through her, but she managed a shrug. "Has something come up?"

"Actually—hey, Jack!" He waved with animation in the direction of the elevators.

Alex's heart jumped to her throat. "Jack?" she croaked.

"He invited me to the UK football game this afternoon. You don't mind if you and I reschedule, do you, dear?"

She did mind, but one look at his shining face told her where and with whom he'd rather spend the day. Her heart squeezed. "Of course I d-don't mind, Dad." Then she tensed, waiting for the appearance of Jack, wishing she'd had more time to prepare for this face-to-face meeting.

The day was rapidly going in the tank.

Looking well-rested and fit in jeans and a gray UK sweatshirt, Jack stepped into the doorway and shook hands with her father. The men made small talk, ignoring her, but giving her time to gather her wits.

Her heart thumped crazily as she scrutinized the length of him, struck by his incredible good looks, remembering their intimate encounter, the things they'd whispered to each other in the throes of passion. Her temperature climbed and the collar of her blouse suddenly seemed warm against her neck.

"Hello, Alex," he said finally, smiling in her direction.

"Hello, Jack," she responded, just as if they had no carnal knowledge of each other whatsoever.

"I brought a few drawings to leave with you," he said, patting a portfolio he held under his arm.

"You kids can chat," her father said. "I'll wrap up a few things on my desk."

"Ten minutes?" Jack asked him.

Her father winked and clapped Jack on the shoulder. "You got it, son."

Jealousy gripped her stomach at the easy camaraderie between her father and this virtual stranger, something she and her father would never have. When Al retreated and Jack walked into her office, she swallowed hard. On the other hand, if she could *sleep* with this virtual stranger, why shouldn't her father enjoy a mere afternoon of football with him?

"Hi," he said, with the smallest smile.

She matched his expression. "I thought we got past that point already."

"I left my jacket at your place again."

Alex crossed her arms, glad for the comforting barrier of her desk. "Along with your teeth print on my leg."

His eyebrow shot up and for a split second he looked proud of himself, then recovered. "Sorry about that."

"That's okay," she said, anxious to put the lapse behind them. "It won't happen again."

He scratched his temple, and nodded. "I agree."

She blinked. "Good." She wasn't sure what kind of reaction she'd expected, but meek acquiescence wasn't on the list. Which obviously meant that he'd found their tryst less than remarkable. To change the subject, she pointed to the portfolio. "You have some drawings to show me?"

He nodded, walking toward her desk.

"Are you limping?"

"Uh, yeah, I twisted it last night when I was leaving."

Alex bit back a smile as she took the portfolio. "Are you okay?"

He looked a little sheepish. "I'll survive. Listen, I overheard your father when I walked up. I didn't mean to take him away from plans the two of you had already made."

"No problem," she said, waving it off despite another pang. "I'm glad to see him doing something fun, and I'm sure he'll enjoy the game with you more than some stuffy old gallery."

"You were going to the Bernard showing?"

Surprised, Alex nodded. "Yes. You've heard of the artist?"

"I own two of her originals."

She stared, agape. "How...interesting." Interesting? More like "astounding."

A light rap sounded at her open door. "Ms. Tremont?"

Alex looked up to see one of the fine jewelry salesclerks. "Yes, Carla?"

"I brought the wedding ring sets you requested."

She motioned her inside. "Excuse me, Jack, this will just take a moment." Alex lifted the lid on one of the two cigar-box-size jeweler's cases, and smiled her pleasure at the dazzling array of gold, platinum and white-gold sets of wedding bands. "Yes, Carla, these are the exact cases I was interested in. Thank you."

Carla left and Alex set aside the open box, noting Jack's pallor. She swallowed a smile, thinking maybe she shouldn't tell him she was considering having him wear some of them in the commercial shoots Monday.

"Have you ever been married, Jack?"

"No."

The one clipped word, along with his shifted gaze, told her volumes. If the mere sight of the rings made the man that nervous, she would skip them. There was something to be said about portraying Jack as the free-spirited bachelor he was. After all, she had certainly found it appealing, hadn't she?

But art collector? She opened her mouth to inquire into this most intriguing bit of information, but her father returned to claim Jack for their afternoon at the stadium. Feeling like a little girl being left behind, Alex followed them to the doorway of her office and leaned against the frame. Hugging herself, she watched Jack as he walked away, talking easily with her intimidating father, and wondered how many other layers this man had to reveal.

But her musings were derailed when Heath appeared in the hallway, walking toward her father and Jack. Her pulse stalled for the few seconds the men conversed, and she experienced the strangest sensation when Jack and Heath shook hands. Engaged to one, fooling around with the other.

And what did that make *her*? Alex exhaled a shaky breath as several unflattering adjectives whirled through her mind. Her engagement ring winked at her, mocking her. She couldn't simply dismiss her betrayal to Heath— she needed to talk to him, the sooner, the better.

Heath gestured to the men's backs when he walked up, fresh-faced and unaware of her turmoil. "I thought you and Al were taking in the gallery today."

"We were."

He scoffed. "He stood you up for a lousy football game?"

"Yes."

"Well, you know I'm not much on this Bernard guy's art, but I'll go with you," he offered.

"She." A feeling of loss stabbed her as the two men walked onto the elevator and the door closed behind them.

"Excuse me?"

Alex looked back to Heath. "Bernard—the artist is a 'she.'"

Heath shrugged. "Whatever. Do you still want to go?"

She visualized giving back his ring, a teary goodbye. "Um, no," she said, suddenly changing her mind. "I think I'll take some flowers out to my mother's grave this afternoon." She needed the comfort of being close to someone who had loved her unconditionally. Perhaps she could sort out all of the mess in her head in the serenity of the shady cemetery.

As expected, Heath backed off immediately, even as he followed her into her office. "I'll let you have some private time, then. Hey, what's with the wedding rings?"

Alex sat in her comfy leather seat and unzipped the portfolio Jack had left, eager to see his new drawings. "I'm trying to work the rings into the new ad campaign."

"Hmm. Any of these you like well enough for me to wear?"

Her head jerked up when his words sank in. "What?"

"Why not?" Heath said, gesturing to the rings. "We've put this off long enough, don't you think?"

14

"WHAT DID YOU SAY?" Lana asked.

Alex sighed into the phone and hooked her legs over the arm of her faithful chair. "I agreed to go away with Heath next weekend to talk about where our relationship goes from here. His timing is uncanny."

"Maybe he senses another buck sniffing around his doe."

"Oh, now that's romantic. If you don't buy the coffee shop, maybe you should start writing greeting cards for a living." At the sound of a distant *ping*, she turned her head toward the balcony door. Seeing nothing, she dismissed the noise. "Any big Sunday plans?"

"I'm working this afternoon. How about you?"

"Cleaning, I guess. Heath left again this morning for Cincinnati. How's your roommate situation?"

"Intolerable. We're not even speaking now, we leave notes. I write mine in pig Latin just to piss her off."

Ping. Alex frowned at the noise, standing this time. "Hold on, Lana, I think I hear something."

"What?"

Ping.

"I don't know." She moved toward the glass door and slid it open just in time for a pea-sized pebble to bounce off her forehead. "Ow!"

"What happened?"

"I have to go."

"Don't leave me hanging—"

Alex disconnected the call and stepped out onto her balcony, barely dodging another pebble before she leaned over the railing.

Jack stood on the ground, two stories below, one hand pulled back in preparation to launch another pebble, the other loaded with enough ammo to pester her for a week. He stopped when he saw her and gave her a boyish grin.

Alex's spirits lifted absurdly. "You almost gave me a concussion," she yelled.

"That's my secret weapon," he yelled back. "Women with concussions are much easier to persuade."

Wary, she crossed her arms. She couldn't imagine what the man might say that would provide the slightest bit of enticement. "Persuade to do what?"

He held up two pink slips of paper. "Tickets to the Bernard showing this afternoon."

Okay, she was enticed.

"Including a reception for the artist."

Alex pursed her mouth. "I...need to change."

He grinned. "Wear riding clothes. The weather is great."

Telling herself that *this* was not a date, this was *not* a date, and this was not a *date*, Alex scoured her wardrobe for something casual and funky. She settled on a pair of black corduroy overalls, a heavy silk coral long-sleeve blouse, and suede slip-ons with a heavy sole. She dumped the contents of her leather tote into a hand appliquéd canvas bag, then dropped in a handful of hairpins so she could twist back her helmet hair once she reached the gallery. At the last minute, she remembered his leather jacket and grabbed it on the way out the door.

Telling herself she was hurrying because Jack was waiting rather than because she was excited, Alex jogged down the hall, slowing when she reached the corridor before Lana's apartment. Hopes that she would make it past without notice were dashed when she rounded the corner to find Lana leaning in her open doorway, filing her nails.

"Got a date?" her friend asked innocently without lifting her gaze.

Alex sighed. "It's not a date. Jack is taking me to the Bernard art show that Dad and I missed yesterday so they could go to a football game."

"Mmm-hmm. One man, one woman, and a place to go. Sounds like a date to me."

"It's not a date," she insisted. "We both happen to have an interest in this artist, that's all."

Lana glanced up. "Jack the Attack is a contemporary art connoisseur?"

"He has two Bernard originals."

Her friend stopped filing. "For real?"

Alex pursed her mouth and nodded.

"Holy husband-hunting, Alex, I'm starting to think there's more to this man than meets the eye—and what meets the eye isn't too shabby."

She shook her finger. "Oh, no, don't read anything into this. We're going to an art gallery, and that's all."

Lana shrugged. "Okay. Just remember you're supposed to set a wedding date this weekend—to marry a different man." She blew on her nails, then stepped inside and closed the door with her hip.

Alex shook her head, then turned toward the exit, although her steps were somewhat more hesitant.

This was not a date.

"SO, JACK, WHO'S YOUR DATE?"

Alex nearly choked on her champagne, but extended

her hand when Jack introduced her to Bernard Penn, the artist whom she'd admired since the woman's first Lexington show nearly six years ago. Jack explained that his father had mentored the unknown local artist before she moved on to make her name in Chicago and Los Angeles. From the looks the quirky young woman was giving Jack, Alex wondered if he himself had mentored her in other areas.

"Jack gave me my first tattoo," Bernard announced, pointing to her bikini area, confirming Alex's suspicions.

"A trade for one of her paintings," Jack added.

"Made you earn the other one, too," the young woman said slyly before moving on to mingle.

Alex lifted her eyebrows over her champagne glass. "Just how large *is* your art collection?"

A slow grin spread over Jack's face. "I stopped counting canvases in ninety-three. Come with me. There's a piece in the atrium I'd like to show you." He clasped her hand and she didn't pull away, casting sideways glances at him as they walked, marveling at how comfortable he seemed in a cultural environment, and how little she actually knew about him.

"Where is your collection?" she asked.

"My place." They moved into the atrium, and Jack pointed out an abstract of musical instruments, commenting on the composition, the striking use of color and light.

"Nice," she said, nodding. "Where do you live?"

"Derek and I turned an older home in Lansdowne into a duplex, but since he and his wife will be needing more space, I'm giving him my side when they return from their honeymoon."

"That's generous of you."

He shook his head. "Derek has carried my weight

around the agency more than once. He's a good man, and it's the least I can do."

"So where will you live?"

He shrugged. "I'll find a place—I mainly use the duplex as storage for my art collection."

Alex angled her head. "So you weren't kidding about having a large collection that you, um, traded for?"

Jack nodded and gave her a crooked smile. "Not in the way you think, though. I've traveled a lot and picked up local pieces for a few bucks, and I've bartered an odd job here and there."

"I'd like to see it sometime," she murmured.

He shrugged. "Why not now?"

"I wasn't fishing for an invitation," she said, averting her gaze and extracting her hand from his.

Jack laughed. "I didn't think you were. Let's go. But I have to warn you, the place isn't exactly a penthouse loft."

She hesitated. The thought of going to his place seemed much too intimate in light of their recent encounter. "I shouldn't," she said, shaking her head. She didn't realize she was fingering her engagement ring until his gaze cut to her hand.

"Still wearing that thing?" he asked lightly.

Her defenses rallied. "Yes."

He made a sympathetic noise. "I never understood the allure of marriage myself."

"Call me old-fashioned," she said, lifting her chin. "But I like the idea of spending the rest of my life with one person."

One side of his mouth drew back. "Okay, Ms. Old-Fashioned, humor me. Let me show off my art collection to someone who actually knows a little bit about the art world."

"I'm sure I don't have your eye, or your expertise," she protested.

"Really? Did you select the Lenux hanging in your bathroom?"

She nodded.

"I have the companion piece."

"You're joking."

"Nope."

"What is it?"

"Come and see for yourself," he urged.

The knowledge that they shared an interest in the same artists left her absurdly pleased. And she had to admit, she was curious to see the man's living space. "Just a tour?"

He held up his hands. "Just a tour. We'll leave whenever you want to."

She wavered.

His eyes sobered. "Alex, I don't have an ulterior motive here to get you alone."

Alex squirmed, feeling foolish.

Jack pressed his lips together, then shifted his weight to his other foot. "I'm sorry our...mistake...Friday night left you in such an awkward position with your fiancé. We both got a little carried away." His color heightened, but his expression remained serious. "And Reddinger won't hear anything from me about what happened."

Alex exhaled, feeling relieved but also a little foolish for thinking that just because they would be alone, they would end up in bed again. Jack seemed as contrite as she about their lapse. They were adults who had learned from their "mistake." Besides, she suspected that for a man like Jack, the lure ended with the conquest. She was safe now. "Let's go," she agreed.

His grin buoyed her, sounding a little alarm in the back of her mind, which Alex ignored.

"Hungry?" he asked.

"A little."

"We can grab some fish sandwiches to go on the way. Sound good?"

She nodded, caught up in his excitement.

"Great. Let's ride."

During the drive across town, Alex tried to concentrate on the sweet-scented autumn air and the delicate orange and yellow leaves that swirled around them, but her senses were keen, making her ultra-aware of Jack's flat stomach muscles moving beneath her hands, of her thighs cradling his, her sex cupped against his buttocks. She told herself that once they arrived at his place, she'd maintain a room's distance from the man. At last he wheeled into the driveway of a large flagstone ranch home, and shut off the engine.

"I think you were more relaxed today," he teased as they removed their helmets.

She smiled, remembering her drive back from the cemetery yesterday, top down, hair flying. She hadn't reached any monumental conclusions during her trip, but she'd felt a little better upon returning. "It's kind of fun once you get the hang of it."

After they stowed their helmets and retrieved the bag of sandwiches, she followed Jack to a side entrance. The grass needed to be mowed, but its deep emerald color was a pleasing background for jewel-toned leaves that had settled around the base of trees and the house itself.

Jack moved casually, obviously much more at ease than she. After opening an aged beveled glass door, he swept his arm for her to precede him. Thrumming with curiosity, Alex stepped inside.

They entered through a tiny retro kitchen with hard-wood floors, charming red tile counters, and white porcelain fixtures. And while the room was stripped bare of furniture and bric-a-brac, she received an immediate introduction to his art collection. Paintings of all sizes, framed and unframed, lined every inch of the anchor wall from floor to ceiling, stretching into a hallway beyond her vision. No theme or color scheme was observed, but each of the pieces was intriguing—landscapes, portraits, abstracts.

"Let's eat outside," he suggested. "Then I'll give you the full tour."

He retrieved a couple of beers from the refrigerator, then elbowed his way through a glass door that led to a brick patio in the backyard. Alex followed, admiring the simple wood table and chairs, also littered with bright leaves. Jack set their food and drinks on the table, then cleared a chair for her and raised the faded green umbrella to shield them from the sun.

"Thank you for taking me to the gallery," she said as they unwrapped the sandwiches.

He passed her an open bottle of beer. "It was the least I could do for taking your father away from you Saturday."

Alex bit into her sandwich and attempted a carefree shrug. "My father is free to spend his time as he pleases."

He dragged a French fry through a mound of ketchup. "You don't have to pretend. I enjoyed spending time with my old man, too. I would have been disappointed if I'd been in your shoes."

She smiled sadly. "It's easier with sons. Dad and I don't seem to be able to connect."

"Except at work?"

Surprised by his interest, she nodded. "Even though

we don't always see eye to eye, it's the one passion we share."

He drank from his beer and settled back in his chair. The off-white shirt he wore looked crisp and new, and suited his coloring. The rolled up sleeves revealed his thick forearms. The man seemed comfortable in any setting. Part of her envied his nonchalance, his ability to move through life on his own terms.

"Alex, is the company really your passion?" he asked. "Or are you simply doing what you think your father expects of you?"

Although rankled, she tried to laugh. "That's a ridiculous question."

"Is it?"

"Yes," she insisted, then focused on removing the label from the cold bottle in one piece. "I mean, maybe at first I wanted to be close to Dad, but now..." She glanced up and sighed. "Well, I've come to realize that Dad doesn't care or even seem to notice how much I do at the store, so now I work strictly for my own fulfillment."

"I'm sure Al loves you very much," Jack said, his voice gentle.

She gave him a wry smile. "So much so that he'd rather spend time with you, a virtual stranger, than his own daughter." Her heart lurched. "You don't know how many times I've wished I'd been a boy."

Jack leaned forward, his mouth curving wide. "If I may say so, what a terrible waste *that* would have been."

She appreciated his attempt to lighten the mood and tingled under his compliment. "I probably sound like a spoiled little girl."

"Not at all," he assured her. "You must have been close to your mother."

"Yes," she murmured. "I suppose most children gravitate more toward one parent."

"I agree. I was closer to my father."

"You miss him." Not a question, because she knew he must.

Jack's smile didn't reach his eyes. "Every day that the sun rises."

So honest, she thought, shaken by his decidedly unmacho topic of conversation.

"But," he added, lifting his beer. "I'm fortunate to have some of Dad's canvases to remember him by. Let's finish up here so I can give you that tour."

His grin restored the cheerful atmosphere. They polished off their food in between discussing details for the commercial shoot the following day. Considering the strange way her body reacted every time she looked across the table at Jack—whom she was beginning to see in a new light—she decided to stick to neutral subjects like the ad campaign.

After discarding the leftovers, they carried their half-full bottles of beer back into the house. With her heart thumping in anticipation, Alex followed Jack slowly from room to room as he commented on the multitude of canvases and pointed out particular favorites of his, especially his father's. Because the rooms were void of furniture, they were free to walk around and admire each one. In one room which was obviously meant to be a small dining room, dozens of canvases were stacked and leaning against one wall.

"My vault," he offered.

"Jack," she breathed, afraid to touch anything, but wanting to see every piece. "You have enough work here to fill a small museum."

His smile was modest. "Maybe I'll open one when I'm

old and gray. Meanwhile, I'll have to put them in storage."

She was struck by the simplicity of his life. A worn couch and chair in the living room, along with a nice stereo system, represented most of the furniture in his house. If he owned a television, it was hidden. A thin layer of dust covered everything, and the air was a little stale. The man was not fastidious—quite a contrast to Heath's compulsively clean, white decor. It was clear Jack spent his money on art, not trappings. And she suspected that over the years he had amassed a collection worth a small fortune.

The last room they came to was his bedroom. Alex hovered in the doorway and tingled as she scrutinized his intimate space, silently admiring the simple lines of the walnut bed and matching dresser, trying to ignore the rumpled nondescript comforter that covered his body at night. Again, canvases claimed every available space on the walls, and were stacked on the floor.

"Is this your easel?" she asked, stepping inside for a closer look at the wooden piece sitting next to the dresser.

"No, it was my father's."

She swallowed at the catch in his throat. "Do you paint?"

He smiled. "No. Unfortunately, I don't have my father's great talent."

"I looked over the drawings you left yesterday—they're quite wonderful."

He seemed pleased, but shook his head. "My work is strictly commercial grade. Besides, I'd rather collect. An artist can become too consumed with his own work to fully appreciate the work of others."

She regarded him, his long, lean frame draped casually in the doorway. An educated, charismatic man who seemed at ease in a corporate boardroom, but preferred to work at his small family advertising agency. An ex-jock who rode a motorcycle, but collected art. She smiled, shaking her head. "You are full of surprises, Jack Stillman."

His eyes changed, and his lips parted, and in a split second the atmosphere changed from comfortably friendly to sexually charged. Her body softened and warmed, and with jarring clarity, she remembered what it was like to be made love to by this man. She panicked, her breath catching when she realized that she wanted him to touch her again. At a loss, she turned her back, feigning fascination in the etching on the dresser mirror.

"Alex." He was behind her, pulling her hair away from her neck.

"Jack," she whispered, leaning back into him. "We shouldn't."

"I know." But the warm succulent kiss he lowered to the curve of her neck sent blood pooling to her breasts and thighs. His erection hardened against the swell of her hip as he reached around to cup her breasts. "I can't help myself," he said. "I want you, Alex." She moaned and lay her head back against his chest, undulating against him.

Within seconds he had unfastened her overalls and freed the buttons of her blouse, exposing her coral-colored lace bra. He pulled down the bra to expose the globes of her breasts, the hardened tips aching for attention. He nipped at her earlobe as he squeezed the pink peaks, mimicking the pressure, layering the sensations until Alex was writhing against him.

"Look at you, you're so beautiful," he murmured into her hair.

Their reflection riveted her, his hands large and tanned

against her creamy skin. Desire buckled her knees, and she knew she was lost. "Jack...make love to me."

He groaned against her neck and slid his hand down over her bare stomach and inside her panties. The movement also served to strip her of the overalls, which she stepped out of, opening herself to Jack's fingers. As he plied her wetness, she reached behind her to tug at his clothing, which led to a frenzy of undressing. When they were both nude, Jack donned protection, then leaned into her from behind, grazing her sensitivity with his erection, whispering how much he wanted her. Already weak with wanting, Alex was riveted to the mirror that reflected their movements from the waist up.

White skin and brown, swollen breasts and big hands, narrow waist and broad shoulders, their bodies complemented each other perfectly, moving in synch, grazing sexes until their passion reached a fever pitch. "Now, Jack," she whispered, wild for the length of him inside her.

He lifted her until she half lay on the dresser for support, then probed her wetness before sliding inside.

"Ahh," he breathed, harmonizing with her moans. Every nerve ending sang as he began to make love to her with deep foraging thrusts. Emotions flitted over his face—need, pain, pleasure. She gave in to the sawing rhythm he set, and her climax burst around her with shocking haste. Amidst the blinding, delicious shock waves, she was aware that he, too, had surrendered to a quick, powerful release, evident by his contracted muscles, guttural moans and intense expressions.

Slowly, slowly, they recovered together. Alex sucked in a sharp breath when he withdrew and lowered her to her feet. He was gentle, making sure she could support her weight before he released her. They dressed in silence, the snaps and scrapes of various fasteners sounding loud in the acoustics of awkwardness.

Alex welcomed the sting of remorse when it hit her, but she didn't waste time berating herself—she'd known what she was doing, knew the ramifications of another encounter with Jack. In for a penny, in for a pound. Indeed, with every look they'd exchanged today, she'd felt herself growing farther from Heath, and closer to Jack. Her desire for him was so great, the certain dead end of the road she was traveling seemed not to matter. She'd never felt more out of control in her life—her newly discovered capacity for self-indulgence scared her to death.

"I—" She jumped at the sound of her own voice. "I think you'd better take me home, Jack."

She wanted him to object, to give her some indication that their fast and furious lovemaking meant more to him than a simple score, but he simply nodded, his expression unreadable.

During the agonizing ride across town, Alex felt worse and worse. She tried to hold on while maintaining as much distance between their bodies as possible. By the time they reached her building, however, Alex had recovered enough to realize it was up to her to repair their working relationship, if possible. After all, tomorrow was the all-important commercial and photo shoot—they'd be together for several hours.

When he stopped the motorcycle, she slid off the bike quickly and unstrapped her helmet as he killed the engine. Dusk was beginning to settle, and his face was swathed in gray shadow.

"Jack—"

"Alex—"

They both stopped and smiled awkwardly.

"Can we just—"

"—forget what happened?"

Alex swallowed, then nodded. "That would be best. My God, I'm engaged and you're..."

"Happily single," he supplied with a wry grin. "Alex, I'm incredibly attracted to you, but you're right—we're moving in opposite directions here. I'm sorry if this has complicated things for you and..."

"Heath," she supplied. "That's none of your concern, Jack." Her tone was more abrupt than she meant it to be, but Jack didn't need to know her plans regarding her compromised engagement. Inhaling deeply, she attempted to change the subject, and the mood. "Thanks again for taking me to the gallery. And for sharing your collection." Other things they'd shared leapt to her mind.

"You're welcome."

Silence stretched between them for several seconds before he said, "I'll see you tomorrow at the studio."

She nodded as she backed away. After a short wave, she turned and, despite her urge to run, managed to walk calmly to the stairwell. But as soon as she was out of sight, she broke into a jog, hating the tears that burned her eyes. Humiliation washed over her in waves as she recalled the incident—humiliation not because she'd once again had sex with Jack, but because she'd enjoyed it. Reveled in it, even.

After slipping into her apartment, she sat in the dark for a few seconds, wondering how her life had swerved so out of control in the past few days. She missed her mother's counsel, and she wished she felt close enough to discuss private matters with her father. Besides, she was all grown up, and vying for a vice presidency—why couldn't she sort out something so simple as her taboo attraction to a rebellious playboy?

Ping.

Alex looked over at the sliding glass window and waited for the second pebble to make its mark before she walked outside to lean over the balcony railing, crazily cheered. "You're determined to break something, aren't you?"

The white of his teeth flashed in the near-darkness. "Sorry to bother you," Jack called up, "but I wanted to say..."

"Yes?" she asked, her heart thumping.

"That I hope Reddinger knows what a lucky man he is."

Stunned into speechlessness, she could only stare as he waved, then climbed onto his bike and drove away.

15

"SORRY I'VE BEEN TRAVELING so much lately," Heath said over the phone. "Do you have a busy day planned?"

Alex doodled on a notepad on her desk, jumpy and miserable, wanting desperately to find comfort in Heath's voice. This was the man who cared about her, the man who shared her views and her values, the man who wanted to marry her. And didn't she want someone to be close to? Someone to grow old with?

Yes, more than anything.

But she'd jeopardized her chance for a trusting, long-term relationship by indulging in foolishness with Jack Stillman. Now what?

Alex tried to sound as normal as possible, despite her teeming unrest. "This afternoon is the commercial and photo shoot."

"That was pretty quick scheduling," Heath said.

"Jack knows the producer, some guy named Richardson. He pulled a couple of strings to get the studio time and, frankly, I'd just as soon get it over with."

"Well, the man will be in his element."

His tone picked at her tangled nerves. "What do you mean?"

Heath scoffed. "He's a natural performer. He knows how to manipulate people to get what he wants out of them—sympathy, admiration, a job."

She bristled at the idea that she was just another person taken in by Jack's undeniable charisma. "Funny, but he strikes me as being a very genuine person."

"Alex," he said, his voice colored with irritation, "I would expect this naiveté from Al, but not from you."

"Naiveté?"

"Come on, Alex, he's been working the two of you from the beginning. Al swallowed his bait hook, line and sinker, but I thought you were more objective. I wouldn't put it past this guy to try to make a pass at you."

Alex swallowed hard. "I think you're giving him a little too much credit."

"Being a con man is a gift. Just be glad he can put his talent to good use for Tremont's in front of the camera."

Funny, she didn't feel glad. And the feeling of non-gladness lasted throughout the morning, her mood matching the lousy weather as black clouds rolled in from the west. Heath's words ran over and over through her head. She'd suspected from the beginning that Jack was playing her father, yet somewhere along the way, she had fallen under his spell, too. Was it his plan all along to seduce her for leverage? And how easily had she played into his hands?

Confused and fidgety, Alex reviewed everything she knew about Jack Stillman, beginning with her first visit to his dilapidated office. He'd told her and everyone else that he'd arranged the conditions purposefully to set up his presentation the next day. She hadn't believed him, but neither had she called his bluff. Perhaps another look at his operations would resurrect all those doubts which had kept her objective and sharp in the beginning. And did she ever need some objectivity.

She glanced at her watch, noting the time she'd have to leave for the studio. But since Jack's mode of transportation would be hampered by the ominous weather, she'd simply leave early and pick him up at his office on the way to the studio. Maybe the stark reminder of his less-than-stellar enterprise would give her a badly needed dose of reality.

Jack Stillman would never be the kind of man she wanted and needed in her life.

JACK CONSIDERED TAKING A CAB to the office Monday morning, but decided the short ride in the driving rain might clear his head of tormenting visions of Alex and their extraordinary lovemaking.

Was he ever wrong.

He arrived at the office around nine-fifteen, soaked, and chagrined to see that Tuesday's and Stripling's cars were both there.

"You're late," Tuesday announced when he opened the door and walked in, dripping.

He removed his leather jacket and shot her an annoyed glance. "I almost drowned getting here, thanks for your concern."

"Don't shake that wet coat in here," she warned. "And my only concern is collecting my money for Friday's daily double."

"Got it right here," he assured her, tossing the coat in the hallway corner, then closing the door. Jack withdrew an envelope, and handed it to Tuesday. "Twelve hundred fifty-five dollars. Pretty good wages for a job that doesn't exist."

She opened the envelope for a quick peek, then sniffed. "I'm worth twice as much," she said, then nodded toward the back. "Tax man's here, a quaking nervous wreck that you didn't bet his horse to place like he told you."

Jack wheeled to walk to the back office, and crashed

through a set of black swinging saloon doors that hadn't been there before. He turned around and walked back through to the front office. "What, may I ask, are these?"

"I decided I need my privacy up here," Tuesday said, stuffing her money deep into the neckline of her dress. "The doors break up the space properlike."

Actually, they looked pretty darn good. "Where did you get the doors?"

"Found them in the Dumpster," Tuesday said. "Slapped a coat of paint on them, and they're as good as new. Marion helped me hang them this morning."

"Marion?" Jack's eyebrows shot straight up. "After nearly crippling the man, you're on a first-name basis?"

"He's feeling much better. I gave him another adjustment last night, and he threw away the board."

"Last night?" Jack asked, then held up his hand. "Wait, I don't want to know." Sounded as though everyone was having success in the romance department except him.

He pushed through the doors again into the back office where Stripling sat, sipping tea, and looking as limber as a willow switch. Tuesday followed him.

"Well?" The man's Adam's apple bobbed. "Did you bet the horse to place? I saw in the paper that she won, and the payout was pretty good."

Making a sympathetic sound, Jack shook his head. "No, Stripling, I didn't bet the horse to place like you told me."

The man's thin shoulders fell.

Jack grinned and whipped out another envelope. "I bet her to win! Seventy-five dollars for a two dollar bet, and I put your entire hundred on her."

Stripling's jaw opened and closed as he lunged for the envelope. "Oh, my goodness! Oh, my goodness!"

"Oh, my goodness is right," Tuesday mumbled, frowning. "If that horse had come in second instead of first, you would have lost his money."

"But if I had bet the horse to come in second—"

"—like he *told* you to—"

"—the payout wouldn't have been as good." He shrugged. "What can I say? I was feeling lucky."

"And just how much did *you* pocket?" she asked.

"Well," Jack drawled as he pulled out the last fat envelope. "I hate to brag, but I cleared just under five gees."

Stripling whistled low. "You're going to have to claim that money on your personal income tax form, you know."

Jack frowned in his direction, then his attention was diverted by the opening of the front door. When had Tuesday hung a bell on it to announce visitors?

"That must be the furniture," Tuesday sang, then strode toward the front.

A few seconds passed before her words sank it. "Furniture?" Jack croaked. "What furniture?"

He jogged to the front just as a huge man in a yellow slicker walked in, holding a clipboard and directing two young men who had a desk hoisted on their shoulders.

"You Stillman?" the man asked.

"Yes. What's this all about?"

The man sucked his teeth, then read from the clipboard. "I got an order here for two desks, two file cabinets and two leather chairs. That'll be three thousand, two hundred dollars, cash on delivery."

"What?" Jack's temples nearly exploded. "I didn't order all this stuff." He whirled to Tuesday. "Did *you* do this?"

She blinked, her face innocent. "I distinctly remember

you saying Friday that you were going to win enough
money to buy the new equipment the agency needed."

"But...but I didn't mean— Hey, watch that leather coat
in the hallway, buddy!"

Tuesday snatched the envelope out of his hand and
counted bills as she talked. "The Salvation Army will be
here in a few minutes to pick up the old furniture, so it'll
be out of the way by the time the computers arrive."

"Computers?" Jack asked wearily.

"My daughter-in-law works at a computer store across
town—I got you a great deal." She handed him the balance of the money, along with two aspirins and a cup of
water.

Jack swallowed the pills dry. "Tuesday," he said, holding on to the wall for support. "Did it occur to you to ask
me first?"

"No," she said matter-of-factly. "Because it's my job to
get things organized around here."

He thought he might pass out—Derek certainly would
when he found out. "There...is...no...*job!*"

ALEX WAS GRATEFUL the showers had subsided enough
for her to dash from the store van into the building that
housed the Stillman & Sons Advertising Agency. With a
rueful shake of her head, she remembered coming here
only last week, marveling at the whirlwind of events that
had taken place since. Had she really known Jack for
only a few days? Odd, but the man had plowed a disrup-
tive furrow through her life that bespoke a much longer
relationship than existed. And a much more meaningful
one.

Shaking off her wayward thoughts, she retraced her
steps down the hall, noting that at least the carpet had
been cleaned, and the sour, mildewed smell was gone.

When she twisted the doorknob, she noticed that the agency sign had been repaired. And when she stepped inside, the transformation was nothing short of remarkable—furniture, plants, music, *cleanliness*. A matronly black woman turned from a file cabinet and flashed a friendly smile. "Now you must be Ms. Tremont."

Alex blinked because she hadn't called ahead. "Um, yes. Have we met?"

"I just knew it from Mr. Stillman's description of you," the woman said. "I'm Tuesday, the agency's office manager."

"Pleased to meet you," she said, extending her hand. The agency must be rebounding if they had hired an office manager. And purchased new furniture. And cleaned. "I should have called—Mr. Stillman isn't expecting me. Considering the weather, I thought I might give him a ride to the television station."

"Well, now that's mighty nice of you," the woman said, beaming. She gestured toward a love seat, covered with a lush moss-green velvet. "Won't you have a seat? I'll let Mr. Stillman know you're here. Would you like some hot tea?"

Alex took the proffered seat and nodded dumbly. "Yes, please."

"Cream and sugar?"

"Both, please."

The woman disappeared through a set of swinging half-doors that she didn't remember. She heard the rumble of at least one male voice, maybe two. A couple of minutes later, the office manager emerged, bearing a cup and saucer. "Here's your tea. Mr. Stillman is on a conference call with a client, but I let him know you were here, so I'm sure he'll be right out."

"Thank you." On a conference call with a client? She

just assumed he was spending all his time on the Tremont's account, but he had mentioned doing business with Phillips' Honey, and after all, his brother was still out of town. Alex picked up the cup and smiled. "What extraordinary china."

Tuesday smiled. "Mr. Stillman insists on nice little touches around here."

The black doors swung out and an older man appeared. "Tuesday," he said, "do you have time for lunch?"

The woman shook her head mournfully. "The phones have been ringing off the hook around here, I'd better not."

So they were busy, Alex thought, sipping her very tasty tea.

"Want me to pick up something for you?"

Tuesday passed on his offer, and when the man left, Alex asked, "That wasn't the other Mr. Stillman, was it?"

"No, that's Mr. Stripling. He only comes in when it gets really crazy around here."

Alex pursed her mouth. Darn—the agency *was* busy. And so different, she found it hard to believe things could have changed so much in a week's time. Was it possible that Jack *had* set her up that first day to lay a foundation for his presentation? "Tuesday, how long have you worked for the agency?"

The woman looked heavenward. "Can't rightly say how long I've been working here—seems like forever."

"And has the office always looked like this?"

"Ever since I've been here." Then she smiled. "Oh, you're talking about that day Mr. Stillman was trying to get your goat." She laughed, slapping her thigh. "That man and his elaborate schemes."

Alex's mouth fell open.

Tuesday's face shone with affection. "Yes, he's a rebel, that one, but it worked, didn't it?"

She couldn't believe it—layers just *kept* peeling off the man.

"My ears are burning," Jack said, strolling in and turning his full-fledged grin toward Alex.

Alex swallowed hard. Funny—just the sight of him set every part of her aflame. "Um, hi. I came by to...um..." Darn it, why *had* she come by?

"To make sure you weren't late to the studio," Tuesday supplied, then disappeared through the swinging doors.

"Right," she parroted, feeling all of twelve years old. Standing, she experienced a bad premonition about the commercial shoot, but a second later she chided herself— she would be watching him from a distance—how dangerous could the man be across a room, surrounded by cameras and lights?

"Give me a minute," he said with a devilish wink, jerking his thumb toward his office. "I just need to grab my thong."

"ALEX," JACK SAID, "this is Sammy Richardson, producer here at the station and an old friend of mine."

Sammy Richardson was not only *not* a man, she was the most female woman Alex had ever seen. Alex suspected that if she'd been a male cartoon character, this would be the point where her eyeballs would bulge out of her head and drop on the floor. Sammy's long, long hair was a thousand shades of natural blond, and her skin was one shade of a natural golden glow. Stunning was the only word to describe her long, curvaceous body, magnificent in jeans and a man's shirt. Old friend?

Yeah, right. "Hello," she managed to say. "I'm Alex Tremont."

"Nice to meet you." Sammy's handshake was firm, her gaze direct and friendly. "Perhaps we can talk about what you're looking for today while Jack goes to hair and makeup."

A frown crossed Jack's face, but he left with an assistant, grumbling. Alex followed Sammy to a makeshift desk a few feet away from a myriad of sets surrounded by cameras and lights. "Okay, let's talk about the shoot," she said without preliminaries. "My people will be here in a half hour, ready to start."

Alex opened her notebook. "Tremont's is considering hiring Jack Stillman as a spokesman."

"Good decision," the woman interjected smoothly.

Bristling at the woman's knowing tone, she said, "We're *considering* hiring Mr. Stillman. The outcome will depend on the success of this shoot."

"What mood are we going for here?"

She squirmed, pushing the tentative slogan across the table: Tremont's. Because clothes *do* make the man. "Um, you know...persuasive, compelling..."

"Sexy?" The woman's mouth curved into a catlike smile.

"Um, yes."

"Jack can certainly handle that assignment," Sammy murmured, seemingly a hundred miles away.

"Yes, he can." Alex agreed pleasantly, ridiculously tempted to let the woman know that she wasn't the only one in the room who knew the particulars of Jack's carnal skills. When she realized how trampy that sounded, she clamped her mouth shut, mentally kicking herself. Trying to steer the conversation back to business, she withdrew a folder of the reduced images Jack had presented at the first meeting, along with a storyboard. "The two female models I requested from the agency we use should be here soon."

Sammy's eyebrows rose. "Just two? Jack *has* settled down."

Alex frowned. "Building on Jack's original ideas, I'd like to focus on four settings—the gym, the backyard barbecue, the office, and the, um, bedroom."

The woman nodded, making notes fast and furious. "Let me call props with this list, and we'll be good to go as soon as Jack is ready and the models get here."

Alex studied the woman while she spoke on the phone, a little awed by her sparkling beauty. Sammy and Jack would make a spectacular-looking couple, she acknowledged, wondering how recently they'd been involved and why their relationship hadn't worked. And her stomach felt strange at the thought of them together.

Sammy hung up the phone and smiled broadly. "The props will be here in ten minutes. Let's take a look at the sets."

"So," Alex ventured as they picked their way around the equipment, "you and Jack go way back."

"Oh, yeah," the woman said. "Way back. We even lived together for a while, but I wanted to get married."

"Oh." Alex paused for casual effect. "And he didn't?"

Sammy laughed, a melodious sound. "Jack? The man is a rolling stone—he'll never commit to anything or anyone. I was astounded when he told me he was working at the agency again." She laughed. "Wonder how long that will last?"

"Long enough to handle our account, hopefully," Alex said, irritated.

"Oh, Derek will take care of you," she said with a dismissive wave. "He's the dependable one. Just be thank-

ful you nailed down Jack long enough for these photos."
She shook her head and made a regretful sound. "He
used to get offers all the time to model, do sports com-
mentary, endorsements. Could have made a boatload of
money."

"He didn't want the money?" Alex asked, dropping all
pretense of disinterest.

"He didn't want the responsibility," Sammy corrected.
"I told you—the man is commitment-shy. He'll work just
long enough to fund his freedom."

"You sound a little bitter," Alex said quietly.

The woman shook her head. "I'm not. Jack didn't de-
ceive me. He told me up front that he didn't ever plan to
marry, but I thought I could change his mind." She
turned, one eyebrow lifted. "When I look back, though,
the one thing I appreciate most about Jack is that he's
honest." Then she laughed. "Well, maybe there are one
or two other things."

Alex squirmed.

"Hey," the woman said, suddenly serious, her gaze direct. "I'm only telling you this to keep you from making
the same mistake I made."

Attempting nonchalance, Alex said, "You're wrong if
you think—"

"I know what I see," Sammy said, her voice gentle but
firm.

Jack entered from the side, wearing a white bathrobe,
flanked by two giggling young women who were still
powdering his nose and patting his hair.

"See," the woman continued. "He's irresistible. Every
woman he meets falls in love with him. But believe me,
don't do it. It took me years to get over him." Sammy
clapped her hands to get the attention of the crew that ap-

peared pushing pallets of furniture and other props, then started belting out directions.

Alex tried to shrug off the woman's well-meaning warning—she had nothing to worry about. But she found herself mesmerized as the shoot commenced and Jack moved through numerous takes like a pro.

He was gorgeously somber in the business suit scenes, striding with purpose across an office setting.

He was charmingly casual in the backyard barbecue scene, tending a grill.

He was breathtakingly sweaty in the gym scene, lifting weights.

And he was knee-weakeningly sexy in the bedroom scene, reclining in boxers, the hand of one of the models on his shoulder.

The photographer took rolls and rolls of film of him in every one of the outfits she'd chosen—including the black thong, which had all the women on the set twitching. Sammy suggested that they get a couple shots with his tattoo showing, which only heightened the mood.

The man was magic, Alex conceded, and the camera loved him. He moved with economy, somehow packing a sense of approachable masculinity into every gesture. Occasionally, he made eye contact with her, and to her consternation, her body leapt in response. After three hours of a slow-burn, Alex had to cross her legs.

Sammy threw her a sympathetic look, then yelled, "Cut—that's a wrap."

16

"Looks to me like your business is just starting to gain some momentum," Stripling said, handing Jack a stack of papers. "So I'm recommending that the penalties and interest be dropped. Coupled with the payment plan I set up, the agency should be caught up on its back taxes within six months."

Jack shook his hand. "Thanks, Stripling. My brother Derek will be so relieved."

The man's smile was genuine. "Good luck, Jack." He tipped his hat to Tuesday, who gave him a fond wink.

When the door closed, Jack wheeled and pushed through the swinging doors. He poured himself another cup of coffee, then dropped into his new leather swivel chair in front of his new wood and metal desk. To his extreme aggravation, Tuesday was on his heels.

"All right, out with it."

Jack frowned. "What?"

"You just got the IRS off your back, you have six new client appointments set up for next week, your brother will be back in a few days to help, and I've never seen such a long face."

Jack drank deeply from his cup. Since Monday, he'd been battling a funk born of proximity to Alexandria Tremont. After the shoot was over, she'd announced she would be in touch once they had the results of the focus group audience, maybe sometime this week. After several days of regular contact with her, he supposed he was suffering from withdrawal. He found himself toying with the phone, or riding his bike near her building on the off chance a legitimate excuse for talking to her would occur to him. One didn't.

He simply couldn't get the woman out of his mind.

"It's that Tremont lady, isn't it?"

"Absolutely not."

"Whew, the fire alarm's going to go off for sure, 'cause liar, liar, your pants are on *fire*."

He rolled his eyes upward to meet her disapproving gaze. "I don't want to talk about it."

"Okay," she sang, throwing up her arms and turning toward the front office. "No one can accuse Tuesday Humphrey of sticking her nose in where it don't belong."

Jack snorted as she moved through the swinging doors, then swiveled his chair around to face the easels of posters he'd drawn for the Tremont's account. He'd lain awake most of the night exploring his state of mind, and trying to get to the root of the problem. He wished he'd never agreed to be the spokesman for the department store, account or no account. Because on top of the increasingly suffocating feeling of being tied to someone else's schedule, there was the little problem of working with Alex.

No, he corrected, the problem wasn't working with Alex—the problem was working with Alex and not being able to take her home afterward. He lusted after the woman with an unprecedented intensity, and he knew they could have fun together for a while. But Alex was engaged to a successful man, and he had nothing to offer her save a pile of paintings.

At the races she'd said she liked the serious, professional side of him. Except the serious, professional side of him that she'd seen had all been a sham, propped up by his lies and Tuesday's corroboration. He had no desire to be serious and professional. Just thinking about being tied to this desk, or to any desk, made him jittery.

What he needed was distance from her. Maybe if he took a trip, gave her time to marry Reddinger...

His phone beeped, which meant Tuesday had patched a call through to his line.

"Jack Stillman," he said into the handset.

"Jack, it's Al Tremont."

"Hey, Mr. T., what can I do for you?"

"Just calling with good news, son. The focus group gave the commercials a big thumbs-up, highest marks possible."

"That's great, sir."

"So, with that little formality behind us, we need to sit down and negotiate a long-term contract with your agency, and for you to be the exclusive Tremont's spokesman! The marketing department is gearing up for billboards, personal appearances, you name it."

Jack's stomach clenched. "Mr. T., I need to talk to you about that. Of course, the agency would be honored to handle your business, but...I'm bowing out as spokesman."

Al made a choking sound. "What? I don't understand."

"I'll honor the contract we signed giving Tremont's permission to use the spots that were filmed, but that's the end of it for me."

"But why, son?"

"It's complicated, sir."

"It's Alex, isn't it?"

Jack blinked. How much did her father know? "I don't know if you've talked to Alex about it—"

"Yes," Al cut in. "I know it puts you in an awkward situation, son, but I was hoping the two of you could work together despite the, um, *problem*."

Damn, maybe they were closer than he'd assumed. "Please don't take offense, sir, but I simply can't work under these circumstances. I'll hand off your account to Derek, and I'm sure you'll find a new spokesperson soon."

Al cleared his throat with a low rumble. "I don't think you understand, son. It's *you* I want, not your agency. I can get just about anyone to come up with a catchy slogan and draw me a few pictures, but I want Jack the Attack representing the store."

Stunned, Jack sat in silence. Just as he'd suspected.

"To put it plainly, Jack—no endorsement, no advertising account. And if it sweetens the pot a little, you won't be working with Alex. You'll be working with our new vice president of marketing and sales, Bobby Warner."

So Alex hadn't received the promotion.

"What do you say, Jack? Are you in?"

Jack sighed, and although anger drummed through his veins, he could imagine the disappointment on Derek's face when he told him they'd lost the account.

"Sure, Mr. T. I'm in."

SHE LOVED HIM. A person got a lot of thinking done in the course of three sleepless nights, and after dissecting Sammy Richardson's advice during the commercial shoot, Alex had come to a frightening conclusion. She, the woman who prided herself on forging a stable future on all fronts, had fallen for a motorcycle-riding rebel who would soon be voluntarily homeless and had no intention of settling down with one woman.

And with the overwhelmingly positive response from

the focus group, it looked as if Jack would not only be their spokesman, but would be handling their advertising account to boot. She'd kept her word to her father, and although she'd underestimated Jack's ability, she was willing to concede that having him as a spokesman might give them the sales boost they needed.

She'd simply have to find a way to disguise her feelings for Jack and work with him until she could arrange to hand off the ad agency liaison responsibilities. The future seemed a little vague, but of one thing she was certain—when Heath returned from Cincinnati this afternoon, she would break their engagement.

Funny, how her feelings for him—or rather, her lack of feelings for him—now seemed so crystal clear relative to her feelings for Jack. She realized how much she and Heath had been robbing each other of a wonderful experience. Heath deserved someone who loved him the way she loved Jack—wildly and unreasonably. If Heath truly loved her, which, upon reflection of their relationship, she doubted, then he would eventually get over her, just as she would eventually get over Jack.

"Alex," her father said, striding into her office without the courtesy of a knock. His face was flushed scarlet, and she was immediately concerned for his health.

"Yes, Dad?"

"I just wanted you to know that you almost cost us an ace spokesman."

She frowned. "What do you mean?"

"I just got off the phone with Jack Stillman, and he was ready to decline a long-term contract for spokesman because he said he couldn't work with you anymore."

Confusion, hurt, anger—her mixed emotions, tripped her tongue. "I d-don't understand."

"You promised me," her father said, his tone low and

accusing. "You promised me that you would work *with* him, and now I find out that you've been so difficult, he doesn't want to work with Tremont's at all."

Difficult? Because she'd slept with him? Did Jack now find the situation too awkward? Her mouth opened and closed, but no sound emerged.

"All because you were determined to sign some high and mighty advertising agency from St. Louis," he added.

"I had no idea Jack felt that way," she murmured, standing on shaky knees. "But if you feel so strongly about having Jack Stillman as spokesman—"

"You know I do!"

She swallowed. "I was planning to step aside and let someone else work with the ad agency."

"There's no need," her father said, laying a memo on her desk. "Bobby Warner was just named vice president of sales & marketing, and he'll be taking over those duties." He exited as he'd entered, without preamble.

Stunned, Alex sat down to read the memo, disappointment coursing through her. Stinging from her father's words and Jack's betrayal, she swung her chair around to face her computer, and put her fingers on the keyboard.

Through a blur of tears, she typed a short letter of resignation from the company she loved. Her father's attitude had made one thing perfectly clear—she could no longer work in this environment, yearning for the love of two men she'd never have.

A few minutes later, a knock sounded at her door. Sniffing quickly, Alex looked up to see Heath stick his head in. "I heard," he said softly. "Can I come in?"

She nodded, her stomach churning. "When did you get back?"

"Just now. I'm sorry about the vice presidency, Alex, but in light of my news, it might be for the best."

She frowned. "What news?"

His smile was a bit shaky. "One of the reasons I've been spending a lot of time in Cincinnati lately is because the bank where the store has its accounts has offered me a job. A great job."

Unable to hide her surprise, she asked, "Why haven't you said anything?"

He shrugged. "I was afraid it wouldn't pan out, and I didn't want you or your dad thinking I wasn't being loyal. I know this company means everything to you."

"Heath, I just typed my letter of resignation."

"What?" His expression changed from surprise to elation. "That's wonderful! Now we can both go to Cincinnati—I know you'll be able to find a terrific job there, Alex."

She looked at Heath, his cheeks pink from excitement, his eyes shining with enthusiasm. They could make a clean break from Tremont's, from Lexington, from her father, from Jack. Could their relationship be salvaged?

Alex bit down hard on her lip, wavering.

17

TO GET HIS MIND OFF ALEX that afternoon, Jack threw himself into the paperwork on his desk, finishing tasks as fast as Tuesday could stack them in front of him.

"I don't know what's gotten into you," she said, finger wagging, "but I hope it's chronic."

Jack sighed. The *last* thing he needed was a persistent dose of the hots for Alex Tremont. "Would you mind labeling folders for the accounts we'll be calling on next week? I need to file some information I found on the Internet."

"One step ahead of you," she said cheerfully, setting the stack of labeled folders on the edge of his desk.

Jack smiled. "Thanks."

"Do you mind if I take off a little early? Reggie wants me to meet his girlfriend tonight, so he's taking us out to dinner."

"Have a great time," Jack said, lifting his hand in a wave. As he picked up the folders, he realized how valuable the woman had become to him and to the business in such a short time. He liked her no-nonsense attitude and her spunk, and he wanted to keep her around.

"Tuesday."

She turned back. "Yes?"

He reached into his pocket and removed a spare door key from his keyring, then tossed it to her. "You're hired."

She caught the key neatly, and a grin spread over her face. "Thank you, sir. I'll see you first thing in the morning." She fairly danced through the swinging doors and a few seconds later he heard the bell on the front door jangle as she left.

Jack turned back to his computer, whistling under his breath, realizing that by hiring an office manager, he'd made a commitment to grow their business. The idea of being spokesman for Tremont's was sinking in—the money would be good, and would allow him to put extra money into the business, to relieve some of the pressure for Derek. And as much as he hated to admit it, being the department store spokesman would still give him a thread of a connection with Alex.

When the bell on the door jangled again, Jack called, "Did you forget something?"

"Yeah," came Derek's voice. "I think I forgot our office address because I don't recognize this place."

Surprised, Jack jumped to his feet and hurried to the front, sporting a wide grin.

Looking tanned and happy, Derek and his new wife Janine stood in the front office, staring at the changes.

"You're home early," Jack said, pumping his brother's hand and lifting the blond Janine off her feet for a bear hug.

"Janine had to get back to see a doctor," Derek said, sliding an arm around her waist.

"Are you sick?" Jack asked, immediately concerned for his new sister.

"No." She beamed. "I'm pregnant!"

Elated, Jack clapped his brother on the back. "That didn't take long."

"Well," Derek said, a little sheepish, "we did have a long honeymoon."

"And a tiny head start," Janine said, holding up her thumb and forefinger.

"Shh," Derek chastised, but grinned anyway.

"Mother will have quite a surprise when she gets back," Jack said.

His brother nodded, then gestured to the office. "Speaking of surprises..."

"Oh, yeah," Jack said, "come on back and I'll show you around. The IRS auditor left this morning—we're in good shape—and Tuesday will be back first thing in the morning."

"Tuesday—you mean that woman who wandered in off the street?"

Jack dismissed his concern with a wave. "You'll love her."

Derek was impressed with the new furniture and equipment, but his first concern, of course, was cost.

"Already paid for," Jack assured him. "Compliments of Keeneland."

His brother laughed, shaking his head. When Janine excused herself to visit the restroom—Derek said she'd been doing a lot of that lately—his brother asked about the Tremont's account.

"The focus group results for the commercials came back today—we're in. Al Tremont wants us to meet next week to negotiate a long-term contract."

"That's great, Jack! Do you have some stills?"

Jack hesitated, then fished out the thick folder of photographs from the Tremont shoot and handed it to his brother.

Derek frowned. "These are all of you!"

"Sit down," Jack said, gesturing to a chair. He caught his brother up on the details of the spokesman-ad account tie-in as quickly as possible, leaving out the sordid details of his association with Alex.

Her brother squinted and scratched his head. "You're modeling now?"

Jack sighed. "It's not modeling."

"Well, whatever, it must have impressed the daughter."

Jack averted his gaze and nodded.

"What?" Derek asked.

"What do you mean, what?"

"That look."

"What look?"

"That I-got-a-woman-problem look."

Jack crossed his hands behind his head. "Not me, man."

Derek leaned forward in his chair and stared at Jack until he squirmed and cracked his knuckles in one sweeping motion. "You did it, didn't you?"

Jack frowned. "Did what?"

"Slept with her."

He stood and walked around to lean on the front of his desk, then sighed. "Okay, yeah."

His brother winced. "Ah, man! Tell me you didn't do it to get the business."

"Of course not!"

"So how will this affect your ability to work on the account? Does her father know?"

"He seems to know—"

"Christ, she *told* him?"

"I don't know, maybe she told her boyfriend, and *he* told her father."

Derek quirked an eyebrow. "Are the two men close?"

Jack cleared his throat. "Her boyfriend is the CFO."

"Oh, now *there's* a smooth move." Derek threw up his hands. "What were you thinking?"

Jack scowled. "That I could have this extremely pleasant conversation when you found out."

Derek shrugged. "Oh, well, if Tremont knows and he offered you the account anyway—"

"I won't be working directly with the daughter anymore." He picked up the minibasketball and tossed it toward the hoop. It bounced off the rim and rolled into a corner.

"And, um, how do you feel about that?"

Jack retrieved the ball and threw it up again. "When did you become a shrink?" The ball glanced off the rim again and bounced back to Derek.

"Since you became a case," his brother said, sending the ball swishing through the net. "If I didn't know better, I'd say you were acting as if you were hung up on this woman."

"And how am I acting?"

Derek crossed his arms and looked around the back office, taking in the new decor and the new computer equipment, the stack of completed paperwork on Jack's desk, and Jack's clothing—part of his Tremont's wardrobe. "Grown up."

"Oh, very funny."

"Enough, Jack," Derek said, his voice low and serious. "Tell me about this woman."

Jack dragged his hand down his face, willing to confess to murder if it would take away the nagging tightness in his chest. "Alex is...different."

"Oh, hell."

"Do you want to hear this or not?"

"Sorry, go ahead."

He sighed, struggling to put into words the kinds of

abstract things that had been floating through his mind like confetti. "Alex is...smart. And straight-laced. And she wears her hair in this tight little bun, except when she's on the bike with me..." He groaned, realizing he sounded like a bad lyricist.

Derek laughed. "I don't believe it. My little brother has fallen in love."

Jack jerked his head up. "Love? Whoa, I didn't say anything about love."

"Who's in love?" Janine asked, rejoining them.

Derek jerked his thumb toward Jack.

"Wait a minute!"

"Who is she?"

"His boss."

"That's not true!"

Janine grinned. "Is she in love with you, Jack?"

He frowned, objecting to the direction the conversation had taken. "I kind of doubt it, seeing how she's engaged to another man."

She slipped her arm around Derek's waist and gave him a squeeze. "Speaking from experience, sometimes a person doesn't realize they're settling until they meet the person they're really meant to love."

Out of respect, Jack didn't roll his eyes.

His brother winked. "You'd better let her know how you feel, Jack."

He scoffed. "Yeah, right."

"I know it sounds scary, but believe me, man, it's the not telling that'll eat you up." He smiled down at his wife and patted her stomach. "Ready to go home, sweetheart?"

She nodded, and they left, arm and arm, heads together, footsteps in synch. Jack watched, marveling at the change in his brother. He always thought his brother would settle down with a demure mouse, not a blond siren. But bubbly Janine had really brought out Derek's lighter side. In fact, they were complete opposites, just like—

On the other hand, lots of people were opposites, and it didn't mean they were in *love.*

Massaging the tightness just below his breastbone, Jack retrieved the basketball and spun it on the tip of his finger as his brother's and sister-in-law's words reverberated in his head. *You'd better let her know how you feel...it's the not telling that'll eat you up.*

But did he love her?

Jack eyed the basketball hoop and pursed his mouth. *L-O-V-E.* Four letters, four baskets. If he made them all, he might call, just to feel her up—er, out. And just to make it fair, he would close one eye and use his left hand.

He tossed the *L* ball.

Swish.

Dammit.

He tossed the *O* ball.

Swish.

Dammit.

He tossed the *V* ball.

Swish.

Dammit.

He tossed the *E* ball.

It rolled around the rim once, twice, three times...then popped out.

"Yeeesssss!" he shouted, pumping the air with his fist. He dropped back into his chair and waited for the relief to wash over him. Instead, his chest resumed its dull ache. He stared at the phone, then the clock. Four-thirty on Thursday afternoon. No doubt she was still at the office, possibly making plans to go out with Reddinger.

He could always call her and say it had been nice working with her, he reasoned, and picked up the phone.

But then she'd know that he knew about her losing the vice presidency. He put down the phone.

Then he brightened—calling to thank her for helping with the commercials would be simple and appropriate. He dialed her office number and drummed his fingers on his desk while the phone rang.

"Tess Hanover."

"This is Jack Stillman—"

"Oh, helloooo, Mr. Stillman."

"Um, hello. I was trying to reach Alex. Is she available?"

"No," she said, her tone a little odd.

He frowned. "Has she left for the day?"

"You could say that."

Jack sighed. "Tess, did she or didn't she?"

"Actually," the woman said, her voice lowered to a conspiratorial level, "I shouldn't be telling you this, but Ms. Tremont resigned."

"What?"

"She and Mr. Reddinger both resigned," she whispered. "I heard that he got a great job offer in Cincinnati."

And Alex was going with him. Jack's heart sank.

"Ms. Tremont and her father had an argument."

He hated to snoop, but the woman seemed anxious to tell him something. "What about?"

"Mr. Tremont barged into her office, and I overheard him blame her for nearly losing you as a spokesman."

Jack swallowed hard. "What did he say?"

"That she'd gone back on her promise to try to work with you, and the reason you had changed your mind was because she was so difficult to get along with."

He closed his eyes. "That's not true."

"He sounded angry. Ms. Tremont offered to step aside and let someone else work with you, but he told her the new vice president would be taking over those responsibilities." Relishing every detail, Tess's voice rolled with inflection. "Then a little while later, Mr. Reddinger arrived and went into Ms. Tremont's office. They came out together and asked me to make official copies of their resignation letters."

He felt as if he'd been punched in the gut. "Is Al still there?"

"Yes."

"Patch me through to him, please." Feeling as if Alex were slipping through his fingers, he stood and paced until Al Tremont's voice came on the line.

"Jack, what's up?"

He wasted no time on formalities. "What's this about you telling Alex I couldn't work with her because she was too difficult to get along with?"

"Well, that's what you said, Jack."

"No, I said I couldn't work with Alex, but I didn't tell you why. We both jumped to conclusions about what the other person meant."

"I'm confused, son. Why can't you work with Alex?"

Sweat broke out on his upper lip, and the pain in his chest escalated to the point of forcing him to sit down.

"Jack?"

"I love her." He leaned his head back, waiting for the fallout.

"What?" Al sounded incredulous.

"I love your daughter."

The man made a few blustery sounds. "Does Alex know?"

"Not unless she's a mind reader."

"Well, son, you'd better get a move on."

"I understand she and Reddinger both resigned."

Al made a rueful sound. "I can replace Heath, but not Alex. I can't believe she's leaving for *him*."

"Maybe she's leaving because she feels unappreciated at Tremont's," Jack ventured.

"Why, that's absurd."

"Is it? I know she was hoping for that vice presidency."

"Jack, just between you and me, I was planning to step down in the next couple of months, and recommend that Alex take over as president. *That's* why she didn't get the vice presidency."

Shocked, Jack asked, "Why didn't you tell her?"

"When she told me she was leaving with Reddinger, I didn't want to muddy the waters. You see, son, I'm more concerned that Alex be with the right man than that she take over the family business." Al laughed with no humor. "I guess neither one of us has been as forthcoming with Alex as we should have been. But I'll make you a deal. If you can talk her into staying in Lexington, I'll offer her the presidency." Al made a regretful noise. "Jack...if you can keep my daughter from leaving me, I would be in your debt."

Jack swallowed. "Maybe you should offer her the presidency first, just to sweeten the deal."

"Sorry, son, I don't want to get in the way here. You're on your own."

18

"DID HE TAKE IT HARD?" Lana asked, licking mocha cocoa cake icing from a silver spoon.

"Who, Daddy or Heath?" Alex sucked down fantasy fudge.

Lana leaned against the couch arm. "Both."

She heaved a sigh, her head still spinning from the day's events. "Daddy didn't make a fuss, said he was disappointed I was leaving Tremont's, but wanted me to be happy." Alex shook her head. "After all these years, he has no idea how much he and the company mean to me. I'm going to be more diligent about spending time with Daddy—even if it means putting up with Gloria—but it's time I move on in my career."

"And Heath?"

She wrinkled her nose. "I think he was more bothered by the thought of living alone in a new city than by the thought of losing me."

"What are you going to do now?"

Alex shrugged. "I don't know. Maybe you and I can buy a coffee shop."

Lana pointed her spoon. "I was talking about Jack."

Her heart clenched. "What does Jack have to do with all this?"

"*Please.* Only that you're in love with the man."

She scraped her spoon against the bottom to get the last trace of chocolate, but it was hard to see through the film of tears. "So is every other woman in the city. If Jack Stillman were open for business, I'd have to take a number to be served."

"Not true. He has a thing for you."

Shaking her head, Alex tried to smile. "Yeah, he called it a 'friendly curiosity.' Besides, he told my father he couldn't work with me, so what does that tell you?"

Ping.

Alex dropped her spoon and jerked her head toward the sliding glass door.

"What's that?" Lana asked.

Ping.

Her heart lifted, tentatively. "Excuse me." She walked to the glass door and opened it in time to take a hit on the top of her head. "Ow!" Crouching low, she made her way to the rail, then leaned over, frowning. "You almost gave me a concussion!"

Jack stopped, then dropped a handful of pebbles next to his bike parked in the grass. He tilted his head back and offered up a tentative grin. "Women with concussions are much easier to persuade."

Refusing to get her hopes up, Alex crossed her arms. "Persuade to do what?"

"To not go to Cincinnati with Reddinger."

Behind her, Lana gasped, but Alex would only allow herself the smallest thrill. "And do what instead?"

He hesitated so long, she thought he wasn't going to respond. "Stay...stay here with me."

Behind her, Lana whimpered, but Alex still had a bone to pick with Jack. "Why would you want me to stay, when I'm so difficult to get along with that you can't even work with me?"

His shoulders fell. "Your father misunderstood. When

I said that I couldn't work with you, I meant I couldn't because..."

"Because why? I didn't hear you."

"Because I love you!"

Behind her, Lana cried out and, at last, Alex allowed her heart to soar. Still, she tried to remain nonchalant. "I'm not sure if I believe you."

He scratched his temple. "I figured as much." Then he turned to his bike and unstrapped a large box. "Okay, I'm coming up."

She watched with delighted disbelief as he marched across the grass beneath the balcony.

"What's he doing?" Lana whispered.

"He's climbing up the fire escape," Alex whispered back. "Scram!"

"No way. I want to see this."

"*Goodbye*, Lana."

"Oh, all right. Call me, would you?"

"Sure."

She thought her heart might come out of her chest. Was it possible? Did this man love her? Slowly he hauled himself and the box up the fire escape ladder. Alex held her breath until his smiling face appeared on the other side of her balcony railing.

His eyes were serious, his expression earnest. "Alex, I don't have anything to offer you except my heart and my devotion, but I want to try to make you happy." He glanced at her hand, then frowned. "Where's your engagement ring?"

"I returned it," she said, feeling herself misting up.

"Why?" he asked, his dark eyes hopeful.

"Because I love you," she whispered.

A grin split his handsome face, then he pulled her mouth to his for a deep, promising kiss.

Suddenly Alex pulled back. "I'm unemployed now."

Jack shook his head. "I don't think so, Madam President."

She frowned. "What?"

"Your father has news. We'll call him," he said simply, then nipped at her neck, "afterward."

Alex tilted her head back, reveling in the thrill of his mouth, his tongue, his teeth on her skin. "Yes, afterward," she murmured. "Are you coming over?"

He lifted his head, as if he'd just remembered he was suspended three stories up. "Absolutely."

"Jack, what's in the box?"

His grin was sheepish. "Um, I bought you a hat," he said, handing her the box, then climbed over the rail to join her. "One that I thought would suit you."

"Can I open it?"

He swallowed, then exhaled noisily, as if gathering his strength. "Go ahead."

Alex bit her bottom lip and lifted the lid, then sucked in a sharp breath.

On a cloud of netting sat a white bridal hat, with a short, pearl-studded veil.

"Oh...oh...oh." Happy tears streamed down her face as she kissed him.

"My brother convinced me that love like this doesn't come around but once in a lifetime," he said. "But before I get down on one knee, I have a confession to make."

Alex swallowed, her joy suspended for a second. "What?"

He winced. "Remember the day you showed up at my office?"

She nodded. How could she forget?

"I wasn't setting you up for my ad pitch. I thought you

were an IRS agent, and what you saw was the way the agency and I really were—a complete mess."

She stuck her tongue in her cheek to suppress her mirth. "So what happened?"

He splayed his hands. "What can I say? You made me want to straighten up my act, and it feels...right. *We* feel right, Alex."

Incredibly touched, Alex cleared her throat. "You were about to get down on one knee?"

He grinned and swooped down in obvious relief. "Alex, will you marry me?"

"But I thought you were against marriage...I thought you said—"

"My knees aren't what they used to be, sweetheart. Is that a yes or a no?"

Alex laughed. "Yes."

His face split into a grin, then he shot to his feet and swung her around, whooping. At last he set her on her feet, then situated the little white hat on her head and kissed her until she was breathless. Warm and alight with his love, Alex finally pulled away, laughing. "Wait...I have to...call Lana."

But Jack shook his head, then leaned over to scoop her into his arms and carry her into the loft. "Afterward."

Epilogue

"ALEX," LANA SAID from the doorway of the dressing room. "Can your father come in?"

Alex tucked an errant strand of hair beneath the bridal hat Jack had given her and smiled at her maid of honor from the dressing vanity. "Yes, Lana, please send him in."

She stood and smoothed the skirt of her gown, simple white silk. Her heart thumped with elation and anticipation. Over the past few months, she and Jack had grown closer every day, their love deepening as their friendship and passion bloomed. She felt very special and extremely blessed to be marrying such a wonderful man.

"If only your mother could see you."

Alex turned to see her father standing just inside the dressing room, splendidly handsome in his tuxedo, beaming.

"She would be so proud," he murmured, his voice catching.

She walked toward him slowly. "But what do *you* think, Daddy?"

He met her in the middle of the room and she was astonished to see his eyes were moist. "I think," he said, his voice throaty, "that I am the luckiest man on this earth to have such an amazing, beautiful, talented woman for my daughter."

Her eyes filled with tears as she lifted her arms to hug his neck, counting yet another blessing—she and her father had grown as close as she'd always hoped. And Alex had even begun to forge a tentative relationship with Gloria.

Her father smiled down at her and stroked her cheek with his thumb. "And I'd say that Jack is the second luckiest man on this earth."

Alex straightened his bow tie. "Thank you, Daddy. And in Jack you're finally getting a son."

Her father's blue eyes turned questioning. "What do you mean?"

She gave him a small smile. "A son, Daddy, like you've always wanted."

A strange expression came over his face. "I couldn't be happier that you and Jack are making a life together, Alex, but whatever gave you the idea that I wanted a son?"

Alex balked. "Well...you're so into sports...and you get along so well with Jack...and I always thought..."

His laugh rumbled out, low and rueful, then he took both her hands in his. "Alex, my dear heart, I would've been glad for any more children your mother and I might have had, but when she first told me she was pregnant, I never imagined having anything *but* a beautiful little girl to love and who would love me in return. I'm sorry if I ever gave you the impression that you weren't *everything* I'd dreamed of in a child. Alex, I love you more than life itself and I'm so proud of you, I'm...speechless."

Her eyes overflowed as she wrapped her arms around his middle. "Daddy, thank you, thank you."

"Hey, you two," Lana said from the doorway. "We're waiting."

They separated, and Alex wiped at her tears.

"Are you ready, my dear?" her father asked.

She nodded, sniffing her tears dry. She claimed her

bouquet, then smiled at her father as he lowered the short veil over her face.

"My last walk with my little girl," he said, extending his arm.

She took his arm, blinking rapidly. "I'll always be your little girl, Daddy."

"Jack's probably wondering if I'm going to keep you," he said gruffly. "We'd better get going."

By the time they reached the doorway of the chapel, Alex had composed herself enough that she could clearly see Jack, stunning in his tuxedo, waiting for her at the altar, his brother Derek by his side. When Jack's face lit up, her heart nearly burst with happiness. Her father squeezed her arm and she began to walk toward Jack, her friend, her lover, her soul mate.

"Happy, sweetheart?" her father whispered.

"How could I not be, Daddy?" she said, squeezing back. "I have the two most wonderful men in the world to love."

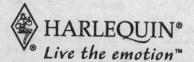

Receive 75¢ off your next Harlequin Temptation® book purchase.

75¢ OFF!

Your next Harlequin Temptation® book purchase.

RETAILER: Harlequin Enterprises Ltd. will pay the face value of this coupon plus 8¢ if submitted by customer for this product only. Any other use constitutes fraud. Coupon is nonassignable. Void if taxed, prohibited or restricted by law. Void if copied. Consumer must pay any government taxes. For reimbursement submit coupons and proof of sales to: Harlequin Enterprises Ltd., P.O. Box 880478, El Paso, TX 88588-0478, U.S.A. Cash value 1/100¢. Valid in the U.S. only.

Coupon expires July 31, 2003.
Redeemable at participating retail outlets in the U.S. only.
Limit one coupon per purchase.

110421

5 65373 00075 5   (8100) 0 11042

HARLEQUIN®
Temptation.

Receive 75¢ off your next Harlequin Temptation® book purchase.

75¢ OFF!
Your next Harlequin Temptation® book purchase.

Coupon expires July 31, 2003.
Redeemable at participating retail outlets in Canada only.
Limit one coupon per purchase.

52604850

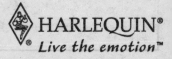

HARLEQUIN®
Live the emotion™

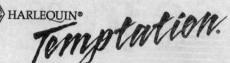
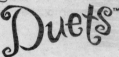
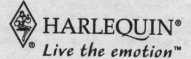

SHOP ONLINE OR DIAL 1-800-SEND-FTD

$10.00 OFF

COUPON

Expiration Date: April 30, 2003

To redeem your coupon:

**Log on to www.ftd.com/harlequin
and give promo code 2197 at checkout.**

Or

**Call 1-800-SEND-FTD
and give promo code 2194.**

Terms and conditions:

NCP2197